PUNISH THE SIN

Peter Balsam sank deeper into the trance. His senses sharpened, he felt the searing flame from each candle; he heard the voice of the devil calling out to him in his head. He felt the heat of hell glowing around him and as his discomfort grew he became frightened. . . . Then he was being drawn downward and he felt angelic hands caress him. He was suddenly cooler, calmer. He began silently repeating the Acts of Faith and Contrition, as his ecstasy grew.
He was joined at last to the Society of St. Peter Martyr.

Only later did he make the awful discovery: On Peter's back, from his shoulders to his waist, were angry red welts. The marks were swollen and stood out in painful relief from the pale whiteness of his back.
'My God,' Margo breathed, as she slipped the robe from his shoulders. 'What happened?'
And then the full horror of it struck him. He began to shake and with the trembling came the terror. 'I don't know,' he sobbed. 'And that's the worst of it. *I don't know where they came from*.'

**Also by the same author,
and available in Coronet Books:**

Suffer the Children

Punish The Sinners

John Saul

CORONET BOOKS
Hodder and Stoughton

For Linda and Jane
The Grey Ladies with the Red Roses

First published in 1978 by Dell
Publishing Co., Inc., New York

Coronet edition 1979

The characters and situations in this book are entirely imaginary and bear no relation to any real person or actual happening

Printed and bound in Great Britain for
Hodder and Stoughton Paperbacks, a
division of Hodder and Stoughton Ltd.,
Mill Road, Dunton Green, Sevenoaks,
Kent (Editorial Office: 47 Bedford
Square, London WC1 3DP) by
C. Nicholls & Company Ltd
The Philips Park Press, Manchester

SBN 0 340 242620

PROLOGUE

He reached up and grasped the doorknob carefully, half-hoping it would be locked. When it wasn't, his eyes widened in anticipation, and he began pushing the door open very slowly. When you are four years old, and you are going to do something that you are not sure you should do, you try to do it either very slowly or very quickly. The little boy was doing it very slowly.

He pushed the door to his parents' bedroom open just far enough for his small body to slip in, then closed it again behind him. He looked around, though he already knew the room was empty. On the other hand, when you are four, very few rooms are truly empty.

He tiptoed across the room to his mother's closet, and again half-hoped the door would be locked. When he found that it wasn't, he made up his mind to go ahead and do it. He pulled the door open and stepped into the closet. There they were: his mother's shoes.

He had seen a picture in a book once – a little boy, all dressed up in his mother's clothes – his tiny feet lost in the immense high-heeled shoes, his body swathed in the folds of a red dress, and his face just barely visible peering out from under the brim of a large sunbonnet. His mother had thought the little boy in the picture was adorable.

So now he stepped into a pair of his mother's shoes, and tried to balance his weight on those tiny little heels. It was difficult, but he managed it. Then, while he was trying to figure out how he was going to get to the hatbox perched almost out of sight on the shelf far above his head, he heard the sound.

It was the click of a doorknob, and even before he heard the next sound, he knew that someone had come into the room. He turned quickly; the closet door was almost closed. Maybe, if he held very still, and stayed very quiet, whoever was in the bedroom wouldn't notice the closet door at all...

He crouched down on the floor of the closet. More sounds. Footsteps, and two voices. It was his parents, and they were both in the bedroom. He heard the bedroom door close.

'I just don't like doing it now,' he heard his mother say. 'It seems so – so dirty, I guess.'

'You mean you don't like doing it in the light.' His father, angry. 'The trouble with you, Ruth, is that you're prissy. You need a touch of the whore in you.'

The little boy wondered what 'the whore' was.

There was a scuffling noise, and then his mother's voice: 'What about the children?'

'What about them?' his father rumbled. 'Elaine's at school, and the kid's outside somewhere doing God knows what.'

The little boy sank farther back into the depths of the closet. Suddenly it was very important that he not be discovered. He wasn't sure why, but he knew it was important.

He listened to more scuffling sounds, and heard some words that he couldn't quite make out. He began to wonder what was happening on the other side of the closet door, but he was afraid to peek out and see.

When his mother began to moan, the little boy conquered his fear. He crept to the crack where the door stood slightly ajar, and pressed his eye close. He could see the foot of the bed, but that was all. His mother moaned louder; he decided to risk pushing the closet door open a little more. And then he saw them.

They were on the bed, and they didn't have any clothes on. His father lay on top of his mother. She was crying or moaning and struggling with his father. But she had her arms around his neck, and between the moans she was saying, 'Yes ... Yes ... Oh, God, yes!'

As he watched the strange scene on the bed, the little boy became frightened. He thought maybe he ought to help his mother, but he was scared of his father. His father had hit him before; he didn't want to be hit again. And he wasn't really sure that his mother wanted any help. Still, her cries were getting louder, and now she really did seem to be struggling. But her arms were still around his father, and she was kissing him.

The little boy's eye was caught by another movement in the room, and he realized that the bedroom door was opening again. He held his breath, then let it out again when he saw Elaine standing in the doorway. She would know what to do, he thought. She was sixteen years old, and almost all grown up. If his mother needed any help, Elaine would be able to provide it. He watched as Elaine moved toward the bed, waiting for her to say something, do something. But she didn't. She just stood there by the bed – watching.

Just as the little boy was about to call out to his sister, he saw her suddenly raise her hands above her head.

He saw the meat cleaver from the kitchen clutched in her hands.

And he saw the cleaver flash down, and heard the sound as the hard metal slashed through his father's skull.

He heard his mother cry out, and he watched in confusion as she tried to struggle free of his father's weight. He wondered why Elaine didn't help his mother, now that she had stopped his father from doing whatever he was doing.

He realized that Elaine wasn't going to help his mother. He watched, horrified, as his sister raised the cleaver again, and brought it down into his mother's face. He thought he heard his mother scream, but it was too quick for him to be sure. Frozen, he watched as his sister raised the cleaver – again and again – bringing it flashing through the air. Long after they had both stopped moving, the knife continued to flash until all he could see was silver and red.

Terrified, the little boy huddled in the closet, wondering if his sister was going to find him and start hitting him, too. But she was standing still now, looking at what she had done. And then she started moving again. She dropped the bloody cleaver on the bed, and knelt down on the floor, as if looking for something he couldn't see.

She stood up again, and pulled a chair to the centre of the room, directly below the light fixture in the ceiling. She climbed up onto the chair and began tying something to the light fixture. It was an electrical cord, the kind his parents used when they needed something longer than the cords that came on the electric things. He wondered why she was tying it to the light fixture. Everybody knew that electric cords have to be plugged in for them to work.

He saw his sister tie the other end of the cord around her neck, and he realized what she was going to do. He'd seen this before. She was going to hang herself. He'd seen pictures of it. But if she hung herself, who would take care of him? He had to stop her. The little boy finally found his voice.

He screamed and as the wail escaped his throat, the girl on the chair spun around and lost her footing. As the chair fell away from her, the closet door swung open, and their eyes met. And then her neck snapped. It was over.

The little boy watched helplessly as his sister swung slowly back and forth. Finally he moved toward her, and reached out to touch her. She felt strange. She didn't feel like his sister anymore. He wondered what to do.

Much later – he didn't know how much later – he heard a scream. He didn't respond to it. He was huddled in the corner of the closet, his knees drawn up under his chin, his arms wrapped around his legs. He thought he heard some other noises too, and even later, he was aware that the closet door was being pulled open. It wasn't until a pair of arms reached down and picked him up that he started crying. When he started, he cried for a long time.

They kept him in a hospital for the first day after the discovery of the gruesome scene in the bedroom. The nuns took care of him, and asked him a lot of questions, but he couldn't answer any of them. He wanted his mother and his father. They didn't come to see him.

On the second day they took him to the convent. He didn't know what a convent was, only that it was a big building, and there were lots of nuns there who fussed over him a lot. And there were other children there, children who lived there. The little boy wondered if he, too, was going to live there.

As he went to sleep the second night, he wondered if his parents would come to see him. And Elaine. He wondered what had happened to Elaine. As he drifted off to sleep, he thought he saw her. She was looking at him, and there was something wrong with her. Her neck looked funny – stretched out and tilted at an odd angle.

When the little boy screamed, a nun hurried into the room and put her arms around him. The nun held him until he went back to sleep.

On the third day they took him to church and the little boy realized that his parents weren't going to come and get him. He realized that they were in the boxes at the front of the church, and that after the boxes were taken away, he wouldn't see them again.

He asked if it would be all right if he looked at his parents before they were taken away, but he was told that he couldn't. He wondered why.

During the funeral service the little boy kept looking curiously around the church, and shortly before the service ended, he tugged at the black folds of the habit the woman next to him was wearing. He knew she was a nun, and that she would take care of him. He tugged again at her habit and she leaned down to put her ear close to his lips.

'Where's Elaine?' he asked. 'Isn't she going to be here?'

The nun stared at the little boy for a moment, then shook her head.

'She can't be here,' the nun said finally. 'You mustn't think about her anymore, or talk about her.'

'Why not?' the little boy asked.

'Never mind,' the nun admonished him. 'Your sister was an evil child, and she has sinned. You mustn't think about her.'

The funeral mass ended, and his parents were taken from the church. He watched them go, and wondered what had happened to them.

And what had happened to his sister.

And why he was by himself.

But, of course, he wasn't by himself. He was in the convent, but no one would tell him why. He heard someone – one of the sisters – say: 'He'll get over it. He'll forget. It will be better that way.'

The little boy did not forget. Not while he was small, and not while he grew up. Always, he was aware that something had happened. Something had happened to his parents, and to his sister. And his sister had caused it to happen.

His sister was evil.

She had sinned.

He knew that God forgave sinners.

But who punishes them?

By the time he was ten, he had stopped asking. Nobody had ever told him the answer.

BOOK ONE

THE SAINTS OF NEILSVILLE

ONE

Peter Balsam trudged to the top of Cathedral Hill and stared up at the forbidding stone façade of the Church of St. Francis Xavier. The desert heat seemed to intensify, and Balsam could feel sweat pouring from his armpits, and forming rivulets as it coursed down his back. He sank down on the steps in front of the church, and stared at the vista below him.

The town was called Neilsville, and it lay shimmering in the heat of the Eastern Washington desert like some dying thing writhing in agony with each tortured breath, unable to end its misery.

There was an aura about Neilsville, an aura that Peter Balsam had felt the minute he had arrived but had not yet been able to define.

A word had flashed into his mind the moment he had gotten off the train two hours earlier. He had put it immediately out of his mind. It had kept coming back.

Evil.

It covered the town like the stink of death, and Peter Balsam's first impulse had been to run – to put himself and all his possessions on the next train east, and get away from Neilsville as fast as he could.

But the next train would not be until tomorrow, and so, reluctantly, he had gone to the apartment that had been rented for him. He had not unpacked his suitcases, not put his name on the mailbox, not tried to order a phone, not done any of the other things that one normally does to settle into a new home.

Instead, he had tried to tell himself that the pervading sense of foreboding, of something desperately wrong in the town, was only in his imagination, and had set out to explore the place.

After two hours he had climbed Cathedral Hill, and now he was about to present himself to the man who had brought him to Neilsville.

He slipped into the gloom of the church, dipped his fingers into the holy water, made the sign of the cross as he genuflected, and slid into a pew. Peter Balsam began to pray.

He prayed the prayers the nuns had carefully taught him in the convent, the prayers that had always before brought him peace.

Today there was no peace. It was as if fingers were reaching out to him, grasping at him, trying to pull him into some strange morass that he could feel but not see.

Balsam concentrated on his prayers, repeating the familiar phrases over and over again, until the rhythms of the rosary overcome the fear within him.

'Holy Mary, Mother of God, pray for us sinners . . .'

In the study of the rectory next to the church, Monsignor Peter Vernon paced slowly back and forth. He had watched Balsam's slow progress up Cathedral Hill, and had expected to hear the faint tinkling that would announce his visitor. Now he realized that Balsam must have stopped to catch his breath after the long climb.

The priest went back to the window, and stared out once more, taking in the familiar dry vista of Neilsville, then focusing on the five girls who were playing on the tennis courts below him – four of them together, one alone. As he continued to stare down at them, each of them, in turn, glanced up at him as if they had felt his disapproving glare. One of them waved impudently, and the priest quickly stepped back from the window, embarrassed at having been discovered watching them, and angry at his own embarrassment.

He resented the girls, resented the way they acted so respectful in his presence, then sneered at him from a distance. When he had been a child, such impudence had not been tolerated. The nuns had demanded respect all the time, and the boys in the convent had given it, unquestioningly. But times had changed, and these girls didn't live at St. Francis Xavier's, didn't have the constant supervision he himself had had at their age. This year, he told himself, things would be different. This year, with the help of Peter Balsam, he would take a stronger stand. This year, he would teach them respect, and humility. It was for this purpose that he had summoned Peter Balsam to Neilsville.

It had not been an easy thing to do. From its inception, the parish school had employed only nuns on the teaching staff, and they had resisted when Monsignor had told them he was bringing in a layman to teach psychology. Psychology, they had told him, had no place at St. Francis Xavier's. It should be left to the public school. And as for a man – and not even a priest at that – teaching at St. Francis Xavier's, it was simply unheard of. Monsignor Vernon had explained to them: he had been unable to find anyone else who could teach both psychology and Latin. Then, when they still resisted, he had invoked his authority as their religious superior. They, like most others, had wilted under the brooding stare of the Monsignor. The priest had invited Peter Balsam to come to Neilsville.

Knowing Balsam's background, Monsignor Vernon had felt it unlikely that his old friend would refuse. Balsam hadn't.

Peter Balsam emerged from the church, recoiling from the hot blast that assaulted him as he stepped into the fierce sunglare. He told himself once again that the fear the town instilled in him was only in his mind. It was just that it was all so different from what he had grown up with, so dry and parched-looking.

He told himself that he should stay, should give Neilsville a chance. He had lived with fear too long, and this time he should overcome it. As he walked to the rectory next to the church, he told himself that the discomfort he was feeling came only from his own imagination. But he didn't believe it, for as he climbed the steps to the porch of the rectory, he again felt something pulling at him, something from outside himself. Something in Neilsville.

He glanced around for the doorbell as he crossed the porch. He was about to knock on the door when he saw a neatly lettered card taped to the inside of the glass panel in its centre. 'Please come in,' the card read. Balsam obediently tried the doorknob, and entered the foyer of the rectory. To his right stood a small table, and on the table rested a silver bell. Balsam picked up the bell, and shook it gently, sending a clear, tinkling sound through the house. A silent moment passed before he heard the click of a doorlatch somewhere down the hall and saw a figure emerge from a room. Then Pete Vernon was striding toward him, tall, purposeful, one hand stretched out in greeting.

'Peter Balsam,' he heard the priest's voice boom. 'How long has it been?' A moment later even before he had a chance to say hello, Balsam found himself being propelled down the hall and into the room from which the priest had appeared a few seconds earlier.

'Pete—' Balsam began tentatively, as Vernon closed the door of what was apparently his study. Suddenly Balsam realized that he was even more nervous than he had thought. Something in his old friend had changed. He seemed taller, and more confident, and there was a brooding quality in his eyes, a darkness that Balsam found unnerving. 'It's been a long time,' he finished lamely. 'Thirteen or fourteen years, I guess.'

'Sit down, sit down,' Vernon said. He indicated two large easy chairs that flanked a stone fireplace, and settled into one of them before Balsam had reached the other. As he sank slowly into his chair, Balsam became acutely aware that Pete Vernon was examining him closely.

'I'm afraid I'm a bit rumpled,' he said, grinning uncomfortably. 'It's quite a hill you have here.'

'You get used to it,' Vernon said. 'At least I have. Welcome to Neilsville.'

The Monsignor saw Balsam's grin fade, and his own brows furrowed slightly. 'Is anything wrong? The apartment not satisfactory?'

Balsam shook his head. 'The apartment's fine. I'm not sure

what it is. It's hard to explain, but ever since I got off the train, I've had this strange feeling. I can't really put my finger on it. I keep telling myself it's only my imagination, but I keep getting the feeling that something's—' He broke off, trying to find the right word. He hesitated over using the word 'evil', though that was the word that kept coming to mind. '—that something's not right here.'

He felt a sudden chill coming from the priest, and realized he'd said the wrong thing. Neilsville had been the Monsignor's home for nearly fifteen years, and the first thing Balsam had done was insult the place. He tried to recover from the blunder.

'But I'm sure I'll get used to it,' he said quickly, and only then realized that he had committed himself to stay. The priest seemed to relax again, and smiled at him.

'And your wife?' he asked smoothly. 'Linda, isn't it? When will she be joining you?'

'I'm afraid she won't be joining me at all,' Balsam said carefully. 'I'm afraid we're separated. Sometimes things just don't work out.'

'I see,' Vernon said in a tone of voice that told Balsam he didn't see at all. 'Well, that's most unfortunate.'

Balsam decided to try to make light of it. There was no point in trying to explain what had gone wrong and no sympathy in the priest's steely gaze. 'That depends on how you look at it,' he said, forcing a smile. 'From our point of view – Linda's and mine, that is – it was the marriage that was unfortunate, not the separation.'

Balsam's smile faded as he watched Vernon stiffen. He had made another mistake: Pete Vernon was a priest, and a failed marriage was nothing to make light of.

'I shouldn't have said that,' he said quickly. 'Of course the whole thing has been very painful, and I'm afraid it will take time.' A lot of time, he thought to himself, but the priest seemed mollified.

'Of course,' Vernon said, his voice suddenly taking on a fatherly quality Balsam had never heard before. 'If there's anything I can do . . .' He trailed off and then he suddenly shifted in his chair. When he spoke again, it was with annoyance.

'I wish you'd told me all this before,' he said. 'Such things make a much bigger difference in towns like Neilsville than they do in bigger cities. It isn't going to make things easier for either of us.'

My God, Balsam thought, is he going to fire me before I even get a chance? Aloud he said, 'I don't really see why my marital status is anyone's business but my own.'

Vernon smiled tolerantly at him. 'I'm afraid you have a lot to learn about Neilsville. Here, such matters are everybody's business. Well, I don't really see that there's anything to be done about the situation. I mean, here you are, and Linda isn't here, and that's that, isn't it?'

Balsam hoped his sigh of relief wasn't audible.

'Pete,' he began, but broke off when the priest held up his hand.

'Since we're talking about the less pleasant aspects of Neilsville, there are one or two more things I should tell you right now. First, while we're old friends, and it's perfectly natural for you to call me Pete, in this parish we tend to be a bit on the formal side. Everybody, and I mean *every*body, calls me Monsignor. It may seem stiff to you, but there are reasons for it. So I'd suggest that you try to get into the habit of using my title yourself.' He smiled wryly at the look of stupefaction on Balsam's face. 'I wish it weren't necessary,' he said, 'but I'm afraid it is. If people overheard you calling me Pete instead of Monsignor, they'd take it as a sign of disrespect.'

'I see,' Balsam said slowly, hoping he'd matched the tone that Vernon had achieved earlier with the same phrase. 'Doesn't that sort of thing tend to isolate you from everyone?'

Vernon shrugged helplessly. 'What can I do? That's the way things have always been done here, and that's the way the people here like it. We have a duty to our flock, don't we?' Before Balsam could reply, the priest stood up. 'Suppose I take you on a little tour?' he suggested. 'We might as well get you used to the lay of the land.' He smiled warmly, but Peter Balsam suddenly wondered just how much of that warmth was real.

Monsignor Vernon led Peter Balsam from the rectory across the tennis courts to the school building. The four girls who had been playing doubles stopped their game and stared at the two men. Peter Balsam grinned at them self-consciously, while the priest studiously ignored them.

The fifth girl, absorbed in trying to serve balls against the wall of a handball court, didn't seem to notice them at all.

'They really gave me the once-over,' Balsam commented when the two men were inside the school building.

'It was me they were staring at,' Monsignor Vernon said stiffly. 'They do it on purpose. They think it embarrasses me.'

'Does it?' Balsam asked mildly, and was surprised when the priest grasped his arm and turned to face him.

'No,' he said, his dark eyes boring into Peter's. 'It doesn't bother me at all. Will it bother you?'

'Why should it?' Balsam asked in confusion, wondering why the priest was reacting so strongly.

The Monsignor dropped his arm as quickly as he'd grasped it. 'No reason,' he said shortly. 'No reason at all.'

But as they began their tour of the school, Peter Balsam was sure that there *was* a reason. He told himself it was nothing more than a function of their common background. Growing up in the convent, neither of them had ever learned how to deal with teen-age girls. And now, in their mid-thirties, it was probably too late for either of them to learn. So, in their own ways, each of them coped with his discomfort – Balsam by grinning foolishly, and Vernon by ignoring them completely. As they began their tour of St. Francis Xavier High School, Peter Balsam put the entire incident out of his mind.

On the tennis court the four girls gave up their game and gathered together. Judy Nelson, a few months older than the other three, was snickering.

'We really bugged him that time,' she said. 'He always tries to pretend we don't exist.'

'Only during the summer.' Penny Anderson shuddered. 'During the year you can't get away from him.' If any of the girls heard her, they didn't respond. They were still watching the two figures as they disappeared into the school building.

'Did you see what happened when I waved to him?' Karen Morton asked. 'I thought he was going to freak. I hate the way he stares at me.'

'Everyone stares at you,' Judy replied, trying to keep the envy out of her voice. 'And the way you flash your body around, who can blame them?' Judy was pleased to see her friend blush.

'She can't help it,' Janet Connally defended Karen. 'We can't all afford to get new clothes every week.'

Karen Morton flushed again, unsure whether her over-developed figure or her poverty was the most shameful, and wishing someone would change the subject. To her relief, the fourth girl in the group did.

'That must have been the new teacher with Monsignor,' Penny Anderson said. 'My mother picked him up at the train this afternoon and took him to his apartment. She says he's weird.'

'Then he'll fit in here just fine,' Judy commented. 'If you ask me, this whole town's weird.' She shuddered a little, but the other three girls ignored it: Judy had hated Neilsville as long as they could remember.

'Are you going to take his course?' Penny asked Judy.

'I wouldn't miss it,' Judy said, a conspiratorial look coming over her face. 'Let's all take it.'

'I don't know if my mother will let me,' Penny said doubtfully. 'She doesn't think they ought to be teaching psychology.'

'Nobody does, except Monsignor,' Janet put in. 'And I keep wondering why he wants it so badly. I mean, it seems like the last thing he'd want us to know anything about.'

'Maybe he had to put it in,' Karen suggested. 'Maybe the Bishop insisted.'

'Oh, who cares?' Judy Nelson said impatiently. 'The point is, if we can all get into that class, and they don't split us up like they usually do, we can get away with anything. I mean, a new teacher, who isn't even a nun? It'll be too much. After the first week he won't know what hit him.'

'It would be fun,' Penny agreed. 'But I'll have to work on Mother.'

'And speaking of mothers,' Judy cut in with a grimace, 'I have to meet mine down at Osgood's to buy a new dress. You want to come along?' The question was addressed to the group, but only Karen Morton responded:

'I'll come. We'll find you something sexy to wear to the party Saturday.'

'As if she'd let me buy something sexy,' Judy groaned. 'She thinks I'm twelve years old.' The two of them wandered off, leaving Penny and Janet alone on the court. After a moment, Judy spotted the fifth girl still silently serving balls to herself on the handball court. She nudged Karen, then turned and called to her friends, loudly enough for the other girl to hear. 'You coming, or are you just going to stand there and watch the elephant play?'

Janet Connally's eyes widened in surprise at her friend's meanness, but she said nothing. She just tugged at Penny's arm, and began walking away. At the other end of the court Judy Nelson was giggling at her own wit.

The object of Judy's wit, Marilyn Crane, wanted to shrink up and die. She'd heard the crack, as she knew she was intended to, and she tried to hold back her tears.

It wasn't her fault she was clumsy, she told herself. It was just the way things were – the way things had always been. All her life, ever since she was small, she'd been too big, and too homely. All her life her mother had read her the story of the ugly duckling, and tried to convince her that someday she'd grow up to be a swan. But Marilyn knew it wasn't true.

She tried to swat another ball neatly against the concrete wall, but missed. She glanced quickly around, relieved to see that she hadn't been observed.

She scooped up her balls and stuffed them into a can. She would have done it much earlier, but the foursome had arrived, and Marilyn hadn't wanted them to think she was leaving just because they were there. Staying had been even worse, since what little skill she had developed over the summer had immediately escaped her with the arrival of an audience. With the stoicism she had developed over her fifteen years of life, she had stuck it out. Now, finally, she was able to make her escape.

She decided to go into the church. It would be cool in there, but more important, in the church she knew she could find solace from her confusion. It was only there, sitting in the chilly gloom, that Marilyn felt she belonged, that no one was laughing at her, or making cruel remarks just loudly enough for her to overhear.

In church, Marilyn would be close to the Blessed Virgin, and the Blessed Virgin always brought her peace.

Indeed, when she sat in the church, staring up at the statue of the Madonna, it was almost as if the Virgin were alive and reaching out to her. Marilyn wanted to reach back, to touch that presence who brought her peace.

But each day, for Marilyn Crane, there was less and less peace. One day, she knew, there would be none at all. And on that day, she would finally touch the Sorrowful Mother, and her own sorrow would be transferred to the Mother of God.

Marilyn slipped into the church, and silently began praying for forgiveness of all her sins.

TWO

As they moved from room to room, exploring St. Francis Xavier's High School, Peter Balsam began to feel increasingly uncomfortable. Most of the parochial schools he had seen had begun to take on the same casual flavour as the public schools, emphasizing secular subjects rather than religious training. But here in Neilsville, the classrooms were stark, decorated only with a small statue of the Blessed Virgin, placed in identical niches in each of the rooms. As the tour progressed, Monsignor Vernon became aware of Balsam's discomfort.

'I told you we were formal around here,' he said with a tight smile. 'I suppose you think we are a bit backward.'

Once again, Peter tried to make light of his feelings. 'I was just wondering how St. Francis Xavier himself would feel about all this,' he said. 'As I recall, the old boy was pretty famous for his lack of formality. In fact, he tended to be pretty merry about most everything, didn't he?'

Monsignor Vernon paused a moment, his hand resting on the doorknob of the only room they hadn't yet inspected. He looked at Balsam for almost a full minute, and when he spoke it was obvious that he was choosing his words carefully.

'Let me put it this way,' he said. 'Despite the fact that St. Francis Xavier was a Jesuit, this is obviously not a Jesuit school. The fact of the matter is that Neilsville, and the people of this parish, myself included, tend to feel much more at home with the Dominicans than with the Jesuits. Do I make myself clear?'

Balsam tried to keep his smile genuine, and his voice easy. 'Perfectly,' he said. 'Although I have to admit that I tend to associate the Dominicans with the Inquisition, I'll do my best to get over it.'

Monsignor Vernon stared at him once more, then a smile began playing around his lips. 'I hope you will,' he said, his voice taking on a warm heartiness. He unlocked the door of the last classroom, then stood aside to let Peter enter. 'This room is going to be yours.'

Balsam looked around the room with more curiosity than he had felt in any of the others. It seemed the same: square, overlooking the schoolyard, a blackboard on one wall, desks perfectly lined up in five rows of six desks each, with his own desk squatting forbiddingly in one corner, so placed that none of the students could ever be obstructed from his view. At the back of the room, as in all the other rooms, there was a niche for the ever-present statue of the Virgin Mary. But in this room the niche contained a different statue. Balsam stared at it for a moment, then turned to Monsignor Vernon. He was surprised to see that the beginnings of a smile had grown into a full-fledged grin.

'I don't get it,' Balsam said finally, moving closer to the statue and examining it carefully. 'Who is he?'

'That,' Monsignor Vernon replied in the jovial voice Peter Balsam remembered from their college days together, 'is St. Peter Martyr.'

When Balsam still looked blank, Vernon continued, 'That's the Dominican you're going to have to get used to. While St. Francis Xavier may have been famous for his merriment, St. Peter Martyr was equally famous for his vigilance in the matter of heresy.'

'Heresy?' Balsam repeated, still not seeing the point.

The grin faded from Monsignor Vernon's face. 'My idea of a joke,' he explained. 'I thought, since you're going to be teaching psychology, and some of the modern psychological theories seem pretty heretical to the Church, that it might be amusing to put St. Peter Martyr in here. To keep an eye on you.'

Balsam shook his head sadly, then looked closely at the man who had once been his friend, trying to determine if the priest really had thought it would be amusing to put the statue in his room, or whether he was trying to say something to Balsam, to warn him about something. It was impossible to tell.

'Well,' the Monsignor said finally, breaking what was fast turning into an embarrassing silence, 'suppose we go back to the rectory for a few minutes? There's a few things we should talk about, and I have some excellent sherry. If it isn't too early?'

'Fine,' Balsam agreed distractedly, not really hearing the question.

They returned to the rectory in silence, Balsam wondering how his friend could have changed so much in so few years. He had remembered Pete Vernon as someone who tended to take life as it came, and make the most of it. Now he seemed to have turned completely around, and taken on an odd stiffness, almost an awkwardness, he'd never had in their school days. Well, Balsam told himself as they reentered the study, I shouldn't have expected him to be the same. We all change, and he has a lot of responsibilities. Balsam decided he was simply going to have to change his perspective with respect to Pete Vernon. Then he smiled to himself slightly as he realized that the change in Pete would certainly make it easier for him to remember to call him 'Monsignor'.

The priest handed him a glass of sherry, then picked up a folder from the desk that sat in one corner of the room, bringing it with him when he returned to the chair opposite Balsam. The two men sipped their sherry in silence for a moment, then the priest spoke.

'I have something here that intrigues me,' he said, tapping the folder. Balsam looked at him inquiringly.

'The synopsis of your thesis,' Vernon continued. 'I keep going over and over it and I get the distinct impression that whoever wrote the summary left a lot out.'

Suddenly Balsam relaxed: he was on familiar territory.

'I can well imagine,' he said. 'You have no idea how much trouble that thesis caused. For a while there, I thought I was going to be tossed out of St. Alban's.'

Vernon fingered the folder. 'I can well imagine.' He read the title of the thesis aloud: '"Suicide as Sin: An Investigation of the Validity of the Doctrine". It almost sounds as if you were challenging the Doctrine. Were you?' He looked pointedly at Peter.

Balsam shrugged his shoulders. 'That depends on what you mean by "challenge". All I set out to do was take a look at the Doctrine of the Church in light of what psychologists now know about the phenomenon of suicide.'

'And that's not challenging the Doctrine?' the priest asked.

'Not in my mind,' Balsam said. 'But I'm afraid at St. Alban's they didn't see much difference between my investigation and an actual challenge.'

'I don't suppose they did,' the Monsignor commented. 'In fact, neither do I.'

'Well, I suppose the best way to explain it is in terms of a trial. What I was doing, I thought, was conducting a preliminary hearing to see if there was enough evidence for a trial.'

'And was there?'

Balsam shrugged. 'Who knows? I found a few conflicts between the Doctrine of the Church and the science of psychology. As to the resolution of the conflicts, I'll leave that to better minds than mine.'

Monsignor Vernon suddenly leaned back in his chair and seemed to relax. For the first time, Balsam realized that the subject of his thesis had disturbed the priest. He decided that a little explanation was in order.

'It's just always seemed to me that the Doctrine of the Church with reference to suicide is a bit inhuman,' he began.

Monsignor Vernon smiled thinly. 'The Doctrines of the Church are concerned with God,' he said. 'That which may seem inhuman isn't necessarily un-Godly.'

Balsam's brows arched. Spoken like a true Inquisitor, he thought. Aloud he said: 'It just seems to me that anybody who is deranged enough to want to kill himself can't be called rational, and certainly deserves the same considerations the Church gives to what we like to call "morons and savages".'

'Your analogy doesn't work,' Vernon replied stiffly. 'Morons and savages are not responsible for themselves, not because they are morons and savages *per se*, but simply because they have no capacity for understanding the Doctrines.'

Balsam decided not to press his point. 'Well, as I said, it's going to have to be left to better minds than mine to decide whether or not the Doctrine should be changed. I took no stand whatsoever in the thesis, which is probably why it passed.'

'And you came to no conclusions of your own?' the Monsignor pressed.

Balsam shook his head. 'As far as I'm concerned, all I did was raise more questions. I don't think I'm qualified enough in either psychology or theology to come up with any answers.'

Monsignor Vernon nodded his head slowly, as if digesting what Balsam had just said. When he spoke again, it took a moment for Balsam to see the continuity.

'I should tell you that there has been a lot of concern expressed in the parish about the course you're going to teach,' he said. 'I'm afraid there's a strong feeling that psychology has no place in a religious school. Frankly, I had some doubts about whether or not I'd chosen the right man for the job.'

'And?' Balsam prompted him.

Monsignor Vernon smiled grimly. 'Let's just say I feel a bit better about it now. A few minutes ago I was about to give you a strong warning against teaching our students anything that is contrary to the Doctrines.'

Which warning you have just given me, Balsam said to himself. 'And you don't think you have to now?' he asked, trying to keep his voice level.

'I think you'll do just fine,' Vernon said, standing up. 'But I think I was wise to put St. Peter Martyr in your room,' he added. Balsam wondered if he saw a light in Vernon's eye. He decided he didn't.

'Maybe I'd better study up on St. Peter Martyr,' he said. 'Since we're going to be roommates.'

Vernon clapped him on the shoulder and Balsam felt himself being steered toward the door. 'Maybe you should,' the priest agreed. 'He was a fascinating man. Believe me when I tell you that he never had any trouble at all in determining what was, and what was not, in conflict with the Doctrines of the Church. If you ever have any doubts about what to teach your class, consult St. Peter Martyr. Or me, for that matter. The sin of pride aside, I have almost as fine a sense of right as St. Peter did.'

'I'll keep it in mind,' Balsam said dryly, and wondered if the priest had heard him. They were near the front door now, and Monsignor Vernon seemed lost in thought.

'You know,' he said, as he opened the front door, 'I was just thinking. I have a study group – pretty informal, for Neilsville – that you might be interested in joining. Particularly if you want to find out more about Peter Martyr. He's our favourite saint. Or have you drifted completely away from such things?' He looked with a sudden intensity into Peter Balsam's eyes. Balsam met the priest's gaze for a moment, then broke away from it.

'Not completely,' he said uncertainly. 'But I think it'll have to wait. I've got a lot of preparing to do for my classes.'

'More than you know,' Vernon said in a tone that made Balsam look inquiringly at him. Seeing the confused look on Balsam's face, the priest continued. 'We decided it should be the junior class that got first crack at the psychology course,' he said. 'And in the junior class we have four girls who will undoubtedly all want to take your course.'

'The four who were playing tennis?' Peter asked, acting on intuition.

'Those are the ones,' the priest said darkly.

'Should I be worried about them?' Balsam asked.

'That's up to you,' Vernon replied. 'But a word of warning. They've been almost inseparable since they were tiny, and most of the sisters have found the only way to handle them is to split them up. Otherwise they band together, and your class becomes nothing more than a gossip and note-passing session. A drawer in my office contains nothing but the notes that have been confiscated from them over the last nine or ten years. Someday I'm going to read them all, just to see what they always think is so important that it can't wait until after class.'

Balsam felt a twinge of concern run through him. Teen-age girls had always made him uncomfortable, and the prospect of confronting a close-knit band of them terrified him. But he wouldn't let his fear show.

'Thanks for warning me,' he said, 'but my instincts tell me it should be interesting to have all four of them in a psychology class.'

'And you always follow your instincts?' Monsignor Vernon asked.

Balsam looked at him steadily. 'No,' he said quietly. 'Not always.'

'Good,' the priest said. 'Then you should fit in well here.' And before Balsam could reply, the priest had quietly closed the rectory door.

For a long time, Peter Balsam stared at the closed door of the stone house. What did he mean by that?

But there were no answers in the stone façade of the rectory. Slowly, Peter Balsam started down the slope that would take him back into the heart of Neilsville. As he walked, he didn't see the town at all. All he saw was an image in his mind. An image of the statue in his classroom; the statue of St. Peter Martyr. It was a warning, he was sure. But of what?

From his window in the rectory, Monsignor Vernon watched Peter Balsam make his way down the hill. It would be all right, he decided. He hadn't been sure, but now that he had talked to Balsam, he knew. Now that Peter Balsam was in Neilsville, everything was going to be all right again.

As he made his way down Main Street, the sense of foreboding that had come over Peter Balsam on his arrival in Neilsville rose again, and he wondered what had happened to his resolve. He had intended to tell Pete – 'Monsignor', he corrected himself – that he wasn't going to stay. But he had not done it. Instead, he had let himself be led by the priest, just as he had always let himself be led. Ever since they had been boys together, it had been like that. Almost as if Pete Vernon held some kind of power over Peter Balsam.

As if the slightly older Vernon knew something that Balsam did not.

Once, indeed, Pete Vernon had said something that had stuck in Peter Balsam's mind: 'Our lives are entwined,' he had said. 'They always have been, and they always will be.' Balsam had dismissed it at the time, told himself that the older boy was only trying to get his goat. But now, nearly twenty years later, here they were, together in Neilsville . . .

He became acutely aware of people staring at him as he walked along the sidewalk, and he resisted the impulse to return their stares. He concentrated, instead, on looking the town over.

Perhaps without the heat and dryness of the desert, Neilsville could have been pretty. Its frame buildings, which would have been attractive set among the maples of the Midwest, looked only stark here in the arid country between the Cascades and the Rockies. They seemed to be waiting for something, some force of nature that would weld them together into a community. But it hadn't happened. Each store, each house, stood huddled into itself, and as Peter Balsam walked among them he wondered if it was only he who felt the odd sense of rejection that seemed to personify the town. Surreptitiously, he began to examine the people of Neilsville.

There was a sameness to them that he had seen nowhere else. They all seemed to be of a type, slightly older than their years – not a healthy kind of age, a wise kind of age, but rather a tiredness. A fear? The same wariness that he had perceived in the buildings was in the people – as if they were waiting for something to happen, and whatever it was, it was not going to be pleasant.

He caught several of them staring at him. They didn't turn away in embarrassment when he confronted them. Instead, they met his eyes, and their lips tightened. Only then would they turn and whisper to their companions. Balsam wondered what they were saying to each other, but he could not hear.

He stopped at the corner of First and Main to wait for Neilsville's lone traffic light to change, and realized that he was standing in front of the office of the telephone company. He went in. Behind the counter, an elderly woman sat pensively at an empty desk. She looked up at him.

'I suppose you'll be wanting to order a phone?' she asked.

Surprised, Peter nodded. 'How did you know?'

'Around here,' the woman drawled, 'everybody knows everything.' She pulled a form out of the top drawer of her desk. 'It's Balsam, isn't it?' she asked. Peter nodded. Without asking him any more questions, the woman began filling in the spaces on the order form. Finally she pushed it toward him for a signature. As he checked over the information she had gleaned from God-knew-where, she suddenly spoke.

'You used to be a priest, didn't you?'

He looked up, startled.

'Not actually,' he said. 'I started studying for the priesthood, but didn't finish.'

'One of those,' the woman muttered. Then, as Peter signed the order for the telephone, she spoke again.

'I understand Margo Henderson got off the train with you.'

Peter decided to ignore the disapproving note in her voice.

'Yes, she did. Very pleasant woman.' More than pleasant, he remembered. Beautiful. And at the same time he remembered Margo Henderson with pleasure, he remembered the woman Pete Vernon had sent to meet him at the station with annoyance. Anderson, her name had been. Leona Anderson.

'Divorced,' the woman behind the counter said, jarring Peter back into reality. He realized she was still talking about Margo.

'Well,' Peter said, smiling, 'there are worse things to be.'

'Are there?' the woman said, not returning his smile. 'We're mostly Catholic in Neilsville, you know.'

'But not entirely,' Peter said. 'I understand there's a public school as well as St. Francis Xavier's. And I think I noticed a few other churches, too.'

The woman behind the counter looked him up and down, and Peter felt her gaze taking in his curly brown hair. Apparently she didn't approve of that, either. 'There's room enough in Neilsville for everyone. If they behave themselves.' Her tone said she didn't think Peter would.

'That's strange,' he said. 'Someone else said the same thing to me earlier today. A woman named Leona Anderson.'

'Leona's a very wise woman.'

'I'm sure she is,' Peter agreed dryly. She had also struck him as a very unpleasant woman, who had made her distaste for him plain, from the look in her eye as she introduced herself to the moment she delivered him to his apartment. 'When will the phone be put in?'

'Four days,' the woman said without consulting a calendar. 'That's how long it takes to process the order.'

Since there seemed to be no room for argument, Peter thanked the woman for her services and left the office. She watched him go. When he was out of sight she picked up the telephone on her desk and quickly dialled a number.

'Leona? That man Balsam you told me about. He was just here, ordering a phone. I think you're right, and you'd better talk to Monsignor. I don't know what it is, but there's something wrong about that young man. If you ask me, trouble just came to Neilsville.'

THREE

Four days later Peter Balsam was beginning to feel a little easier about Neilsville. He had created a space for himself: his books were neatly arranged on the bricks and boards that nearly covered one wall, and he had spent more than he had intended on the plants that now hung from hooks in the ceiling and brackets on the walls. And, of course, there was the telephone. He stared at the green instrument on his desk, and wondered why the installation of the phone that morning had made him feel 'connected'. It wasn't as if he had anyone to call, nor was there much likelihood that anyone would call him. And then, surprisingly, the telephone rang. He stared at it uncomprehendingly for a moment, then picked it up and spoke a tentative hello, ready for whoever had called to discover he had dialled a wrong number and hang up.

'Peter Balsam?' A woman's voice, vaguely familiar, somewhat shy.

'Yes,' Peter answered, wondering if he should recognize the voice.

'It's Margo Henderson,' the woman continued. 'From the train?' Balsam felt a surge of pleasure run through his body.

'Hello,' he said again, this time with warmth.

'That's better,' Margo said. 'For a minute I thought you didn't remember who I was.'

'I didn't,' Balsam admitted. 'Actually, I thought it was going to be a wrong number. I just had the phone put in this morning. It usually takes a few days before anybody can get the number.'

'Not in Neilsville.' Margo laughed. 'You're the most interesting thing to happen in years.' She paused for a second, and Peter was about to respond when she plunged ahead. 'I was wondering if maybe you'd like to take me out for dinner tonight,' she said.

Peter was momentarily nonplussed, then recovered himself.

'I'd love to,' he said. 'But I have a problem. No car.'

'That's no problem. I happen to have a very serviceable Chevy. If you're not too proud to allow yourself to be picked up by a woman, I'll see you about seven-thirty.'

'Well, fine,' Peter said, not really sure if it was fine or not, but willing to give it a chance. 'Do you know where I live?'

'Let me see if I can figure it out,' Margo replied. 'If you don't have a car, you must be within walking distance of St. Francis Xavier's. So you must live in that new apartment building on Third Street, just off Main.'

'A regular Sherlock Holmes,' Peter said.

Margo chuckled. 'Not really. See you at seven-thirty.'

Balsam was about to say something else when he realized he was holding a dead phone in his hand. He stared at it, wondering why she had hung up so abruptly, then decided she had probably been calling from work, and someone had been waiting for her. With a shrug, he turned his attention to other things.

An hour later, Peter Balsam found himself walking slowly up the hill to St. Francis Xavier Church. As he walked, he noticed that Neilsville, though still bleak, no longer seemed as threatening as he had originally thought. Familiarity, he thought: he was getting used to the town. He was no longer seeing only the strangeness of the structures in Neilsville. Now he was noticing their uniqueness as well. Some of the houses, he was beginning to realize, were rather interesting in their own way. Yards were, for the most part, neat and well tended, as if the people of Neilsville, knowing that the surrounding landscape was always going to be barren, had decided to create some green oases within the desert. But it wasn't until his third day in Neilsville, when he had decided to venture away from Main, that Peter had discovered this softer side of Neilsville. Now he walked purposefully along, enjoying the shade of the tree-lined streets and enjoying, too, the privacy the side streets afforded him. On Main Street, he had been too aware of the constant stares of the people of Neilsville as they tried to size up this stranger in their midst. But on Elm, if people watched him from their windows, Peter Balsam was blissfully unaware of it.

He reached the top of the hill and made his way into the cool, dark church. Just inside the entrance he dipped his fingers in the font and genuflected, then moved down the aisle, genuflected once more, and sank into a pew. For a few moments Balsam simply sat, absorbing the serenity of the church, letting his eyes adjust from the glare of the summer afternoon to the soft light filtering through the stained glass of the clerestory windows.

Slowly he became aware that he was not alone. A few pews ahead of him, near the alcove dedicated to the Blessed Virgin, a girl sat motionless, her head bowed. He recognized her as the girl who had played alone on the handball court.

Her lips moved silently in prayer, and her fingers worked at the beads clutched in her hands. Balsam watched her for a few minutes, then began to feel as if his stares were intruding on her privacy. Self-consciously, he forced himself to concentrate on his own meditations, and ignore the lonely presence of the girl.

Thirty minutes later they met at the door of the church. He hadn't seen her rising from her pew at the same time as he had risen from his own, and he had almost forgotten her presence. But as the two of them emerged from the shadows of the church into the white hot afternoon, and the somnolence that he always felt in church left him, Balsam smiled at the girl. She looked at him uncertainly, and seemed about to hurry away, so he spoke.

'Hello,' he said.

Marilyn Crane looked at the man mutely, and tried to find her tongue.

'You seem to come here as often as I do,' Balsam continued. 'It makes a nice break from the heat of the day, doesn't it?'

Her eyes widened, and Balsam wondered if it was possible that the girl hadn't noticed him yesterday and the day before, as the two of them silently sat in the church. Apparently she hadn't.

'I'm Peter Balsam,' he said, offering her his hand.

Marilyn Crane stared blankly at the proffered hand. Then, as if coming out of a daze, she grasped it and introduced herself.

'I'm Marilyn Crane,' she said. 'You're the new teacher, aren't you?'

Balsam nodded. 'Are you going to be one of my students?'

She smiled shyly and bobbed her head, almost as if she was apologizing for her presence. 'Latin Three,' she said. Then she added, as an afterthought: 'And the psychology course, I hope.'

'You hope?' Peter repeated. 'All you have to do is sign up for it.'

'I don't know if I can,' Marilyn said softly. 'I asked my parents if I could take it, but they said they'd have to talk it over.'

'Well, you can tell them for me that I promise not to put any crazy ideas in your head,' Balsam said, grinning.

Suddenly the girl seemed to relax, and the two of them began slowly walking back down the hill toward town.

'How did you know that was what my parents were worried about?' Marilyn asked suddenly, when they were halfway down the hill.

Balsam tapped his head. 'I'm a psychologist,' he said darkly. 'I have ways of knowing things.'

Marilyn looked at him sharply, then, as she realized he was kidding her, she laughed, a hesitant, hollow sound. Listening to it, Balsam was sure he knew the reason it sounded strange: this child rarely laughed.

'You spend a lot of time in church, don't you?' he said mildly.

Marilyn nodded. 'I like it there. It's so cool, and quiet, and I can be by myself but not feel lonely, if you know what I mean.'

'I know exactly what you mean,' Balsam replied. 'I feel the same way.'

Marilyn looked at him wonderingly, and for the first time in her life felt that there might actually be someone else in the world who understood how she felt.

'I usually pray to the Sorrowful Mother,' she said. 'For some reason, she always seems to make me feel better.'

Balsam didn't respond right away, and Marilyn glanced quickly at him to see if her words had put him off. But no, he merely seemed to be thinking about something, so she continued walking beside him in silence. It was a nice silence, she thought. Not like the silences that so often fell over groups of her acquaintances as she approached.

Had Peter Balsam been aware of the silence he probably would have broken it. But he was thinking about what the girl had said, or, more accurately, of the way she had referred to the Blessed Virgin. The Sorrowful Mother, she had said. It had been a long time since Balsam had heard that appellation applied to the Holy Mother. He wondered briefly how she had happened to use it, but quickly decided not to question her about it. Not yet, at least. The child seemed nervous, like a rabbit on the alert, ready to shy away at the least provocation. And Balsam felt that it was important that she not shy away. Important for him, and important for her.

'Well,' he said finally as they approached the corner of Third Street, 'this is where I get off.' He pointed down the street. 'I live down there,' he continued. 'In the new apartment building.'

A look of comprehension came over Marilyn's face, and she bobbed her head. Peter suddenly realized that she had been afraid he was rejecting her. He smiled at her, saying, 'Come over and see me if you want to. I'm always home, or most always, and my name's on the mailbox.'

'Oh,' Marilyn gasped. 'I – I couldn't do that – ' she stammered.

Balsam looked blank. 'You couldn't?' he asked. 'Why on earth not?'

Now Marilyn appeared totally flustered. 'I – I don't know,' she floundered. And suddenly Peter understood. There had never before been a teacher in Marilyn's life who didn't wear a habit or live in a convent. What he had just suggested was so totally beyond her experience as to be almost incomprehensible.

'Well,' he said briefly. 'Don't worry about it. And don't forget to give my message to your parents. I think the psychology class is going to be very interesting, and I'd like to have you in it.'

As Marilyn looked dumbfounded, Peter smiled at her once more, and started down Third Street. After he had gone a few yards, he turned and waved, and suddenly Marilyn waved back. Peter Balsam continued down the street toward his apartment.

For a few seconds longer, Marilyn watched the retreating figure of the new teacher, then continued home. Suddenly the world did not seem so bleak to her. She liked the new teacher, and she would talk to her parents again about taking his psychology course. Then she suddenly stopped, and there on the sidewalk of Main Street, Marilyn Crane crossed herself, and silently repeated a prayer of thanks to the Sorrowful Mother for bringing Mr. Balsam to Neilsville. Then she opened her eyes and continued walking. Across the street, Judy Nelson watched her from the drugstore window, and smiled.

The bell rang at precisely seven-thirty. Peter Balsam opened the door to find Margo Henderson smiling at him with a brightness that was almost too cheerful. He held the door for her to come in, and closed it firmly behind her. As the door clicked shut, the smile faded slightly, and she laughed nervously.

'I feel like a wicked woman,' she said, shrugging off the light jacket she had thrown over her shoulders and glancing quickly around the apartment. 'Do you happen to have a spare drink around here?'

'Scotch or bourbon?' Peter said, wondering if he should offer her wine instead, and wishing he'd thought of a clever retort.

'Scotch, with about ten splashes of water.' She gave the

room a more careful inspection while Peter mixed two identically weak highballs. 'I like this,' she declared as she took one of the glasses from him. 'Books and plants – the two things I can't live without.' She tasted the drink. 'And you make perfect drinks, too. Maybe we should get married.'

Peter choked on the mouthful of scotch-and-water he had been about to swallow, then realized she had been kidding. As his face reddened, Margo laughed again.

'I'm sorry,' she said. 'I didn't mean to kill you off.' She patted him on the back until his coughing subsided. He sank to the couch and looked at her. And then, when he saw the twinkle in her eye, he suddenly began laughing.

'I am *so* glad to see you,' he declared. 'You haven't any idea.' Then he looked at her quizzically. 'What did you mean, you feel like a wicked woman?'

'This is the first time in my life I've ever asked a man for a date. Now, maybe you have women calling you all the time, but for me this is a new and daring experience. In fact, I'd give odds such a thing has never been done in Neilsville before.'

'Well, I'm glad you called,' Peter said. 'If I sounded a little strained earlier, it was just out of surprise that the phone rang at all. I'd been staring at it, feeling very plugged into the world, when I realized nobody in town was likely to call. And then it rang, and here you are. Where are we going for dinner?'

'I'm not sure,' Margo said, suddenly pensive. 'I'd thought about Clyde's, where the food is good and the music isn't too offensive, but then it occurred to me that it might be the better part of valour to go out of town.'

'Out of town?' Peter repeated blankly.

Margo nodded. 'Maybe I'm being paranoid, but considering you're brand new in town, and teaching at St. Francis Xavier, and I'm divorced, and . . . well, all things considered, I think we might do better to go somewhere where neither one of us will be recognized. If you aren't starving, I thought we might drive over to Moses Lake. It's forty minutes away, but I know a good Italian place there.'

Balsam started to protest, but then he remembered the frown on Leona Anderson's face when he had accompanied

Margo off the train, and the remarks Monsignor Vernon had made about the 'formality' of Neilsville. 'Formality', he thought, was the wrong word. He was getting the distinct impression that Neilsville was downright narrow-minded.

'Fine,' he agreed, finishing his drink. Then he smiled at Margo mischievously. 'Do you want to meet me around the corner, or shall we risk walking out to your car together?'

'Not to worry,' Margo said sheepishly. 'I parked in the alley.'

The restaurant hunched shabbily in the middle of an asphalt parking lot, lit garishly by a sign advertising the name of the place – Raffaello's – and, in much larger letters, Olympia Beer. But inside it had been decorated in checkered red-and-white tablecloths that somehow managed not to be cute. And the food had been delicious. Peter leaned back in his chair, picked up the cup of cappuccino in front of him, and looked at Margo. He decided she was really quite beautiful.

'Feel better?' she asked him, winking over the rim of her glass as she drained the last of her wine.

'What makes you think I wasn't feeling good to start with?' Peter countered.

She shrugged slightly. 'I don't know,' she mused. 'There was just a look about you. Like something was panicking you. I supposed at first it was me, but I've changed my mind. I think it was Neilsville.'

Balsam nodded guiltily. 'You hit it right on the head,' he admitted. 'I have to confess that I've been getting pretty nervous about the whole thing. At least until yesterday. Yesterday I finally decided to take a chance and walk on a street other than Main. Behind the scenes, Neilsville doesn't seem quite so bleak as it does on Main Street.'

'I guess most towns are like that,' Margo agreed. 'You don't really get a feel for them from the downtown area. You have to see where the people live. And even then, it's not easy. People in small towns aren't as friendly as they're supposed to be. Unless you're a native, of course. If you're not, forget it. You're a newcomer for at least twenty years.'

'I thought that only happened in New England,' Peter laughed.

Margo shook her head. 'Small towns are small towns, wherever you go,' she said. Then she changed the subject. 'How did you find your friend the Monsignor?' she asked, and Peter thought he detected a trace of acid in her voice.

'Not the same as I remembered him,' he admitted. 'But I don't suppose I was the same as he remembered me, either.'

'Mmmm,' Margo mumbled, avoiding his gaze.

'You don't like him, do you?' Peter said suddenly.

'I don't know.' Margo was pensive. 'I suppose Monsignor is something of a reflection of the town. And I'm not going to try to tell you that the town hasn't been hard on me. At least the Catholic part of it.' She looked across the table at Peter, wanting to say something more, but not wanting to risk offending him. But he seemed different from the rest of the Catholics she knew, and she decided to take a chance. 'There's something evil about them,' she said hesitantly. 'Or maybe that's the wrong word. But ever since I was divorced, and pretty much excommunicated from the Catholic community, I've noticed something. I can't put my finger on it, but I'm sure it's there. They stare at you. They talk about you. They make you feel like a freak. And your friend Monsignor Vernon is the worst of them. Every time I see him, I feel his eyes on me, boring into me, as if he's examining me, and finding me lacking. And the rest of them aren't much different.' She suddenly felt embarrassed, as if she'd said too much, and tried to put on a cheerful face. 'I'm doing all right, though,' she added quickly.

Balsam shook his head in wonder. 'I don't know,' he said slowly. 'It all seems so strange to me, almost medieval.'

'It is,' Margo said bitterly. Then she brightened. 'Let's talk about something more cheerful. Have you seen your classroom yet?'

Balsam grinned crookedly at her. 'I thought we were going to talk about something more cheerful,' he said.

'Well, there must be something cheerful to talk about,' Margo laughed. 'Neilsville isn't all that bad.' She paused thoughtfully, then brightened. 'Let's not talk about Neilsville at all. Why don't you tell me about you?'

Peter hesitated a split second, then decided there was no reason not to tell her about his childhood.

At least the part of it he could remember, the part after he was taken to the convent.

He began telling Margo about growing up with the Sisters, then deciding to enter the priesthood.

'And that, I suppose, was the first of the mistakes,' he said.

'Mistakes?'

'Sometimes it seems like my life was a series of mistakes. I only entered the priesthood because it seemed the natural thing to do. But I soon found out it wasn't for me, so I left the seminary and went to St. Alban's.' He grinned. 'Remind me to model my robes for you sometime.'

'You still have them?'

'In the bedroom closet. I guess nobody ever throws things like that away. Anyhow, I took a degree in psychology, and then went to California on a counselling job. But it didn't work out any better than the priesthood. So I decided to go back to St. Alban's, and get a master's degree. And I got married.' A frown creased Margo's face. 'Didn't I tell you that?' He hurried on. 'I thought I had. Not that it matters. I'm separated.'

'Does Monsignor Vernon know?'

'I told him. He didn't seem too pleased.'

'I'll bet,' Margo agreed. 'What happened? To your marriage, I mean?'

'I'm not sure. Looking back on it, I don't think Linda and I ever should have gotten married in the first place. I suppose we needed each other at the time – we were both pretty lonely people. Anyway, she found someone else not to be lonely with.'

There was a note of bitterness in his voice, and Margo decided not to press the matter. 'What brought you to Neilsville?'

'Monsignor Vernon. I got a letter from him, asking me if I could teach both Latin and psychology. When I wrote back and told him I could, he offered me the job here. So here I am.'

'And you don't like it.' It was a statement, not a question.

Peter moved uncomfortably in his chair. 'I don't know. I get what they call bad vibes from the town. It's as if there's something going on here, something under the surface, that's always about to erupt, but never does.'

Margo stared at him. 'That's it, exactly,' she said. 'That's exactly how I feel. But I thought I was the only one.'

'Well, now there's two of us.' Peter smiled. He reached for the cheque and stood up.

An hour later, when they pulled up in front of his apartment house, he took her hand, squeezed it, and opened the car door.

'Next time,' he said, 'it's going to be your turn. I want to know as much about you as you know about me.' Then he got out of the car, closed the door firmly, and turned to go into the building. Margo waited for him to turn and wave. When he didn't, she felt slightly disappointed.

As she drove home, Margo decided she liked Peter Balsam. She liked him very much. Next time, she would tell him about herself. And she was sure there would be a next time, even if she had to call him again. But she didn't think she would. Next time, she was sure, Peter would call her.

Later, as she was preparing to go to bed, Margo suddenly remembered that there was something Peter hadn't told her. On an impulse, she reached out to pick up the phone, but it rang before she touched it. It was Peter.

'I hope I didn't wake you up,' he said.

'No. As a matter of fact, I'm glad you called.'

'I'm not really sure why I called.'

'Maybe because I wanted to talk to you.'

'You mean, you made me call you?'

'Maybe I did,' Margo said mysteriously.

Peter chuckled. 'I don't believe in that kind of thing.'

'Don't you? Maybe you should.' Then: 'Peter?'

'Yes?'

'I was wondering about something. When you were a child – how did you get to the convent in the first place?'

There was a silence, and then Peter's voice, sounding

slightly hollow, came over the line. 'I don't know, really. The sisters never really tell you where you came from.'

Twenty minutes later, as Margo was trying to fall asleep, she was still thinking about what he had said, and wondering where, thirty-some years ago, Peter Balsam had come from.

FOUR

If the first day of school at St. Francis Xavier High School did not engender the same enthusiasm as the last, it was not only because the first day marked the beginning of another nine months of regimentation. It was, as far as the students were concerned, much worse than that; it meant another nine months of being reminded of their constant failure to live up to the standards set by Monsignor Vernon and the Sisters, another nine months of constant invasions of their privacy as the Sisters swooped down on them, demanding to know exactly what it was they were whispering about, or inspected their lockers, or suddenly seized their notebooks to determine exactly what was being written in them, or subjected them to any of the other minor or major indignities that plagued their lives. And, of course, the first day was the worst, for they had only just gotten used to the freedom of summer when it was torn from their grasp.

And, of course, there was Monsignor Vernon, ever-present, ever-watchful, constantly ready to criticize, seldom ready to praise. He had been there this morning, waiting on the steps of the school, watching them return for yet another year. There he would remain for the next nine months, if not on the steps, then in the corridors, his black-garbed figure looming over them, his piercing black eyes boring into them, discovering in them – each of them – minute flaws to be condemned.

As they walked together down the stairs to the first floor of the school and made their way slowly toward Room 16, neither Judy Nelson nor Karen Morton was in the best of moods. They stopped in front of Judy's locker, and she began working the dial. As usual on the first day of school, it took her three tries before the metal door suddenly clicked open. Judy pulled the door wide open and tossed her history book inside. She stared at it bitterly.

'Do you suppose Sister Kathleen meant it when she said we'd go through that whole thing in the first semester?' she asked of no one in particular. The three inches of history sat depressingly thick on the floor of the locker.

'Who reads it?' Karen said, tossing back her long blonde hair. 'All you have to do is glance at the headings, and study the quizzes at the end of the chapters. Everybody knows Sister Kathleen hasn't made up a test of her own in forty years.'

'She gives me a pain,' Judy groused. 'Did you believe her this morning? She thinks we spent the whole summer "being carnal", as she puts it. Is that the same as screwing?'

Karen giggled, but her face turned red, and Judy wondered if she'd touched a nerve. She decided to press the point, and see what happened.

'I mean, the way she was talking, she must think we don't do anything except talk about sex, or dream about sex, or *have* sex, for that matter. Well, if you ask me, that says a lot about where her head's at.' By now, Judy was pleased to note, Karen was showing definite signs of nervousness. Now, she thought, was the time to pounce. 'Of course,' she mused, trying to sound as if she didn't have anyone in particular in mind, '*some* of us do have a few sins to worry about, don't we?'

'I wouldn't know,' Karen said sarcastically. 'But personally, if I have any talking to do on that subject, I'll do it in the confessional. Not to Sister Kathleen, and certainly not to you.' Then, before Judy could reply, Karen caught sight of Marilyn Crane coming down the hall, and said, 'You know, maybe it wouldn't be so bad being like Marilyn. At least the Sisters never seem to worry about *her* "losing her soul in sin".'

Judy slammed the locker shut, and glanced down the hall to the spot where Marilyn stood trying to work the combination to her locker. 'If I were her,' she said acidly, 'I'd really be in trouble.' She smiled wickedly at Karen. 'After all,' Judy purred, 'isn't suicide supposed to be the worst sin of all?'

'Judy – ' Karen breathed, her eyes widening at her friend's cruelty. 'That's an awful thing to say. I mean, I don't like her any better than you do, but still – ' Before she could finish what she was saying, a sharp scream interrupted her. She whirled to see Marilyn Crane staring into her locker, one hand clapped over her mouth to stifle the scream. If she hadn't turned so quickly, perhaps Karen would have seen the tiny smile that was playing around the corner of Judy Nelson's mouth. It was not a pleasant smile.

Twenty feet away, Marilyn Crane stared, horrified, into the depths of her locker. There, where earlier had been only a neat pile of books, lay a frog.

Or at least what had once been a frog. The creature was spread out on a dissecting board, its legs pinned as if it had been crucified, the contents of its belly laid artfully around the corpse. Penned in neat letters across the bottom of the dissecting board was a message. 'Jesus Loves You – But No One Else Does.'

Marilyn felt a wave of nausea rise in her stomach, and pressed her hand harder over her mouth. Who could have done it? And why? It was crazy. It was sick. *She* was sick. Then she got hold of herself.

No, she told herself. Don't get sick. That's what they want. Don't give them the satisfaction. She heard a noise behind her, and turned to see three of the Sisters hurrying toward her. Her first impulse was to wait for them, and show them what was in her locker. But there would be a fuss. They would question her. Eventually, they would find out who had put the frog in her locker – and she would only get blamed for being a tattle-tale. Thinking quickly, she scooped up the dissecting board and shoved it into the large carry-all that served her both as purse and book-bag, praying the frog wouldn't make too much of a mess before she could get downstairs to the girls' room and get rid of it. She slammed the locker shut and turned to face the three nuns who were now gathered behind her.

'What happened?' The voice was cold, accusing. Marilyn looked up at the cowled face of the nun who had spoken, and recognized Sister Elizabeth. Helplessly, she turned to the others. Sister Marie's countenance seemed gentlest, so it was to her that Marilyn directed her answer.

'Nothing,' she said slowly. 'I – ' She cast around for a likely-sounding excuse for her short scream. I pinched myself on the hinge of the locker, she finished, holding up an undamaged finger as proof that the accident had been more frightening than harmful.

Sister Elizabeth looked at her sceptically, and opened her mouth to challenge the girl. But before she could speak, the third nun, the same Sister Kathleen who only moments ago had been the subject of conversation for Judy and Karen, reached out and patted Marilyn gently.

'Some day, Marilyn,' she said softly, 'you're going to have to learn to be less clumsy.'

Ordinarily such a statement would have hurt, but this time Marilyn was grateful. For once, her reputation for awkwardness had served her. She smiled sweetly at the nun, and in her mind begged forgiveness for the lie. Down the hall, she noticed that Karen Morton and Judy Nelson were losing interest in her plight.

'That's Marilyn,' Karen commented. 'She'll probably slam her locker on her nose before the week's over.' The two girls laughed, and started on down the hall toward Room 16.

At the end of the corridor a door shut softly as Monsignor Vernon turned back into his office.

Inside Room 16, Peter Balsam was nervously awaiting the arrival of the psychology class. So far, the day had gone remarkably well. After all, Latin was Latin, and most of his students had taken it before. They knew what to expect. But the psychology class was different. All morning he had felt a certain electricity coming from some of the Latin students; he assumed these were the ones who had registered for the new course as well, and they were trying to size him up, trying, from the way he handled the Latin classes, to figure out what the psychology course would be like.

And, of course, there had been Sister Elizabeth, the rather stern-looking nun who had stormed into Room 16 between first and second periods to inform him that in her opinion his course was a mistake, and that, even before it had begun, it was already disrupting the school. She was having discipline problems, she declared, and he was to blame. The students were so busy talking about him, and his new course, that they paid no attention to her. Balsam, realizing that humour would be useless with Sister Elizabeth, solemnly promised her that he would see to it that his course created no more disturbances. Sister Elizabeth, carrying an air of scepticism with her, had marched wordlessly out of his room.

Then, between the second and third periods, Sister Marie had stopped in. In contrast to Sister Elizabeth, Sister Marie had been all smiles. When he had promptly called her Sister, she had held up a hand in protest, and asked him to please, at least when they were alone, just call her Marie. And, she had confided in an excited whisper, despite what the others might say, she herself thought it was about time they started teaching something useful at St. Francis Xavier's. Then her face had taken on a slightly wistful look and, as if suddenly realizing she might be on the verge of complaining, she had beaten a hasty retreat.

Finally, just a few moments ago, it had been Sister Kathleen. She had marched into the room, checked to be sure it was empty, then closed the door firmly behind her.

'It's my duty to speak to you about an unpleasant subject,' she had announced. Without waiting for any response from Peter Balsam, she had plunged ahead.

'I'm sure you are aware that it isn't easy for us to maintain a suitable moral climate for the children here,' she said, looking him in the eyes. Then her gaze shifted, and Balsam had the distinct feeling that she was suddenly losing her nerve. He thought he knew what was coming, and he wasn't disappointed.

'The modern world is not all I might wish it to be,' Sister Kathleen continued. 'I'm afraid the moral laxness that seems to have invaded the rest of the world has succeeded in penetrating St. Francis Xavier School, if you know what I mean.' She looked at him darkly, and Balsam looked right back at her, trying not to reveal that he had, indeed, caught her meaning. She decided he was obtuse, and she would have to be more specific.

'What I'm trying to say,' she went on uncomfortably, 'is that I hope you have no plans to discuss anything – well, *carnal* is the word, I suppose – in your psychology course.' She spat the word psychology out, as if it were extremely distasteful.

'It's a psychology course, Sister,' Peter had reassured her softly. Then he couldn't resist his impulse. 'Not a course in sex education.' He almost chuckled out loud as the nun turned scarlet and fled from the room.

A moment later he had heard the sharp scream from the hallway, but by the time he had reached his door the three nuns who had paid him visits that morning had the situation well in hand. Also, he was sure, all but Marie would resent his intruding into the matter. So he had retreated back into Room 16, to await his students. And one by one, they were drifting in. He recognized some of them and noted that as they came into the room they headed directly for the seats they had occupied in earlier classes in Room 16. One of these, Janet Connally, had started for the third-row seat she had occupied earlier, then, as if remembering something, moved up to the front rank, and carefully set her books on one of the adjoining seats, her sweater on the other. When Peter Balsam caught her eye, she smiled at him, then self-consciously glanced around the room, nodding in recognition to her friends.

A moment later a pretty, dark-haired girl came into the room, glanced quickly around, then went directly to the seat on which Janet Connally's sweater was resting, picked up the sweater, and sat down. She handed the sweater to Janet, and whispered something in her ear. The two girls giggled, and Balsam wondered what had been said. Sister Elizabeth, he realized, would have found out immediately, probably with an intimidating look. Balsam had neither the assurance nor the technique to make such a ploy work, so he simply pretended not to hear the giggles.

A few minutes later Karen Morton and Judy Nelson breezed into the room, waved at Janet Connally and the dark-haired girl (who Balsam decided must be Penny Anderson) and took two of the remaining seats in the front row. The fifth seat next to Karen Morton, was stacked with Karen's books. Balsam wondered whom it was being saved for. Just before the bell rang signifying the beginning of the class period, he found out.

Jim Mulvey, his hair a bit too long, and his clothes looking slightly rumpled, slouched into the room, shoved Karen Morton's books to the floor, and sank into the last seat of the front rank. While Mulvey fixed Balsam with a slightly sullen look, Karen glared at her boyfriend and retrieved her books from the floor. When Jim turned to her, she was all smiles.

Peter Balsam picked up the roster and noted that there was one more name on the list than there were students in the room. Though he was already familiar with almost half the class, he began calling the roll. Before he'd even begun, he knew who was missing. Marilyn Crane. He glanced at the list once more. Yes, her name was on it. He looked out at the twenty-nine faces in front of him. Marilyn's was not among them. He began calling the roll, half concentrating on matching names to faces, half wondering what had happened to Marilyn.

When he was halfway through the list, the door to Room 16 creaked open, and Marilyn Crane crept into the room and slid into the single vacant seat in the back row. At the sound of the door opening, every head in the room had turned. And then, starting from the point where Judy Nelson and Karen Morton sat together, the whispering and giggling began, rippling through the room, swirling toward Marilyn. Balsam stopped calling the roll, and stared out at the teen-agers, waiting for them to notice the sudden quiet.

When the silence finally came, he fixed his gaze on Karen Morton and Judy Nelson. Judy regarded him steadily, with an almost challenging look in her eyes. But Balsam was pleased to see that Karen Morton had the good grace to blush and quickly find something fascinating in her notebook. He resumed calling the roll, taking care to give Marilyn Crane a reassuring wink when he got to her name. In another minute, he was done. He set the list down on his desk, and looked once more at the class.

'Well,' he said, 'I suppose we might as well get to it. This class isn't going to be like any of the others, so those of you who think you have me all figured out from Latin classes can forget it.' That should throw them off, he thought, and was pleased to see the looks of consternation he'd produced. There was a rustling in the room, as thirty teen-agers suddenly realized they were going to have to reassess things. The four girls in the front row glanced nervously at each other.

'As some of you know,' Balsam continued, looking at them placidly, 'I generally seat my classes alphabetically.' An almost inaudible groan went through the room, and several of the students began gathering their belongings in preparation for the seating shift. 'However,' Balsam continued, 'this class is different. In this class you can sit where you want, and you needn't feel you have to use the same seats every day. It may make it a little harder for me to learn your names, but don't worry about it. So, if any of you want to change seats now, feel free.'

About half the class began trading seats. Nobody in the front moved, nor did Marilyn Crane: the front row had already decided where to sit, and Marilyn Crane had no reason to move – no one had invited her to sit by them. Balsam noticed, however, that the boy who eventually did sit next to Marilyn – Jeff Bremmer, if his memory served him correctly – smiled and spoke to her. While they resettled themselves, Balsam wondered how many, if any, of his students had figured out that he had just gotten them to tell him something about themselves without saying a word. He knew they would continue to tell him about themselves as they rearranged themselves through the term. It would be particularly interesting to watch the front row, the four girls Monsignor Vernon had mentioned to him, and the boy, Jim Mulvey, who was apparently Karen Morton's boyfriend.

When they were finally settled in their new seats, Balsam began telling them what he hoped to accomplish in the psychology course. He would not, he told them, be spending too much time on the field of abnormal psychology, though he would delve briefly into some of the more exotic forms of madness. That earned him an appreciative laugh.

But what he was most interested in, he told them, were the possibilities the course offered for them all to get to know themselves, and each other, better. In this class, he announced, he intended to stay as far away as possible from the formalized teaching methods that were the norm at St. Francis Xavier's. Instead, he hoped the students would learn from each other as much as from him. At the same time they were teaching each other, he told them, they would be teaching themselves. If they all worked together, it should prove an interesting and valuable year.

Balsam glanced at the clock, and saw that he had only fifteen minutes left. Behind him, where it had been for forty-five minutes now, a map of the Holy Roman Empire covered much of the blackboard. Balsam now directed the attention of the class to the map.

'Behind the map,' he told them, 'there is a picture. I'm going to raise the map for just a second, then pull it down again. Then we'll talk about what you saw.'

Quickly, before the students could begin buzzing among themselves, Balsam raised and lowered the map, exposing for not more than a second a large black-and-white print, done with a pen in great detail.

'Well?' he said, turning back to the class. 'How about it? What did you see?'

In the front row, Judy Nelson's hand slowly rose.

'Judy?' Balsam said, then, as she started to stand up, he waved her down. 'Not in this class,' he said, smiling. 'Let's save the calisthenics for Latin, shall we?'

Judy's eyes widened in surprise; this had certainly never happened at St. Francis Xavier's before. Not only she, but the entire class seemed to relax. She sank back into her seat.

'Well?' Balsam prompted her.

Judy started to speak, then giggled self-consciously, 'I'm sorry,' she said. 'It's just not easy to answer questions sitting down. None of us has ever done it before.'

Again the class laughed, and Balsam was pleased. So far, everything was going exactly as he planned it.

'That's all right,' he said easily. 'You'll get used to it. Now, if you haven't forgotten completely, what did you see in the picture?'

'Well,' Judy said slowly. 'I think it was a skull. At least that's what it looked like to me.'

Balsam nodded. 'Anybody else see a skull? Raise your hands.' All the hands in the room went up, except one. Marilyn Crane sat, her hands folded on the desk in front of her, her face betraying the shame of having missed out on something.

'We seem to have a dissenter,' Balsam said, trying to let Marilyn know with a smile that it was all right with him if she hadn't seen a skull. 'What did you see, Marilyn?'

The girl looked as if she was about to cry. She didn't want to be the only person who hadn't seen what everyone else had seen. But she'd seen something different, and she wasn't going to pretend she hadn't.

'I – I suppose it sounds silly, but all I could see was a woman looking at herself in a mirror.'

Another ripple of laughter passed over the class, but it was derisive, not happy. Before it had died away, Balsam had reached behind him and let the map roll upward into its case, exposing the picture. And then, as they studied it, the class stopped laughing, for Marilyn had been right. A second look revealed that the picture was, indeed, a highly detailed drawing of a woman peering into a mirror. It was captioned 'Vanity.' Balsam let them absorb the lesson in silence for a moment.

'You see?' he said at last. 'Nobody was wrong, and nobody was right.' The class looked at him, baffled, and Balsam realized he had presented something totally new to them – a situation in which there was no wrong and no right.

'What you've just seen,' he told them, 'is what we call an experiment in stimulus response. As you may have noted, not everyone reacts to a given stimulus with the same response. How one responds to a given stimulus depends on one's psychological make-up.' And then, realizing that only Marilyn Crane had responded differently from the rest, he decided to add something for her benefit. 'The fact that only Marilyn didn't see the skull is interesting, isn't it? You must be an awfully morbid group.' He winked at them, so they would know he was only kidding. But he'd made his point; no one turned to stare at Marilyn. Instead, they stared at each other.

Balsam glanced at the clock; there were still five minutes left.

'You know,' he said, directing his attention to the class once again, 'you all surprise me. For fifty minutes now, I've had something carefully concealed on the desk. And not one of you has asked me what it is.' The students looked at each other uncomfortably. 'I hope that will change by the end of the term,' Balsam continued dryly. 'A little curiosity may have killed the cat, but it never hurt a student. So gather round.'

He pulled a cloth away, and the students clustered around his desk to see what it was that they should have asked about. It was a wooden box, with a glass top, known as a Skinner box. Under the glass was a white rat. As the students looked on, Peter Balsam flipped a switch on the side of the box, and the rat began pounding at a small lever inside the box. Each time it hit the lever, a small pellet of food fell into the box. The rat promptly gobbled it up.

'Conditioned response,' Balsam told them. 'The rat has learned that the food will only come out when the light is on and he presses the lever. So every time the light goes on, he presses the lever.' He switched the light off; the rat sat still.

Around him, the students were talking among themselves,

and speculating on the possibilities of the experiment. In the middle of their discussion, the bell rang. Immediately, the discussion ended, and the students began moving back to their seats to gather up their books and notebooks.

'And that,' Balsam said loudly enough to attract their attention, 'is another example of conditioned response. See you tomorrow.'

They stared at him for a moment, then burst into spontaneous laughter. As Balsam watched them drift out of the room, he decided it was going to work. The psychology class was a success.

He pulled open the bottom drawer of his desk, and took out the brown bag that contained his lunch. Then, as he began slowly munching on a sandwich, a vague discomfort came over him. At first he couldn't pinpoint the cause of his anxiety, but as he continued eating his lunch it all came clear to him.

It was the picture, and the way the class had reacted to it. Why, out of thirty students, had all but one of them seen the image of death? Why had only Marilyn Crane, of all the students, seen a woman and a mirror? The ratio was wrong – the class should have been fairly evenly split in their initial perception of the picture.

But they weren't.

FIVE

Inez Nelson heard the telephone ring, and glanced toward her husband. His eyes remained fixed on the TV. It rang again, and Inez glanced at the ceiling, as if expecting to be able to see Judy running toward the upstairs extension. When it rang for the third time, Inez sighed, got up from her chair, and walked into the kitchen, half-expecting it to stop ringing before she could pick it up. It didn't.

'Mrs. Nelson?' Inez immediately recognized the voice as Karen Morton's. 'Is Judy there?'

'Just a minute,' Inez said. She laid the receiver on the kitchen counter and went to the foot of the stairs.

'Judy!' she called. 'For you! Karen Morton!'

'In a minute,' Judy's muffled voice called back. Inez walked slowly back to the kitchen and picked up the receiver. 'She'll be here in a minute,' she said. She stood by the phone, idly waiting to hear her daughter's voice before she hung up.

'Karen?' Judy's voice came on the line. 'I was just going to call you.' Her voice dropped slightly, and her tone became confidential, 'I saw him today. I mean he *spoke* to me.'

'Who?' Karen asked without much interest.

'Lyle,' Judy said, as if Karen should have known. 'Lyle Crandall. Isn't he gorgeous?'

'If you like that type,' Karen said. She was not about to admit that she agreed that Lyle Crandall was, indeed, gorgeous.

'I think he's neat,' Judy went on. 'He looks just like Nick Nolte, only better. Is he coming to your party?'

'I suppose so,' Karen said, sounding bored. 'I mean, I guess he'll show up with Jim Mulvey, and you better believe Jim's coming.'

'But he's not coming with any of the girls?' Judy asked.

'It's not going to be that kind of party,' Laren said. Then, after a slight pause, she added, 'At least not at first. But you never know what might happen, do you?'

Judy felt a wave of anticipation run over her, and wondered if the party was really going to turn out the way Karen had implied. 'What about your mother?' she said. 'Isn't she going to be there?'

A slight snicker came over the wire. 'She has to work Saturday night,' Karen replied. 'At first she told me I couldn't have a party if she couldn't be here, so I told her I was only going to have some girls in. She thinks we're going to make fudge or something.'

'What if she finds out boys are going to be there?' Judy wanted to know.

'She doesn't get off till midnight,' Karen said confidently.

'By then we'll have gotten everybody out of the house.' Then, in a near whisper: 'Did you tell your mother you were coming over early?'

'Of course,' Judy said. 'You don't think I'm going to wait till everyone's there and then change my dress, do you?'

Karen giggled. 'That might be interesting,' she said.

'Maybe for you,' Judy said archly. 'I'm a little more modest.'

'In that dress?' Karen said. 'I didn't think you bought it because you thought it was modest. I thought you bought it because you thought it was sexy.'

'It is, isn't it?' Judy breathed. 'Do you think Lyle will notice?'

'How can he miss?' Karen said sarcastically. 'With that neck line, and the way it fits, everyone will notice you.' Then she paused a moment. 'What if your mother finds out which dress you bought?'

'She won't,' Judy said confidently. 'Besides, even if she does, I can talk her into letting me keep it.' Then, remembering that her mother sometimes stood at the foot of the stairs listening to her when she was on the phone, Judy glanced down the stairwell. No one was there, but she decided enough had been said about the new dress.

'What do you think of Mr. Balsam?' she asked, changing the subject.

'I guess he's okay,' Karen replied, not wanting to commit herself to an opinion until she found out how her friends felt about the new teacher. 'At least he's different from the Sisters. But he'll probably change. In a week his class won't be any different from the others.'

'I don't know,' Judy said, suddenly thoughtful. 'Janet says he's completely different in Latin than he is in psychology. She says it's like having two different teachers.'

'Really?' Karen was suddenly curious. 'What do you mean?'

'I'm not sure,' Judy said. 'I guess he teaches Latin the same way the nuns do, making you stand up to recite, and all that. Janet says she thinks it's because he doesn't really know Latin very well, and he's trying to cover up.'

Karen giggled. 'Maybe he's just crazy, and he's trying to cover that up by teaching psychology. You know what they say about psychologists – most of them need one.'

Now both girls laughed, but in the middle of the laughter Judy thought she heard a click, as if someone had picked up the other phone in the kitchen.

'Well, I have to go now,' she said, cutting into the laughter. She hoped Karen would pick up her signal. 'So I'll come over an hour earlier on Saturday, and help you get ready, all right?'

There was a short silence while Karen tried to fathom why Judy was breaking off their conversation so suddenly. And then, with the antennae that teen-agers share, she knew what was happening. 'That'll be great,' she said. 'If I can get Penny and Janet to come early too, it'll almost be like having two parties. See you tomorrow.' She hung up the phone, congratulating herself on how quickly she had caught on and helped Judy fool whoever was eavesdropping on them.

Judy Nelson replaced the phone on its cradle, then stuck her tongue out at the instrument, as if it had been responsible for her mother's violation of what Judy regarded as a personal and confidential conversation.

But the click she had heard had not been her mother picking up the downstairs phone; rather, it had been Inez finally replacing the receiver. Now she was back in the living room, and she was fuming. She glanced at her husband, and saw that he was still intent on the baseball game. Well, there wasn't any use in trying to talk to him anyway. He would simply rebuke her for listening in on something that was none of her business, then tell her that, since tapping telephones is illegal, she couldn't use anything she had heard against Judy. That, she thought, is what I get for marrying a lawyer. Purposefully, Inez moved to the stairway. George Nelson glanced up.

'Going upstairs?' he said.

'I have to talk to Judy,' Inez said, certain that if she told her husband what she was going to talk about, he would stop her. 'It won't take a minute.'

'Tell her if she wants, I'll beat her at backgammon in about a half hour,' George said. Then his eyes locked once more on the TV screen. Inez stared at him for a moment, then shook her head grimly. There would be no cozy games between father and daughter *this* evening, not if she had anything to do with it. She marched up the stairs, entered Judy's room without knocking, and closed the door behind her.

From the bed, Judy looked at her mother, and was about to complain about her having come in without knocking, when she realized something was wrong. Her mother was angry. And then she knew. The phone. The click hadn't been her mother picking up the phone. It had been her mother hanging up. She had heard the wrong part of the conversation.

'I see you know why I'm here,' Inez began. Judy weighed the chances of bluffing it out. Just how much had she said about the dress? She tried desperately to remember. Too much.

'Do I?' Judy countered.

'I think you do,' Inez could feel her temper rising. 'I heard you talking to Karen just now.'

Judy stared defiantly at her mother.

'You bought that dress, didn't you?' Inez demanded, her voice accusing.

'Which one?' Judy stalled.

'Don't talk to me that way, young lady,' Inez snapped. 'You know very well which one. The one I distinctly told you you couldn't have. You bought it, and stashed it away at Karen Morton's, didn't you?'

'Well, what if I did?' Judy blurted out. 'That dress you wanted me to buy made me look twelve years old. And the other one looked nice.'

'Nice enough to help you get into trouble with Lyle Crandall? Well, it isn't going to work. Tomorrow afternoon you're going to get that dress and return it to the store.'

'Oh, all right,' Judy said, giving in on the theory that simply returning the dress was a comparatively mild punishment.

'And you can forget about going to that party,' Inez added.

'Mother – ' Judy began, but Inez cut her off.

'Don't!' she said, holding up her hand. 'If I were you, I'd

think more about my sins than how I could get around my mother!'

Judy stared at her in bafflement. 'Sins?' she said blankly. 'What are you talking about?'

Inez's eyes narrowed. 'Do you want me to count them out for you? You can start with the lie. You lied about the dress.'

'I didn't,' Judy said defensively. 'You never asked me which one I'd bought.' It was a technicality, she knew, but she hoped it would work. It didn't.

'You would have lied about it, if I had asked you,' Inez snapped. 'There's a commandment about honouring your father and your mother, you know.'

Suddenly it was too much for Judy. She leaped up from the bed, and stood staring at her mother. And then she burst into tears.

'Don't say that,' she screamed. 'Wanting to grow up doesn't have anything to do with you. It's something I want to do for me, not to spite you! Can't you understand that?' Then, as she saw that her words had had no effect on her mother, Judy fled to the bathroom and locked herself in. She felt the anger well in her, and wished it would resolve itself into more tears. But, instead, it turned into more anger, and she suddenly felt trapped. Trapped like that rat in Mr. Balsam's box. Well, she'd show her mother. She'd find a way to get even, and her mother would be sorry.

Outside the bathroom, Inez Nelson stared at the closed door. She listened for a moment, hoping to hear a sound that would tell her what was happening inside. But there was no sound, and she knew that Judy was sulking again, something that seemed to be happening more and more lately. Well, this time she wouldn't give in, and she would see to it that Judy didn't find a way to get her father on her side. But she hadn't reckoned with her daughter's determination.

The thought had crossed Peter Balsam's mind that it might not be a bad idea to give Margo Henderson a call, and invite her out for a drink. Then the call had come from the rectory, and he had found his plans for the evening abruptly changed.

Monsignor Vernon – he was still having trouble with that; he had almost called the priest 'Pete' – had asked him to come up to the rectory for a 'chat'. Something in his voice told Peter it was a summons, not an invitation; it was a command. So he had trudged up the hill and arrived at the rectory at precisely nine o'clock. Monsignor Vernon had met him in the foyer, as before, and led him down the hall to what apparently was his private den; at least, if others used it, Peter Balsam hadn't seen them yet. The Monsignor had closed the door behind them, and offered Balsam a glass of sherry. This, Balsam realized, was a ritual, and he wondered if he was expected to decline the offer. Well, if he was, it was too bad. The least the priest could do if he was going to ruin Balsam's evening was give him a drink. Peter accepted the sherry and took one of the comfortable chairs by the fireplace without waiting for an invitation.

'Well,' Monsignor Vernon said amiably, sinking into the other chair and holding his glass up to the light. 'This is nice.' Balsam was unsure if he was referring to the sherry, or things in general. He grunted noncommittally.

'How did it go?' the Monsignor asked him suddenly. 'The first day of school, I mean?'

Balsam shrugged. 'As well as can be expected, I suppose.' Then he grinned. 'I mean, I'm still alive, and nobody even shot a spitball at me.'

Monsignor Vernon smiled icily. 'They wouldn't,' he said shortly. 'We leave that sort of thing to the public schools.'

Balsam nodded sombrely, a sudden image of Sister Elizabeth flashing into his mind. With her around, he imagined, discipline problems were kept to a minimum at St. Francis Xavier's.

'I suppose I should get to the point,' the priest said, shifting in his chair. So I was right, Balsam thought. This was a command performance. He waited quietly for the Monsignor to begin.

'I had a chat with Sister Elizabeth this afternoon,' the priest began. 'She seemed a little upset about you. She thinks you have what she called a "cavalier attitude".'

Balsam smiled at the term, but when he saw that the priest was not smiling, his expression quickly sobered.

'And you agree with her?' he asked carefully.

'I'm not certain,' the priest said pensively. 'That's why I wanted to talk to you this evening. I've been thinking about the talk we had the other day, about your thesis. It occurred to me that I'm still not sure where you stand.'

'Where I stand?' Balsam repeated, trying to fathom the Monsignor's meaning.

'I suppose this will sound strange to you,' Vernon said, trying to smile, with very little success. 'But I must know exactly where you stand with reference to the teachings of the Church.'

'Well, I haven't left it,' Balsam said.

'No, you haven't, have you?' Monsignor said speculatively. 'But then, there are various ways of leaving the Church, aren't there? And it seems to me that your thesis was certainly a step, however, tentative, in that direction.'

He paused then, as if waiting for a response from Balsam. When none was forthcoming he continued. 'Well,' he said abruptly, 'there's no point in beating around the bush. We're here to determine whether you do, or whether you do not, accept the Doctrines of the Church. Since you seem to be particularly well versed in at least one of them, we might as well begin with that one.'

Balsam's first instinct was to simply stand up, walk from the room, proceed down the hill, pack his things, and catch the first train out of Neilsville. Then he thought about it, and decided that there was no point in evasion. If the issue was so important to the priest, he would face it.

'Fine,' he said at last. 'Where do you want to begin?'

'I thought I just made that clear,' the Monsignor said. 'Do you accept the Church's Doctrine that suicide is a mortal and irredeemable sin?'

'I thought I told you the other day that I don't think I'm qualified to make any judgments at all about that.'

'Are you qualified to have faith?' the priest countered.

'I don't think it's a question of faith,' Balsam replied quietly.

'Then let me put it in purely intellectual terms,' Monsignor Vernon said. Unexpectedly, he stood and took Balsam's glass. 'More?' he asked. Surprised, Balsam nodded. The priest refilled the glasses, handed one to Peter, and regained his chair.

'There are reasons why we have the Doctrines, you know,' he said, and Peter could tell from his tone that he was about to receive a lecture. He nodded anyway, on the off chance that it might cut the lecture short. It didn't.

'The Doctrine against suicide exists for many reasons,' the priest said. 'Most important, of course, suicide is in obvious conflict with natural law, since it involves the destruction of natural order.' Balsam was tempted to bring up the phenomenon of lemmings hurling themselves periodically into the sea. He decided against it. The Monsignor would merely say there could be no comparison between human self-destruction and subhuman self-destruction. During this sequence of thoughts Balsam had lost track of the priest's line of reasoning. He seemed to have shifted from the subject of natural order to the subject of absolution.

'You realize,' Vernon was saying, 'that one of the greatest problems a suicide presents to the Church is the problem of absolution . . .'

Not to mention the problems the suicide is causing for himself, Balsam thought. He went on listening.

'. . . The very act of suicide, if it is successful, precludes the possibility of confession and absolution for the sin. There can't be any question but that the suicide has separated himself from the Mother Church, and, therefore, from God.'

'*Extra ecclesium nulla salus*,' Balsam muttered.

'Pardon me?' the priest said.

'Outside the Church there is no salvation,' Balsam translated for him.

'I know the Latin,' Monsignor Vernon said dryly. 'I simply didn't hear the words clearly.' Then he paused, and stared hard at Balsam. 'Do you have "problems" with that Doctrine as well?'

Balsam shrugged. 'I hadn't thought about it,' he said

wearily. He leaned forward in his chair, and decided to try to explain his thinking to the priest.

'Look,' he said, 'I don't know what's been going on here in Neilsville, but everywhere else, at least everywhere I've been, a lot of people are raising questions. And these aren't people who have left the Church, or are contemplating leaving it. They're simply some thoughtful people who would like to see the Church bring itself a little closer to the twentieth century.'

'And that includes challenging the Doctrines?' Vernon asked darkly.

'Not necessarily,' Balsam said. Was there no getting through to this man? Pete Vernon had always seemed so reasonable in school. What had happened? He made one more try. 'It's not really a matter of challenging the Doctrines,' he said. 'It's simply a matter of bringing the Church more in touch with the needs of people.'

'The Church is concerned with the needs of God,' Monsignor Vernon said stiffly, his voice taking on a coldness that almost frightened Peter.

'There are those of us who don't think the needs of God and the needs of man are any different. And we would like to see the Doctrines reflect that.' After he spoke he realized that he had taken a stand. The Monsignor was glaring his disapproval.

'The Doctrines are infallible,' Monsignor Vernon declared. 'They do not need modification. Or do you also challenge the Doctrine of Infallibility?'

Balsam found himself suddenly angry. The man sounded like a medieval Inquisitor. 'The Doctrine of Infallibility itself is only about one hundred years old,' he pointed out, trying to contain himself. 'And, unless my memory is way off, I don't think there was any kind of unanimity when that particular Doctrine was adopted.'

Suddenly the priest was on his feet, glaring down at Balsam with an intensity that frightened him.

'Peter Balsam,' the priest hissed, his eyes glinting, 'it is exactly the sort of thinking I have heard from you tonight that is destroying the Church. We will not tolerate it at St. Francis Xavier's. I do not know, and do not particularly care, what your private thoughts may be – obviously you are very close to falling from grace – but I will not stand for your contaminating the children of this parish with your ideas. It has been my duty and privilege to protect my flock from ideas such as those you've expressed, and I will not fail in my duty now. Do I make myself clear?'

Now Balsam stood up, and gazed at the priest levelly. 'You do,' he said tightly. 'And I have to tell you that what I'm hearing sounds as if it came straight out of the thirteenth century.'

Suddenly the priest relaxed a little, and moved away from Balsam. When he turned to face Peter again, there was a slight smile on his lips that could have been genuine. Peter doubted it was.

'If you've studied your history, you know that there were a lot more saints in that century than in this. Maybe we should consider that fact before we talk with such self-satisfaction about our "modern times".'

'We know a bit more about human beings now,' Balsam said.

'Perhaps,' Monsignor replied. 'But they certainly knew something we've forgotten – how to deal with heresy and sin.' He paused, and when he continued it was more to himself than to Peter. 'Or at least some of us have. Not all of us.'

Ten minutes later, as he walked back down the hill, Balsam was still trying to figure out what had happened to his old friend, Pete Vernon. Though a definite physical resemblance remained, Monsignor Vernon had nothing else in common with the Pete Vernon with whom Petre Balsam had grown up.

As he was leaving, the Monsignor had urged him once more to attend a meeting of the study group he led. Perhaps he should, Balsam decided. Perhaps it was the study group that had affected Monsignor Vernon so strongly, and made his religion so rigid. What was it the priest had said they called the group? The Society of St. Peter Martyr. The same saint whose statue stood in the alcove of Room 16, keeping tabs on him.

Peter Balsam decided to attend the next meeting of the Society. If he was still in Neilsville.

After Balsam left the rectory, and he had carefully locked the front door for the night, Monsignor Vernon returned to the den, carefully locked that door as well, and lit the fire that was already laid in the fireplace. Then, unaware of the uncomfortably high temperature that was turning the small room into an oven, he began to pray. He prayed for a long time, and by the time he was finished, the flames had died. All that remained in the fireplace was a bed of coals, glowing hotly in the darkness. A bed of coals, he thought, that glowed for the heretics and sinners. Smiling contentedly, Monsignor Vernon took himself to bed. He would sleep peacefully tonight. Tomorrow he would begin his work.

SIX

The next day, a subtle shift had taken place in the seating pattern of the psychology class. Though the same five people still ranged across the front row, Judy Nelson was not sitting next to Karen Morton. Today she had moved herself to the end of the row, and Penny and Janet had each moved in a seat. Balsam had wondered, when he first noticed this, if something had happened between Karen and Judy, or whether the four girls were in the habit of changing places, and sharing each other. That, he knew, was unlikely – in many ways adolescents tended to be much more rigid than adults.

Today, Balsam hadn't bothered to cover the Skinner box. As he talked to the class, he occasionally glanced down at the rat, which sat calmly gazing back up at him, almost as if it knew it was going to be called upon to perform, and was awaiting its cue.

Balsam was talking to the class about frustration, and he had tried to put a capital 'F' on the word when he had first used it.

'Frustration,' he had said, 'might be defined as the feeling one gets when one has to sit and listen to a psychology lecture when one would rather be doing almost anything else.'

The class had chuckled nervously, as if they were a little embarrassed at being caught out. But at least they were all paying attention; all that is, except Judy Nelson, who seemed lost in her own world. From what Balsam could observe of the sullen expression on her face, it was not a pleasant world.

He was right. Judy was still sulking about the scene she had had with her mother the night before. She had spent most of an hour locked in the bathroom, waiting for the slight tap at the door, and her mother's plaintive tone asking her if she was all right – the signal that she had won, that her mother had given in. But it didn't come. Finally, Judy had given up the bathroom in favour of a frontal assault. She had gone downstairs to play backgammon with her father. But he had only looked at her coldly and announced that he had changed his mind – there would be no backgammon that night. Judy, bursting into tears, had fled back to the bathroom. There she had waited. And waited. Eventually she had heard her parents come upstairs, and heard them call her a cheerful good-night. Then she had heard their door close as they retired for the night. Judy had considered throwing another tantrum, but had discarded the idea. Instead, she had taken her anger to bed with her, where she had no trouble at all in transferring it to Karen Morton.

The 'if onlies' had begun: If only Karen hadn't called her. If only Karen hadn't begun talking about the party. If only Karen hadn't mentioned the dress. Ignoring the fact that she, too, had talked about the party, bragged about the dress, Judy had quickly decided that the whole thing was Karen's fault. So, today, she had snubbed Karen in the morning, then carefully seated herself two seats away when they had arrived at Room 16. Now, as Mr. Balsam droned on, she glanced across at Karen, and mentally criticized everything about her, from her bleached hair and plucked brows to the too-tight dress that was stretched across her too-large bust. It was all Karen's fault, Judy told herself again. And then she saw all the students standing up and moving to the front of the room, and realized she hadn't heard a word Mr. Balsam had said. Coming out of her reverie, Judy got up and joined the group clustered around the strange box with the rat in it.

'Now,' Peter Balsam was saying, 'watch carefully. As you can see, I've arranged a maze in the box. A simple one. Two correct choices, and it's easy to get through. For you and me, anyway. But it looks different to the rat, since he can't see the whole thing, and wouldn't know what to think of it, even if he could see it. Now, watch what happens.'

He dropped a pellet of food at one end of the maze, and placed the rat at the other. Then he replaced the glass top on the box. The rat sniffed a couple of times, caught the scent of food, and began snuffling around. It started through the maze, came to a dead end, snuffled some more, retraced its steps, and got back on the right track. Then it missed the second turn, and came up against another dead end. Unfazed, it backtracked again. This time its efforts were rewarded.

'Let's try it again, and see what happens,' Balsam said. He opened the box, lifted the rat out, and put in another food pellet. The rat made it to the food with only one wrong turn. The third time he repeated the experiment, the rat went directly to the food. It had learned the route.

'Okay,' Balsam said. 'I'm sure everyone understands what's been happening. I've encouraged the rat to learn by rewarding him with food. So far, so good. Now let's try something else. He picked up a small piece of wood from the desktop, and held it up for the class to see.

'Let's add a new element,' he said. 'Let's put this into the maze right here.' He carefully added the new barrier to the maze.

'But if you put it there,' Janet Connally pointed out, "he won't be able to get through at all.'

Balsam smiled at her. 'Exactly,' he said. 'Now let's see how the rat reacts.' He put the rat back in the box, and quickly replaced the glass top. The rat hurried through the maze until it suddenly bumped into the new barrier. It sniffed at the barrier a couple of times, and tried to prod its way past. The barrier held. Then the rat began moving more rapidly, poking in every corner, frantically searching for a way past the barrier. When it found none, it leaped against the barrier a couple of times, then strained upward and clawed at the glass. Finally, it sat very still, trembling, immobile.

'What happened?' a voice asked softly.

'I frustrated it,' Balsam said. 'And when it couldn't find any outlet for its frustration, it threw in the towel.'

'You mean it just stopped trying?' Balsam recognized the voice now. It was Marilyn Crane. He glanced up at her, and saw an expression of compassion on her face.

'That's right,' he said. 'It stopped trying. It will probably try again in a few minutes, since it can still smell the food. But it will stop again, and unless I take the barrier away it will just give up completely.'

'But I still don't understand what happened.' Penny Anderson looked worried.

Balsam smiled at her. 'I led it to expect something,' he said. 'I taught it that if it went through the maze in a certain way it could expect a reward at the end. And then, just as it had gotten used to the game, I changed the rules. All of a sudden it doesn't know what to expect, and finds that it isn't even in control of the situation. So it's frustrated. Unless I relieve the frustration, it will get neurotic. In fact, if I tried, I could drive that rat completely crazy. All I'd have to do is keep changing the rules on it, let it learn the new rules, then change them again. Mainly, it's a matter of being inconsistent. As long as the rat knows what to expect, he's all right. It doesn't bother him that he can't get food when the light is out. He just waits for the light to come back on. I set the rule long ago, and never varied it. With the maze, I did something different. I was inconsistent.'

'I think I see,' Janet said carefully. 'It's like with my parents. As long as they do what I expect them to do, I feel safe. But every now and then they do something unexpected, and it upsets me.'

'That's it,' Balsam said. 'It's all a matter of consistency. Lack of consistency leads to frustration, and from there on it's a downhill slide.'

Just then the bell rang, and the class, without thinking, began moving to their desks. One or two laughed self-consciously.

'Conditioned response,' Balsam heard Janet Connally whisper to Penny Anderson. Then the two girls were gone, disappearing into the hall with the rest of the class. When he turned back to the rat, Judy Nelson was staring blankly down into the box. Balsam watched her in silence for a moment, wondering if she was aware that the room had emptied. She seemed to be lost somewhere in the depths of the maze, as she had been lost somewhere in another world during his lecture. When he finally spoke, she looked up in surprise.

'Has he moved yet?' Balsam asked her.

'No,' she said uncertainly. 'He just sits there. It's too bad, isn't it?'

'What is?' Balsam inquired.

'I'm not sure. I mean, it just seems like it's too bad the rat doesn't have more control over his surroundings. It's like he wants to do something, but just can't do it.'

'Exactly,' Balsam said, moving closer to her and looking down at the rat. The rat, still trembling, stared balefully back at him, almost as if it were reproaching him.

'That's one of the things that make rats nice for experimentation,' he explained. 'Because they don't have much control over their environment, it's much easier to get dependable results. Or magnified results.'

Judy peered at him now, a puzzled expression on her face.

Balsam began again. 'If the rat were human it wouldn't be nearly so easy to reduce it to a point of total frustration. For instance, if the rat were a person, it would have first gone over the entire maze, making sure it hadn't taken any wrong turns. Then it would have investigated the barrier, trying to figure a way to get through. And then, if that failed, it would have started figuring a way to break the glass, so it could go over.'

Judy nodded her head. 'And if that didn't work?' she asked quietly.

'Who knows?' Balsam shrugged. 'If I were that rat, I suppose I'd be busy tearing that cage apart, or I'd kill myself trying.' His attention had wandered back to the rat again, but as he finished what he was saying he glanced once more at Judy. There was an odd look on her face.

'Is something wrong?' he asked her.

Judy shook her head negatively. 'No,' she said shortly. 'I – I'm fine, really.' She glanced at the clock. 'I'm going to be late if I don't hurry.' She moved to her chair, and quickly began gathering her belongings. As she was about to leave the room, Balsam stopped her.

'Are you sure you're all right?' he said.

She nodded quickly, and started for the door.

'If something's wrong, I wish you'd tell me what it is,' Balsam tried again. 'Or maybe you should talk to Monsignor.'

At the mention of the priest, Judy suddenly turned back, and stared at Balsam.

'Monsignor?' she said blankly. 'You must be kidding!' And then she was gone.

Balsam stared after her, her words echoing in his ears. '*You must be kidding*.' And the look on her face, a mixture of resentment, bafflement, and, it seemed, contempt. And why not? Balsam reflected. Why had he suggested she talk to the Monsignor? Certainly the priest was the last person Balsam would go to if he had a problem; why should the students feel any differently? Perhaps he should have suggested one of the nuns. But which one? Sister Elizabeth? Hardly. What about Sister Kathleen? All Judy would have gotten was a lecture, a warning about her sins. And, if she had been sinning, a lecture wasn't what she needed.

Then he came, in his mind, to Sister Marie. Of course. Quickly, Balsam stepped into the hall and looked up and down. But Judy was gone. He went back into his room, fed the rat, and pulled his lunch bag from his desk. He took one bite and put his sandwich down. Maybe he could convince Sister Marie to talk to Judy and find out what was wrong. Because something *was* wrong. He was sure of it.

He found the nun in the library, deeply engrossed in a copy of *Christian Century*, which she quickly closed when she realized someone was approaching. Then, when she saw who it was, she smiled and waved. As Balsam drew nearer she laughed, and reopened the magazine. Inside was another magazine. Balsam saw that the nun had been engrossed in the theatre column of *The New Yorker*.

'Catching up on your religion?' he grinned, sitting down across from her.

'It's terrible, isn't it? I always feel so guilty about it, but I do love the theatre, there's no sense denying it.'

Peter glanced once more at the magazine that was so neatly concealed inside the *Christian Century*. 'Unlikely reading material for St. Francis Xavier's,' he commented.

Sister Marie nodded emphatically. 'If you promise not to tell anyone – and I mean *any*one – I'll let you in on a secret.'

'Who would I tell?' Balsam said.

'Well, this is my own guilty secret. I've never told anyone until now. But I think it'll be safe with you.' Her eyes were twinkling merrily, and Balsam decided he'd been right. If anyone should talk to Judy Nelson, it was Sister Marie. Her voice dropped conspiratorially.

'The library gets *The New Yorker* every year as an anonymous gift,' she said.

'From you?' Balsam said.

'Oh, no, I couldn't,' Sister Marie said, horrified at the suggestion. Then she went on, 'My sister, however, could, and does. Every year, when Monsignor gets the notice of renewal, he talks about cancelling it. But he's afraid to, because he thinks it would get back to whoever donates it, and they might cut off any other donations they're making to the Church.'

'And would she?' Balsam asked.

'Heavens, no,' Sister Marie said, laughing happily. 'That's the best part of it. My sister happens to be a Baptist. She sends in the subscription each year as a favour to me. She doesn't give a nickel to the Church. In fact, she says I'm the only Catholic she can put up with at all! Isn't it wonderful?' The two of them laughed for a moment, then Peter grew serious. He decided he liked Sister Marie very much.

'I wonder if you could do me a favour,' he said slowly.

'Of course,' Sister Marie responded. 'Unless it's something wicked. Then I'd have to confess afterward, but I'd probably do it anyway.'

'You're impossible,' Peter said, smiling at her.

'I try.' Then, as his smile faded, she grew serious. 'What is it?' she asked.

'I'm not sure, really. But I thought you might be able to find out. It's one of my students, Judy Nelson.' The nun nodded shortly, acknowledging that she knew Judy.

'Something's bothering her,' Balsam continued, 'and I can't get her to tell me what it is.' Briefly, he told Sister Marie what had transpired after his class and that he had suggested that Judy talk to Monsignor.

'She wasn't too receptive to that idea,' he finished.

'No, I don't imagine she was,' Sister Marie said briefly, and Peter Balsam thought he detected a bitterness in her voice. He thought she was about to say something about the priest, then appeared to change her mind. She smiled at him reassuringly.

'I'll see what I can do,' she said. 'Mind you, I'm not guaranteeing anything. Sometimes I think our habits get between us and the children. I think we scare them. But I'll find her this afternoon, and see if I can find out what the trouble is. All right?'

Suddenly Balsam felt better. He smiled at the nun, and stood up.

'I'm sorry to dump this on you,' he began, but Sister Marie held up a hand.

'Don't be sorry,' she said. 'Try to do what you think is right, and try not to worry too much about the consequences. If things go too far wrong, God will take care of them.'

Balsam started to reply, then changed his mind. He smiled at her once more, then turned to go. Behind him, he heard her voice.

'Mr. Balsam?' He turned around. The twinkle was back in her eye. 'There's something else you should know. One thing you can count on with Judy – if she can find a reason to be dramatic, she'll *be* dramatic. Whatever it is, I'm sure it's not serious.'

Balsam nodded, then made his way back to Room 16. He finished his sandwich, sharing it with the rat, and prepared for his next class. Latin III. By the time the class convened, he was totally immersed in conjugating irregular verbs in the past perfect.

He had forgotten about Judy Nelson.

At a quarter to four that afternoon, Marilyn Crane hurried down the hall toward the lockers. She was late and she still had to stop at church before she went home. As she began spinning the dial on the lock, hoping it would open on the first try, she was vaguely aware of someone leaning heavily against the wall a few feet away. She didn't look up; not enough time. She turned to the last digit, and grasped the handle of the locker. It wouldn't move. Quickly, she twirled the dial again, until she felt a slight click. She tried the handle once more, and this time it moved. Marilyn pulled the locker door, and started to put her books inside. Then she gasped, and her hand flew to her mouth.

Inside was a crucifix, suspended upside down from one of the coathooks at the top of the locker. The face of Christ had been smashed. She looked frantically for a note, some explanation, but there was none. She stared vacantly at the dangling, obscenely defaced crucifix, then slammed the locker shut and closed her eyes tightly, but the image stayed before her. Then, as she began silently praying, she felt the eyes on her. She opened her own, and looked around, recognizing the person of whom she had been vaguely aware a moment earlier. It was Judy Nelson, and she was leaning against the wall, staring at Marilyn. Marilyn looked quickly away.

Judy Nelson! Would Judy have done something like this? She knew Judy didn't like her. None of that group did. Marilyn remembered the frog yesterday. Was Judy in the biology class? She could feel the other girl's eyes still on her.

No, Marilyn told herself, don't think that. Judy wouldn't do something like that. It has to be someone else; someone I don't even know. She wanted to believe it, believe that only a stranger could be so heartless. She forced herself to turn and look at Judy Nelson.

It was then Marilyn realized that something was wrong. Judy hadn't moved, nor had her expression changed. It came to Marilyn that Judy wasn't looking at her. but beyond her, at something off in the distance. She wondered if she ought to speak to Judy. Probably not. But she couldn't just walk away, could she?

Why not? Hadn't Judy said mean things to her?

So had everyone else. And Judy seemed to need help.

Marilyn closed her eyes again, and silently begged the Sorrowful Mother to give her strength. And she thought she felt strength flowing into her. She moved down the hall until she was next to Judy.

'Judy?' she asked. 'Are you all right? Is something the matter?'

Judy Nelson seemed to come out of her reverie. She looked coldly at Marilyn, as if she hadn't noticed her before.

'I'm fine,' she said; her tone told Marilyn she wasn't.

'Can I help?' Marilyn offered, determined not to be put off by Judy's coldness.

Judy stared at her again, and Marilyn thought she was going to walk away without saying anything. But then she seemed to change her mind. Her face went slack, and suddenly looked very tired.

'Nobody can help me,' she said. Then she turned, and silently walked away, down the hall. For a moment, Marilyn was tempted to follow her, and try to find out what was wrong. She watched until Judy disappeared around the corner. Then, shrugging, Marilyn walked down the hall the other way, and left the school building to go into the church. As she sat in the pew, silently praying to the Blessed Virgin, she imagined she heard music in the background. It was a singsong sound, like Gregorian chants, and Marilyn wondered where it was coming from. When it stopped, she realized that it hadn't been coming from anywhere. It must, she was sure, have been coming from inside her head. She left the church, and walked down the hill toward home.

Inez Nelson heard the front door open and then close, and wiped her hands on her apron. 'Judy?' she called. 'Is that you?' She started toward the front of the house, glancing at the clock to determine how late Judy was. But before she had gotten halfway down the hall she heard her husband's voice.

'It's me,' George Nelson called out. He stepped into the hall, almost bumping into his wife. 'Judy not home yet?'

'No, she isn't,' Inez said, suddenly worried. Why would she have been calling Judy, if Judy were already home? Didn't he *think*?

'Maybe she went over to Janet's or Penny's,' George suggested.

'She should have called if she did,' Inez pointed out, when, as if on cue, the phone began to ring. George looked triumphant.

'See?' he said, and picked up the receiver. 'Nelson residence.'

'Mr. Nelson?'

'Yes,' George said, a little uncertainly. He didn't recognize the voice.

'This is Mrs. Williams, at the emergency room of the hospital.'

'The hospital?' George repeated blankly.

'Neilsville Hospital,' Mrs. Williams repeated. 'I'm afraid I have to ask you to come down here. Your daughter's here.' Then, when George failed to respond, she continued, 'You *are* the father of Judy Nelson?'

'Yes,' George said weakly, the colour draining from his face. 'What's happened? What's wrong?'

He listened, trembling, then quietly dropped the receiver back on the hook and turned to his wife.

'What is it?' she said. 'What's happened?'

'I'm not sure,' George said slowly. 'She says – ' he faltered, then blurted out, 'Judy tried to kill herself.'

SEVEN

Judy Nelson lay propped up in bed, glaring at the nurse who was adjusting the bandages on her wrists. In one corner of the room her bloodstained clothes lay in a pile: she had refused to allow them to be taken away, and rather than provoke a scene the nurses had decided the clothes could wait.

'Your parents will be here any minute now,' one of the nurses said gently, patting Judy on the hand. 'How are we feeling?'

'I don't want to see them,' Judy muttered, pulling her hand away.

'Of course you do,' the nurse smiled. 'We all want to see our parents, don't we?'

Judy glared at the nurse. '*I* don't,' she snapped. 'Why don't you leave me alone?'

The nurse didn't answer her, merely moved to another chair, a little way from the bed. She ignored Judy's sullen stare and occupied herself with several unnecessary readings of Judy's chart.

In the reception area of the emergency room, Mrs. Williams was trying to explain the situation to Inez and George Nelson. George seemed to be listening carefully, but Inez was tapping her foot nervously, as if waiting for all the 'nonsense' to be over with, so she could see her daughter.

'We don't really know what happened,' Mrs. Williams was saying. 'Or perhaps I should say we don't know *why*. Judy won't talk to anybody about it, and until she does, well ...' Her voice trailed off, and she shrugged eloquently.

'Could you tell me exactly what you *do* know?' Inez asked sharply.

Mrs. Williams sighed. These things were so difficult. Thank

God they practically never happened. Brusquely she began telling the story to the Nelsons.

'Apparently Judy didn't leave the school this afternoon. Instead, she went to the girls' locker room, off their gymnasium, and waited until she thought everyone had gone home. Then she found a razor blade, and cut her wrists.' When she saw the colour draining from Inez's face she hastened to explain. 'It isn't as bad as it sounds,' she rushed on. 'As a matter of fact, it's next to impossible to do enough damage to yourself with razor blades to die, except under certain circumstances. Mostly it just hurts a bit, and causes a lot of mess. Anyway, Judy must have gotten scared as soon as she cut herself, because she called the police right away. Of course the police called us, but by the time our ambulance got there, it was all pretty much over with.'

'Over with?' George asked. 'What do you mean, over with?'

'One of the janitors at the school found her,' Mrs. Williams said. 'Fortunately, he wasn't the kind to get upset at the sight of blood, and he had her wrists bandaged before anybody else could get there. It wasn't the best bandaging job I ever saw, but it wasn't the worst, either. Doctor put in a few stitches and rebandaged the wrists, and Judy should be fine in a day or so.' Mrs. Williams tried to smile brightly, as if the whole incident were no worse than a scraped knee.

'I want to see her,' Inez said suddenly.

'Yes,' Mrs. Williams began. 'I . . . I'm sure you do. But I'm afraid you'll have to talk to the doctor first.' Now she was showing definite signs of discomfort.

'The doctor?' George said. 'Which doctor?'

'Dr. Shields,' Mrs. Williams said nervously.

'Shields?' George Nelson repeated. 'He's a psychiatrist, isn't he?'

'Yes – ' She started to explain. Inez cut her off.

'A psychiatrist? Just to bandage Judy's wrists? I don't understand.' Mrs. Williams was sure she did understand; she just didn't want to face it.

'I'm sure you do,' she said. Suddenly, since the issue was

met, she felt on firmer ground. 'With wounds like Judy's, calling in a psychiatrist is standard procedure.'

'Wounds like Judy's?' Inez said vaguely.

'I think she means self-inflicted wounds,' George said quietly. Inez's face remained blank. Shock, George realized; she must have gone into shock and blocked out the details of what happened. He signalled Mrs. Williams aside.

'Is Dr. Shields around?' he whispered. 'I'd like to talk to him, and I think he should probably have a look at my wife, too.'

Suddenly understanding his meaning, Mrs. Williams stole a glance in Inez's direction. She was gone. Quickly she looked up and down the hall. Inez was striding purposefully toward Judy's room.

'Mrs. Nelson,' she called, but it was too late.

Inez Nelson pushed open the door to the hospital room, and stepped in. She didn't see Judy at first but she heard her.

'Get her out of here,' Judy screamed. 'I told you I didn't want her in here!'

Inez whirled, and saw her daughter propped up in bed. She could barely recognize her. Judy's face was contorted with anger, and she was tearing at the bandages at her wrists. Inez started to move toward the bed. Before she could get there Judy had pulled the bandages off, and ripped at the stitches. Blood spurted from her wrists. She began screaming at her mother again.

'I hate you,' she shouted. 'Get out of here! *Leave me alone!*'

Inez tried to put her arms around her daughter, but Judy wriggled away, leaving Inez's blouse bloodied. She stared down at herself, and the horror of it washed over her. Inez, too, began screaming, and a moment later, after she'd pressed the emergency bell, the nurse began trying to separate mother and daughter. It took her only a second to realize that of the two, the mother was far worse off than the daughter. Inez was hysterical; Judy, screaming and struggling against her mother, seemed to know exactly what she was doing. Just as the nurse herself was beginning to panic, help arrived in the form of Mrs. Williams and George Nelson, followed by a press of orderlies and nurses, who crowded into the room, creating further confusion. Three burly orderlies were attempting to pull a shrieking Inez Nelson away from the bed when Dr. Shields arrived, sized up the situation in an instant, and began issuing orders. Within minutes, sedatives were administered to both Judy and Inez Nelson.

'I'm sorry, Doctor,' Mrs. Williams said when the room had been cleared, 'I tried to keep her away but I couldn't.'

'It's all right,' Dr. Shields said calmly. 'I don't see that there's much damage done.'

'Keep her out of the room?' George Nelson repeated. 'Keep her out? Why did you want to keep Inez – my wife – out of the room?' He looked from Mrs. Williams to the doctor, then back again.

'It was my fault, really,' Dr. Shields said. 'Judy said she didn't want to see her mother right now, and I should have been here when you arrived to explain it to you. I'm sorry. The whole thing was really my fault.'

But George Nelson hadn't heard the last. 'Didn't want to see her mother? Why? I don't understand.'

Dr. Shields looked at him sympathetically, seeing the man's confusion and helplessness. 'Could you wait a couple of minutes?' he asked George. When George nodded mutely, Dr. Shields patted him on the back. 'Fine,' he said. 'Mrs. Williams will get you a cup of coffee, and by the time it's cool enough to drink, I'll be back. Then I'll try to tell you what's happening, and what's going to happen next.' When a look of fear came over George's face, the doctor felt compelled to add: 'It isn't as bad as it looks.' Then he smiled reassuringly, and disappeared down the hall. George Nelson sank into a chair, prepared to wait. He wondered why he suddenly felt that this was just the beginning. He was sure that it *was* as bad as it looked – and probably much worse.

Peter Balsam heard about Judy Nelson from a very agitated Sister Marie, who called him as soon as she heard about it from Sister Elizabeth – who had gotten all the details from the janitor. Sister Marie seemed to think the whole thing was her fault – she had been unable to find Judy during the afternoon. And now this had happened. Sister Marie felt terribly guilty. Balsam assured her that no matter what had happened, there was no reason for the nun to blame herself. He did not add, since he could see no reason to increase her worries, that he, too, felt responsible for Judy. Perhaps if he had tried a little harder to talk to her, if he had spent a little more time with her . . .

On an impulse, Balsam decided to go to the hospital.

Mrs. Williams looked up at the man who hovered uncertainly over her desk, and put on her best professional smile.

'Yes?' she said. The young man in front of her looked very uncomfortable. 'Do you need to see a doctor?' she added solicitously.

'Me?' Balsam said in surprise. 'Oh, no . . . no, I'm fine. I was just wondering if I'm in the right place.'

'That depends on the problem,' Mrs. Williams smiled. 'What can I do for you?'

'I wanted to find out about Judy Nelson,' Balsam said. He was vaguely aware that the two men who sat huddled together a few feet away had stopped talking and were staring at him. 'Is she still here?'

Mrs. Williams nodded. 'Oh, yes,' she said. 'I'm afraid she isn't allowed any visitors yet.' She paused, then continued, 'Are you a friend of the family?' Dumb question, she admonished herself. If he knew the family, he'd be talking to Mr. Nelson, not to me. In front of her, the young man was shaking his head.

'Not exactly,' he was saying. 'I'm one of her teachers. My name is Peter Balsam. Why don't you just tell Judy I was here—'

He started to turn away, then stopped. The two men who had been seated were now standing.

'Mr. Balsam?' one of them was saying now. 'The psychology teacher?'

Balsam nodded.

'I'm George Nelson,' the man said, offering his hand. 'Judy's father. This is Dr. Shields.'

Balsam took the proffered hand and smiled an acknowledgment to the doctor.

'Hello,' he said. 'How is she? Is she all right?'

'She's going to be fine.' The doctor answered for George Nelson. 'We were just talking about the whole situation. Why don't you join us?' He indicated the chairs, but Balsam waited until the other two were seated before he sank into the third chair.

'What happened?' Balsam asked. The two men looked uncomfortably at each other.

'That's just what we were trying to figure out,' Dr. Shields said. 'I'm afraid we don't really know.'

'I heard the janitor found her in the gym,' Balsam said softly. 'With her wrists – cut.' He had almost said 'slashed,' but the word seemed too graphic.

'It was in the locker room,' Dr. Shields corrected him, 'and fortunately it isn't serious. Now we're trying to figure out why.'

'Why?' Balsam repeated the word bluntly.

'Why she cut herself,' George Nelson said miserably. 'She just never seemed like the kind of girl who would do something like that.'

The word 'dramatic' popped into Peter Balsam's mind. Sister Marie had used it, at lunchtime. She had said Judy tended to be dramatic. He wondered if he should mention it to the two men. They seemed to be waiting for him to speak.

'Has she talked about it?' Balsam asked.

The doctor shook his head. 'No. All she's said is that she doesn't want to see her mother. Frankly, I don't think the situation is all that serious. In my experience, which I admit is very limited, someone who really wants to commit suicide doesn't call the police immediately after the attempt.'

'She called the police?' Balsam asked.

George Nelson nodded. 'That's right. And the cuts aren't deep. But we still think there must be a reason for it. I mean, a sixteen-year-old girl doesn't just *do* something like that, does she?' He looked from the doctor to Balsam, then back to the doctor.

'Did you see her today?' the doctor asked Balsam, ignoring Nelson's question.

'Yes, of course,' Peter said. 'She's in my psychology course.'

'Did anything seem to be bothering her?' the doctor pressed.

'I'm not sure,' Balsam began uncertainly. He didn't want to raise any false alarms. 'I mean, I think something was on her mind, but I haven't the slightest idea what it was. She stayed for a minute or two after class, but when I tried to draw her out, she wouldn't talk about it. So I suggested she talk to Monsignor.'

'Monsignor?' the doctor asked.

'Monsignor Vernon,' George Nelson filled in. 'The priest who runs the school. Did she talk to him?'

'I don't know. Frankly, I'd pretty much forgotten about it until Sister Marie called me.'

Dr. Shields looked at Balsam questioningly, and Peter felt compelled to continue.

'After I suggested Judy talk to Monsignor, I got to thinking maybe she'd be better off talking to a woman. I tried to catch up to her, and suggest that she talk to Sister Marie, instead. But she was gone, so I found Sister Marie, and asked her to try to talk to Judy.'

'And did she?' the doctor prompted him.

'I wish she had,' Balsam said unhappily. 'But she didn't. She said she looked for Judy after school, but couldn't find her.'

'She must not have looked very hard,' George Nelson said bitterly. 'Judy was there all afternoon.'

'What happens now?' Peter asked, deciding not to pursue the question of whether or not Sister Marie had made a proper search for the girl.

The doctor shrugged helplessly. 'I'm keeping her here for observation,' he said. 'Standard procedure. But whether she'll start talking about what happened is anyone's guess. With kids, sometimes it's hard to get through.'

Suddenly there seemed very little left to say, and Peter Balsam began to feel uncomfortable – there must be things the doctor would want to talk about with the patient's father. He stood up uncertainly, grateful when the two men also rose from their chairs. The doctor extended his hand.

'I'm glad to have met you,' he said with a smile. 'I hope we see each other again.'

'But in happier circumstances,' Peter replied, accepting the doctor's hand. He turned to George Nelson.

'I can't tell you how sorry I am about this,' he said softly.

Nelson tried to smile at him, but found it difficult. 'Thanks for coming,' he said. 'I'll tell Judy you were here. Or someone will.'

A few minutes later Peter Balsam was walking slowly back through the streets of Neilsville. As he approached his apartment, he had a feeling of something left undone, as if there were someone he should talk to. He glanced up toward Cathedral Hill, and saw the short spire of St. Francis Xavier Church. Monsignor. He should talk to Monsignor. Peter Balsam didn't stop at his apartment. Instead, he increased his pace, and hurried up the hill.

He let himself into the rectory, and rang the silver bell. He waited. When there was no response, he rang the bell again. Still no response. He was about to leave when he noticed a thin band of light gleaming from beneath the door to the den. Balsam made his way down the hall. He stood quietly for a moment, listening.

At first there was silence, but a second later he heard the sounds of praying. An odd sort of praying: not the steady rhythms of the rosary, but short, staccato bursts of religious ejaculations. He listened for a moment, and had started to move away from the door when he heard another sound, a sound he hadn't heard since his childhood days in the convent. He stared at the door, wondering if he was really hearing what he seemed to be hearing. It was then that he noticed that the door was slightly ajar. Before he quite realized what he was doing, he had pushed the door partway open.

In the centre of the room, kneeling on the floor, Monsignor Vernon was praying. He was staring heavenward, but from where Balsam stood, it almost seemed as though the priest was praying to the chandelier that glowed dimly above.

He was stripped to the waist, and sweating profusely, whether from the heat of the fire that flickered on the hearth, or from religious fervour, Balsam was unsure. In one hand the priest held a rosary; in the other was clutched the flagellum. With each ejaculation, Monsignor Vernon was beating his naked back with the whip. It was not the soft, symbolic flagellation the nuns Balsam had grown up with indulged in. Monsignor Vernon was punishing himself, and the welts on his shoulders showed vividly against the pale white of his skin. Embarrassed, Peter Balsam quickly pulled the door closed and backed away, wishing he hadn't seen the strange ceremony within.

Then the praying stopped, and a strange silence fell over the rectory. Balsam picked up the small silver bell and rang it once more. He thought he heard a movement in the den, but he wasn't sure. He turned away, about to leave the rectory, when he heard Monsignor Vernon's voice.

'Hello?' The voice sounded muffled, and uncertain.

'It's me,' Balsam called. 'Peter. I can come back ...'

'No,' the voice came again. 'I'll be right with you. Just give me a moment.'

Balsam wondered how the priest would look, if his fervour and exertions would show in his face. But when Vernon appeared a moment later, he seemed relaxed, as if he had been doing nothing more strenuous than reading a book. Looking at him, Peter wondered if he could possibly have imagined the strange scene of a few minutes earlier.

'Peter,' Monsignor Vernon greeted him with a joviality that Balsam had not heard since their college days. 'Come in, come in. I was just praying, and didn't hear the bell.'

In the den, the lights had been turned up, and the fire, with another log thrown on it, was dancing brightly.

'A little warm for that, isn't it?' Balsam asked. The priest grinned self-consciously.

'I guess so,' he said. 'But every now and then I want a fire, and it doesn't seem to matter how hot it is outside.' Then the brief flash of joviality faded, and Monsignor Vernon's face took on a serious expression. 'I suppose you want to talk about Judy Nelson?' he asked in a tone that told Balsam that despite what he might wish, the priest did not want to discuss the matter.

'I just came from the hospital,' Balsam said tentatively.

The priest's brow arched. 'Did you?'

'No one knows what happened. Judy won't talk about it.'

'I don't imagine she would,' Monsignor said in a disapproving tone. 'But I imagine she'll talk to me about it.'

'Oh?' Balsam inquired. The priest nodded, almost imperceptibly, but did not explain.

'I was wondering,' Balsam said carefully. 'Did you happen to talk to her today?'

'I did,' the priest said, 'but the conversation is confidential. I heard her confession this afternoon.' Then he looked sharply at the teacher. 'What made you think I might have talked to her?'

'Because I suggested it,' Balsam said nervously. 'I mean, I didn't suggest she confess, but I told her I thought she ought to talk to you. Or to someone.'

'I see,' the priest said. He folded his hands carefully. 'Was there a reason? For your suggesting she talk to me?'

'I – I thought she needed someone to talk to, and since she didn't seem to want to talk to me, I suggested you.'

The priest considered this for a moment, then asked what had caused Peter's concern.

'It was her manner, more than anything,' Balsam began, trying to recreate the scene in his mind. 'She stayed after my class.' He recounted as best he could the conversation he had had with Judy. When he was finished, the priest seemed to think it over, then asked a question.

'Was there anything you said, anything at all, that might have caused this?'

Balsam thought. He didn't think there was. And then he remembered. It seemed so insignificant. He hadn't meant anything by it. But now, considering what had happened, he decided he'd better tell the Monsignor about it.

'There was one thing,' he said carefully, trying not to attach any great importance to his words, and succeeding only in making them sound even more important. 'We were talking about an experiment I conducted during the class today. It had to do with frustration, and I was demonstrating a point with a rat and a maze. Judy seemed a bit distracted during the lecture, but when I started the experiment she perked right up. Then, while we were talking, she asked me what I'd do, if I were the rat. And I told her, I think, that I'd probably do what I could to relieve my frustration, even if it killed me. Or die trying. Something like that. I can't remember my exact words.'

The priest was staring at him coldly. 'Let me get this straight,' he said. 'Am I to understand that, while talking to a student you knew was having a problem you talked about dying as a solution to the problem?'

Balsam felt a knot form in his stomach, and his mind reeled. No, he told himself, that's not what I did. Or, at least, that's not what I intended.

'It wasn't exactly like that,' he said aloud, but the priest cut him off.

'Then exactly how was it? Exactly what did you say?'

Balsam thought hard, and the words suddenly came back to him, as if they were written in front of his eyes. 'I said: "If I were that rat, I'd be busy tearing that cage apart, or I'd kill myself trying."' Suddenly the words sounded ominous.

'Kill yourself,' the priest said. Then he repeated it. 'Kill yourself. Well, I suppose that tells us what put the notion into Judy's head, doesn't it?' The priest shook his head sadly. 'Well,' he said, 'what's done is done, isn't it? And when it comes right down to it, the final responsibility rests with Judy herself, of course.' He smiled at Balsam, but Balsam felt no warmth from the smile. 'You shouldn't feel guilty about it,' the priest continued. 'She may have already had the idea. Still, it was an unfortunate phrase to have used. If I were you, I'd be a lot more careful in the future. Children can be so – suggestible.' He stood up, and Peter was grateful for the signal that the conversation was over. He, too, rose from his chair.

'You know,' the Monsignor said as he walked Balsam to the rectory door, 'you ought to think about a couple of things.' Balsam looked at him questioningly. 'You might be wise to try to find a little more faith within yourself. Faith in the Church.' When Peter looked puzzled, the priest continued, 'The Devil works in strange ways, just as does the Lord. Granted, talking about how a rat might react, given a chance and some brains, certainly doesn't seem particularly significant. Talking about suicide is a different matter.'

'I wasn't talking about suicide,' Balsam snapped, his anger rising. 'I was only using a figure of speech.'

'So said many a heretic,' Monsignor Vernon said softly.

'Heretic?' What are you talking about?' Balsam cried. He gazed at his old friend, but nothing in the priest's eyes revealed what was going on in his mind. 'I'm sorry, but I can't see how any of this could possibly be construed as heresy – or anything even resembling heresy.'

'Don't you?' the priest said. 'Pray, Peter. Pray for guidance. You might try praying to St. Peter Martyr. I find he can be very helpful.' And then the door of the rectory closed, leaving a furious Peter Balsam standing helplessly on the front porch. Fuming, he began the walk back to his apartment.

Peter Balsam closed the book slowly, and put it back on the shelf. He had not taken Monsignor Vernon's advice; had not prayed for guidance to St. Peter Martyr. Instead, he had looked the saint up, to see just who it was that Monsignor seemed to think could be so helpful. What he found was one of the old Italian Inquisitors. St. Peter Martyr, it seemed, had been one of the zealots who had dedicated a short thirteenth-century life to the eradication of sin and heresy from the Christian World. And, from what little Balsam had been able to find out, St. Peter Martyr had been personally responsible for the imprisonment, torture, and death of hundreds of heretics. In the end, though, he had lost: he had been assassinated by two heretics, thus earning for himself the title, Martyr.

Balsam sat for awhile, staring off into space and wondering what it was about St. Peter Martyr that appealed to Monsignor Vernon. What was it that had made the priest into a fanatic?

Then Balsam paused. Maybe the priest wasn't a fanatic. Maybe he, Balsam, was being oversensitive. He didn't know. Suddenly, he wasn't at all sure there was any way of finding out.

EIGHT

There was a tension in the air of St. Francis Xavier High School the next morning, the sort of tension that can only be brought about by a particular kind of shock. It was almost as if Judy Nelson were not coming back; as if she had been kidnapped, or murdered, or died in an accident. Perhaps, had Judy been a student at the public high school, the tension would not have been quite so great. There would have been a certain relief that she hadn't died, mixed with the horror at what she had done. But at St. Francis Xavier's the attempt was as shocking as the completion of the act would have been.

The Sisters sensed it immediately, and dealt with it in the only way they knew how – they ignored it. Judy's absence was noted in the records of attendance, but was not commented about, at least not in the classrooms. Of all the Sisters, Elizabeth had the fewest problems in the classroom. Her students, accustomed to her strict discipline, contained their urge to talk; more conscious than ever of Sister Elizabeth's sharp tongue and equally sharp ear, they saved their whispers for the breaks between classes, doing their best to vent their pent-up feelings in the five short minutes they had to move from one classroom to another.

Karen Morton was feeling the tension more strongly than

anyone else that morning. She and Judy had most of their classes together, and while Karen had often resented the slightly edged comments Judy had been in the habit of making about both her appearance and her boyfriend, Karen missed her friend. And she was also finding that she had become the object of the other students' curiosity, as though her closeness with Judy made her privy to the answer to the question that was on everyone's tongue that morning: Why? Why had Judy done it? And what was going to happen to her now?

Karen felt everyone watching her as she moved through the halls. She lowered her eyes and wished once more that she had dressed differently this morning. Suddenly her sweater felt too tight, and she was uncomfortably aware of the way her skirt hugged her hips. Somewhere, in the back of her mind, something was telling her that she should be in mourning. And then she realized that was ridiculous – Judy was in the hospital, not the mortuary. She turned the corner into the hall where all four of the girls had managed to be assigned lockers, and was relieved to see that Penny Anderson and Janet Connally were waiting for her. She tried to smile at them but couldn't.

'Karen?' Janet said as her friend approached. 'Are you all right?'

Karen nodded mutely, and wondered for a minute if she really was all right. 'People just keep staring at me,' she said. 'I feel like Marilyn Crane.'

'They stare at you for different reasons, though,' Penny Anderson put in. Then she couldn't contain herself any longer. 'Why do you think she did it?' she said. 'I mean, if anybody was going to try to kill herself, you wouldn't think it would be Judy.' She shuddered a little. 'It's too weird.'

'I don't know,' Karen said. 'But everybody looks at me like it's my fault. And Sister Elizabeth! She *glared* at me this morning! I wanted to crawl under my desk.'

'That's just Sister Elizabeth,' Janet Connally said comfortingly. 'She glares at everybody. You should have heard Sister Kathleen this morning. She spent the whole hour talking about sin. She wouldn't mention Judy's name at all. But she sure got her message across. The way she was talking, Judy might as well have –' She broke off, as she realized what she had been on the verge of saying. 'I mean,' she went on lamely, 'Sister Kathleeen kept talking about how the intent is as sinful as the act, and all that stuff. But I don't see how it can be.'

Karen Morton shrugged. 'I don't understand half of what they tell us. Sometimes I think they're trying to scare us.'

'Well, they certainly succeeded with Judy,' Penny Anderson said. 'My mother says they probably won't let her come back to school.' It was a thought that hadn't occurred to either of the two other girls, and they stared at Penny in dismay.'

'Not let her come back?' Janet said softly. 'Why?'

'Mother says what Judy did was even worse than getting pregnant,' Penny said. 'And you know what happened to Sandy Taylor last year.'

The three girls looked at each other. Sandy Taylor had simply not been at school one day. They had all been told that Sandy had 'gotten sick', but it hadn't taken much effort to figure out the truth, especially when Sandy's boyfriend had left school a couple of days later. It seemed to them that there was, indeed, a strong possibility that Judy Nelson might not be allowed to return to school.

It was then that Marilyn Crane appeared at the end of the hall. Janet Connally started to wave to her, but felt a nudge from Penny. Immediately, her hand fell back to her side. Behind Marilyn, the figure of Monsignor Vernon loomed, authoritarian and scowling.

Marilyn, unaware who was behind her, approached the group excitedly. She had something to say that they would want to hear; she was bursting with the story of seeing Judy the previous afternoon, just before she had – Marilyn couldn't say the words, even to herself. *Before she did what she did.* She quickened her pace, but then, abruptly, the three girls turned away. The look of eagerness fell away from Marilyn's face, and she stopped. She tried to pretend she hadn't been about to approach them at all, that she had some other urgent business in this part of the school. She spun around, and nearly collided with Monsignor Vernon.

'Oh, she said in surprise. 'I'm sorry. I – I didn't know you were there.' She looked helplessly at the scowling priest, bracing herself for the scolding she was sure was about to fall upon her. But it didn't come. The Monsignor seemed not to notice her. He merely stepped around her, and continued down the hall. A few feet away, the girls who had been clustered together scattered like leaves before a breeze. She had been so hopeful. Now, again, she was alone. Holding back her tears, Marilyn decided she would skip lunch that day, and spend the time in church, consoling herself under the comforting presence of the Sorrowful Mother.

A few minutes later, Marilyn Crane slipped into the one empty seat in the back row of Room 16. She could see that there was also an empty seat in the front row: the seat Judy Nelson had occupied the day before. No one had sat in it today, and she didn't think it was likely that anyone would sit in it tomorrow, either.

Peter Balsam surveyed the class. The same thing was on their minds that had been on the minds of his last class, and the one before that. But the psychology students didn't stop buzzing among themselves when they came into the room, as the other classes had. And he had himself to thank – if 'thank' was the word – for he had certainly done his best to let them know that they were not expected to behave here the same way they were expected to behave elsewhere at St. Francis Xavier. They had believed him. They were talking about Judy Nelson, and they weren't making much of an attempt to keep him from knowing about it. He decided, on an impluse, to face the issue squarely.

'Well,' he said, 'I guess there isn't much question what we're going to be talking about today, is there?'

His words silenced them. They stared at him, consternation clouding their faces, a wariness passing over them, as though they weren't sure what to expect.

'I know it's on all your minds,' he said calmly, 'and I don't suppose you've had a chance to talk about it in any of your other classes. Since what happened to Judy Nelson is definitely of a psychological nature, let's talk about it, get it all out in the open, and then maybe tomorrow we can get back down to business.'

When the class continued to stare at him mutely, Balsam was taken aback. He had expected a flood of questions. Instead he was getting nothing. Finally, almost tentatively, one hand rose. It was Janet Connally.

'Yes, Janet?'

'Did – did Monsignor tell you to talk to us about Judy?' Her voice quavered, and Balsam was aware that she was almost frightened of her own question. He shook his head, and smiled at them.

'This is between you and me. In fact, I have an idea that Monsignor might prefer me not to mention the subject at all. But this class is for you, not for Monsignor. So why don't we get on with it?'

The ice broke. Immediately, five hands went up, and Balsam was hard-pressed to decide whom to call upon first. He chose Karen Morton, telling himself that her hand had been just a shade faster than any of the others. But he knew he had really called on her first because she was one of Judy's friends. 'Karen?'

'I – I don't really know what I want to ask,' she began uncertainly. 'I mean, there's so many questions, I don't know where to start.'

'Start anywhere,' Balsam said gently.

'Well, can you tell us what happened?' Karen asked. 'I – well, we've just heard so many rumours that we don't really know how bad it is.'

'It isn't bad at all,' Balsam said. 'The cuts aren't deep, and Judy is only in the hospital now so the doctors can keep an eye on her.'

'You mean they're afraid she might do it again?' It was Penny Anderson, and she hadn't bothered to raise her hand. She had simply blurted the question out. That pleased Balsam

'No, I don't think anyone's afraid she'll do it again. It's simply that whenever anyone attempts to take his own life, he's kept under observation for a few days. In fact, I think it's a state law. Basically, it's not so much out of fear that the victim will try it again, as out of a desire to let the person calm down, and try to find out what led him to do it in the first place.'

'Why did she do it?' This time it was Janet Connally.

'Well, Judy might know,' Balsam said. He wondered if they would rise to the bait. Jim Mulvey did, and Balsam was surprised. Maybe he'd underestimated Mulvey.

'Might?' Jim said. 'What do you mean? I should think if anybody knows why she did it, Judy would.'

'That's what you'd think, isn't it? But what Judy did, what anyone who tries to kill himself does, isn't particularly rational. Usually it's an impulsive act, and after it's over the person wonders why he tried it in the first place. Unfortunately, all too often, it's too late. Judy was lucky. She's going to be fine.'

'But what makes someone do something like that?' Balsam heard the question, but wasn't sure who had asked it.

'Any number of things,' he said. 'Haven't you ever gone to bed at night and thought how nice it would be if you just didn't wake up in the morning?' All of them squirmed uncomfortably. 'Well, sometimes people decide not to take a chance. They decide to see to it that they won't wake up. But more often than not, what they're really trying to do is cry out for help. They don't want to die. Not really. They just want someone to help them. So they do something to attract attention to themselves.'

'But it's a sin,' Marilyn Crane's voice said softly from the back of the room. Everyone turned and stared at Marilyn. She did not notice. She was concentrating on Peter Balsam.

There it was: *It's a sin.* How was he to answer it?

And then he thought he saw an answer. 'I'm not so sure,' he said carefully. 'What I mean to say,' he continued into the shocked silence, 'is that I'm not sure that a suicide *attempt* should be considered a sin. I mean, if the act isn't completed, then where's the sin?'

'Sins thought and considered are no different than sins committed, are they?' Again, Marilyn Crane.

'Well, that's certainly what we've all been taught,' Balsam began. And then he stopped.

It took a moment before the class realized what had happened. Monsignor Vernon was coming slowly toward Mr. Balsam, a scowl creasing his forehead, his black eyes flashing. A hush fell over them. Something was about to happen. When it came, though, it seemed anticlimactic.

The priest reached the front of the room and turned to face the class. He made the sign of the cross and blessed them. Then he dismissed them. Monsignor Vernon watched in silence as the room slowly emptied. Then he turned to Peter Balsam.

'We will go to the rectory,' he said.

Inez Nelson hurried into the main entrance of Neilsville Hospital, and glanced quickly at the clock. She was right on time, noon sharp.

Inez followed the green arrows to the psychiatric area, no more than three rooms, that served the mental-health purposes of Neilsville. She glanced nervously around, hoping not to see any familiar faces. There would be enough talk as it was, without her being seen going into this section of the hospital.

No one seemed to be around at all, so Inez seated herself in the small waiting area. A minute later she heard a door open, and looked up. Margo Henderson was standing in the doorway, smiling at her.

'Inez,' Margo said genially, 'I'm so glad to see you.' At the look of consternation on Inez's face, Margo continued hurriedly, 'Of course, I wish it could have been under happier circumstances, but Dr. Shields tells me that Judy's going to be just fine.' She paused a moment, hoping there would be some response. 'Well,' she said, 'Dr. Shields will be with you in just a minute. Why don't you sit down?' Margo indicated the chair Inez had risen from, then seated herself at the desk. So, Inez wasn't going to speak to her. Margo tried not to be bitter about it. Of course Inez was under a strain, but still . . . And then Margo remembered that Inez Nelson was Leona Anderson's best friend. And it had been Leona who had been the prime force in squeezing Margo out of St. Francis Xavier parish. Leona and Monsignor Vernon. Well, damn them both, Margo told herself. She picked up a pen, and began moving some papers around on the desk. She could feel Inez's eyes on her.

'It was an accident,' Inez said suddenly in the silence. 'I want you to know it was an accident.' Margo looked quickly up at Inez, and saw the desperation in the other woman's eyes. Who was Inez trying to convince, Margo or herself? 'Of course,' she said shortly, and returned to her work. A moment later a buzzer sounded on her desk.

'Dr. Shields is ready for you now,' she said, in an even, professional tone. 'Right through there.' She indicated the door she had recently emerged from, and watched Inez until her former friend had disappeared from view. Then Margo shook her head sadly, and went back to work.

Inez Nelson felt no better when she left Dr. Shields's office than she had when she entered. She still wanted to see her daughter; she was not to be allowed to do so. Instead, she had been forced to listen to a lot of psychological doubletalk. She was Judy's mother, and she was sure she knew better than any of them what Judy needed. And yet, she was frightened and feeling very unsure of herself. Maybe the doctor was right. As she hurried out of the hospital, Dr. Shields's words rang in her ears.

'Judy's being manipulative,' he had said. And he had been right. But Inez was sure there was more to it than that. There had to be something else. Dr. Shields, himself, must have thought so. If not, why would he have said what he did?

'*Always look for the reason. Somewhere, there will be one. It may not make sense, but it will be there.*'

What was he talking about? What did that mean? Inez Nelson felt more baffled, and more frightened, than ever.

NINE

Peter Balsam sat glumly in the den of the rectory, and wished Monsignor Vernon would open the window. He glanced around, and became aware that the den, which he had thought comfortable so short a time ago – only days ago – now seemed oppressive and crowded. He glanced at his watch, wondering how long this meeting was going to last; he had already been here for most of an hour, and the priest had yet to say a word. Instead, the Monsignor had alternately prayed, then glowered at Balsam. Once, Balsam had risen as if to leave. Monsignor Vernon had curtly told him to sit down. Balsam had sat, reluctantly at first, then angrily, and finally with curiosity.

Then, with a suddenness that startled him, the priest spoke.

'You're a stubborn man, Peter,' he said. 'But so am I. Except that I prefer to think of myself as tenacious. Tenacious in my beliefs, tenacious in my determination to do what is right, and tenacious in my determination to see that those around me do what is right.'

'I was doing what I thought was right,' Balsam said softly.

'Right?' The priest almost shouted, '*Right?* Don't deny what you were telling your class; I heard it. Every blasphemous word of it!'

'Don't be ridiculous,' Balsam snapped. Immediately he regretted his choice of words. The priest was turning scarlet. 'I'm sorry,' he went on, trying desperately to remove his anger from his voice. 'I didn't mean that quite the way it came out.'

'But you did mean it, didn't you?' Monsignor Vernon said icily.

'I don't know.' Balsam felt weary. 'Let me try to put it this way. I was brought here to teach psychology, not the catechism. And today my students needed to understand what happened to Judy Nelson, and why it happened, and they needed reassurance. They did not need to be told that what Judy Nelson did was a mortal sin, and that her soul is forfeit, and a whole lot of medieval nonsense!'

The priest was on his feet now, towering over Balsam. 'Let us say,' he snapped, 'that is what *you* thought they needed. *I* say they needed something quite different, and I am in a much better position than you to define the needs of the students in this school.' Peter felt himself sink deeper into the chair as the priest raged on. 'The last thing in the world my students need is a lot of confusing, self-contradictory, pseudo-scientific claptrap. Perhaps, if these students were going on to college, they might need a small dose of what you call "psychology". But for the most part they aren't going anywhere. What they need are the tools to make their lives easier right here, in Neilsville. That is what the Church is for. To give people faith, and through faith, salvation.' He paused and Peter could see the priest's effort to calm himself. 'The world is a complex enough place without confusing our children and undermining their beliefs. In fact, it is exactly such talk as I've heard from you that is responsible for the decay of our society. You leave people nothing to cling to, nothing to console themselves with. And I will not tolerate it. Do you understand me?'

'I think I understand you perfectly,' Balsam replied coldly 'And I think it might be best for both of us if I resigned my position here immediately. As it is, there is no way I can teach my class effectively.'

Something almost like fear flashed over Monsignor Vernon's face, but was gone in an instant.

'That's a foolish stance,' the priest replied, 'and I think you know it.' The rage he had been displaying only a moment earlier vanished, to be replaced by a countenance that seemed almost genial. He took his chair opposite Peter's once more, and leaned forward, his elbows on his knees, his head resting on his clasped hands. 'Peter, why can't you understand that you are not dealing with an enormous high school in an urban area? Why can't you understand that the needs of our students are not the same as the needs of students in, say, Philadelphia? We are not dealing with sophisticated people here. It isn't just because of me, and what I'm sure you think is my narrow-minded outlook. It's much deeper than that. It has much more to do with the people who live here than it does with me. In fact,' he went on, a conspiratorial smile taking form, 'I don't know if you're aware of it, but there was a great deal of pressure put on the Bishop not to add your course to the curriculum at all. All I'm asking you to do, really, is exercise a certain amount of caution. Surely there's enough material so that you can do a little judicious picking and choosing, isn't there?'

'You mean censor my material?' Balsam asked warily, feeling his resolution weakening and resenting it.

Monsignor Vernon sighed. 'Yes, if that's the way you want to put it.'

'So much for freedom of thought,' said Balsam.

'I didn't tell you to stop thinking,' Monsignor said. 'All I've done is suggest you put some limitations on what you say to your students.'

'Isn't it the same thing? How can my students think, if they're given nothing to think about?'

'Is it really so important? Frankly, what our students need is a lot more faith, not a lot more to think about.'

'Ignorance is bliss?' Balsam remarked.

'In some cases, yes,' the priest replied, his voice taking on a softness Peter hadn't heard before. 'I know it sounds strange to you, but it's quite true. Living here for twelve years has opened my eyes to a lot. There was a time when I would have agreed with you – I wanted to know the truth about everything. But as I've grown older, I've discovered that the truth, or what we try to tell ourselves is the truth, is a very difficult thing to live with. And I've discovered that Truth – God's Truth, as taught by the Church – is a much better thing. It gives me peace, and it gives peace to my flock. If it all strikes you as a restriction on your freedom, let me remind you that God puts many restrictions on all our freedoms.'

Listening to him, Balsam thought it all sounded quite reasonable, put in those terms. But the bottom line still read 'repression.' Repression of thought, of ideas.

'Well,' he said, standing up again. 'I still have the feeling I'm not the right man for the job here. I'm sorry, but you'd better start looking for a replacement. If there's one thing I've always valued, it's freedom. Not only my own freedom, but the freedom of those around me. People have to be exposed to all kinds of ideas, and have the freedom to choose among them.'

'That's nonsense,' Monsignor snapped. 'And, frankly, you surprise me. You were raised to be a good Catholic, and I would have thought your faith would be stronger.' His eyes were flashing again, and Peter once more wanted to draw away from the force of the priest's faith. But there was no place to go. 'Is it faith and belief in the word of the Lord that brings salvation, not any kind of self-serving "science" that does nothing but provide excuses for the worst kinds of immoral behaviour,' Vernon was saying now, 'and as for your resigning your post here, if I were you I'd think twice about that, and then twice more.' He paused, a weariness coming into his voice. 'It wasn't easy for me to bring you here, Peter, and one more failure on your record is not going to help you. You have a history of not finishing things, and I'm beginning to understand why. You hide from reality. You refuse to face things as they really are, and prefer to find what you call evidence to back up your own weaknesses. If I were you, Peter, I'd think about it, and pray about it, before I made up my mind to leave Neilsville. God had a purpose when He sent you here. You have no right to turn your back on that purpose, and on the Lord, until you have completed whatever task He sent you here to perform. And I think I know what that task is.'

'Direct line?' Peter said, but Vernon went on, ignoring the sarcasm, his voice building as he spoke.

'I think He sent you here to help me. This is not an easy time to live in, and the Faith of the Church is under attack from every direction. I think He sent you here to me, not to turn and run again, but to be shown the powers of the Faith, and be restored to the Church.' Balsam stared at the priest. 'Yes,' the Monsignor intoned, as if he were no longer aware of the other man's presence, 'that is it. He sent you to me to help me carry on the work of St. Peter Martyr. To help me bring the heretics back to the fold. To punish the sinners.' And suddenly he looked directly at Peter Balsam, his eyes glowing. 'Pray Peter,' he said urgently. 'Pray for guidance, and stay here with me. Together we will finish what was begun so long ago.'

Monsignor Vernon fell to his knees, and began to pray. For a moment Peter Balsam wondered if he was expected to join in the prayers. But the priest seemed to have fallen into a reverie, and Balsam suspected he was no longer aware of his surroundings. He looked at Vernon with concern, and pity. He would pray, and try to find some guidance. And he would think.

Peter Balsam walked slowly down the hall, and left the rectory. A minute later, he stepped into the cool freshness of the church.

He sat quietly in the gloom for a while, trying to gather his thoughts together, and make some sense out of the confusion. What had the Monsignor been talking about when he asked Balsam to stay and help him finish what had been begun 'so long ago'? And all the talk of 'bringing the heretics back to the flock' and 'punishing the sinners.' It reeked of the Inquisition. Had Peter Vernon, somewhere on the way to becoming a monsignor, also become a fanatic? It certainly seemed so. Still, some of what the priest had said had made sense. Balsam had run away from things, and did like to find what the priest had called 'excuses' for his, failures. Except Balsam noted to himself with wry amusement, he preferred to call them 'rationalizations.'

A figure suddenly brushed past Balsam. Marilyn Crane. He glanced quickly in the direction from which she had come. Yes, she had been praying to the Blessed Virgin. Balsam hoped the girl had found more comfort in the saint than he had been able to give her in class. He glanced around the church, wondering if others had sought sanctuary from the sun and their problems. But the church was empty now. Peter Balsam began wandering through the side aisles, looking at the statues of the various saints.

It wasn't until he had paced almost to the altar that he noticed it. Then, quickly, he crossed the nave and examined the statues in the opposite alcoves. It was the same. Except for the obligatory statues of the Blessed Virgin and St. Francis Xavier, for whom the church was named, all the other saints, at least the ones he was familiar with, were Dominicans of the thirteenth and fourteenth centuries. There was St. Dominic himself, and St. Peter Martyr, and a statue of the Blessed James the Venetian. And the Portuguese St. Sanchia, who had originally welcomed the Dominicans into Portugal. There were others, some of whom Peter Balsam vaguely recalled. There was one who was totally unfamiliar. Saint Acerinus. Balsam searched his memory and couldn't remember the saint at all. That was no surprise: there were so many saints, and he had never been particularly interested in keeping track of them. In fact, he was rather pleased with himself for recognizing as many as he did. What disturbed him was that they were all Dominicans, all of the period of the Inquisition. And it had been the Dominicans who had been primarily charged with carrying out the Inquisition. Hadn't it crossed his mind, just minutes ago, that Monsignor's ramblings had 'reeked of the Inquisition'? Balsam stared around at the statues of the saints. Suddenly he had an urge to get out of the church, to get away from the sanctified visages that seemed to be glowering down at him, accusing him.

He hurried out of the church, and back to his classroom. A few moments later, at exactly one o'clock, the bell rang. The afternoon was about to begin. Peter Balsam was sure it was going to be a long afternoon.

When the doorbell rang Peter Balsam glanced up from the book he had been reading, but didn't leave his chair. He looked at the clock: it couldn't be Margo – she was just getting off work. The doorbell rang again.

'Peter?' Margo's voice came through the door, a bit muffled, but definitely Margo's. 'Are you in there?'

Now he jumped out of the chair and threw the door open.

'You're early,' he said. Then he reached out to take the bag that seemed about to spill from her arms. 'Let me take that.'

He peered into the bag. 'Good Lord, are we expected to drink all this?'

'That depends,' Margo grinned. 'It depends on how serious your problem is, and how long it's going to take to solve it. If there's any left over, I'll think up a problem of my own for another night.' She winked at him, making the wink seductive. 'Besides, it might be a long night.'

She had closed the door, and was taking off her jacket. Peter watched her, watched the sensuousness of her movements, and enjoyed the manner in which she managed to be sexy without being lewd. He felt desire growing in him. As Margo hung her jacket in the closet, Peter's eyes never left her.

'I took off early,' he heard her saying. 'Whatever's wrong, you made it sound so serious when you called that I decided Dr. Shields's reports could wait.' She looked around as if she expected to see his problem lurking in a corner somewhere. Then she surveyed Peter carefully.

'Well, the apartment's in one piece, and so are you, so it can't be nearly as awful as you made it sound on the phone. Maybe I should reclaim those bottles immediately.'

Suddenly, now that she was in the room with him, the problems didn't seem nearly so heavy. In fact, the entire afternoon was already fading into a haze, like a half-remembered nightmare. But it wasn't, it was real. He had a decision to make, and he wanted Margo's input before he made it.

'I'm thinking about quitting,' he announced. He moved into the kitchen and opened the wine she'd brought while Margo digested this bit of information. When he came back into the living room and handed her a glass, she looked at him speculatively.

'Aw, heck,' she said cheerfully. 'And you just got here, too.' Then she turned serious. 'I don't understand, Peter. What happened today?'

He told her about his talk with the Monsignor, and about the class session that had preceded it, and when he was finished she looked at him blankly.

'I don't see what the problem is,' she said.

'Oh, come on, Margo. You're bright. Can't you see? The man's crazy. He's a fanatic.'

Margo considered his statement. When she spoke, she seemed to be making a very conscious choice of words.

'Peter,' she began. 'I don't know if Monsignor Vernon is crazy, or a fanatic, or what. But I do know that while what he said to you this afternoon may have *sounded* fanatic, or crazy, or whatever, it isn't. Not here. Now, whether the town gets its ideas from Monsignor Vernon, or he gets his ideas from the town, I can't say. The kind of thinking that goes on around here actually gets scary sometimes. Do you know, there were several times after my divorce when I actually thought I should leave town? Really, it's true! All the people I thought were my friends – Inez Nelson for example. I saw her today, at the hospital. She'd hardly even speak to me, even when I was working. She thinks I'm a sinner. Can you imagine that? In this day and age? A sinner. But that's the way things are around here.' Then she flashed him a smile. 'Maybe you can help change things.'

Peter shook his head sadly. 'Not me. Either I fit in, or I run away. That's the kind of person I am.'

'You can change.' Margo shrugged. 'If I can change, you can change. And let me tell you, I've had to change a lot in order to survive the last couple of years. Every time I hear Leona Anderson make a crack loud enough for me to hear, I just turn around and wink at her. I used to cry though.' She stared into her drink, and swirled the liquid around. Then she looked up at Peter. 'Winking is better,' she said softly. 'It doesn't hurt so much when you wink. For me, it was either wink or run. Learn to wink, Peter.'

'I don't know,' Peter said. 'I'm just not sure what to do. I don't like what Monsignor's doing, and I don't like what his kind of religion is going to do to the kids. But what can I do? There's a little matter of obedience, you know. It's not like I have a union to complain to. All I have is the Church, and I'm sure you know they don't take kindly to underlings griping about their superiors.'

'But what if you're right?' Margo asked. 'What if Monsignor is crazy, or a fanatic? Shouldn't something be done about it?'

'Sure, but how do you prove that someone who professes total faith in the Church has too much faith? It's self-contradictory.'

Margo thought about it, and wasn't sure she grasped his idea. So she changed the subject. They made small talk, the kind of talk people make when they're consciously avoiding something, and ate dinner. It wasn't until they'd finished washing the dishes and opened the second bottle of wine, that the subject of the Church came up again.

'Have you ever looked at all the saints in the church?' he said suddenly. Margo looked at him questioningly, then shrugged.

'I wouldn't know one saint from another,' she said. 'Why? Is something wrong with them, too?'

Peter chose to ignore the hint that he was reaching a bit far to find fault with St. Francis Xavier. Instead, he tried to explain his misgivings.

'They're all right out of the thirteenth and fourteenth centuries,' he said. 'Dominicans. Which is odd right there, when you consider that the church was named for St. Francis Xavier, who happens to have been one of the original Jesuits.'

Margo frowned, as if she was trying to remember something. 'You know,' she said finally, 'it seems to me that I remember a time, about five years ago, when I noticed one day that we had different saints in the church. As though the ones I was used to had suddenly been replaced. But I didn't pay much attention to it. At the time I told myself I just hadn't really noticed them before. But maybe he changed them.'

'Changed them? Who?'

'Monsignor Vernon. Five years ago, when he became Monsignor. Maybe he changed them. Didn't you tell me he's big on the Dominicans? Which ones are they? The ones there now?'

'Mostly Italians,' Balsam said. 'St. Dominic, and Monsignor's special favourite, St. Peter Martyr, who also graces my classroom, and a few others. Then there's St. Sanchia, who wasn't Italian, but helped the Dominicans establish themselves in Portugal. And one I've never even heard of, someone named St. Acerinus. I haven't any idea who he was, but he probably fits right in with the rest of them.'

'You don't sound like you approve of them.' Margo grinned. 'Aren't all the saints supposed to be wonderful, lovable people?'

Balsam chuckled. 'That depends. For instance, take St. Peter Martyr. I looked him up the other day. If you check him out in *The Lives of the Saints*, he seems to be a wonderful fellow. Teacher, priest; spent a lot of time convincing heretics that they should come back to the fold. Spent hours and hours, arguing with them, showing them the error of their ways.'

'What's wrong with that?' Margo asked.

'Nothing. Except it turns out that Peter Martyr's idea of arguing with someone often involved torture, imprisonment, or burning at the stake.'

'Good God,' Margo breathed. 'That's horrible.'

Balsam nodded. 'They were all like that. Most of the saints in St. Francis Xavier Church were part of the Inquisition. I haven't read much about it, but what I have read chills my spine.'

'The Inquisition,' Margo said with a shudder. 'And "heretics". What a word! It sounds archaic.'

'It didn't when Monsignor used it today,' Peter said. 'You know,' he went on, 'I get the strangest feeling when I talk to Monsignor. He doesn't seem the least bit worried about the Inquisition. In fact, I get the feeling he wishes it had never come to an end.'

'Maybe it hasn't come to an end for him,' Margo mused. Then she brightened. 'That saint you've never heard of. Can't you look him up?'

'I already tried,' Balsam said, smiling. 'Apparently I'm not the only one who never heard of him.'

'What do you mean?'

'See those books over there?' He pointed to four thick volumes on his desk. Margo glanced at them, and nodded. 'Those are *The Lives of the Saints*. The nuns used to give them to us for Christmas. And as far as I can tell, they've never heard of St. Acerinus, either.'

'You're kidding,' Margo said.

'Look for yourself. The complete index is in the fourth volume.'

Margo picked up the book, and flipped through the pages. When she couldn't find the saint she was looking for, and was convinced that St. Acerinus, indeed, was not listed in the index, her eye ran up and down a couple of columns. Then she paused, startled. 'Hey!' she exclaimed.

'Oh, God,' Peter groaned. 'You found it.'

'You're a saint!' Margo cried. 'Here's your name, right here. Saint Peter Balsam. What does it say about you?'

'Never mind,' Peter said. 'He's an early one. Third century.' But she hadn't heard him. She was busy picking up one of the other volumes, searching for the entry headed 'Peter Balsam.' He fell silent and watched her read the page devoted to the saint whose namesake he was. When she finished, she closed the book and grinned at him.

'Well,' she said mischievously, 'that settles it.'

'Settles what?'

'Your problem. You aren't going anywhere, Peter Balsam. You're going to stay right here in Neilsville.' Her voice suddenly turned serious. 'Saint Peter Balsam didn't knuckle under, and he didn't run away. He stuck to his guns, and stood up for what was right.'

Balsam smiled wryly. 'And look what happened to him.'

'Well, of course he died, but that was a long time ago.'

'Was it?' Peter said. 'When I talk to Monsignor, nothing seems long ago.'

But he knew she was right. He would stay in Neilsville, as long as he could. He had a feeling his students needed him.

And of course there was Margo. She needed him too. Or did he need her? He decided not to worry about it. Instead, he opened another bottle of wine.

'Here's to Saint Peter Balsam,' he said, and raised his glass.

Margo did not go home that night.

TEN

The rest of the week passed slowly in Neilsville, almost as if the town were waiting for a signal, something to tell it that a crisis had passed. The signal did not come. Judy Nelson was very much on their minds.

By Saturday her closest friends, Penny Anderson, Karen Morton, and Janet Connally, had all been to visit Judy, first separately, and then together. They had seen that she was not dying; indeed, she seemed to them to be in fine shape – she questioned them about classes, wanted to know what work she'd missed, and made them promise to fill her in on all the details of the party on Saturday that she would not be able to attend.

The subject all her friends wanted to talk about was carefully avoided. No one wanted to be the first to bring it up, and Judy herself didn't mention it. But the bandages on her wrists kept it at the front of all their minds.

Since that first day, Peter Balsam had resolved to make no further mention of Judy Nelson's attempt on her own life. For the moment, he told himself, it was better to let it drop. He was sure he had gotten his point across in the few minutes before the Monsignor had suddenly appeared. Balsam had kept a careful eye on the class, particularly on Judy's friends, with the intention of talking privately with any who seemed overly disturbed by the incident. But they all seemed to be doing fine. Every evening he was seeing Margo, and that helped. Monsignor Vernon had apparently forgotten the stormy session earlier in the week, for he treated Balsam the same way he had from the beginning, with a formal cordiality that induced a certain respect but no warmth.

Harriet Morton, Karen's mother, had considered cancelling her daughter's party, but after consulting with Leona Anderson had decided to let it continue as scheduled. After all, it was only going to be the girls, and they probably needed the diversion. Cancelling the party, she and Leona had decided, would only draw attention to a situation best ignored. Now she glanced impatiently at her watch.

'Karen?' she called up the stairs. She reached in her purse and fished for her keys, keeping one eyes on the stairs as she waited for her daughter to come down. She heard Karen moving around on the floor above, and called again. 'Karen! I have to go now. Will you come down here?'

'Coming,' Karen called, and a moment later appeared on the stairs.

'Now, is everything all set for the party?' Harriet asked anxiously. Karen shrugged.

'Not yet. Penny's coming over early to help me. Can I use your punchbowl?'

Harriet sighed. 'You'd better wash it first.'

Karen looked as though having to wash the bowl might well dissuade her from using it. 'Then *don't* wash it,' Harriet said. 'You can all get dust poisoning, if there is such a thing.' The two of them laughed, and Harriet realized with a rush how much she loved her daughter. She gave Karen a quick squeeze and a kiss, and hurried out the door. 'Have a good time,' she called over her shoulder, 'and I'll see you all later.'

'By then it'll all be over,' Karen said, waving. It had better be, she thought with a twinge of guilt. No telling what might happen if her mother came home and found the boys there. She closed the door after her mother, and went back upstairs, where she continued working on the dress that Judy Nelson had intended to wear that night. Just a few alterations, and it would fit Karen perfectly.

An hour later, as she bit off the last thread, Karen heard the doorbell. 'It's unlocked,' she called down the stairs, and a moment later heard Penny Anderson's voice.

'Hi! Are you upstairs?'

'Come on up. I just finished my dress for tonight, and you can tell me if it fits right.'

A minute after that Penny appeared in the doorway, and gasped at the sight of the black dress Karen was proudly holding up.

'Where did you get it?' Penny breathed. 'It's beautiful. But it must have cost a fortune!'

'It's Judy's, really,' Karen told her. 'She wasn't supposed to buy it, but we snuck it over here so her mother wouldn't find out. She was going to return it to the store on Monday, so I just—' She hesitated, then blurted out the truth. 'Well, I took it in at the hips a little, since now she won't be wearing it at all. Do you think the store will notice?' She offered the dress to Penny for inspection.

Penny looked at the new seams critically. 'If they don't look at it too closely,' she decided. 'The new seams are perfect. Of course, you can still see where the old ones were. But why should they even look? Put it on.'

Karen slipped into the dress and modelled it for Penny.

'It's great,' said Penny. 'Really sexy. I wish I had a figure like yours.'

'Be glad you don't,' Karen said. 'Nothing fits me right, and I always look like some . . .' She trailed the sentence off, unwilling to use the word 'tramp.'

'Not in that dress, you don't,' Penny assured her. 'And you know what? I'll bet if you take off that makeup, and just let your hair fall, you'll look really great.'

Together, the two girls began experimenting with Karen's hair and face. Half an hour later they surveyed the results in the mirror, and Penny giggled. 'You know what? You look just like Judy always wanted to look. If she could just see you in that dress she'd die!' Then she realized what she'd said, and the two girls stared at each other.

'Why do you suppose she did it?' Karen asked. 'Have you asked her?'

Penny shook her head. 'I don't think I want to know. It's creepy, if you ask me. And it must have hurt like crazy.'

'I don't know,' Karen mused. 'I guess if you're feeling so bad you want to die, you don't care.'

Penny shuddered a little. 'I don't think I could do it. I couldn't stand the pain.' Then she smiled. 'But I could sure stand to get the treatment Judy's getting. All she does is lie there in bed, and get waited on hand and foot, while she watches television all day.'

'Yeah,' Karen said slowly. 'But suppose she'd died? What do you suppose that would be like?'

'Don't you ever think about it?' Penny asked her. 'I think about it all the time. I like to picture my own funeral sometimes.'

The thought had never occurred to Karen. Now she saw a picture in her mind's eye. 'That could be kind of neat,' she said. 'I think I'd want a very small funeral. Just you and Janet and Judy, and my mother. And Jim, of course. It would be horrible for him, and he'd probably throw himself on my coffin.' The prospect pleased her – a devastated Jim Mulvey, his own life forever destroyed by the untimely death of the girl he had hoped to marry, prostrated on the casket, crying openly over his loss.

'My funeral would be much more dignified,' Penny said. 'Of course, everyone would be there, and there'd be masses of flowers. And my parents would be in the front row. I don't think they'd cry. Instead, they'd be helping everyone else get through it. You know how my mother is; she'd be trying to take the attitude that life goes on, but of course inside she'd be a wreck. And it would kill Daddy, though he wouldn't let anyone know it. They'd probably be dead themselves within a year. After all, what would they have left to live for?' Then, as the dramatic image of her parents wasting away with unexpressed grief faded, Panny snickered. 'Can you imagine Marilyn Crane's funeral?' she giggled. 'Three faded roses, and everyone there to make sure she was dead.'

'Who'd even care if she was dead?' Karen said flippantly. She began taking off the black dress. 'We'd better get started, or we'll never be ready by the time everyone shows up.' She hung the dress up carefully, and pulled on a pair of jeans. 'Come on,' she said. 'You can help me wash the punchbowl.'

An hour and a half later, the party was in full swing, except that so far, none of the boys had arrived. Then, as Karen and Penny were joking about having spiked the punch (they hadn't) the front door opened, and Janet Connally arrived. With her was Jeff Bremmer.

'Jeff was helping me out with a science project this afternoon, so I invited him along,' Janet explained. Jeff looked around the room, and saw that he was the only male in sight.

'I don't know,' he said uncertainly. 'Maybe I shouldn't have come.'

'Don't be silly,' Penny said. 'Everyone else is coming. Someone had to be first. Just don't tell anyone you were here. Karen's mother thinks this is a hen party.'

Now Jeff was really unnerved. 'I think I'd better go,' he said. But a moment later a car pulled up in front of the house, and Jim Mulvey and Lyle Crandall appeared at the door. Suddenly, Jeff felt better about the party.

'Hey,' Jim Mulvey said, whistling at Karen. 'Now that's what I call a dress.'

'You like it? It's the one Judy was supposed to wear tonight.'

'Looks better on you,' Jim assured her. Then he winked. 'I got some beer here. Can I put it in the ice box?' When Karen looked uncertain, he reached out and squeezed her around the waist. 'Come on,' he said. 'It's only a little beer. Us guys get thirsty.' He pulled out a can of Olympia and held it up in Lyle Crandall's direction. 'Want one, Crandall?'

'Sure', Lyle said. 'And give me one for Jeff.' Jim Mulvey tossed him another can and Lyle opened both of them. 'Try this on for size. Jeff,' he said, handing him the can.

Jeff considered the possibility of giving it back. Then he changed his mind. He held the can up to his lips, and the bitter fluid choked him. He flushed a deep red as the other two boys laughed at him.

'So what's been coming down?' Jim Mulvey asked of nobody in particular as he popped the tab on his own beer.

'We were talking about Judy Nelson,' a voice said from somewhere in the background. 'And killing yourself in general.'

There was a wave of laughter through the room. Judy Nelson had become something to joke about.

'The guy next door killed himself years ago,' Lyle Crandall put in.

'You're kidding,' Jim said. 'Who was that?'

'I can't remember their names anymore, and his wife moved away right after it happened.'

'What'd he do?'

Lyle laughed and began to tell the story but Janet Connally cut him off.

'Ugh,' she said with a shudder. 'That's horrible. Let's talk about something else.'

'I think it's interesting,' Jim Mulvey grinned. 'If you were going to kill yourself, how would you do it?'

Suddenly they were all talking about the best way to commit suicide. Pills, it was decided, were best, and after that gassing oneself. The more painful ways were discarded, as either too scary or too messy. And then, when they had exhausted that subject, they turned to speculating upon who in their classes were the most likely candidates for a suicide. No one mentioned any of the people at the party. If anybody noticed, nobody commented on it. When they were done, they agreed that if anybody at St. Francis Xavier's was actually going to kill himself, it should be Marilyn Crane. As Jim Mulvey put it, 'She should do herself a favour.' Everyone laughed, and someone suggested that Marilyn could even invent a new method – she could bore herself to death. Everyone laughed at that, too, except Jeff. He felt sorry for Marilyn, and decided that coming to the party had been a mistake. He argued with himself about leaving, but in the end he went to the refrigerator and helped himself to another beer. By the time it was half drunk, he felt much better about everything.

Just before nine o'clock, the telephone rang. Karen motioned for quiet before she picked up the receiver, then, after she had spoken into the phone, waved to everybody. 'It's all right,' she cried. 'It's Judy.' As the party resumed, Karen chatted with Judy Nelson. When she finally hung up, she waved again, until she had everyone's attention.

'Judy has a wonderful idea,' she said. Then she began explaining what Judy's wonderful idea was.

At exactly nine o'clock the telephone rang at the Crane home. Geraldine Crane picked it up, and was pleasantly surprised when a voice asked for Marilyn.

'For me?' Marilyn said curiously, coming into the room. 'Who is it?'

'Don't know.' Geraldine shrugged. She handed the phone to Marilyn, and sat back down in the chair she had vacated when the phone rang. She picked up the book she had been reading, but didn't open it. Instead, she listened to Marilyn's side of the conversation.

'I don't think so,' Marilyn was saying. 'It's getting awfully late, and I think I'd better stay home.' There was a silence, then: 'No, really – I'm not feeling well. Thanks anyway.' Then she hung up the phone and started out of the room.

'Who was that, dear?' her mother said.

'No one.'

'Don't be silly. It was someone. Who was it?'

'Karen Morton,' Marilyn said. She made another attempt to get out of the room, but again her mother stopped her.

'Well, what did she want?'

'Nothing.'

'Marilyn, she must have wanted something. It sounded like she wanted you to go somewhere. Where?'

'Over to her house.'

'Really?' Geraldine was elated. Marilyn was rarely invited to go anywhere, and almost never by people her own age, except that nice Jeff Bremmer. 'What for?'

'She said it was a party. A come-as-you-are party. They want me to come.'

'Why that sounds wonderful,' Geraldine said enthusiastically. She remembered going to that kind of party herself, years ago, and it had been lots of fun. People had shown up in the most ridiculous outfits.

'Well, I'm not going,' Marily said quietly.

Geraldine decided to take the bull by the horns. It was time Marilyn started mixing with the other children, she thought. 'Of course you're going,' she said. 'Why on earth shouldn't you?'

'It's late,' Marilyn said. 'It's nine o'clock, and I want to go to early Mass tomorrow.'

'You can go to a later one, and sleep in,' Geraldine replied.

'But Mother, look at me. I'm a mess.'

'That's what makes come-as-you-are parties fun,' Geraldine said, more sharply than she had meant. 'Now put on your coat and I'll take you right over to Karen's.'

Marilyn surveyed herself in the mirror. She had been about to go to bed with a book, and she was wearing a flannel nightgown and an old pink bathrobe that she had insisted not be given to the Goodwill. Her hair was in curlers, and her face was covered with cream.

'I don't want to go,' she insisted. But Geraldine was adamant. She brushed Marilyn's objections aside and packed her into the car.

Five minutes later, with a coat covering her bathrobe, and slippers on her feet, Marilyn Crane was deposited in front of the Morton house. Without giving her daughter time to voice any more objections, Geraldine Crane drove away. She was sure that finally her ugly-duckling daughter was going to be accepted by the flock. Marilyn, sure that the flock was playing a trick on her, moved slowly up the walk to the door. The house seemed dark, suspiciously quiet. She reached out, and tentatively rang the bell.

At ten-thirty Saturday night, Harriet Morton glanced around the diner where she and one other waitress had spent the evening with very little to do. Only two tables were occupied, and they were both in the other girl's station. And something was nagging at her. She had a feeling that she should be at home. She glanced at the clock, then heard the voice of the other waitress behind her. 'Why don't you call it a night?' Millie was saying. 'You've been jumpy as a cat all night, and it's not as if I can't handle it by myself.' It was a tempting offer, but Harriet thought about the tips she might miss. Millie read her mind. 'Tell you what I'll do. I'll punch you out when I leave, and we'll split any tips that come into your station between now and closing. Which, if we're lucky, should come to about twelve and a half cents each. Go home, will you? I can tell you're worried about something.'

'It's probably silly,' Harriet replied. 'It's just that Karen's having a party tonight, and it's the first time I've ever let her have one when I wasn't there.'

'Afraid it's turned into an orgy?' Millie grinned. 'Go on, take off. I'll handle the mob.' She looked sourly at the two lone diners who were poking unenthusiastically at the mess of potatoes and gravy that was billed as 'real home cooking.'

Five minutes later Harriet was in her car, and ten minutes after that she was pulling into the driveway. From the outside, the party seemed to be over – the house was dark. And then, as she closed the car door, she heard the music. Soft music, not the loud rock she had expected. She tried the door. Unlocked. As she snapped on the lights, she heard the sounds of scuffling in the living room. And there they were.

Harriet surveyed the guilty-looking teen-agers who were scattered around the living room trying to look as though they hadn't been caught – except that their clothes were mussed and the girls' makeup had somehow transferred itself to the boys' faces. Well, it was bound to happen someday, Harriet told herself. They *are* growing up. She steeled herself to give them the lecture she knew her husband would have given them, had he been alive. Of all the kids, it was her own daughter who was staring at her with the most resentment. The others looked properly ashamed; Karen, however, looked mad. It didn't occur to Harriet that Karen's anger was not so much directed at Harriet for the lecture she was giving, as at the fact that Karen was afraid of what the other kids might say when it was over. Karen could see her stock slipping. Her mother, she had always said, let her do what she wanted. Now the truth was coming out. Harriet Morton was just as strict as all the rest of the mothers of Neilsville.

Karen whispered into Jim Mulvey's ear. 'We'll sneak out when this is all over with,' she said softly. 'Then maybe we can finish what we started.' Jim felt a sudden tightness in his groin. Was it really finally going to happen? All of a sudden he was a little bit afraid.

Peter Balsam steered Margo's car into her driveway, and came to a stop. He turned and smiled at her.

'Are you coming in for a nightcap?' Margo asked.

Balsam shook his head. He wanted to accept, wanted to take her in his arms, but something held him back. 'Not tonight,' he said, avoiding the hurt look in her eyes. 'I've got some reading to do.' Then: 'You're sure you don't mind if I take the car?'

Margo smiled. 'Not if you bring it back in the morning. And I figure the best way to guarantee my seeing you in the morning is to loan you the car. Somehow, you just don't strike me as a car thief.' She kissed him quickly, then got out of the car. 'See you in the morning. Shall I fix some breakfast?'

'That'd be great,' Peter said. 'And Margo? Thanks for riding along with me.'

She grinned at him. 'I was just looking out for my car. Next time you decide you have to drive to Seattle, you can do it alone. Trip's too long for me.' She waved at him and disappeared into her house. A moment later she heard him put the car in gear and back out of the driveway. Five minutes later, Margo Henderson was in bed.

Balsam made his way slowly through the back streets of Neilsville. He didn't want to be seen driving Margo's car. He suspected there was already a certain amount of gossip and he didn't want to fuel that particular fire. He was only five blocks from home, and beginning to relax after the trip, when he saw the figure sitting forlornly on the curb. As he drew abreast of the odd apparition, a face peered up at him and he recognized Marilyn Crane. His foot hit the brakes bringing the car to a fast enough stop to send the books piled neatly on the back seat tumbling to the floor. Peter Balsam backed the car up, and rolled down the window.

'Marilyn?' he called. 'Marilyn, is that you?'

She had been about to walk away, hoping to disappear into the shadows, when she recognized his voice. Uncertainly, she turned, and Peter could see that she had been crying. She peered at the car, as if unsure whether to come closer or run away. Peter opened the door and got out. He started around the car.

'Marilyn? It's me, Mr. Balsam. What's wrong? What are you doing wandering around in a bathrobe?'

'I – I'm all right,' she said, but it was obvious she wasn't. And then she remembered the day they had walked from the church into town together, and how Mr. Balsam seemed to understand her. Suddenly her tears started flowing again. 'No, I'm not all right. I'm terrible, if you really want to know. Can I get in your car?'

'Of course you can.' Instinctively, he reached out and took her arm to guide her into the car. By the time he shut the door firmly behind her, she was sobbing uncontrollably. He hurried around to the driver's side. Then, instead of driving away, he pulled the car closer to the curb, and turned off the engine. He reached out to touch the unhappy child and she clutched at his hand.

'What is it, Marilyn?' he said softly. 'Can't you tell me?'

'It – it was awful,' she said. 'They were all so mean.' She looked at him beseechingly. 'Why are they all so mean?'

'I don't know,' Peter said gently. 'Why don't you start at the beginning?'

Marilyn nodded vigorously, and did her best to control the sudden fit of crying that had overtaken her, as she told Peter Balsam what had happened to her that evening.

'It was awful, Mr. Balsam,' she said, reliving the experience. 'I stood there, and rang the bell, and I knew it was some kind of horrible joke, and I waited, but no one answered the door. And then, when I was about to leave, Mother drove away, so I didn't have any choice. So I rang the bell again, and then I could hear them inside. They were all giggling, and I knew they were giggling at me. And finally Karen opened the door, and asked me to come in. I wanted to run away right then, but I hoped that maybe – well, maybe it wasn't a joke at all, and that Karen had dressed up so that *everyone* would look as bad as I did, and she'd be the only one there that looked nice. So I went in. And they were all waiting for me. All of them – Penny and Janet, and Lyle and Jeff – all of them. And there I was. And they were laughing at me. I tried to tell Mother – I knew it was going to happen!' She began crying again, and Peter let her cry, knowing that nothing he could say could take away her humiliation. He let her cry it out. Then, when her sobbing eased off, he squeezed her hand.

'Would you like me to take you home?' he said softly. Marilyn seemed terrified.

'No,' she said. 'Not yet. I can't go home yet. Mother'd be furious with me. She'd tell me I was being too sensitive, and that I should have laughed right along with everyone else, then stayed and had a good time.'

'Maybe you should have,' Peter suggested gently.

'But I couldn't have. Don't you see? They didn't invite me because they wanted me. They only invited me so they could laugh. Once the joke was over, they didn't want me to stay. Oh, God, I wanted to die! It was so awful!'

'I'll tell you what,' Balsam said. 'Why don't we go somewhere, and I'll buy you a Coke?'

Marilyn looked at him hopefully, then her face sagged in disappointment. 'Like this? I can't go anywhere looking like this.'

Balsam couldn't help grinning at her now, but he was careful not to laugh.

'You managed to get here looking like that, didn't you?'

'That was different. I just had to get away from Karen's.'

'How long ago was that?'

She shrugged listlessly. 'I don't know. A half-hour. Maybe an hour.'

'Do you mean to tell me you've been wandering around like that for an hour?' She nodded. 'And you don't want to go home yet?' She shook her head. 'All right, then, we'll go to a drive-in, and you can stay in the car while I buy a couple of Cokes. How's that sound?'

She looked at him gratefully. 'Could we?' she implored him. 'I just don't want Mother to find out what happened. She wouldn't understand at all, and she'd just get mad at me, and tell me I did everything wrong.'

'It's all right,' Balsam assured her. He started the car, and a few minutes later he pulled it into the back corner of the parking lot at the A & W. He went inside, and felt curious eyes on him as he bought two Cokes. When he returned to the car, Marilyn had calmed down considerably.

'You don't know what it was like,' she said, sipping on her Coke.

'How do you know?' Peter said. 'You're not the only one who's ever been caught in something like that.' Then he proceeded to make up a story about his own past, in which he was made to look as ridiculous as Marilyn had been made to look tonight. He told himself that it didn't matter that the story wasn't true. What mattered was that Marilyn realize that she wasn't the only person who had ever been humiliated in public. She listened to him in silence. When he finished, there was just the tiniest trace of a smile at the corners of her mouth.

'That story wasn't true, was it?' she said.

'No,' Balsam admitted. 'But it could have been, and the stories that are true are still too painful to talk about.' He thought about his wife, Linda, and the other man. The man he had found her with. That, he thought, was humiliation. But he couldn't tell Marilyn about it.

'What'll I do now?' she suddenly asked him. 'I mean, how can I face them at school on Monday?'

'Don't worry about it,' Balsam said, 'Just act as if nothing happened, and I'll bet nobody will mention it at all. And listen carefully in my class on Monday. I think I'll have a special lecture – a little talk about people who feel good by making other people feel bad. With no names mentioned, of course. And don't be surprised if I act like you don't exist. I wouldn't want anyone to think you and I had planned anything in advance.'

It worked. Marilyn smiled at him now, and the tears were gone.

'Thanks for finding me tonight,' she said softly. 'I guess you're the only person in the world I really needed to talk to tonight.' She handed him her empty paper cup, and Peter Balsam got out of the car to throw it away, along with his own. Then he drove her home, in a comfortable silence.

'Marilyn?' her mother called from the living room as she closed the front door behind her. 'How was the party?'

'Fine, Mother,' Marilyn responded. She saw no reason to let her good feelings be dissipated by a lecture from her mother.

'Who brought you home?'

Before she could think of anything else to say, Marilyn blurted out the truth.

'Mr. Balsam?' Geraldine Crane repeated. 'How on earth did that happen?'

'He – he was just driving by, and saw me walking,' Marilyn said, stretching the truth only a little. 'He offered me a ride, and since I felt silly walking dressed like this, I accepted.'

Geraldine Crane considered this for a moment. She wasn't sure she approved. After all, the man was practically a stranger 'Well, I wish you wouldn't do things like that,' she said. 'If he ever offers you a ride again, turn him down.'

'Oh, Mother,' Marilyn said, 'For heaven's sake, he's one of my teachers.'

'But we don't really know him, do we?' Geraldine asked darkly. 'Better to be safe than sorry.'

But Marilyn had already slipped up the stairs. She didn't hear what her mother had said.

Leona Anderson wondered if she should call Geraldine Crane that night, or the next morning, or at all. It had been quite shocking. It was a good thing her bridge game had run late, and that she had happened to drive by the A & W just when she had, or she wouldn't have seen it at all. There they were, just as brazen as trash, that Mr. Balsam and Marilyn Crane. And her in her bathrobe, no less! And in Margo Henderson's car. It really was too much.

And then, on reflection, Leona Anderson decided not to call anyone that night. She would wait until morning, and then tell Inez Nelson at church. Between the two of them, she and Inez would be able to decide what should be done. Leona had no doubt that something should be done.

Peter Balsam glanced at the clock as he entered the apartment. Nearly midnight. He was weary from the long drive, but he'd gone all the way to Seattle just for these books and they beckoned to him now. He picked up the most formidable of them, Henry Lea's *The Inquisition of the Middle Ages.*

He opened the book to the index, and began running his fingers down the columns. Then he began leafing through the book, reading a paragraph here, a page there, consulting the index once again.

Peter Balsam did not sleep at all that night. By dawn he knew much more about the saints that adorned St. Francis Xavier church than he had at midnight. What he had discovered wouldn't have let him have much sleep even if he had gone to bed. As the sun rose above Neilsville, and the intense heat of the last days of summer baked the town, Peter Balsam continued his reading. And every now and then, as if it were winter, he shivered.

ELEVEN

Karen Morton was walking up Cathedral Hill alone. Usually, on Sunday mornings, she waited at the foot of the hill, at the corner of First and Main, for Penny Anderson, Janet Connally, and Judy Nelson. But this morning Judy would not be coming. This morning Karen had no desire to see Penny or Janet. Or anyone at all. She wished she were home, closed comfortably into the security of her bedroom.

It had not been an easy morning for Karen, and it was not showing any promise of getting better.

She had thought of staying in bed, pleading illness, but quickly decided that wouldn't work. She had sensed, even before she saw her mother, that no excuse would be accepted today. She was going to have to get up, have to face her mother's anger, have to go to church. She was going to have to confess her sins. That was what was frightening her, for Karen knew she had a lot to confess. And so, even earlier than usual, Karen had gotten up, dressed, and gone downstairs. There just hadn't seemed any point in prolonging it.

Her mother had been in the kitchen. She hadn't spoken to her when Karen came down for breakfast. She simply stared at her, then turned back to the stove where she was frying eggs. Finally, her back still to Karen, sne had asked the question Karen hadn't wanted to hear.

'What time did you come in last night?' she said quietly.

'I'm not sure,' Karen hedged.

'Well, I am,' Harriet snapped. 'It was after two o'clock. Where were you all that time?'

'Jim and I went to – to the A & W,' Karen said. She knew immediately she had made a mistake.

'Did you?' It was an accusation, not a question. 'Did you,

indeed? It must have been interesting, sitting there in the dark. The A & W closes at midnight.'

Karen sank into a chair next to the kitchen table, and waited in silence for the onslaught of her mother's wrath. But it didn't come. Instead, Harriet Morton silently continued fixing their breakfast, silently set the plates on the table, and silently sat down. For Karen, the silence was much worse than any lecture.

'I'm sorry,' she had whispered finally. Again, her mother stared at her. Then, at last, Harriet Morton began to speak.

'I don't know what to say,' she began, and Karen had a sinking feeling in her stomach. Those were the words her mother always used when she was about to invoke Karen's father. She waited.

'If your father were alive,' Harriet had gone on, 'I could leave this whole matter up to him. But he isn't alive, and I have to deal with it. I suppose, when it comes down to it, that I shouldn't blame you. I know it can't be easier for you, not having your father around, than it is for me. But I'd hoped you were old enough to be trusted by now. Apparently I was wrong. Apparently all the things your father and I tried to teach you went in one ear and out the other. Well, there isn't anything I can do about it now. But there are a few things I can do about the future. First, there won't be any more parties. Since I won't be able to supervise them, you won't have them.'

'For how long?' Karen asked softly. She had been expecting this.

'How long?' Harriet had said, looking at her blankly. 'Why, until you're eighteen, of course. As long as you're my responsibility.'

Karen had gasped. 'But Mother—'

'And of course you won't be seeing Jim Mulvey any more,' Harriet went on. She looked deeply into Karen's eyes, and added, 'Unless, of course, you have to get married. I've been praying all night that that won't happen. But if it does, it's a cross we'll both have to bear.'

Karen stared at her mother in dismay, and then burst into

tears and fled the table. Her mother found her lying on her bed, crying.

'It's time for church, Karen,' she said softly.

'I'm not going,' Karen sobbed into her pillow.

'Of course you are,' Harriet said. 'Isn't it more important for you to go this morning than ever before? You need the church this morning, Karen. Now get off that bed, change your clothes, and go.'

She was nearing the top of Cathedral Hill. Other worshipers were streaming toward the church of St. Francis Xavier. Karen did not join in their Sunday-morning chatter, and there was an air about her that kept people from calling a greeting to her. Karen Morton had something on her mind.

She made her way up the steps, and through the foyer. Then she dipped her fingers in the font, genuflected, and started down the aisle to the pew she and her mother usually occupied. Behind her, someone whispered a quick greeting. Karen didn't reply. She sank to her knees, and began the prayers she repeated every Sunday morning. Then she sat on the pew, and tried to pay attention to the Mass.

An hour later, when the Mass was over. Karen stood up reluctantly. Now was going to be the worst time. Now she was going to have to go to the confessional. She knew it was supposed to make her feel better; she knew that her sins would be forgiven. Until this morning, going to confession *had* always made her feel better. But this morning was a special morning. This morning she had a difficult confession to make. Karen steeled herself, almost lost her resolve, then slipped quickly into one of the confessionals that stood to the left of the doors. She clutched her beads, made the sign of the cross – 'In the name of the Father, and of the Son, and of the Holy Ghost. Amen.' – and knelt.

'Bless me, Father, for I have sinned,' Karen began. 'It has been a week since my last confession.' Then she paused, wondering where to start. 'I am guilty of the sin of lust,' she said softly. She heard the slightest intake of breath from beyond the grille. and was immediately fearful.

'What are your sins, my child?'

Karen knew the voice. She had heard it in the halls of the school for too many years not to recognize it, even when it was pitched to the low level of the confessional. It was Monsignor Vernon.

'I – I –' Karen wanted to run from the tiny confessional, run out of the church and down the hill. She tried to get hold of herself. From the other side of the grille the Monsignor's voice inveighed her to begin.

'But it isn't easy . . .' Karen faltered.

'Nothing in this world is easy, my child,' the priest said softly. 'But we must confess our sins. What have you done?'

She told him. She began telling him all that had transpired during the week, and during the week preceding. She confessed to being deceitful, and told him first about helping Judy Nelson with the dress. Then she began telling him about the party the night before, and about being deceitful toward her mother. She told him about the trick she had pulled on Marilyn Crane, and the hurt she had caused Marilyn. And then she told him about the last hours of the night, when she and Jim Mulvey had sat in his car, hidden in the darkness.

'I – I let him touch me, Father,' she whispered. She felt the heat between her legs once again just as she had felt it last night, and a wave of guilt swept over her.

'You let him touch you?' Monsignor asked. 'Let him touch you where?'

'I – I'm not—' Karen stammered. Then she blurted it out. 'I let him touch me all over.'

There was a long silence from the other side of the grille. Then the Monsignor spoke again.

'Exactly what do you mean when you say you let him touch you all over?'

In the darkness of the confessional, Karen Morton flushed a deep scarlet, and wished for a moment that she could die.

'Bless me, Father, for I have sinned,' she mumbled again.

'I cannot forgive sins that have not been confessed,' the inexorable voice came out of the darkness. Karen squirmed in embarrassment.

'He – I let him touch me on my chest. And between my legs,' she said miserably.

'And did you touch him?' the priest continued relentlessly.

'Yes.' The word was almost inaudible, and Karen wondered if she had been heard. But she couldn't bring herself to repeat it. Then the voice began talking to her.

'Lust is a most grievous sin, my child. Your soul is in grave danger, and you must be on your guard against the evil that is within you.'

'I am trying, Father,' Karen said miserably.

'The Devil walks among us,' she heard the priest saying. 'He is constantly with us, leading us out of the paths of righteousness. Guard yourself against him, my child, and be wary. He will appear as a friend, but he will lead you astray.' Then the voice fell silent, and Karen wondered about the words. What was the priest trying to tell her? Was he saying that Jim Mulvey was the Devil? It didn't make sense. Then he spoke again.

'Is there anything else?' he said.

Karen searched her mind. It was almost over. Soon, she would be absolved of her sins, and free to go. She tried to remember if she had left anything out of the confession, but the strain of it had left her confused.

'No, Father,' she said finally.

'Your sins are many, child, and your penance must be heavy.'

Karen felt her heart sink. Many times she had seen people come out of the confessional and walk down the aisle toward the altar. There they would kneel, and spend the rest of the day. Often, she had wondered what prayers they were saying. Now she was sure she was about to find out.

'You will leave the confessional on your knees, and approach the Holy Virgin. For your sins, say one hundred Rosaries, and between each Rosary, recite the Apostles' Creed. Do you understand your penance?'

'Yes, Father.' Karen wanted to cry. Leave the confessional on her knees? She didn't remember anyone ever having done that before. People would stare at her. They would know that she must have done something terribly wicked. She wished she could die. Then she realized the priest was saying the words of absolution. Quickly, she repeated the Act of Contrition. 'Oh my God,' she began, the words coming automatically through her confusion, 'I am heartily sorry for having offended Thee, and I detest all my sins because I dread the loss of heaven and the pains of hell; but most of all because they offend Thee, my God, who are all-good and deserving of all my love. I firmly resolve, with the help of Thy grace, to sin no more and to avoid near occasions of sin. As she finished, she heard the words of absolution.

'I absolve you from your sins, in the name of the Father, and of the Son, and of the Holy Ghost. Amen. Go in peace, my child.' The shutter closed over the grille, and Karen Morton was alone in the confessional. She sat for a long time, wishing she had the courage, or the cowardice to ignore the penance, to leave the confessional and walk out of the church into the sunlight. But Karen Morton was in fear of her Lord, so she grasped her beads firmly, pushed the door of the confessional open, and, still on her knees, crept out into the church. She stared at the image of the Holy Virgin and kept her eyes firmly fixed on that peaceful face as she made her pitiful way down the aisle. By the time she reached the statue, and began telling her beads, the pain in her knees was almost as great as the agony in her mind. Her lips moving silently, she began the Apostles' Creed.

Peter Balsam stared out into the morning sunlight and wondered what he should do next. His first impulse was to call Margo Henderson, and he had already reached for the phone when he realized what he must do instead. He must go to church. He must pray. He must make his decision for himself. He knew that, in the light of what he had read last night, it was not going to be easy to pray this morning, not going to be easy to sit below the glowering countenances of the Saints of the Inquisition – the Saints of Neilsville – and come to a decision that made sense. But this morning, not much made sense to Peter Balsam. His long night's reading had shaken him to the core. Now, he had to find out if his faith had withstood the shaking or if it had crumbled.

He left his apartment, carefully locked the door behind him. and began the climb up Cathedral Hill.

He entered the church just as Karen Morton came out of the confessional and looked on in horror as she slowly made her way down the aisle to the alcove dedicated to the Blessed Virgin. For a split second he had wanted to go to her. When he saw the rest of the parishioners ignoring her, he changed his mind. He was still staring at her when he heard the voice behind him.

'I'd hoped you'd be here earlier,' Monsignor Vernon's voice said softly into his ear. Peter Balsam jumped back, startled, then turned to stare at the priest.

'What on earth is going on here?' he demanded.

Monsignor Vernon looked at him impassively, almost as if he hadn't heard the question.

'Why did Karen Morton just go down the aisle on her knees?'

The priest smiled clamly, a look of peace in his eyes.

'That's between her and her Lord, isn't it?'

'Is it supposed to be some kind of penance?' Balsam demanded.

'It doesn't concern you,' the priest countered. He turned, as if to move away, then turned back. 'Will I see you at the next Mass?' he asked Balsam.

Balsam glanced again at Karen Morton, who was now engrossed in prayer, before he answered. Then he turned to the priest, and shook his head.

'I don't know,' he said. 'But I need to talk to you.'

'To me?' Monsignor Vernon asked. 'Very well. Shall we go to the rectory?'

'If you don't mind, I'd rather we went somewhere else. How about my classroom?'

The Monsignor shrugged indifferently and led Peter Balsam out of the church. A few minutes later he put his key in the door to Room 16, and stood aside to let Balsam enter first. Then he followed the teacher in, and pulled the door closed behind him.

'Is something wrong?' The question was not so much an inquiry as a prod. Balsam decided not to allow himself to be prodded. Instead, he approached the statue of St. Peter Martyr, and stood silently staring at it for several minutes.

Then he turned quickly and spoke.

'He was a prize bastard, wasn't he?' Balsam had intended the words to be shocking. He succeeded. The priest immediately made the sign of the cross. Then his eyes flashed angrily at Balsam.

'I beg your pardon?'

'I've been reading up on him,' Balsam said calmly. 'On him, and on all the other saints you've got scattered around here. Almost all of them come straight out of the Inquisition, which I've also been reading up on.'

The priest sat down on the edge of Peter Balsam's desk, arms folded in an attitude of exaggerated patience.

'I have a lot of Dominican saints here, yes,' he said pensively. 'And I suppose you're right – a lot of them do date from the period of the Inquisition. But I don't get your point.'

Balsam felt his resolve beginning to crumble. 'It's just this,' he said, suddenly uncertain. 'I got curious about the saints in the church and I decided to do some research. And then, the more I read, the more I realized that the kind of intolerance all these saints represented wasn't much different from the sort of thing we were talking about the other day. The day we were we were discussing what I can, and what I cannot, teach in my class.'

The priest smiled dryly. 'You think the Inquisition's being revived, right here in Neilsville?'

'In a word, yes, that's exactly what I think.'

'Before I even argue the point with you,' Monsignor Vernon said wearily, 'may I inquire what the purpose of this meeting is?'

'Certainly,' Balsam retorted. 'This is to tell you that I've changed my mind. I don't think I can stay in Neilsville.

In fact, after the reading I did last night, I'm not even sure I can stay in the Church.'

Suddenly the priest looked stricken.

'You're not serious,' he exclaimed. 'You aren't really considering leaving the Church?'

Now that he'd said it, Balsam was suddenly no longer sure he meant it. He glanced nervously at the Monsignor, then back to the image of St. Peter Martyr.

'I don't know,' he said uncertainly. 'It's just that I can't stomach the sort of thing people like him stood for. And it seems to me that the Church hasn't really progressed very far since his day.'

'Of course it hasn't,' the priest intoned. 'Why should it? Faith is absolute, and the Truth of the Lord is absolute. There is room within the Faith for differences of opinion.'

As Balsam stared, the Monsignor's voice softened and he returned to himself. He smiled. 'Peter, I know we've had differences of opinion. They are not at an end. We have always had our differences.' He paused, as if weighing the prudence of what he was about to reveal, then continued with a sigh, 'I hadn't intended to tell you this, but I selected you for the job here because of those differences.' He left the edge of the desk, and began pacing the room, speaking as he moved. 'I've been following your career very slosely, Peter, much more closely than you ever knew. And I've worried about you. Of all of us, you've seemed to me to have had the most trouble, not only within the Church, but within yourself. I suppose some of it has to do with your childhood –'

'Forget that,' Balsam snapped. 'It has nothing to do with all this.'

'Doesn't it?' the priest said quizzically. Then he smiled again. 'Well, maybe it doesn't. At any rate, it's all academic. If you wish, I'll take the matter of your resignation under consideration. I will do it reluctantly, but I will do it. In the meantime, I wish you'd do me a favour. I wish you'd examine your own conscience, and I wish you'd make a greater effort to understand what the Dominican saints were all about.

Their methods may seem a bit harsh today, but don't forget that some of the tales of that period have been grossly exaggerated. Primarily, they helped people to keep the Faith. And that, I think, is at the root of your problems right now. I think you're having a crisis of faith.' He put his hand on Peter's shoulder. 'It happens to us all,' he said gently. 'It's happened to me, since I've been here. But I've come through it. Of course I had the Society of St. Peter Martyr to help me. The Society could help you, too.'

Balsam looked at the priest curiously. 'Exactly what is the Society of St. Peter Martyr?' he asked.

The priest smiled enigmatically. 'Come and see,' he said. 'We meet tomorrow night.' When Peter seemed hesitant, he added: 'What harm can it do? It might even help. If nothing else, at least you'll understand us better. Then, if you still want to leave, I'm sure we'll be able to arrange it.'

Balsam sighed heavily. He had a feeling that something was wrong – that the talk had not gone as he had intended it to. He shrugged off the feeling and smiled at the Monsignor.

'Okay,' he said. 'Tomorrow night?'

'Seven-thirty, at the rectory.'

The two men left the classroom, and walked together out of the school. 'Will I see you at Mass this evening?' the priest asked.

'I don't know,' Balsam answered honestly. 'But I suppose so. If I miss it, I can always confess.' He regretted the facetious remark as soon as he'd made it, but the Monsignor was not listening.

'Then if not before, I'll see you tomorrow night,' He turned and disappeared into the rectory.

Peter Balsam started down the hill. Then, as if remembering something, he went back to the church. There, still on her knees in front of the Holy Virgin, was Karen Morton, her fingers playing over the beads, her lips reciting the Rosary. As Balsam left the church and started again down the hill, he wondered how long she would be there.

If he had known Karen Morton would be in the church, praying on her knees, for the next eight hours, he might have changed his mind once more, and left Neilsville that afternoon. But it was already too late; things had already gone too far, and Balsam was already too enmeshed in it. The punishment was beginning.

BOOK TWO

THE SOCIETY OF ST. PETER MARTYR

TWELVE

Inez Nelson hurried up the steps, and through the main doors of St. Francis Xavier School. She was late, and she knew that Monsignor didn't like to be kept waiting.

She turned into the reception room and glanced nervously at the door that led to Monsignor's private office, wondering if she should tap at the closed door. Just as she decided against it she heard the click of the latch and looked up, relieved to see the priest smiling at her.

'Come in, come in,' he said expansively. 'It's a good thing you're late – Mondays are always my busy day. The work seems to pile up over the weekend, even though there isn't any school. Or maybe I just don't work hard enough on Fridays.' He closed the door behind Inez, and offered her a chair. Then he moved behind his desk and sat down. His smile had disappeared.

'I suppose you've been to the hospital?' he asked.

Inez nodded. 'I spent nearly an hour with that Dr. Shields—'

'The psychiatrist?' Monsignor interrupted her.

'Yes.' Inez paused, choking back a sob. 'Oh, Monsignor, I'm so confused and it's been worrying me all weekend. He says Judy is doing fine. But she won't talk about why she did it. All she'll tell him is that she's fine now, and that it won't happen again.'

'And what does she say to you?'

Inez squirmed uncomfortably. 'Well, that's just it, Monsignor. That's why I felt I had to talk to you. About so many things. But primarily about Judy. You see, she won't see me.'

Monsignor Vernon's eyes opened in surprise. 'Won't see you? What do you mean, she won't see you?'

'Just that,' Inez said unhappily. 'She absolutely refuses to see me.' She was fighting tears. 'And it's only me,' she went on, her voice beginning to quaver. 'She sees everyone else. Her father. Her friends. But she won't see me. And everyone says she's fine.'

'Do they?' The priest's tone suggested to Inez that he didn't believe Judy could possibly be fine. 'If she won't see you, I wonder how fine she could be?'

'That's exactly what I thought, too,' Inez said. Suddenly she felt much better. 'But I don't know what to do. If only I could talk to her, I know I could find out what's the matter.'

The priest shrugged. 'Frankly, I don't see what the problem is. Judy is only sixteen, and you *are* her mother. If you want to see her, I don't see how anyone can stop you.'

Inez nodded vigorously. 'That's exactly what I've been saying. But no one agrees with me. Oh, not that I can't see her if I demand to. Everyone says I can do that. But they all think it would be unwise. Dr. Shields and George – my husband – both seem to think I should just wait. They say eventually she'll see me, and I suppose they're right. But in the meantime nobody seems to be taking my feelings into consideration. I feel like – well, I feel like such a failure.' She looked guiltily at the priest. 'Do you know what I've been doing? I've been going to the hospital every day at visiting hours, and visiting total strangers. Well, not total strangers, of course, but people I wouldn't normally go see in the hospital. Then I tell them that I was there visiting Judy, and I just decided to drop in.' Now the tears came, and Inez stared miserably at the priest. 'I just don't know how long I can stand it, Father,' she said. 'If it ever gets out that all this time Judy has been refusing to see me – well, you don't know what an awful feeling it is.'

Monsignor Vernon offered her a Kleenex, and a smile. 'It's difficult, I know,' he said softly. 'Sometimes I think everything is topsy-turvy these days, and we're expected to give in to our children all the time.'

'I know,' Inez said, sniffling into the tissue and trying to regain control of herself. 'But I was beginning to think I was the only one who thought so.'

'You aren't,' the Monsignor replied, 'although sometimes I think there are very few of us left who refuse to be manipulated by our children.'

Inez looked sharply at the priest. *Manipulated.* The same word Dr. Shields had used. 'That's it exactly,' she said. 'I feel like I'm being manipulated by Judy. As if she's trying to punish me.'

'And that's undoubtedly exactly what's going on,' Monsignor Vernon said emphatically. 'You have no idea what it can be like here.' He turned his chair, gazing out the window as he talked. 'I have to have my guard up all the time. They're smart, you know. Brighter than we were, when we were young. But it isn't a good kind of brightness. It's a clever kind of brightness. They're always testing me, pushing me, to see how far they can go before I crack down on them. It must be even worse in the public schools. They have so few controls anymore. Thank God the Church recognizes the function of discipline in the raising of children! But it gets harder each year. Every year, they strain me more. Every year, more of them try to corner me. Well, I don't intend to tolerate it! This year, the children will find out who runs this school, and they'll find out it isn't them!' He suddenly spun the chair around again, and seemed almost surprised to see Inez Nelson sitting opposite his desk. He had almost forgotten she was in the office, and that it was to her that he was talking. Now she sat very still, unnerved by the intensity with which he had spoken. He broke the moment with a quick smile. 'I'm sorry,' he said, chuckling a little. 'Sometimes I get quite carried away. Well, what were we talking about?'

'Judy—' Inez said distractedly. 'We were talking about Judy. Which brings me to the other thing I wanted to discuss with you. Dr. Shields tells me that she'll be fine by the end of the week, and that she can come back to school a week from today. Next Monday,'

'I see,' Monsignor Vernon said carefully, licking his lips nervously. Inez Nelson noticed the gesture immediately.

'That's right, isn't it?' she said quickly. 'I mean, there isn't going to be any problem, is there?'

'Actually, I don't know,' Monsignor Vernon said hesitantly. 'I mean, we've never before been faced with something like this, and I haven't quite been able to find out what to do about it yet.'

'Do about it?' Inez asked blankly. 'What's there to do? I don't understand.'

'Well,' the priest said slowly, 'it isn't really the same as if she'd simply been sick, is it? What she did comes very close to sacrilege. Judy will have to confess and be absolved before she can return to school.'

'Before?' Inez asked. 'Why before?'

'Because of the nature of her sin. You must be aware that suicide is one of the most grievous sins that a Catholic can commit. Only God can forgive it, not the Church.'

Inez was suddenly alarmed. Was Judy to be excommunicated?

'But she didn't—' she began. 'I mean, she didn't actually do anything, did she?' she asked desperately. 'I mean, yes, I suppose she tried, but Dr. Shields says he doesn't think she really meant to kill herself, and in any case, she isn't dead, is she?'

Monsignor gave the distraught woman his most tolerant look. 'I'm afraid that isn't the point. The point is that she did, indeed, intend the sin. That she didn't succeed was only a matter of luck, not intent. And I'm sure you're aware that a sin intended is every bit as offensive to God as a sin committed.'

Inez Nelson stared at him helplessly. 'But what's going to happen to her?'

'I'm afraid I can't answer that. There are grave philosophical and theological questions involved. I simply haven't the answers yet. But I intend to put the entire case before my study group tonight, and I'm sure that among the six of us we'll be able to find the answer. The Lord, through St. Peter Martyr, will guide me.'

He rose from behind his desk, and led Inez out of the office. As she was leaving, he called to her, and she turned back, her face pale and her eyes beseeching him. He raised his hand in the sign of the cross. 'May the Lord bless you and keep you, may the Lord make his face to shine upon you, and give you peace.'

But as she walked out of the school, and slowly made her way to the parking lot, Inez Nelson knew there was going to be no peace for her. For her, or her daughter, or anyone else in Neilsville. As she got into the car, a cloud passed over the sun. Summer had come to an abrupt end in Neilsville.

The final bell had rung, and the students had poured out of the classroom into the halls. All but Marilyn Crane. She sat alone in the room, except for Sister Elizabeth, who was straightening up her desk.

It had not been an easy day for Marilyn; if she had had her way she would not have come to school at all. But her mother had insisted, and Marilyn had dragged herself up the hill. It had seemed steeper today than ever before, and when she had finally reached the school she had had to force herself to go in. All through the day she had heard the snickers, and the whispers, as the story of her humiliation on Saturday night spread through the halls. Everybody had heard. Suddenly it wasn't just her own classmates who snubbed her and turned away at her approach. Now the younger children, the children who had always been at least a little respectful, were pointing at her and giggling together.

She tried to ignore it all, tried to do as Mr. Balsam had suggested, and pretend that nothing had happened. She had spent the entire day waiting for the final bell, and how it had rung. But she still didn't leave her desk. Instead, she stared miserably down at the paper that lay accusingly in front of her. It was a test and it was marked B-minus.

The grade itself wasn't really bad. What hurt most was the note pencilled next to the grade. There, in Sister Elizabeth's flowing script, was the real condemnation: 'This is very disappointing. I know you can do better.'

Marilyn wanted to cry. What did they want from her? She tried, she knew she tried. But, once more, she had failed.

As she stared at the grade, and the note beside it, anger

churned in her. She fought it back. After all, who was there to be angry at, besides herself? She was the one who had gotten the grade. She was the one who hadn't lived up to Sister Elizabeth's expectations. Her anger turned to frustration. What *did* they want, anyway? And even if she knew, why should she live up to their expectations? Why should she?

Why should she do anything at all?

And then, realizing the magnitude of the thought that had just gone through her mind, she quickly begged forgiveness. She decided to go to church. Things were always better in the church. The Blessed Virgin didn't demand anything of her.

Marilyn gathered her things, and left the room. As she did, Sister Elizabeth glanced up, looked at her curiously, and decided something was wrong with Marilyn Crane. She made a mental note to discuss Marilyn with Monsignor Vernon. Monsignor would know what to do. Sister Elizabeth went back to her work and put Marilyn out of her mind.

Peter Balsam arrived at the rectory punctually at seven-thirty. He let himself in, picked up the small silver bell, and rang it. When there was no response, he walked down the hall and tapped lightly at the study door. It was opened immediately by a man he didn't recognize, but who seemed to know who he was.

'Peter Balsam,' the man said, opening the door just wide enough for Peter to slip through. He held his finger to his lips. 'Monsignor is saying the blessing.'

The study was dimly lit, and as Peter looked around he realized that of the six men gathered in the small room, the only one he recognized was Monsignor Vernon. All the others were strangers, but he had the distinct feeling that he was no stranger to them. They stared at him and he felt as if he were being measured – and found wanting. As he pondered the possible significance of this, Monsignor Vernon finished the blessing, and smiled at him.

'Peter,' he said expansively, 'let me introduce you to the Society.' He took Peter by the elbow and introduced him to the members of the Society of St. Peter Martyr one by one.

All were priests, and all were from parishes outside of Neilsville. But as the Monsignor introduced them Balsam realized that, though they were all considerably older than Vernon, they shared certain traits with him. There was a tightness to their faces, particularly to Father Bryant, whose expression seemed frozen in disapproval. Father Martinelli, the eldest of them all, peered out from deep-set eyes that were almost invisible under bushy brows. He grunted a greeting to Balsam, but there was a note of displeasure in it, as if he felt this introduction should not be taking place. Father Prine, gnarled with rheumatism, extended his hand, but pulled it painfully back before Peter could shake it. The other two, whose names Peter didn't catch, greeted him formally, but offered no particular welcomes.

When the introductions were completed, Monsignor Vernon invited Balsam to sit down. The chair near the fireplace, the one he had occupied every time he had been in the study, had been left vacant. He wondered briefly whether this was by design or coincidence, deciding that either way he was grateful for the familiar touch.

'I've heard a lot about you,' he said to the group in general. They stared. Just as the silence was becoming uncomfortable, Father Prine spoke.

'And we've heard a lot about you.' There was something in the voice that told Peter that not all they heard had been good.

'All bad, I suppose,' he grinned. The humour was lost on the old priest, who turned dourly to Monsignor Vernon.

'You'll have to forgive us,' the Monsignor said to Peter. 'We are a closed group, and we observe strict rules about speaking. While you are among us, you will observe them, too. But you are not to consider yourself a member of the Society of St. Peter Martyr. Not yet, at any rate. Whether or not we decide to initiate you into our order will depend on many things.'

Peter was about to challenge the priest's use of the word 'order' but he remembered the sanction against questions. He felt his temper rising, and had to fight down an impulse to leave. He restrained himself. He had come to the rectory for a reason. Here, he might find out just exactly how it was that Monsignor Vernon had changed from the rather casual student Balsam remembered from the seminary into the rigid dogmatist he had become. And if Balsam was to make any kind of adjustment to St. Francis Xavier's, he needed to understand his superior. He fought down his impulse to leave and sat quietly in the chair by the fireplace.

And the questioning began.

The questions seemed simple enough, at first, and Peter soon began to feel like a child being put through the Catechism.

He was asked to repeat the Apostles' Creed.

He was examined about his knowledge of the Immaculate Conception.

But as the questioning continued, each of the priests taking his turn, Balsam realized that they wanted more of him than a simple statement of his knowledge of the beliefs of the Church. They were trying to determine if there were flaws in his faith: if there were areas in which he was not in agreement with the Doctrines.

'Do you accept the Church as the true vessel of the Word of God?'

'Do you accept the Infallibility of the Pope?'

'Did you leave the priesthood because of doubts as to the Faith, or only as to your vocation?'

The questions rang in his ears, and he began to find himself agreeing with everything they asked, telling them what he knew they wanted to hear, not because he wanted to please them, but because, as they droned on, the questions lost their meaning. He began to feel that they were not asking him for his own responses, which would have been too complicated and ambiguous to fit into the narrow structure of their questions. Instead, they were inundating him with their own beliefs, and taking reassurance as he reflected those beliefs back to them.

An hour went by. Peter began to realize that he was no

longer hearing the questions, that they no longer made sense to him. He held up a hand.

'Wouldn't it be easier if I just talked?' he asked. 'I know what you're driving at, but at this rate we'll be here all night.'

Father Martinelli glared at him. 'You know nothing,' the old priest quavered. 'Answer the questions, please. If we wish your comments we will ask for them.'

The questioning continued.

And then it was over. As if an unseen signal had been passed among the priests, the questioning suddenly stopped. Peter searched the faces, one by one, trying to read in their expressions their reactions to his answers. The faces were impassive.

Then he heard Monsignor Vernon speaking.

'It's time we took up the discussion for tonight,' he said softly. 'Which is, of course, the problem of Judy Nelson.'

Balsam was baffled. Judy Nelson? Why was she to be discussed here? What possible concern was she to this group? The answer came soon enough. For the next ten minutes, as Peter listened in silence, the priests discussed what penance should be placed on Judy when she returned to school. The question of whether or not she should be allowed to return at all was disposed of very quickly; since she had not put herself beyond redemption, she was to be brought back into the fold. But the question of penance was not so easily resolved. Finally, as the discussion seemed to be getting nowhere, Peter interrupted.

'Don't you think it might be a good idea to talk to Judy before you decide on anything?' he suggested. Father Martinelli gazed at him with a detached curiosity.

'Not relevant,' the ancient voice crackled. 'Of what possible interest could anything she might say be to us?'

Peter was astounded. 'It seems to me that it might be wise to find out why she did it, before you began handing down penances,' he said.

'Nonsense,' Father Bryant snapped. 'Her motivations are of no concern to us. She has sinned, and in the eyes of the

Church, it is the sin that matters, not the motivations of the sinner.'

The five other priests nodded solemn agreement.

Balsam started to get to his feet. 'Then you really have no need for me, do you? I'm a psychologist, not a priest, and certainly not a judge.'

'Sit down,' Monsignor Vernon said. Peter sat. 'You are here for a reason. We have found, over the years, that a strictly structured examination of our own faiths has often served to reinforce that faith. That is what we have provided you with. But you are also here to discuss a specific problem that we don't feel qualified to handle.'

Six pairs of eyes bored into Peter's. No one spoke until Peter broke the silence.

'What problem?' he asked.

Father Prine took over now.

'We are concerned for the safety of our children,' he said, his voice muted but steady. 'We can see no reason why young Judy shouldn't be allowed to return to school, yet we feel that somehow the other children must be protected from whatever—' He groped for the word, then found one he seemed reluctant to use. '—whatever evil is lurking in Judy.'

Balsam wanted to tell the old priest that he was certain there was no 'evil' lurking in Judy, that she was simply the victim of some psychological problems. He knew it was useless. It was not what they wanted to hear. He addressed himself instead to the thrust of the question.

'I'm not sure what could be done,' he said slowly, 'I mean, short of isolating Judy – and that would simply focus attention on the whole situation. It seems to me that the best thing to do is try to act as if nothing had happened, and hope things settle down of their own accord.'

The priests appeared to be pondering the wisdom of this course. Finally Monsignor Vernon broke the silence.

'I wonder,' he began. 'I heard about something, or read about it. Relaxation therapy, I think it was called.'

Peter Balsam's attention was suddenly riveted on the priest. Where had he ever heard of relaxation therapy? But the

Monsignor didn't notice the sudden tension in the teacher, and continued talking, softly, reasonably.

'I was just wondering if it could be of any possible use in this situation. The students have been pretty keyed up lately. Do you think there's any way we can use this relaxation therapy to calm them down? Before Judy comes back next week, I mean?'

Balsam's mind was suddenly racing. There was danger here, but he couldn't define it. All he could put his finger on was the incongruity of the priest's suggestion. Of all people, Vernon was the last one Peter would have expected to suggest the use of what was, at best, an experimental process. His instincts told him to move carefully.

'I don't know,' he said honestly enough. 'I'm afraid I don't know much about the process, and from what I've read, I don't think it would accomplish much.'

'But you don't know?' Father Bryant pressed.

'No,' Peter said reluctantly. 'I don't.'

'In fact,' Monsignor Vernon said, 'it might indeed help them, mightn't it?'

Peter felt suddenly trapped. 'I suppose it might,' he admitted.

'Well, then,' the priest said affably. 'Why don't we leave it at this? You sleep on it, and do whatever you think best.' He stood up, and Peter realized he was being dismissed. 'I want to thank you for coming tonight. I think it's been good for all of us.'

It wasn't until the door closed quietly behind him that Peter was sure his part in the meeting was over. Confused, he stood in the hallway for a moment, then, as he began to walk slowly toward the front door of the rectory, he heard the chanting begin. It was soft at first, then grew louder. Gregorian chanting, but somehow slightly wrong. As he left the rectory, Peter Balsam attributed the peculiar sound of the chanting to the fact that the participants were old, and their voices had weakened with age.

But as he walked slowly down Cathedral Hill, the sound of

the chanting stayed with him, ringing in his head, embedding itself in his mind.

He tried to figure out just what the Society of St. Peter Martyr was all about. He was sure it wasn't the simple 'study group' Monsignor had claimed it to be. No, it was something else. He racked his memory. 'Order.' They had called it an order. Surely, in this day and age, they weren't attempting to begin a new order, one tied to the memory of a thirteenth-century inquisitor? That was absurd.

And there was something else that bothered him, something he thought about long after he got home that night. As he was drifting off to sleep, it came to him. The Society of St. Peter Martyr had not acted like any 'study group' he knew of. No, the Society of St. Peter Martyr had acted like a tribunal.

Peter Balsam found it very disturbing. When he slept, his dreams were filled with the sound of chanting, and the strange, intolerant visages of the members of the Society of St. Peter Martyr.

THIRTEEN

As his class began drifting into Room 16, Peter Balsam realized that he had been anticipating this hour all morning. His mind had been on his Latin classes even less than usual. The Latin students had sensed his distraction, and had taken advantage of it, spending the previous three hours mistranslating their lessons, winking at each other every time he failed to catch their deliberate errors, and passing the word, one class to the next, that today was a good day in Mr. Balsam's class – anything went! By fourth period, the psychology students were looking forward even more than usual to their offbeat class, and they came into Room 16 carrying an air of anticipation. It was almost as if they knew that Balsam had been lax with the other classes because he had something special planned for them.

Now, as the classroom slowly filled, Balsam had a sudden feeling of trepidation, his first such feeling since the decision had come to him. What he was about to do was an experiment, and an experiment he was unfamiliar with. He had gotten up early this morning, filled with a sense of purpose, and reviewed what little material he could find on the subject of relaxation technique, quickly realizing it was little more than a very light form of hypnosis, a period of induced relaxation, using both music and the human voice to put the subjects – a word Balsam hated – into a state resembling light sleep. Almost light sleep, but not quite. The music would be important and he had made his selection carefully from his limited collection of records and tapes. Feeling inspired, he had chosen religious music, a recording of Gregorian chants made by a small order of nuns in France. If the chanting of the Society of St. Peter Martyr the previous evening had put the suggestion into his head, he was unconscious of it. He busied himself setting up the record player as the last of his students hurried into the room.

The last to come in were Karen Morton and Marilyn Crane. Though they entered the room together, it was obvious to Balsam that it was only a matter of coincidence. Marilyn seemed almost unaware that anyone else was in the room. And Karen completely ignored Marilyn as she walked slowly toward the front row of desks. This morning she didn't seat herself immediately; instead, she piled her books on top of the desk, and approached Balsam, a little smile playing around the corners of her mouth. Balsam had a distinct feeling that she was about to play some kind of a game with him, and decided to end it before it got started.

'Take your seat, please, Karen,' he said shortly, not seeing the hurt look that came over her at his rebuff. 'We're already late getting started, and there's a lot I want to accomplish today.' Then he turned his attention back to the class, and particularly to Marilyn Crane, who had moved lifelessly to her usual place at the back of the room.

As he finished setting up the sound system, Balsam began explaining what relaxation technique was all about, without telling them what he hoped to accomplish with it. He was afraid that if they knew he was planning more for them than a simple experiment, their guard would be up, and they wouldn't be responsive to the technique. A hand went up in the front row, Janet Connally's.

'Janet?'

'I'm not sure I understand,' Janet said slowly. Then she grinned mischievously. 'I mean, it sounds like I might fall asleep.'

Balsam returned her grin. 'You might,' he agreed. 'But don't worry about it. Today marks a momentous event at St. Francis Xavier's. Sleeping in class is permitted. In fact, a lot of you might wind up snoring through this whole thing, so let's get rid of the desks. Let's push them all over against the walls, and make enough room so everybody can lie down on the floor. If we're going to relax, we might as well go all the way.'

The class exchanged looks, startled, then quickly began moving the furniture. When the job was half-complete, the door suddenly opened, and Monsignor Vernon appeared, his eyes quickly taking in the activity in the room. The activity stopped. It was almost as if someone had suddenly thrown a switch, and the motion had frozen. But instead of asking what was going on, the priest simply stared at Balsam, smiled briefly, and disappeared again.

When the door was safely shut, the clearing of the furniture continued.

There was a lot of giggling and whispering as the class settled itself on the floor, and Balsam didn't try to stop it. He wanted them to be relaxed, and if giggling and whispering would help, that was fine with him.

'All right,' he said when they seemed as settled as they were going to be, 'let's begin. I'm going to put on some music, and I want you to let yourselves float with it. As I said earlier, don't worry about falling asleep. There's no better relaxation than sleep, and that's what this is all about.'

He set the needle on the record, and the music began. At the first notes, another wave of giggling went over the class, but it soon subsided. Slowly, one by one, each of the students succumbed to the persistent rhythm and monotony of the chanting. Balsam walked among them and saw that their eyes were closed. One or two of them were displaying that odd flutter of the eyelids that comes with light sleep. He began talking to them, telling them to become aware of their breathing, to imagine with each breath that they were sinking into the floor. Deeper and deeper into the floor. Breathe evenly. Listen to the music. Sink into the floor. Deeper. Deeper . . .

He went back to the front of the room and was about to continue when once more the door opened, and Monsignor Vernon came silently into the room. This time he was not alone. Behind him, the Society of St. Peter Martyr filed into Room 16. Almost before Balsam was aware of what was happening, the six priests ranged along the back wall, silent observers of whatever was about to happen.

Balsam looked quickly at the class; none of them had noticed the intrusion of the elderly clerics and their young leader. Their breathing remained even and deep, their eyes closed. Balsam began turning the volume of the music down, until it was an almost imperceptible background. And then, trying to keep his voice on an even tone that wouldn't interrupt the state of near trance that had come over the class, he began to speak.

'Relaxation,' he began, 'is a technique designed to relieve internal pressures through the release of physical pressures. Basically, it helps us the way sleep does. But in simple relaxation, we try to put our bodies in a state almost resembling sleep while we let our conscious minds roam about, sorting out our anxieties and dissipating them harmlessly. What we are doing today is a little like lying in a hammock on a sunny afternoon, daydreaming. Daydreams, which we may think are just idle fantasies, are really much more. They're a means of bolstering our own identities, or reinforcing ourselves against the everyday pressures of life.' He glanced quickly over the class, noting that so far nothing had disturbed any of the students. Jim Mulvey was snoring gently. Vaguely amused, Balsam wondered if any of the students were hearing him. He glanced at the back wall, where the Society stood impassively listening. Then he contined his lecture.

'Though we may sometimes feel that daydreaming is a waste of time, psychologists have known for years that it's a very important means of releasing pressures. It's a sort of safety valve. The human mind, of course, has developed many safety valves. One you're all familiar with is dreaming. Dreaming is really the unconscious mind clearing up the debris it has been otherwise unable to cope with. Daydreaming is similar, except that it occurs on the conscious level.'

The class was still quiet, but the Society had shifted its attention. Their interest had moved to the class. They seemed particularly intent on two of the girls: Karen Morton and Marilyn Crane.

Feeling strangely uneasy, Balsam stepped up the pace of his talk.

'Occasionally,' he went on, 'the safety valves the mind builds for itself fail to operate. When this happens, we begin to see all kinds of things happen, as the mind attempts to cope with its problems. Things like nervous tics develop, or a person becomes unable to concentrate. Or irrational behaviour can begin to occur. Some people, when their safety valves fail to relieve internal pressure, begin scratching themselves, almost uncontrollably.

Balsam heard a faint rustling sound in the room and tried to pinpoint where it had come from. Karen Morton seemed to be fumbling in her purse. Then she settled down again. The members of the Society of St. Peter Martyr still stood impassively against the back wall. If they were listening to him as intently as Balsam suspected, they showed no outward signs of it. He tried to pick up his train of thought.

'Sometimes,' he continued, keeping his voice low, 'all of our safety valves malfunction, and when this happens the results can be very serious indeed. The end result, of course, can be self-destructiveness.'

With a shock Balsam realized what he had just said, and stopped abruptly. His eyes went to the dour faces of the Society. Now, instead of the almost blank expressions they had been wearing, they were staring at him with an intensity that almost frightened him. He was getting too close to the sort of thing the Society would brand as heresy, and Peter Balsam ranged around in his mind for a way out. He found it almost too easily.

'The Church,' he continued smoothly, 'has recognized this for centuries, long before the social sciences began to study the mechanisms of the human mind. From its very inception, the Church has realized the importance of releasing the pressures and problems that can impair the functioning of the mind. To provide a mechanism for the release of pressure, the Church instituted the ritual of the confessional.' He glanced quickly at the six priests and was relieved to see that they had resumed their impassivity. Then, as Balsam continued his lecture on the function of the confessional in the psychological health of those who used it properly, Monsignor Vernon smiled encouragingly at him, and led the five elderly priests out of Room 16. When they were gone, Balsam felt a sudden surge of relief. He continued his lecture, only now he felt free to concentrate on what he felt was the area of primary importance. He talked to them about Judy Nelson, and this time he was sure that his lecture would not be interrupted.

He told them that what had happened to Judy was simply a matter of too much pressure having been allowed to build up, with no release. When it had become too much for her to bear, she had behaved irrationally – she had become self-destructive. He tried to tell them that Judy was more to be pitied than blamed, and then, as he continued talking softly, he urged them to do their best to be kind to her when she returned to school, to try to understand and not to dwell on the details of what she had done.

He glanced at the clock, and saw that only ten minutes of the hour remained. He turned to the sound system, and quickly changed the record. The soft chanting was replaced by the discordant sounds of acid rock. Gradually, he began turning the volume up, until the room was filled with the vibrant sounds of the music. Soon a stirring was noticeable in the room, as the class began to come out of their almost stuporous state and become aware of their surroundings.

All of them, that is, except one.

Marilyn Crane, a strange look on her face, her eyes wide open and her mouth hanging slack, had risen to her knees. Her hands were clasped before her, and as the class stared, she began to pray.

Karen Morton noticed the blood on her hands while she was opening her locker. It was just a slight stickiness at first, and she would have ignored it except that when she removed her fingers from the lock, the brilliant redness of fresh blood remained. That was when she looked at the palms of her hands.

The odd part was that it didn't hurt, and she didn't know how she had done it. There, in the centre of each palm, the skin was broken, and the flesh had a strange pulpy look as if she had been gouging at it. She glanced around to see if anybody had noticed her, but no one was near. She pulled a Kleenex out of her purse, and hastily wiped the stains off her locker. Then she hurried toward the stairs, wanting to get downstairs to the restroom before anybody saw that she was bleeding and asked for an explanation.

Safe inside the restroom, Karen examined the wounds closely. She felt something hard in one of them, and washed her hands carefully. When the blood was gone, she held up the injured hand and found something stuck in the wound. She worked it carefully loose, and rinsed it off. It was the broken point of a pencil. She washed both hands once more, dried them, and searched her purse. There, at the bottom, was a pencil, covered with blood, its point broken off. Sometime during the hour, she realized, she had fished the pencil out of her purse, and begun gouging herself with it. But she had no memory of any of it; none whatsoever.

She burrowed further into her purse and found a couple of battered Band-Aids she had been carrying around with her for months. She stripped the wrappers off and began applying them to her injured hands. It was while she was applying the Band-Aids that the pain began. It was very slight, at first, but quickly searing sensations began to shoot up her arms. By the time she had finished with the makeshift bandaging, Karen had made up her mind. She was going home for the rest of the day. She told no one where she was going, or why. She simply left the restroom, walked up the stairs, and out of the building. For the rest of the afternoon she worried about what had happened to her. As the afternoon wore on, Karen Morton became increasingly frightened.

'Marilyn?' Peter Balsam asked when he saw that there was no one left in Room 16 but himself and the girl. She gave no sign that she had heard. 'Marilyn?'

Slowly her head swung around, and she stared at him in silence for a long time. Then her lips began to move, but no words formed.

'I saw her,' she whispered finally, with a great deal of effort. 'I saw her.'

'Saw her?' Balsam repeated, baffled. 'Saw who?'

And suddenly Marilyn was smiling, her face taking on a look of radiance that almost transformed her homeliness into beauty.

'The Virgin,' she whispered. 'I saw the Blessed Virgin. She came to me!'

'It's all right,' Balsam said soothingly. He tried to keep his voice steady, but he felt his stomach lurch. Something had gone wrong; Marilyn had not come out of the semi-trance along with the rest of the class, and there was no one to turn to for help. Telling himself to stay calm, he decided to try to talk her back into reality.

'What did you see?' he asked quietly.

'She was beautiful,' Marilyn said dreamily. 'Only she wasn't smiling at me. It was as if she was in pain. And then, while I was watching her, she showed me her hands. They were bleeding. It – it was as if she had been – as if she had been—' She trailed off, unable to say the word.

'Crucified?' Peter Balsam asked softly. Marilyn nodded mutely.

'What does it mean?' she asked him, and for the first time Balsam was sure she was aware of his presence. 'She was trying to tell me something, I know she was, but I couldn't figure out what it was. What was she trying to tell me?'

Balsam took Marilyn's hand and held it gently. 'It's all right,' he said soothingly. 'It's all over now. You fell asleep and dreamed. That's all.'

'No,' Marilyn objected, pulling her hand out of his. 'I know I wasn't asleep. I heard everything you were saying. You were talking about safety valves, and releases, and what happens when the safety valves don't work. And that's when she came to me. But I still heard you. You went on talking, and the priests of the Sanhedrin were here, listening to you, and watching the Sorrowful Mother, and then they went away. And then you talked about Judy Nelson, and the Virgin went away too. I know I wasn't asleep. Mr. Balsam. I *know* it.' Marilyn stood up and began putting the room in order, and Balsam realized that whatever had happened, it was over now. But what had happened? Marilyn, at least, had been aware of the six priests' presence. He decided to probe a little further.

'You saw the priests?' he asked her. Marilyn nodded emphatically.

'The priests of the Sanhedrin. The Jews who condemned our Lord. They were here, six of them, and they were watching the Sorrowful Mother. But she wasn't paying any attention to them. She wanted to talk to me. But I don't know why.'

Balsam wondered if he should tell Marilyn that the priests she had seen were very real. No, it would probably only upset the girl more. Instead, he decided to try to convince her that it was nothing but a dream.

'There was no one here, Marilyn,' he assured her. 'What happened was simply a mixture of a dream and reality. It isn't uncommon. With part of your mind you're aware of what's going on around you, but part of your mind is drifting. And things start to get mixed up. The real world gets mixed into your dream, and your dream seems all the more real.'

'But it wasn't a dream,' Marilyn insisted. 'I know it wasn't a dream. I saw the Blessed Virgin, and her hands were bleeding!' Then, seeing the disbelief in Peter Balsam's face, she ran from the room, as if leaving his scepticism would confirm the reality of what she had seen.

Alone in Room 16, a deeply disturbed Peter Balsam sat thinking. A few minutes later he reluctantly concluded that he must discuss the incident with Monsignor Vernon.

Balsam wasn't surprised when he found the Society of St. Peter Martyr gathered in Monsignor Vernon's office. It was as if they had expected him, and when he entered the office they rose as one to greet him. As usual, the Monsignor acted the spokesman.

'Well, Peter,' he said, smiling almost warmly. 'We are pleased with the way you handled your class today.'

Balsam smiled wryly. It was odd indeed that he was finally receiving praise for the one class that had gone totally wrong.

'I'm afraid I handled it very badly,' he said. Monsignor Vernon looked at him questioningly, and Balsam related as well as he could what had happened to Marilyn Crane. The priests listened in silence. When Balsam finished they looked to Monsignor Vernon. The priest frowned as he thought over the implications of the odd incident.

'It would appear that Marilyn thinks she's had a religious experience,' he said carefully.

Balsam nodded. 'I tried to explain to her that it was much more likely that she simply fell asleep, but she wouldn't listen. And the more I think about it, the more worried I get.'

'Worried?'

'I've been thinking about Marilyn and her entire personality structure,' Balsam began. But before he could finish his thoughts, the Monsignor interrupted him.

'Marilyn's always been one of our best students, and one of our most religious ones, too.'

'I'm sure she has,' Balsam said dryly. 'But I wonder how much of it is real.'

'Real?' Vernon repeated. 'I'm not sure what you mean.'

'Marilyn doesn't seem to be a very well-balanced child. She had practically no friends, and the other kids shun her. It's almost as if they take a malicious pleasure in making her feel bad.' He told them what had happened at the party the previous Saturday night. They listened, again in silence. 'If you want my opinion,' Balsam finished, 'Marilyn uses her studies and her religion as an escape. Since she isn't particularly well accepted by her peers, she chooses to get her acceptance from her teachers and the Church.'

'Is that so bad?' Father Bryant asked. 'There are worse ways to compensate.'

Balsam shrugged. 'There are all kinds of ways to compensate, and I'm certainly not about to suggest that Marilyn has picked unhealthy ones. But any compensation, carried to an extreme, is unhealthy.'

'I see,' Monsignor Vernon said slowly. 'You believe Marilyn's faith is questionable. You believe that what she thinks she saw this afternoon stemmed from – what? – hysteria?'

'I think it's possible,' Balsam said, glad that the priest seemed to understand it so well. But then the Monsignor's expression changed, and the cold light that Balsam had come to recognize shone in his eyes – the cold light of his religious fanaticism.

'I disagree,' he said flatly. 'I've seen this sort of thing before. She's clever, you know, A very bright child. This is nothing more than an attempt to manipulate us. All of us. You, me, her friends, the sisters, everyone. Mark my words, an investigation of this matter will prove me right. You may call it hysteria if you wish. To me it is nothing more than a very clever kind of manipulation. It is out of wariness born of experience that the Church has set up machinery to investigate just such phenomena as Marilyn Crane claims to have experienced.' And then, as quickly as the light of fanaticism had come into the Monsignor's eyes, it was gone. Suddenly he was smiling genially at a horrified Peter Balsam.

'It really isn't anything to worry about,' he said now, the hardness in his voice gone. 'Things like this happen all the time. I imagine that Marilyn will forget all about it by the end of the day. And if she doesn't, I'll have a talk with her.' Then he paused for a moment, as if a thought had occurred to him. 'And we mustn't forget,' he said softly, 'there's always the chance that the Blessed Virgin did visit Marilyn.'

FOURTEEN

Peter Balsam heard his front door open and called from the kitchen. 'I'm in here, throwing together something that I hope won't poison us. Come in and fix us some drinks, will you?'

'I'm already here,' Margo Henderson replied from the doorway. She surveyed the suit he was still wearing with distaste. 'One of these days we're going to Seattle again, just to get you a new suit. Why don't you change? Just looking at you makes me feel uncomfortable.'

'Can't,' Peter said, grinning at her. Now that she was there, he was beginning to feel a little better. But not much; the grin faded. 'I have to go to a meeting tonight, and it isn't the kind of meeting where you show up in jeans and a tee-shirt.'

'As if you owned such things in the first place,' Margo commented as she pried a tray of ice loose from the freezer. 'What's the big meeting?'

'You won't approve,' Peter said. He wrestled with a can opener, then helplessly handed the mangled soup can, together with the opener, to Margo. 'It's the Society of St. Peter Martyr.'

Margo glanced at him briefly as she took the can and completed the job Peter had botched. 'I thought you were all through with them,' she said levelly.

'I didn't say that,' Peter hedged.

'No?' Margo's eyebrows, arched. 'Strange. That's the distinct impression I got last night.'

Peter looked at her sharply. 'Last night? I didn't talk to you last night.'

'Of course you did,' Margo said. 'All right, so it was early this morning, if you want to get technical. But I call anything before dawn "last night".' Then, seeing the look on Peter's face, she frowned. 'You really don't remember, do you?'

'There's nothing to remember,' Peter declared. 'I came home from the meeting, went to bed around eleven, and slept all night. I thought about calling you, but decided not to; it was too late.'

Margo finished with the can, then mixed drinks for both of them before she spoke again. As she handed Peter his scotch-and-water, she looked at him carefully, trying to decide if he was playing some kind of a joke on her. She decided he wasn't.

'Well then,' she said, biting her lower lip speculatively, 'you've taken up some rather odd habits. Do you always make phone calls in your sleep? Because you *did* call me last night.'

Peter searched his memory, but could find no recollection of any such thing the previous night. He felt a slight knot of fear in his stomach, but fought it down. 'What did I say?' he asked, trying to keep his voice light. 'Was I interesting?'

'No,' Margo said shortly, 'you weren't. All you said was that you'd gone to the meeting of that silly society of Monsignor's and that you weren't going back.'

'Did I call it "that silly society," or are you editorializing?'

The smile crept back to Margo's face. 'All right, so I didn't quote you exactly. If you want to know, I don't recall your exact words. I mean, it was late, and I was asleep and, well, you know how groggy people can get in the middle of the night. Anyway, I got the definite impression that you were not impressed with Monsignor and his funny friends.'

'Funny friends?' Peter repeated. 'I don't suppose those were my exact words either, were they?'

'No,' Margo said again, beginning to feel exasperated, 'they weren't. But if you ask me, any friends of Monsignor's have to be funny.'

'I wish they were,' Peter replied in a tone Margo found suddenly disturbing. 'But I'm not sure there's anything funny about them at all.' Briefly, he told her about the meeting of the Society the previous night, and the events of the afternoon. Margo listened to him carefully, and when he was finished she shook her head.

'But why do you want to go back again tonight?' she asked. 'It seems to me you'd want to stay out of the whole thing.'

'I don't know,' Peter mused, as if trying to explain his feelings to himself as well as to her. 'I can't figure out what they're up to. But I know they're up to something. Last night, just before I left their meeting, Monsignor Vernon told me I had been invited for a reason - to have my faith reinforced. And he was right. When I woke up this morning, I felt much better than I did last night.'

'Better about what?' Margo asked.

Peter shrugged. 'The Church. Until this morning I was almost ready to throw the towel in on the whole thing. But this morning I felt different. I felt I'd missed something, that there was something, somewhere, that would make everything clear to me. And I think that something may just be in the Society. Anyway, I decided I have to give it a chance.' He smiled at Margo, hoping to erase the look of concern that had come over her face. 'I don't see what harm it can do, and it might answer a lot of my questions.'

Margo looked doubtful. When she spoke, skepticism edged her voice. 'A miraculous transformation, Peter? Something happened to you last night, because you've certainly changed your tune.'

'A man can change his mind,' Peter said, trying to keep his voice light.

'Or have it changed for him,' Margo pointed out. Silently, she decided to be waiting for Peter when he returned home that night.

He was let into the study, as the previous night, by one of the old priests – Father Martinelli, if he remembered correctly – and once again found Monsignor Vernon deep in prayer. But the room looked different to Peter Balsam, and he soon realized why. Tonight no lights were on. The curtains had been drawn tightly shut. The only illumination was provided by a fire glowing in the fireplace and tall red candles placed around the room. Seven chairs had been carefully arranged in a semicircle around the fireplace – the two large comfortable chairs and five others. Monsignor Vernon was kneeling at one of the chairs, using it as a makeshift prie-dieu. The other chair, opposite the one Monsignor Vernon knelt at, was waiting for Peter Balsam. He took the chair silently, steeling himself for another inquisition.

But tonight it was different. There was no discussion before the ritual got under way. Instead, as soon as Monsignor Vernon finished the silent prayers, the chanting began. The Monsignor led it, and with each phrase one of the other old priests joined in, the sound swelling until all the ancient clerics were chanting out the cadences.

At first Peter Balsam wondered if he was expected to join the chanting, but as he listened he realized that he couldn't participate: the phrases were unfamiliar. As he tried to follow the words, he discovered that it was not the thinness of the voices that made the chanting unintelligible; it was the language, a tongue sufficiently like Latin to sound familiar, but different enough – twisted enough, Peter thought with a shiver – to remain beyond his grasp.

As the cadences mounted, surrounding him, invading him, Peter Balsam felt his mind begin to wander. The fire flickering on the hearth almost seemed to recede into the distance, and the dancing shadows of the shimmering candles cast strange images on the walls. He began to feel as if he was being transported back in time to another age, an age where faith alone could transport a man into raptures.

Images began flitting through his head. His eyes, almost closed, drifted from one face to another, but instead of the five elderly priests and the youthful Monsignor, Peter Balsam saw the faces of ancient saints come suddenly to life. They were smiling on him and beckoning to him. A feeling of camaraderie came over him, and Peter Balsam happily gave himself over to the companionship of the small group.

Some time later, he became vaguely aware that the chanting had stopped, and that the Society was now involved in responsive prayers. He was dimly aware of Monsignor Vernon's voice, resonating softly through the room, and the thin, reedy voices of the five elderly priests as they made the responses. He tried to concentrate on the words, but, like the chanting, they were in a not-quite-Latin that he was unable to translate. Yet, like the chanting, the prayers held an insistent rhythm, a rhythm, that grew, bearing a spiritual message that was very clear: Peter Balsam, the steady intonations seemed to whisper, you are in the presence of God. Be humbled, Peter. And be comforted.

And he was. As the rhythms overcame him once more, Peter Balsam uttered a silent prayer of thanksgiving to be part of this wondrous ceremony.

Time almost stopped for him then, and his thoughts ceased to flow as he gave himself up to the religious experience that was unfolding around him. As he sank deeper and deeper into a state of trance, his senses sharpened. He felt the searing heat from each individual candle; the tongues of fire on the hearth seemed to be licking at his feet. He heard the voice of the Devil calling out to him in his head, and tried to close out the beckoning whispers. He began to feel the heat of hell glowing around him, and as his discomfort grew he became frightened. And then, as he felt himself being drawn downward, he felt the hands of angels upon him. He was suddenly cooler, and his mind's eye saw the fires receding into the distance. As the angelic hands caressed him, he felt a calm come over him, and he began silently repeating the Acts of Faith and Contrition. Slowly, his ecstasy grew.

The fire still burned in the fireplace, as high as it had when the evening had begun. The candles were shorter, but how much shorter he couldn't discern. Around him, the six priests were gathered, sitting calmly, almost expectantly, in their chairs, watching him. Peter Balsam had no idea what time it was, nor how long he had been closeted in the study with the six priests. He discovered, to his own fascination, that he was not thinking about the ceremony at all; instead, he was almost entirely possessed by a feeling of fulfilment, as if he had, somehow, received answers to questions that he could not now even formulate. And he was tired, with the weariness of a man who had just run several miles. Somewhere in the back of his mind a memory stirred, then disappeared.

He wondered if he was expected to speak. He looked from one face to another, and for the first time tonight saw each of the priests distinctly. In the warm glow of the candlelight the gnarled old faces took on a kind of beauty, and Peter Balsam realized that there was a gentleness in these men that he had not seen before. They were smiling at him, and he returned their smiles.

'Welcome,' Father Martinelli said softly.

'Welcome?' Peter repeated, just as softly. Suddenly, it was a word of many and marvellous meanings.

'We are glad to have you among us,' Father Prine murmured.

Monsignor Vernon nodded agreement. 'Once again we are seven. Now we can continue our work.'

Balsam frowned slightly. 'Work?' he asked. 'What work?'

Monsignor Vernon shook his head. 'No questions,' he said quietly. 'Not now.'

The meeting of the Society of St. Peter Martyr was over. Peter Balsam had become a part of the Society.

He walked back to his apartment slowly, savouring the night air, and the first feelings of true peace that he had felt in a long time, certainly since he had come to Neilsville. He breathed deeply of the warm, dry air, and looked to the sky in search of the stars he felt should have been there. The sky was black, except for a pale, almost ghostly glow where the full moon far above the clouds shone weakly through the mists. By the time Peter Balsam reached his home, the rain had begun to fall.

Light glared in the living room, hurting his eyes. Squinting, he stepped inside, then drew back. Margo was lying on the couch, sound asleep, an open book sprawled across her breast. While he was wondering whether to wake her, her eyes popped open, and she jumped off the couch.

'What are you—' she began. Then she glanced wildly around and sank back down on the sofa.

'What am I doing here?' Peter asked, grinning at her. 'I live here, remember?'

She looked up at him sheepishly. 'I'm sorry,' she said. 'I was going to be here waiting for you, all bright-eyed and bushy-tailed, and dying to hear all about what happened at that meeting. So what do I do? I fall asleep. What time is it?'

Peter suddenly realized he didn't have the vaguest idea what time it was. When he looked at his watch, he wasn't sure he believed it.

'That can't be right,' he muttered, holding the watch up to his ear.

Margo looked at him quizzically. 'What can't?' she said. 'What time is it?'

Peter sank down on the couch beside her. 'My watch says three o'clock,' he breathed. 'But it can't be. I was only gone an hour or so.'

Margo looked at him speculatively. 'You've been gone seven hours, Peter,' she said calmly. 'What happened?'

'I don't know,' Peter said blankly. He tried to explain to Margo what had transpired at the rectory that evening, but in the telling none of it made sense. It all sounded like a dream, like disconnected fragments out of some religious fantasy. Margo listened to the story quietly.

'Why don't you go get out of those clothes?' she said when he'd finished. 'They look like they've been slept in. I'll put on some coffee and we'll try again.' She grinned at him mischievously. 'So far, it all sounds exactly like what I thought it would be. A bunch of silliness.' But inside, she was more concerned than she had shown.

As she put the kettle on, Margo wondered if she was making a mistake. Perhaps Peter wasn't what he seemed to be. Perhaps he wasn't the nice, simple rather straightforward person she had become so fond of. She spooned instant coffee into two mugs and tried to clear the last remnants of sleep from her mind while the water came to a boil.

A few minutes later, as she started into the living room with the two steaming mugs, Peter appeared in the doorway his face pale.

'Margo—' he began.

She set the cups down quickly, and hurried to him. 'Peter, what is it?'

'I don't know,' Peter gasped. 'When I took off my shirt, I—' He broke off again and unconsciously touched the belt of his robe.

'What *is* it?' Margo said, more urgently. He clutched his robe tighter around his torso, and stared at her, wild-eyed. Peter was frightened. Very frightened. She moved closer to him.

'Let me see, Peter,' she said gently. His hands fell to his sides, and he let her untie the cord around his waist. Then she opened the robe, and let it fall to the floor.

On Peter's back, from his shoulders to his waist, were angry red welts. Though the skin was not broken, the marks had swollen and stood out in painful relief from the pale whiteness of his back.

'My God,' Margo breathed. 'What happened?'

Peter shook his head mutely, 'I don't know,' he said. And then the full horror of it struck him. He began shaking. And with the shaking came the tears.

'I don't know, Margo,' he sobbed. 'And that's the worst of it. I don't know where they came from!'

'They did something to you,' Margo kept insisting. 'While you were in that trance, or whatever it was, they did something to you.'

Balsam shook his head in despair: 'They couldn't have,' he repeated yet again. 'I would have remembered it. I wasn't unconscious. I was in some kind of odd state, I know, but I was conscious of my surroundings.'

'But you thought you were gone only an hour or two, and it was seven hours. *Seven hours*, Peter! If you really remember everything that happened, how could you have lost five or six hours?'

'I don't know,' Peter said helplessly. 'I suppose something happens to your time sense when you go into a trance. But I know I wasn't unconscious. I know it.'

As the dawn came, they gave it up. They were both too tired to retrace the same ground. Peter went to the window, and watched the sun rise slowly over Neilsville. The clouds had gone, but there was a heaviness in the air that said they would be back soon. Peter turned back to Margo.

'You'd better go,' he said. 'It's awfully late.'

She nodded dully, 'I know.' Her voice was lifeless. She looked at his tired eyes and she wanted to put her arms around him, to feel his arms around her. 'Oh, Peter,' she said, the words choking her a little. 'What are we going to do?'

He tried to smile at her, but the attempt failed. 'I don't know,' he said Then a touch of irony crept into his voice. 'I don't seem to know much of anything, do I?'

Now she did go to him and put her arms around him. 'Yes, you do,' she said softly. 'There's an explanation for all this. And we'll find it. Really we will.'

Peter wanted to believe her; he told himself that he did. But inside, he wasn't sure. Inside, he was terribly frightened, and terribly alone.

He sent Margo on her way, then sat for an hour trying to fight off the sleep he was suddenly afraid of. At seven o'clock he called the school and told them that he had become ill in the night, and would not be in today. Then he went to bed and spent the day sleeping – and dreaming. In the dreams, there were many explanations of the strange marks on his back. But when he woke up every now and then, none of them made sense. Or maybe they did.

FIFTEEN

'You look like hell.'

Dr. Shields stared at Margo and motioned her into a chair.

'I feel like hell,' she admitted, 'I was up all night.'

The psychiatrist put the report he had been reading into the top drawer of the desk, and leaned back in his chair.

'Peter Balsam?' he asked.

Margo nodded mutely, then, reluctantly, began telling him about the discussion with Peter that had kept her up all night. At first the psychiatrist listened in silence. Then, as she continued her story, he began interrupting her with questions. When she was finished, he sat with his hands folded in front of him, lost in thought.

'Do you want some advice, or did you just want to talk it out?' he asked finally.

Margo shrugged helplessly. 'I don't really know. If you have any advice, I suppose I might as well hear it.'

The doctor nodded noncommittally, then looked sharply at Margo. 'Just how much does Peter Balsam mean to you?'

'I don't know,' Margo said dully. 'A lot, I thought. But after last night, I'm not so sure. The whole thing sounds so weird, I'm not sure I want to be involved at all.

'Well, it's not that bad,' Dr. Shields said gently. 'After all, you aren't involved with his problems. Yet.'

'Yet?' she repeated.

'Yet. I mean, so far, everything that's happened to Balsam has only happened to him. Any time you get too uncomfortable with it, all you have to do is stop seeing him.'

'But I'm not sure I want to do that. I want to know what's happening, before I make the decision. Does that make any sense?'

Dr. Shields nodded. 'So how can I help? What's bothering you most?'

She looked at him levelly. 'The marks on his back. The welts. Dr. Shields, you have no idea what they look like. They're awful!'

He leaned forward now, and stared at her intently. 'Tell me about them.'

She closed her eyes, and as an image of the strange markings on Peter's back came to her, she did her best to describe them. As she talked, a chill passed through her. When she was done, she looked at the doctor.

'Well?'

'You're sure the skin wasn't broken? Not even abraded?'

'I'm positive. And they didn't hurt him, either.'

'That figures. It sounds to me like their origin is hysterical.'

'Hysterical?'

'It's not an uncommon phenomenon. Although in this case it seems to me to be a rather bizarre manifestation. Essentially, it's the same thing as psychosomatic illnesses. The wish becomes the reality.'

'It doesn't make sense,' Margo said. 'Are you telling me Peter has a subconscious desire to be beaten?'

The psychiatrist shrugged eloquently, but when he saw the expression his gesture brought to Margo's face, he tried to reassure her.

'It doesn't necessarily indicate that at all,' he said. 'The subconscious works in all kinds of strange ways. And don't forget the circumstances of the manifestation. If what you say is true – and I don't have any reason to doubt it – it sounds to me like Balsam's got himself mixed up with a pretty crazy bunch of priests. Do you think they practice flagellation?'

'As far as I know, priests don't do much of that anymore,' Margo said, trying not to sound as defensive as she felt. 'Besides, even when they did do it, it was ritual. They never used the kind of force that would leave marks like Peter has.'

Dr. Shields's brows arched in scepticism. 'Under normal circumstances, of course, they don't. But what about other circumstances? From what you've said, that society sounds like an odd group. And your Peter Balsam could fit in very well with them. Isn't it true that he once studied for the priesthood?'

'That was years ago,' Margo said vehemently. 'And he gave it up.'

'Right,' Dr. Shields pounced. 'Gave it up to go into psychology. And you know what people say about us. No one's as crazy as a psychologist.'

'Including you?' Margo asked.

'Did I ever say I was sane?' Dr. Shields replied, the first traces of a grin playing around the corners of his mouth. 'I'll tell you what,' he said. 'Let's forget about it all for the time being. Well, not really forget about it, but I don't really think any of us, including your friend Balsam, knows, enough about what's going on to make any reasonable judgments. So let's just keep our eyes open, and see what happens next. And tell Balsam that if he'd like to talk to me. I'm willing.' Then he had an idea. 'You know,' he mused, 'it would sure help if we knew what really went on in those meetings of the – what do they call it?'

'The Society of St. Peter Martyr,' Margo said dully.

'Lovely name,' the psychiatrist said sarcastically. He gave her a reassuring smile. 'Go home and get some sleep. And Margo,' he added as she opened the door to the outer office. She turned. 'Be careful,' he said seriously. 'You don't really know very much about Balsam, do you? He might be very different from what you think he is. Granted, he seems like a nice guy. But he could be crazy, couldn't he?' Margo stared at him wordlessly, then closed the door behind her. Dr. Shields sank back into the chair behind his desk, and stared thoughtfully at the closed door. He liked Margo, and didn't want to see her hurt. He hoped he was wrong. But inside, he didn't feel he was. And if Peter Balsam was, indeed, as sick as Dr. Shields suspected, it could only mean trouble.

Then he remembered Judy Nelson, still a patient in the hospital. And who had come to the hospital right after she had been admitted? Peter Balsam.

For the rest of the afternoon, Dr. Shields tried to convince himself that Balsam's visit had been nothing more than the concern of a teacher for one of his students, that there was no connection between Peter Balsam and Judy Nelson's attempt on her own life. But when he went home that afternoon, he was still unconvinced. There *was* a connection. He was sure of it.

Geraldine Crane heard the front door slam, but went right on with her ironing. A moment later she glanced up to see her daughter come into the kitchen.

'You're early,' she commented. Marilyn set her books down on the table and opened the refrigerator. 'Don't spoil your appetite,' she heard her mother say.

She poked around the refrigerator, then decided that a carrot would do for a snack. She moved to the sink and began peeling the carrot into the disposal.

'All the vitamins are in the peelings,' Geraldine said. 'If you peel it, there isn't any use in eating it.'

Marilyn silently continued peeling the carrot, and wished her mother would leave her alone. Her wish was not granted.

'I was cleaning your room today,' Geraldine said tonelessly. Marilyn wondered if she was going to be criticized for not keeping it clean enough, or if it would be something else. It turned out to be something else.

'I found your history test,' Geraldine said in an accusing voice. 'You might have shown it to me.'

'I didn't want to,' Marilyn said.

'I can see why.' Her mother's voice stabbed at Marilyn. 'Since when do you get B-minuses?'

Marilyn threw the carrot into the sink. Suddenly she didn't want it.

'It's only one test, and not an important one,' she said defensively.

'One test?' Geraldine asked. 'It may be only one test to you, but to me it says you aren't trying hard enough.' She put down the iron, and turned to face her daughter. 'I don't know what to do with you, Marilyn. It seems like no matter what I want for you, it never works out.'

Marilyn was on the verge of tears. 'It's only one test, Mother,' she pleaded. 'And it isn't that bad a grade. Greta got worse grades than that all the time.'

Geraldine nodded. 'Your sister didn't go to college,' she said. 'Greta got married.'

'Well, maybe I will too,' Marilyn blurted, regretting the words as soon as they'd been said. She had just opened a whole new can of worms, and she knew it.

'You have to date before you get married,' Geraldine pointed out acidly. 'And so far I don't see you doing much in that department, either.'

'All right,' Marilyn exclaimed. 'I'm sorry, Mother! I'm sorry I'm not like Greta, I'm sorry I'm not popular, I'm sorry I'm a disappointment to you. I'm sorry, I'm sorry, I'm sorry.'

Geraldine Crane sank down into one of the chairs by the kitchen table, and pulled Marilyn down into another. Suddenly she wished she hadn't spoken so sharply to her daughter, and now she tried to make up for it.

'There's nothing for you to be sorry about,' she said gently. 'I'm really very proud of you. I just want you to be happy.' She paused a minute. 'And you spend too much time in church,' she went on. 'You're too young to be spending all your time in church. Time enough for that when you're older.'

'But I like it in church,' Marilyn said through the lump that was suddenly blocking her throat. She didn't want to cry; she hoped she wasn't going to. 'Maybe I should go into a convent.'

'Don't be silly,' her mother said. 'That's no kind of life for you. All you need to do is make some friends, and try to get out of yourself a bit. No wonder you're not happy. If I spent as much time by myself as you do, I'd be miserable, too.'

Marilyn could no longer hold the sobs back, but neither could she let herself go in front of her mother. She felt too alone. Before her mother could stop her, she had fled from the kitchen. Geraldine Crane sat silently at the kitchen table and listened to her daughter pound up the stairs. Then, though there was no one to see it, she shrugged helplessly and went back to her ironing. Bringing up Greta was so easy, she thought. Why is it so difficult with Marilyn?

She picked up another of her husband's shirts, and began pressing the sleeves, her mind on her daughter. The iron went back and forth over the same spot. It wasn't until she saw the brown of the scorch mark that Geraldine realized she was drifting, and put her mind resolutely back on the task at hand. It didn't occur to her that the same kind of preoccupation that had just caused her to ruin the shirt might also have caused her daughter to get a B-minus on the history test.

She heard Marilyn coming down the stairs a few minutes later, and wondered if she ought to call her into the kitchen and try to talk to her. But before she could make up her mind, Marilyn appeared at the door.

'I'm going to the hospital,' Marilyn said in a voice that left no room for argument.

'The hospital?' Geraldine asked. 'Whatever for?'

'I'm going to visit Judy Nelson,' Marilyn said in a voice that was almost defiant. 'If you want me to have friends, I guess visiting Judy is a good enough way to start.'

'But I thought you didn't like Judy,' her mother said curiously. 'I thought you didn't like that whole group.'

'Judy wasn't at the party,' Marilyn said sullenly. 'Then, unexpectedly, she came over to her mother, and kissed her on the cheek. 'I'm sorry,' she said. 'I know I'm not what you always wanted for a daughter, but I'll try to do better. I shouldn't let myself get so upset.'

Before Geraldine could make any response at all, Marilyn was gone, Geraldine looked out the window, and saw her daughter get on her bike and pedal off. She frowned a little, with a vague feeling that something important had just happened and she had missed it. Then she put it out of her mind and went back to her ironing.

Marilyn saw them before they saw her. She stood inside the door and looked out on the half-dead garden behind the hospital. Penny Anderson and Judy Nelson were chatting together while Karen Morton flirted with one of the orderlies. Marilyn's first impulse was to leave, and either forget about the whole thing or come back another time. She fought the impulse down and stood inside the building, watching the group of girls and the orderly.

Then, after a couple of moments, Judy and Penny joined Karen. Marilyn could see their lips moving but couldn't hear their voices. She wondered what they were talking about.

'Don't look now,' Penny was saying, 'but I could swear that Marilyn Crane is standing just inside that door.' The other girls started to turn, but Penny spoke again. 'I said don't look now. What do you suppose she's doing here?'

'If she's watching us, she probably came to visit me,' Judy said acidly.

'After Saturday night?' Penny asked. 'I wouldn't think she'd want to see any of us, after what we did to her.' She began giggling to herself, remembering the expression on Marilyn's face as she had realized why they had invited her to the party.

'She doesn't know I had anything to do with it,' Judy said. 'I was right here in the hospital, remember?'

'I wonder what she wants?' Karen said. Then, feeling the pressure of the orderly's leg against her own, she suddenly stood up. Things were going too far.

'Let's get out of here,' Karen said nervously. 'Marilyn isn't going to come over as long as we're here, and I don't want to talk to her anyway. Her pimples might rub off.' She was pleased when the other girls laughed.

'Okay,' Judy grinned. 'You two get out of here, and I'll call you as soon as she leaves.'

'That should be good for a laugh,' Penny said. Then she and Karen wandered off, trying not to look at the door where Marilyn still hovered.

Marilyn watched them go, and reached out tentatively to

push the door open. Then something told her to forget it, to leave the hospital without talking to Judy. Too late. Judy was waving at her.

'Hi,' Judy called. 'What brings you out here?' Her voice sounded friendly, and Marilyn felt encouraged. Maybe this hadn't been such a bad idea after all.

'I – I thought you might want some company,' she said hesitantly. She offered Judy the stack of fan magazines she had picked up in the drugstore on her way to the hospital. 'I brought these for you.'

Judy glanced idly at the covers. 'Thanks,' she said laconically. She stared at Marilyn, waiting for the other girl to speak.

'When are you going home?' Marilyn eventually asked.

'Who knows? As far as I'm concerned, I could go home today. But they won't let me out of here until I tell them why I did it – and I don't want to tell them.'

The orderly looked sharply at Judy, and seemed about to say something. Judy didn't give him time.

'Why don't you leave us alone?' she said to him. 'I mean, how can we talk with you sitting listening to every word?'

'I'm not supposed to leave you alone,' the orderly replied. 'You know that.'

'Oh, that's stupid,' Judy snapped. 'Can't you just go over there and sit by yourself? That way you can still see me, but at least I can talk to Marilyn.'

'Well ...' the orderly began, on the edge of agreeing to Judy's request. Judy pushed him a little harder.

'Then go on,' she urged. 'Just for a few minutes.' She took on an appealing little-girl look, and before the orderly could decide if it was sincere, he had taken the bait.

'Okay,' he said, standing up. 'But only for a few minutes. Then you have to go back to your room.'

Judy pouted a little, but the pout disappeared as soon as the young man's back was turned. She grinned conspiratorially at Marilyn. 'I have him wrapped around my little finger.' she whispered. But Marilyn wasn't listening. She was thinking about something.

'What was it like?' she asked.

'What was what like?'

'What you did,' Marilyn said. 'You know—' Her voice trailed off, and she was afraid she'd said the wrong thing. A dreamy expression had come over Judy's face.

'It was weird,' she said. 'You know what? I really don't know why I did it. I was mad at my mother, but certainly not that mad.'

'You didn't seem made when I saw you in the hall that day,' Marilyn mused. 'You seemed more – sad.'

Judy looked at her curiously. 'You? I don't remember seeing you.'

'Don't you remember?' Marilyn asked her. 'It must have been just before you went to the gym and – and did it.'

Judy shook her head slowly. 'I don't remember anything like that at all,' she said. 'All I remember about that day is talking to Mr. Balsam. Then it all gets kind of fuzzy. But I remember being in the locker room, and I remember cutting myself. It didn't hurt at all. I just cut myself, and the blood started coming out. And I felt so peaceful. It was – well, it was almost like I feel sitting in church sometimes, listening to Monsignor celebrate Mass. A strange feeling comes over me, and I feel like I'm not in my body anymore. That's how it felt when I cut myself. Like I was watching it happen to someone else. And then I suddenly realized what I'd done. I mean, I suddenly realized it was me it was happening to. And I got scared. That's when I called the police. And then Mr. Jenkins found me.' Judy paused, eyeing the other girl. 'The rest was horrible.'

'Horrible? What do you mean?' It seemed to Marilyn that the cutting would have been the hard part.

'They all wanted to know what happened. Why did I do it? How do I know why I did it? It just seemed like a good idea at the time. Now they're all afraid I'm going to try it again.'

'Are you?' Marilyn asked, her voice serious. Judy shook her head emphatically.

'Not a chance. I suppose if I'd really wanted to kill myself, then I might try again. But I don't think I wanted to die. I think I just wanted to see what it felt like. But it's all over now.' She grinned suddenly. 'I've got too much to do. Who has time to die?'

Then the orderly was back, and Judy was standing up.

'Nap time,' she said, with a hint of a sneer in her voice. 'They treat you like a baby around here.'

'If you act like a baby, you get treated like one,' the orderly pointed out. Judy stuck her tongue out at him, but he ignored it. The two of them started walking toward the building. Suddenly Judy turned back.

'Thanks for coming,' she said. Then, just before she disappeared into the hospital, she spoke again. 'Killing yourself is really kind of neat. You should try it sometime.' And then Judy Nelson began to laugh – a laugh that lingered in Marilyn's ears long after Judy disappeared into the shadows of the building.

Marilyn Crane sat alone for a long time, staring at nothing and trying to figure out the meaning of everything Judy had said. Then, she didn't know how much later, she finally left the bench and went back to her bike.

Before she mounted the bike and rode away from the hospital, Marilyn reached into the carryall. Her hand closed on a small object. She took it from the carryall and stared at it.

A small packet of razor blades.

Marilyn had no memory of having purchased them.

No memory of putting them in the carryall.

Yet there they were. She stared at them mutely, part of her mind wondering where they had come from, part of her mind accepting the fact of them. Carefully, she replaced them in her bag.

From a window on the second floor of the hospital, Judy Nelson watched Marilyn. There was a small smile on Judy's face as Marilyn pedalled away toward town. Judy watched until Marilyn disappeared, then got back into bed. She picked up the telephone, dialled, and waited while it rang.

'Penny? Marilyn just left.'

'What did she want?'

'Who knows? Who even cares? But I'll tell you one thing. Something's going to happen to that girl!'

SIXTEEN

The Bishop glanced once more at the calendar on his desk, and noted the neatly inked appointment for five o'clock. 'Golf,' it read, 'Joe Flynn.' He had been looking forward to it all week until an hour ago, when his secretary had come in and calmly pencilled in another appointment above the golf date: 'Peter Balsam.' His raised eyebrows had only produced a shrug and the explanation, 'Fellow says it's urgent.' So now he was going to be late for his golf date, and while he knew Joe Flynn would forgive him, he wasn't certain he would forgive this Peter Balsam for delaying him. Golf, after all, was important. The Bishop glared up at the clock on the wall, hoping the man would be late, even if only by a minute. During that minute he would have a legitimate excuse for slipping out of the door behind his desk. He was counting the last fifteen seconds when the buzzer on his intercom sounded.

Muttering to himself, he pressed the switch. 'Yes?' he barked as loudly and testily as he could, hoping to intimidate the unwanted visitor.

In the secretary's office, Father Duncan winked up at a nervous Peter Balsam and held a finger to his lips. Then he spoke into the intercom.

'Mr. Balsam is here to see you, Your Eminence. Shall I bring him in?'

'What're the chances of his going away if I say no?' the Bishop's voice growled from the box. Balsam felt himself turning red and wanted to flee. Father Duncan just grinned at him.

'None whatever,' the priest said severely. 'And I already called Joe Flynn and explained, so you can stop worrying about being late.'

'Oh, very well then, show him in. But I wish you'd explain things to me the way you do to Joe Flynn. After all, you're *my* secretary.'

Father Duncan stood up and beckoned Peter Balsam to follow him. 'He always plays golf on Wednesday, so don't be surprised if he's a bit grumpy. And try to keep the meeting short. The later he is, the grumpier he gets. But his bark is much worse than his bite.' Then, before Peter could reply, he pushed the door open and stood aside so that Peter could precede him into the Bishop's office.

Bishop O'Malley did not get up when Balsam entered his office, which surprised Balsam just a little. He heard the secretary make the introductions as he crossed the room to kneel in front of the Bishop. But he didn't make it.

'Must we?' the Bishop said, anticipating Peter. 'Why don't you just sit down so we can get this over with as fast as possible, all right?'

An abashed Peter Balsam sank into the visitor's chair on the near side of the desk, and the Bishop smiled to himself. Threw him off with that one, he thought; score one for me. While Balsam recovered from the assault, the Bishop tried to decide which demeanour would prove most effective in getting this young man out of his office. He settled on a stern-superior image, and frowned across his desk.

'Father Duncan tells me you arranged this meeting yourself,' he said severely, though the secretary had told him nothing of the sort. 'Ordinarily, you would need the intervention of Monsignor Vernon in order to get this far.' He watched Balsam squirm, and added another point to his side.

'I'm sorry, Your Eminence,' Balsam said. 'But I'm afraid I couldn't go through Monsignor—'

'Couldn't, or wouldn't?' the Bishop broke in. 'There's a difference, you know.'

'I do know,' Balsam said, more sharply than he meant to. 'I'm a psychologist.' The Bishop mentally erased the two points he had scored for himself, and chalked up one for Balsam. Then he decided to give up keeping score – it just wasn't going to be his day. He smiled at Balsam.

'Sorry,' he said. 'Father Duncan didn't tell me that.' Balsam took the statement as the sign of truce it was. He relaxed again.

'I couldn't go through Monsignor Vernon, sir, because I would have had to tell him what I wanted to talk to you about.'

Bishop O'Malley picked up a pencil from the desktop and leaned back in his chair. He tapped his front teeth with the pencil for a moment, surveying the man across from him. 'I gather you want to talk to me about Monsignor?' he inquired mildly.

Balsam nodded. 'I don't know who else to talk to, or I wouldn't have bothered you. And I'm not sure it's really Monsignor Vernon I want to talk about. It's his society.'

'His society?' the Bishop repeated. 'I'm not following you.' He glanced surreptitiously at the clock. Yes, he was going to be late.

'The Society of St. Peter Martyr,' Balsam said, wondering if he was going to have to explain the whole thing to the Bishop.

'Oh, that bunch,' the Bishop said nonchalantly. Suddenly he felt much better: this could be disposed of in a couple of minutes, and he could be on his way to the country club.

'Then you know about them?' Balsam asked eagerly.

'Well, they aren't any secret, are they? Seven old priests who get together every now and then to talk about "the good old days".' He looked at Balsam curiously. 'You really came all the way over here to talk about the Society of St. Peter Martyr? I think you wasted your time.' He stood up, ready to end the meeting. But Peter Balsam didn't move.

'I think there's more to it than that,' he said softly. The Bishop stared at him for a moment, then sank back into the chair behind the desk. He was going to be late after all.

'More to it? What makes you think so?'

'Have you ever been to one of their meetings?' Balsam countered.

When the Bishop shook his head, Balsam began to describe

the two meetings of the Society he had attended. The Bishop heard him out in silence, but throughout the entire recital the pencil drummed on the edge of the desk.

'Is that all?' he said when Balsam eventually fell silent.

'More or less,' Balsam said equivocally. He'd left out the last part of the story, unable to bring himself to tell the Bishop about the strange marks on his back.

'It sounds like more,' the Bishop commented dryly. 'It sounds like you don't really remember too much about the meetings, and you're reading a lot into the Society that simply isn't there. Frankly, it doesn't seem to me to be in the least remarkable that seven old priests with not much to do have decided to entertain themselves by forming a discussion group.'

'You keep saying seven,' Balsam put in. 'There are only six.'

The Bishop smiled easily. 'There used to be seven. Until Father George Carver died last year. Now it looks like they're trying to recruit you to round the number out again. Are you thinking of joining them?'

'According to them. I already have,' Peter said hesitantly. The Bishop noted the hesitation in his voice, and picked up on it.

'Is there something you haven't told me?'

Balsam shifted uncomfortably in his chair, wondering whether he should tell the Bishop about the marks on his back. He decided against it.

'I really came here more to ask some questions than to tell you about the Society. I'd hoped you knew more about it than I do.'

'I see. On the assumption that the Bishop is the source of all knowledge in the diocese. Well, I'm afraid that's a myth. If I tried to keep up with everything all my priests are doing, I'd never have time for the important things.'

Like golf? Balsam wanted to ask, but didn't.

'Like golf,' the Bishop grinned, reading his mind. 'As for the Society of St. Peter Martyr, I'm afraid I know very little about it. As far as I knew it was simply seven old priests—'

'Monsignor Vernon isn't exactly old,' Balsam broke in.

The Bishop peered at him over his glasses; this Balsam was showing a lot more spunk than he liked. On the other hand, he was finding it refreshing, in an odd way.

'Not in years, perhaps, but his thinking is a bit old-fashioned As for the rest of them, well, their years match their thinking, for the most part.'

'What do you mean?' Balsam asked. He thought he knew, but wanted the Bishop to spell it out for him.

'How can I put it?' the Bishop mused aloud. Then he put the pencil down and leaned forward in his chair.

'The Church is in a constant state of paradox,' he began. 'On the other hand we tell our flock, and each other, that we hold the keys to the absolute truth. But on the other hand we realize that there is no absolute truth. Truth changes along with the times. The trick to being comfortable within the Church is to balance tradition with change, and try to change tradition to keep up with the times. Unfortunately, all too many of us find it easier to cling to the traditions than move with the changes. All too many of us fail to see that keeping up with the times isn't destroying the Faith. And that, as I see it, is the basis of the Society of St. Peter Martyr. They're old-fashioned in their thinking, and they don't get much support from the Church, at least not in my diocese. They want to *Believe*. They need to lean on each other for support.

'They're terribly dogmatic, of course, and quite frankly I don't spend much time with them. I don't mean as the Society of St. Peter Martyr; I don't spend any time with the Society at all – I mean as individuals. I'm afraid I just can't be quite as – what's the word? religious? – as they'd like me to be. And, though I know I shouldn't say it, Monsignor Vernon's the worst of them.'

The Bishop smiled wryly, then went on. 'Young man, every time I talk to Vernon I thank my lucky stars I'm getting older. By the time that man gets to be my age, he's going to be absolutely impossible. In fact, I have to keep reminding myself that he's your age, not mine. He seems old already.'

'I know,' Balsam felt himself warming to the Bishop. 'I

went to school with him. He was just Pete Vernon then, and you wouldn't have recognized him.'

'Wouldn't I? Don't forget, I've been watching him in Neilsville for twelve years now. I remember the young man who came out here from Philadelphia. He's a lot different now. Neilsville, I suppose. Towns like that do things to people. Too small. Inbred. I suppose it's inevitable that the clergy gets caught up in it too. I've often wondered if I'd have stayed with the Church if they'd sent me to a place like Neilsville.' Then he brightened a bit. 'Who knows? Maybe if I'd wound up in Neilsville, I'd have started a Society of St. Peter Martyr myself. Just between us, being stuck in Neilsville is certainly my idea of martyrdom.'

'I know what you mean,' Balsam replied. Then he picked up on something else. 'Did Monsignor start the Society of St. Peter Martyr?'

'You mean you didn't know?'

Balsam shook his head. 'I know he's their leader, but I'd assumed the Society had been going on for years.'

'Not at all. Vernon started it about five years ago, at about the time he became Monsignor. I suppose it was his way of proving to himself that he'd "made it".'

'Seems a strange thing,' Balsam commented.

'Petty conceit, I'd call it,' the Bishop snapped.

'Conceit?'

Now the Bishop regarded him quizzically. 'You mean you haven't figured it out?'

'You've lost me again,' Balsam admitted.

'The names, man, the names, the Bishop cried. 'Monsignor Vernon named the Society after himself!'

Balsam stared at the Bishop blankly. 'Named it after himself?'

'You mean you didn't know?' The Bishop chuckled. 'St. Peter Martyr's name was Piero da Verona. Now if you were to translate that into English, what would you come up with?'

'Peter Vernon,' Balsam said slowly. 'Or something close enough to that so it wouldn't make any difference. Is that what you mean?'

The Bishop nodded. 'It makes you wonder, doesn't it?' Then: 'What an unpleasant person he must have been.'

'Who?'

'Piero da Verona. St. Peter Martyr.'

Balsam's brows arched in surprise. 'I beg your pardon?'

'You've read the story, haven't you? About how one of the so-called heretics was finally pushed too far by Verona's persecutions, and killed him one night?'

' "So-called" heretics?' Balsam wanted to smile. He didn't.

The Bishop looked at him sharply, wondering if the young man was pulling his leg. 'Oh, come on. I think we all have to admit that during the Inquisition the Dominicans were denouncing everyone who disagreed with them as heretics. But calling them heretics doesn't make them heretics, does it?'

'No,' Balsam agreed, 'it doesn't.' Then he changed the subject. 'What happened to the man who killed Verona?'

'Ah,' said Bishop O'Malley, standing once more. 'Now there's a wonderful case of the mysterious ways of the Lord. The murderer is a saint too!'

Balsam's eyes widened in astonishment. 'Once more?'

'Possibly.' Bishop O'Malley laughed. 'I don't know what the truth of the matter is, and I don't suppose anybody else does either, but the story is that the man who killed Verona – his name escapes me if I ever knew it – repented, joined an order himself, and was eventually canonized. Not as fast as Verona, of course, who I think holds the record for quick canonization, but he eventually made it.'

'As Saint who?'

'I haven't the slightest idea. There's so many saints I can't keep up with them.' He glanced at the clock and, was surprised to see how late it was. 'If you'll excuse me,' he said to Balsam, 'I'm going to be very late for my game.'

Balsam leaped to his feet. 'I'm sorry for having taken so much of your time,' he apologized. The Bishop clapped him on the back, deciding he quite liked this young man.

'None of that,' he said. 'Any time. But next time, please go through proper channels. If you have to, lie to Vernon about it. Better that than having him find out you circumvented him entirely. Let him get wind of that, and you'll really find out what the Inquisition was like.' Then a thought struck him. 'You know, young man, maybe that's what they're up to. Maybe the Society of St. Peter Martyr is actually trying to resurrect the Inquisition. If they are, Neilsville would certainly be the place to start. It's always struck me as the kind of town that would love to have an Inquisition. Or a witch-burning. Tell you what, why don't you join up with the Society, and see if you can find out what they're up to? Who knows? It might prove to be interesting.'

Bishop O'Malley opened the door to his office and walked with Peter Balsam from the rectory to the car that Balsam had borrowed from Margo Henderson. He waved to Balsam as the younger man drove away, and decided that he did, indeed, like the boy very much. Feeling quite good, Bishop O'Malley got in his own car and set out for his golf game.

Had he known about the marks on Balsam's back, he would not have felt nearly so good. He would have known that something was happening in Neilsville.

Instead, he went happily to his golf game, where Joe Flynn beat him by three strokes. Which wasn't too bad; Joe Flynn usually beat him by five.

Peter Balsam entered his apartment and tossed the car keys to Margo Henderson.

'Not a scratch on it,' he said. 'You ready for the dinner I promised?'

Margo nodded, relieved to see that he seemed to be in a good mood. 'Shall I fix you a drink first?' she asked.

'Sure. Then I'll tell you all about the Bishop. Right now I'm going to change my clothes.'

He walked quickly into the bedroom and stripped to his shorts. As he'd done this morning, he glanced in the mirror to check the welts on his back. This morning they had been as angry and red as ever.

Now they were gone.

He looked again, and tentatively touched the skin of his back.

No trace. Not a scar. Not a mark. His back was as clear as it had ever been.

When Peter Balsam returned to the living room a few seconds later and took the drink Margo offered, his mood had changed. The merriment was gone, and in its place was a certain thoughtfulness.

By the time dinner was over Peter Balsam had made up his mind.

He would join the Society of St. Peter Martyr.

Margo wasn't sure it was wise, but Peter insisted. Reluctantly, and only because the Bishop had suggested his joining the Society, Margo agreed. Despite her falling-out with the Church, she instinctively trusted the Bishop. And she was beginning to suspect she loved Peter Balsam.

But she didn't like it. She didn't like it at all.

SEVENTEEN

Peter Balsam found the note in his box on Thursday morning:

The Rectory
Friday Night
8.00 p.m.

There was no signature, not even any initials, and it was written – lettered almost – in a flowing script that appeared to have been produced by a quill. And yet, despite the lack of details in the note, Balsam was sure he knew what it was: the summons to his final initiation into the Society of St. Peter Martyr. He stared at it silently for a moment, then slipped it between the pages of the book he had been carrying. When he turned, he saw the smiling face of Sister Marie watching him quizzically.

'Is something wrong?' the nun asked.

'Wrong?' Peter repeated, somewhat startled. 'No, nothing's wrong.' He started to move away, but the nun stopped him.

'Are you sure? You look pale. Almost as if you'd just seen a ghost.'

Peter hesitated for a moment, then suddenly pulled the note from the book he was carrying. He handed it to the nun. 'What do you make of this?'

Sister Marie took the note from Balsam's out-stretched hand and examined it carefully. She turned it over, glanced at the back of it, then returned it to Balsam.

'Odd,' she said.

'Do you recognize the handwriting?'

Sister Marie looked puzzled, as if she wanted to say something but wasn't sure it was proper. Balsam pressed her. 'You do recognize it, don't you?'

'I'm not sure,' Sister Marie said slowly. 'It was like a

déjà vu. When you handed me the note, I had the strangest feeling that the same thing had happened before. But then, before I could remember, it was gone.'

Balsam felt a pang of disappointment. He had hoped the nun would be able to tell him whose hand had written the message. Then she brightened, and asked to see the note again. This time she examined it even more carefully, and held it up to the light. When she finally gave it back to him she looked even more bewildered.

'I don't know,' she said, hesitating in a way that made Balsam suspect she did. 'I can tell you where the paper came from,' she said. 'That's easy: Monsignor Vernon. But you knew that, didn't you?'

'It seemed likely,' Peter grinned.

'It's the hand that bothers me,' Sister Marie said. 'I know it isn't Monsignor's; I also know I've seen it somewhere before. But there's something amiss. Something on the edge of my mind that isn't quite right. It's as if I've seen it before, but it was different, if you know what I mean.'

It's like Neilsville, Balsam thought to himself. You've seen it all before, but here it isn't quite right. Here, there's always something more than what can be seen. Aloud he said. 'Try to remember, will you?' At his voice, the nun's expression changed from bewilderment to concern.

'Is it important?' she asked, not seeing how a simple summons to the rectory could be of that much concern to anyone.

'I wish I knew,' Peter said. 'It might be, and it might not be. I wish I knew who wrote this note.'

'Well, don't worry about it too much,' the nun smiled. 'It'll probably come to me in the middle of the night, and if it does I'll write it down before I forget it.'

'In the margin of *The New Yorker*?' Balsam asked mischievously.

'That, or something even worse,' Sister Marie tossed at him. Then, before he could draw her out, she was gone.

Several times during Thursday and Friday, Peter Balsam spoke briefly with the Monsignor, and each time he wondered if he should mention the odd note. But the Monsignor never mentioned it, nor did there ever seem an opportune moment for Peter to bring it up. He wasn't sure, but he had the feeling that Monsignor Vernon was deliberately preventing him from asking any questions.

Late Friday afternoon, Balsam went looking for Sister Marie. When he found her, he had the distinct feeling that she wasn't particularly glad to see him. Her usual cheerful smile was nowhere in evidence, and the twinkle in her eye had faded.

'Sister Marie?' he said, as if he wasn't quite sure it was her. She seemed to jump a little, as if she hadn't seen him, though he was standing right in front of her.

'Mr. Balsam,' she said, and Peter noted the use of his last name. Her eyes didn't meet his.

'You've been hiding from me today,' he said, forcing a lightness into his voice that her manner did nothing to encourage.

'No, I don't think so,' the nun said softly. Her eyes flitted from one part of the room to another, as if seeking escape.

'I was wondering if you'd remembered where you saw that handwriting before,' Peter said as casually as he could.

'Handwriting?' the nun repeated too quickly. 'What handwriting?'

'On the note,' Balsam said, beginning to feel just a bit exasperated. The nun continued to look blank. 'The note I found in my box yesterday morning? Surely you haven't forgotten?'

'Oh, that,' Sister Marie said, laughing nervously. 'I'm afraid it slipped my mind completely!' Again she glanced around the room, and Peter had the distinct impression she was about to dart off somewhere. He was right.

'I'm afraid you'll have to excuse me,' she exclaimed. 'I promised Sister Elizabeth I'd help her with some things this afternoon.' Then, as if she were too aware that the excuse was lame, she added quickly: 'Some tests. I promised to help her grade some tests.' And then she was gone.

Though they'd made no plans to have dinner together Friday evening. Peter wasn't surprised when Margo Henderson appeared at his apartment shortly after he got there himself, nor was he surprised that she was carrying a couple of steaks that nearly matched the two he'd picked up himself on his way home. What did surprise him was that as soon as she was inside his apartment he gathered her into his arms and kissed her. She returned the kiss warmly, then pulled away from him.

'Now that was something new,' she said. 'I could get used to being greeted like that.'

'Good,' Peter replied. 'Since we have two extra steaks, why don't you plan on being greeted that way again tomorrow night? And tomorrow night we can spend the evening together.'

'They cancelled the dance?' Margo asked. Peter snapped his fingers impatiently.

'Damn. I'd forgotten all about it.' St. Francis Xavier's was holding its first dance of the school term that weekend. He grinned at her. 'What do you think they'd say if you showed up with me to help me chaperone?'

'Me at St. Francis Xavier's? Monsignor'd have to exorcise the place after I left. But I'd love to have dinner.' She paused, frowning prettily. 'Although I have to admit I'm beginning to feel like a corporate wife – I have dinner with you, then sit by myself while you run around to meetings and social events.' The glint in her eye told Peter that she was teasing, but he decided to take it seriously. He took her hands in his.

'It isn't fair, I know. And you don't have to do it, Margo. In fact, I wish you wouldn't.'

The smile faded from her face and she grew serious. 'Of course I don't have to do it, Peter, and you're very sweet to worry about it. But I'd rather have dinner with you and spend the rest of the evening worrying about you than spend the entire evening with anyone else. I thought you knew that.'

'Maybe I was fishing,' Peter said, the beginning of a grin playing around the corners of his mouth. Margo's face remained serious.

'Or maybe you were trying to tell me you care about me, in your own way. Well, all right. I know you care about me, and you know I care about you. That gives me the right to spend an evening worrying about you now and then. I will worry about you tonight – unless I can talk you into changing your mind.'

Balsam smiled gently. 'Why don't you wait for me and do your worrying here? Then, no matter how late I get back, we can find out what's really going on with the Society of St. Peter Martyr. Tonight I'm going to record the whole thing.' He held up a small cassette recorder. Margo stared at it in silence. Suddenly she wasn't sure she wanted to know about the Society. In fact, she was almost sure she *didn't* want to know what went on at their meetings. But at the same time, she *had* to know. She made up her mind to be waiting when Peter came home that night. Silently, Margo began fixing dinner. There just didn't seem to be much to talk about.

The Society of St. Peter Martyr was waiting. All six of them were in the foyer, standing formally in a semi-circle – expectant. He closed the front door behind him and stood looking at them. There was a long silence as the six priests surveyed him, and then Monsignor Vernon spoke.

'Peter Balsam,' he said sonorously, 'we have met, and it is our decision that you shall be initiated into the Society tonight.'

'I see,' said Balsam softly. He decided to risk a question. 'Even though I'm not a priest?'

The Monsignor smiled faintly. 'We have never had a ... layman in the Society before, but we are prepared to make an exception for you. Our reasons,' he declared, anticipating Peter's question, 'will eventually become clear to you.'

Peter remained silent. But he wondered why the Monsignor had hesitated over the word 'layman.' What other word had come into his mind?

The six priests turned suddenly, and began filing down the hall toward the study. Balsam quickly reached into the inside pocket of his jacket and activated the recorder before falling in behind them.

As before, the study was lit only by candles and the uneven glow of the fire. Once again the chairs were arranged in a semi-circle in front of the fire, with the two easy chairs opposite each other, reserved for Monsignor and Balsam. In a few moments the seven men were seated.

The catechism began again, each of the priests in turn questioning Balsam's knowledge of the Faith. He answered the questions easily, giving the correct responses, careful to keep his voice level, to give no hint of his true feelings whenever he was mouthing a doctrine he questioned. As the inquisition went on – and he had the distinct feeling that it was, indeed, an inquisition – he wondered to what purpose it all was. The questions were the same ones he had answered before, and his answers were the same. No, he realized with a start, the answers were *not* the same. The first time he had sat in this room to be questioned by the six priests, it had taken him a while to realize what they wanted to hear. Tonight, he had known from the beginning. And his tone had been different that first night. He had made no effort to conceal his doubts about certain aspects of his faith. Tonight, Peter Balsam was acting the part of the true believer. And as he played his role, letting himself be led through the Doctrine and listening calmly to his own responses, he began to wonder if the role wasn't taking over the actor, to wonder how much of his earnestness was feigned and how much was real.

It was over, finally, though Peter Balsam didn't realize it at first. He looked from one stern face to another, wondering from which of them the next question would come. Eventually he realized there would be no more questions. The six clerics were looking at him with satisfaction; he had apparently passed their test. He wondered what would come next.

Suddenly they were standing, looming over him. 'Peter Balsam,' they asked in one voice, 'what do you want of us?'

The question echoed in his mind. *What do you want of us?* His brain searched for the answer. He knew there *was* an answer; one single answer that they were looking for, and that if he was unable to give it, there would be no second chance.

He was still trying to decide what to say when he heard his own voice answering.

'Solace in my Faith.'

'And what do you offer us?'

'My body and my mind, for use in your holy work.'

They reached out to him then, taking each of his hands, and drawing him to his feet. They offered him wine.

He had passed.

He was one of them.

He had told them what they wanted to hear, and he was glad.

The Society of St. Peter Martyr, once more seven strong, began to pray.

The same chanting he had heard before began once again, but this time Peter Balsam was aware that he was somehow able to take part in it. He mouthed the strange words easily, his lips and tongue forming one syllable after another as if he had been saying the unfamiliar Latin-like words all his life. As he chanted in unison with the others, part of his mind tried to reason out the source of his ability to match the priests word for word. He told himself that it was simply because he had heard the service once before, and it had remained imprinted on his memory. But another voice inside him told him there was more to it than that; that one hearing of the service was not enough for him to have it flow so easily from his lips.

He put the disturbing thoughts from his mind, and concentrated instead on trying to follow the service. It sounded, at first, much like the praises of the Lord that had been sung in the convent he grew up in. But, again, there was something different. The praises were there, but there were overtones of other things. Things in the odd not-quite-Latin that he could almost get a grasp on, but then would lose. Eventually he stopped trying to understand the words and began to feel them instead. They were words of exhortation. The Society was praising the Lord, yes, but it was also exhorting Him. To what purpose? Faster now, and faster, until individual words escaped him and there was only the rhythm.

The rhythm, insistent, inexorable, caught him up in its mysticism, transporting him into the same state of religious ecstasy he had experienced once before in this room. He began to lose consciousness of his physical surroundings, and was only aware of the presence of the light, and the warmth, and the spirituality of his companions. They were moving now, the circle closing in on him, surrounding him, and as the service grew more intense Balsam had the feeling of being at one with them, of joining them in an experience that was both frightening and exhilarating, as if, for the first time, the core of his soul was being touched by God.

And then the voice began.

It sounded far away at first, but it grew steadily louder until its throbbing tones echoed through the room. The glow of the candles and the heat and flicker of the fire held him but the chanting had stopped. Only the throbbing sound of a single voice filled his ears now. And then that, too, stopped. In the sudden silence, Peter Balsam reached out to touch the priest who was closest to him. In the odd light the priest seemed to glow white as an angel, and Balsam was sure he would find the support he was seeking. He tried to speak, but his mouth refused to open. From somewhere he heard another voice: 'He is with us. Saint Peter Martyr is with us.'

And then the deep tones of the oddly disembodied voice once more filled the room, using the strange language that Peter could not quite understand, He was able to follow the meaning now and then, but only in snatches.

'You must find him for me . . .

'You must punish . . .

'They are everywhere . . .

'Celebrate . . .

'Punish . . .

'Sin . . .

'Sin . . .

'Celebrate . . . Punish . . . Sin . . .'

And then the voice was gone, and the chanting began again. And once more the strange trance came over Balsam, and he lost track of time, and of place, and of what was real and what was not. All was religion, and religion was all. And the chanting went on . . . and the celebration went on . . . and sometime during the long night, Peter Balsam felt himself slipping away, drifting in a fantasy that he had neither the will nor the desire to define.

Three hours before dawn, it ended. As before, Peter Balsam had no idea of what had happened. Only impressions, and a feeling of both exhilaration and exhaustion.

And, of course, a tape. As he left the rectory he felt the miniature recorder, still in the pocket of his jacket, still running. He switched it off, though he knew it must have stopped recording hours earlier. But the first two hours of the meeting were on the tape. At least it would be a beginning. But a beginning of what? He hurried his step, and by the time he got home he was almost running.

Margo was waiting for him, a strange expression on her face.

They listened to the tape together.

Margo sat at one end of the sofa, Peter at the other, and Peter was intensely aware of the distance between them. They only listened to snatches of the first part of the tape; the part that had recorded the catechism. Ten minutes after it began, Margo commented softly that whatever else was on the tape, Peter had certainly started out sounding like a good Catholic. He glanced at her, wondering what the remark meant, but her eyes were turned away from him. He reached down and advanced the tape through the rest of the first hour to the point where the chanting began.

When the first strange sounds of the almost religious music came out of the tiny speaker, Margo spoke again.

'There was a silence,' she said suddenly. 'What was happening during the silence?'

'You mean when they were accepting me into the Society?'

Margo nodded.

Peter thought back to the moment, then remembered.

'Wine,' he said. 'Monsignor Vernon passed a chalice of wine around.' Margo's brow furrowed, and she fell silent.

They listened to the tape, watching the cassette player almost as if it were producing a visual image as well as emitting the peculiar sounds.

'It sounds almost like Latin,' Margo said.

'I know. But it isn't. Not quite. It's close, but just different enough to make it mostly unintelligible. I can pick up a word here and there, but most of it sounds like another language.'

'Like Spanish, sort of,' Margo said.

'Spanish?' Peter said. He listened more closely, and suddenly the rhythms made more sense. And then it came to him. It wasn't Spanish at all. It was some kind of strange Italian.

'That's it,' he said softly.

'What?' Margo asked, looking at him for the first time.

'That's it!' Peter exclaimed. 'It's not Spanish, Margo, and it isn't quite Latin. It's some kind of Italian! And it makes sense, too. Not the words. I can't understand them, but I know what we're listening to! They're using a language that's between Latin and Italian.'

Margo looked confused, and he tried to explain.

'The Romance languages all stem from Latin. French. Spanish. Italian. But languages change slowly. So what would early Italian sound like? It would be somewhere between Latin and modern Italian, wouldn't it? And St. Peter Martyr was an Italian from the thirteenth century! The Society is using the language of St. Peter Martyr! That must be it. Of course we can't understand all of it, any more than we can understand all of Chaucer's English.'

'But where would they have learned it?' Margo asked.

'Who knows?' Peter said. Suddenly he felt much better about everything; the chanting had lost a lot of the mystery it had held in the flickering light of the rectory.

'How much of this do you remember?' Margo asked him suddenly.

'Not much,' Peter said. 'It all sounds vaguely familiar to me, but not nearly as familiar as it should. I mean, only a few hours ago I was taking part in that chanting.'

Margo stared at him. 'I thought you said you couldn't understand the words.'

'I couldn't. And I still can't. But at the time I was able to keep up with it, without even trying. It was like the words just flowed out of me ...' His voice trailed off as he realized that now, in his apartment, the rhythms that had seemed so simple in the rectory seemed incredibly complicated.

And then he heard the voice.

It boomed sonorously out of the recorder, resonant and compelling. He recognized it immediately, and wondered why he hadn't known it during the service. It was Monsignor Vernon.

'What's he saying?' Margo asked. She, too, had recognized the priest's voice.

'I'm not sure,' Peter said slowly, trying to conceal the sudden fear that was clutching at his stomach. 'I ... When I was there, I thought I was hearing the voice of St. Peter Martyr. It never occurred to me that it was Monsignor. And I can't understand most of what he's saying. It has to do with sin, and punishment, and celebrating. I don't know. I should be able to understand the Latin – I teach it. But it isn't quite Latin anyway. It's more like Italian and my Italian doesn't exist.'

And then the booming voice stopped, and the chanting began again, accompanied now by a different sound. Slowly the chanting faded away, and the new sounds grew in volume. They began as a series of small whining noises, but as the tape ground on, the whines turned into moaning, mixed with heavy breathing, and other sounds that seemed familiar to Peter but that he couldn't quite identify. Occasionally a cry of ecstasy penetrated the steady moaning.

Peter knew what he was hearing, but didn't want to admit it to himself. He listened to the tape, trying to shut it out, but at the same time fascinated. And he began to remember some of the images he had experienced in the rectory.

The angels, seeming to glow whitely in the flickering candlelight.

The closeness among the seven of them that he had thought was a spiritual closeness.

The caresses that he had thought stemmed from a religious experience.

Naked men, priests stripped of their vestments, stripped of everything, their bodies intertwined not spiritually but carnally, caressing each other not religiously but sexually.

He was listening to the sounds of an orgy, an orgy he knew he and six other priests had participated in only hours earlier.

And then he heard his own voice crying out in that tight ecstasy that only comes with a sexual climax. His stomach knotted and he knew he was going to be sick. As he lunged toward the bathroom his right hand flew out, knocking the tiny recorder from the coffee table. But it didn't stop: the sickening sounds continued as he fled the room.

He stayed in the bathroom for a long time, waiting for the nausea to subside, not wanting to go back into the living room, not wanting to face Margo. Then, as he was beginning to hope that she might have left, he heard her rapping at the door.

'Peter?' she said, her voice quiet and gentle. 'Peter, are you all right?'

All right? he thought. All right? How could I be all right? My God, what have I done? He sank to the floor of the bathroom, laying his cheek on the cool tile. He heard the click of the door opening, and realized that Margo had come in. Then he felt her touch him on the cheek.

'It's all right,' she said softly. 'Peter, it's all right.'

He stared up at her, wanting to believe her, but sure that nothing would ever be all right again.

Darkness closed around him.

EIGHTEEN

Margo's first impulse was to call the hospital. Before she got to the phone, she had changed her mind. What could she tell them? They wouldn't believe her. Even if she played the tape for them, she was sure they wouldn't believe her. And besides, Peter had only passed out. She told herself that it wasn't anything serious: he had simply been overcome by exhaustion and the emotional shock of discovering what he had participated in.

She went back to the bathroom, and started moving Peter Balsam's unconscious body toward the bedroom. She would put him to bed, and then she would lie down on the couch and wait for him to wake up. Under the circumstances there just didn't seem to be anything else to do.

He didn't stir at all as she pulled and shoved him into his bed, but he looked so uncomfortable that she decided to undress him.

The first thing she noticed were the marks. The same marks that had been there a few days earlier. They were back, and they were identical to the earlier ones standing red and angry all over his torso. She pulled his trousers off, then his underwear. The last garment seemed damp, and at first she thought he had simply been sweating profusely. But there was more. From Peter Balsam's body an odour emanated. The sweet muskiness of semen.

Margo Henderson buried her face in the soiled undergarment and cried. As the tears came, she realized that she had still been hoping. She had been clinging to a hope that the evidence of the tape had been false, that what she had heard was something entirely different from what she now knew was the truth. She had stumbled into a mess. And yet, even as she lay on the bed next to Peter, sobbing softly into the pillow, she realized she was not going to walk away; she would not – could not – leave him.

It wasn't Peter's fault, she told herself, forcing back the sobs. He didn't know what he was doing. He didn't know what they were doing to him. You watched his face as he listened, and he was shocked. So don't blame him; help him.

Margo rose from the bed, then pulled the covers up over Peter's naked body. She looked down at him, and realized how vulnerable he must be right now. When he woke, she must be close to him. He mustn't feel that she had abandoned him.

She went out to the living room, and stretched out on the sofa. The first glow of dawn was beginning to light the sky outside as Margo fell into a fitful doze interrupted by dreams that took all the peace from her sleep ...

She was outside the rectory, and she knew what was going on inside. But she couldn't stop it. She could only crouch in the darkness outside, listening to the sounds, hearing first the chanting, and then the moaning, knowing that Peter was inside, that he was in the middle of that group of six strange priests, and that they were seducing him. Their hands were touching him, and their lips kissing him in a way that only her hands should have touched him, only her lips should have kissed him.

Then she was suddenly inside the rectory, inside that oddly lit room, watching the naked priests, their wrinkled bodies glistening sweatily in the candlelight as they stripped Peter's clothes from him, their fingers greedily playing over his smooth skin, their tongues clucking away in that strange language. And then they were holding him down and Monsignor Vernon, grown suddenly to a towering height, stood over Peter, his monstrous organ thrusting toward Peter's gaping mouth. The priest began advancing toward Peter, and Margo looked on in horror. She wanted to scream, but couldn't make any sound escape her lips. She tried to lunge forward, tried to rescue Peter from the grasp of the old men, but she couldn't make her feet move. They seemed to be mired in heavy mud. All she could do was look on in mutely fascinated horror as Monsignor Vernon, suddenly enveloped in a halo, forced his penis into Peter Balsam's mouth. And finally, as the immense glans disappeared between his lips, she screamed.

Margo woke up to the sound of her own scream, and felt her body shaking uncontrollably. She could feel a clammy sweat covering her like a wet sheet. And then she felt a hand touch her, and her eyes snapped open. Peter Balsam was bending over her. She stared silently at him for a second or two, suddenly unsure whether she was awake. And then she realized she was awake, and he was real, and she threw her arms around him.

'Oh, God, Peter,' she cried into his ear. 'I saw it all. I was there, right there in the room, and those priests – those six awful priests – they were naked and they were – they were doing the most disgusting things to you. And then the Monsignor – Monsignor Vernon – he – he—' She broke off, unable to continue.

'It's all right,' Peter said softly, holding her closer. 'It was only a dream. You had a bad dream.'

She lay still in his arms for a moment, and her panic passed. And then she remembered, He should have been in bed. She had put him to bed, then lay down to doze, only a few minutes ago. What was he doing up? How could he be up already? She wriggled free of his arms and sat up. The sun was pouring brightly in the front window.

'What time is it?' she asked.

'Almost eleven,' Peter said. 'I woke up half an hour ago and decided to let you sleep. I guess I shouldn't have.'

The dream came back to her, and she looked at him, tried to separate him from the Peter Balsam in her dream. But she couldn't quite do it, and she had to tell him why.

'Peter,' she said softly, 'there's something I didn't tell you last night. Part of my dream just now wasn't a dream. It was a memory. Last night I – well, I got so nervous waiting for you here that I decided to go for a walk. And I found myself walking up the hill. To the rectory.'

'Is that why you looked so strange when I came in last night?'

She nodded miserably. 'I already knew what had been going on at the rectory, long before I heard the tape. I must have been outside the window of Monsignor's study for hours, listening.' She looked at him beseechingly. 'You have no idea what it was like. I didn't want to listen, but I couldn't make myself go away. I stayed until it was almost over. I only got back here about forty-five minutes before you did.'

'Why did you stay?' Peter asked gravely. 'I don't think I would have.'

'I had to. I had to see you, to see if you knew what was going on up there. And you didn't. I could tell from your face.' Her voice rose. 'Oh, Peter, they're doing such horrible things to you.'

She flung her arms around his neck and clung to him. Only this time, Peter picked her up and carried her into the bedroom, kicking the door closed behind him.

'What are you going to do?'

It was an hour later, and they lay in bed, her head resting on his stomach.

'I'm not sure,' Peter said. 'I have to stop it. I can't let them keep doing what they're doing.'

'But what can you do?'

'I don't know. I suppose I could take the tape to the Bishop, but frankly, I don't think he'd do anything. The only thing he could do is talk to Monsignor and the rest of them, and of course they'd deny they were doing anything wrong.'

'But those sounds . . .'

'Religious ecstasy,' Peter said, trying to make light of the whole mess. 'The sounds we were making thirty minutes ago weren't much different.'

Margo blushed, remembering, then spoke again.

'But you have to do something.'

'I know,' Peter said. 'And I'm going to have to do it alone. No one's going to believe what's on that tape.'

'I can back you up,' Margo said softly.

Peter shook his head violently. 'I'm going to have to do it on my own. I'll talk to the Bishop again, but I don't think anything will come of it. And believe me, I won't be going to any more meetings of the Society of St. Peter Martyr.'

'What about the dance tonight?'

'I'll go, of course. That's going to come under the heading of acting as if nothing had happened. And all of a sudden I think it's important that I be there. Important for me, and important for the kids.'

Then he remembered Sister Marie, and her strange evasiveness yesterday morning.

'And there's someone I have to talk to,' he said softly, thinking: Someone who knows more about all this than she's told me.

He decided not to tell Margo about Sister Marie.

The gymnasium of St. Francis Xavier High School had that look of slightly seedy festivity produced by high-school students valiantly trying to convert a gymnasium into a ballroom. The crepe-paper streamers, already beginning to go limp as the dance was beginning, hung unevenly from the light fixtures and the basketball hoops, serving more to accentuate the unsuitability of the room than to lend their intended air of gaiety.

Marilyn Crane sat unhappily in one corner of the gym, the corner farthest from the door, and wondered for the tenth time why she had come. For the tenth time she answered herself; she was here to make her mother happy, and because her sister Greta had always come to the dances in the gym. The fact that Greta always had a date had not struck her mother as particularly relevant. So Marilyn sat in her corner, half hoping to be left alone and unnoticed, half hoping someone – anyone – would come over to talk to her. No one did.

The room began to fill up, and Marilyn watched the sisters in their black habits cruising among the students like so many dignified black swans in a flock of brightly coloured, raucously quacking ducks. Marilyn wondered how they did it; wondered if that mystic self-confidence was issued to the sisters along with their habits. Marilyn particularly liked to watch Sister Marie, her wimple framing her pretty face in a way that seemed to accentuate her beauty rather than lend her an air of remoteness.

Sister Marie, unaware of Marilyn's scrutiny, was standing by the main entrance, greeting each of the students, as he came in, and doing her best to keep her right toe from tapping to the music too obviously. Years of practice in front of a mirror had taught her the precise amount of movement she could make under the heavy folds of her habit without causing the telltale swaying of the material that had constantly given her away during her novitiate. But she still tended to get carried away, particularly since the advent of the rock era. Rock music always set her foot to tapping far in excess of the tolerance of her habit. She saw Janet Connally coming in, and smiled easily.

'All by yourself tonight?' she grinned.

'I get to meet more boys if I come alone,' Janet said. 'Besides, Judy couldn't come, Karen's here with Jim, and Penny is working the refreshment table with Jeff Bremmer.'

'How is Judy?' Sister Marie asked, genuine concern in her voice.

'All right, I guess,' Janet said slowly. 'She came home yesterday, and she's supposed to be back in school on Monday.'

'That'll be nice,' Sister Marie said emphatically. 'I've missed her.'

'Sister Marie,' Janet began. She wanted to ask the nun if she knew what was going to happen to Judy, but suddenly, without really knowing why, changed her mind.

'Yes?' the nun prompted her.

'Nothing,' Janet said. Suddenly she felt nervous, and wanted to be elsewhere. 'I think I'd better say hello to Penny.'

She moved off quickly, and her place was taken by Monsignor Vernon, who had been standing a few feet behind her.

'Monsignor,' Sister Marie greeted him gravely, her cheerful smile disappearing.

'Sister Marie,' the priest acknowledged her greeting, looking dolefully around the room. 'Well.' The word was uttered in a tone that conveyed deep disapproval.

'I think it looks nice,' Sister Marie said tentatively.

'I wonder if it's the sort of thing we should be encouraging.'

Sister Marie knew what was coming, knew how the Monsignor felt about frivolous activities – sinful activities. She knew about St. Peter Martyr, and about the Monsignor's fascination with the saint. Often, in the lonely privacy of her cell, she had wondered where that fascination had come from, and where it would lead the priest. And sometimes it frightened her. As it had frightened her when she finally remembered where she had seen that odd handwriting on the note Peter Balsam had shown her a few days ago.

Now, sensing that the Monsignor was about to launch into one of his tirades, she glanced quickly around for a diversion.

'I think I see Penny Anderson waving to me,' she said, moving away from the priest. 'I'd better see if she needs any help.' Before Monsignor Vernon could make a reply, the nun was gone, gliding through the crowd, smiling and nodding to the students as they danced around her. The priest watched her go, his eyes noting the contrast between her dark habit and the brightly coloured dresses of his charges. He felt his anger surging up, silently wished he could turn the clock back, turn time back to an easier day, when girls dressed modestly and a priest was respected.

Monsignor Vernon's expression grew even more severe as he watched the teen-agers merrily greeting Sister Marie as she made her way through the room. Not one of them had spoken to him. He turned, and walked back into the foyer of the gym, glad to be away from the glittering lights and festooning crepe.

Peter Balsam glanced at his watch as he hurried up the steps of the gymnasium: he was already ten minutes late, and he had intended to be at least that much early. He burst through the door into the foyer, and almost collided with the Monsignor. He felt his heart pound at the sight of the priest, and hoped his voice wouldn't give his feelings away. He wanted to back away, then turn and flee, but he forced himself to stand his ground and smile a greeting.

'Monsignor,' he said. 'Nice evening, isn't it?'

The priest seemed pleased to see him, and Peter began to relax. Maybe he was going to be able to pull it off after all.

'Sorry about last night,' Vernon was saying. 'I'm afraid time just slips away from us sometimes. I hadn't intended for the service to go nearly that late.'

'Well, it was Friday night,' Peter said, forcing his voice to remain neutral. 'I'm afraid I slept in a bit this morning, though.' He waited for the priest to respond, then became aware that the Monsignor was no longer looking at him, but seemed to be concentrating on something behind Peter. Peter turned, and saw Karen Morton and Jim Mulvey coming in the door. He smiled a greeting to his students, but they hurried by, studiously ignoring him. It wasn't until they had disappeared into the gym, that he realized it hadn't been he they were avoiding; it had been Monsignor. The priest was glaring after them.

'Karen seems like a nice girl,' Peter said, trying to keep his voice easy.

'Do you think so?' the priest said icily. 'Then you aren't as perceptive as I thought you were. Excuse me, I'd better have a word with Sister Elizabeth.'

Puzzled, Peter made his way to the door of the gym, and let his eyes wander over the crowd. Eventually he saw the Monsignor bending down to whisper into Sister Elizabeth's ear, and pointing toward a spot where Jim Mulvey and Karen Morton were dancing. A moment later, Sister Elizabeth was striding toward the couple, a ruler in her hand.

He watched curiously, wondering what the ruler was for. Then, as he looked on, Sister Elizabeth put the ruler between

Karen and Jim, She looked at them severely when the ruler wouldn't quite fit, and pushed them slightly apart. When they were a foot apart, and the ruler could be passed between them without touching either of them, Sister Elizabeth was satisfied. She glared at each of them once more, then moved on to another couple.

Balsam almost laughed at the performance. The fact that Sister Elizabeth had not been kidding with her measurements made him stop. He looked around and saw that all the nuns were carrying rulers, and that they were all circulating through the room, meticulously making certain that the boys and girls were maintaining a foot of open space between them. All, that is, except Sister Marie, who was standing at the refreshment table chatting with Penny Anderson and Jeff Bremmer. Peter Balsam decided to have a cup of punch.

The nun saw Peter approaching, and had an impulse to hurry away. But then she changed her mind, and made herself smile at him.

'Some punch, Peter?'

Balsam's brows rose. 'No more Mr. Balsam?' he said. The look of hurt in her eyes, and a sudden flicker of what he thought was fear, made him wish he hadn't said it. 'I'm sorry,' he said quickly. 'I didn't mean it to sound sarcastic. I'm just glad to see you smiling at me again.' He decided to change the subject. 'Where's your ruler?' He gestured toward the nuns who were still steadily circulating through the room, measuring the gaps between the students.

'Oh, I have one,' Sister Marie said, her sense of mischief getting the best of her. 'But I use it differently.' Deftly, she slipped the ruler from the sleeve of her habit, and stirred the punch with it. Then she looked at Balsam, and her manner changed slightly. 'Could I talk to you for a minute?'

He followed her to a quiet corner.

'What is it?' he said gently. He thought the flicker of fear he had seen earlier was back, and growing.

'It's probably nothing,' Sister Marie said nervously. 'But I have to tell you about it. I'm sorry about the way I acted yesterday, when you asked me about the handwriting in that note. I told you I'd forgotten all about it. I lied. I didn't forget; I remembered. But for some reason, when I remembered, the strangest fear flowed over me. I almost felt like – well, never mind,' she broke off.

She saw no point in telling Peter Balsam that she had felt like killing herself. Besides, it had only been an impulse, and it had passed almost immediately. But it *had* frightened her. Frightened her badly.

'You remembered the handwriting?' Balsam said, his heart suddenly pounding.

'Yes,' Sister Marie said, nodding. 'But I don't know what it means. It's very strange.'

'What is it?' Balsam said impatiently. He had to know.

'It was years ago,' Sister Marie said. 'I was in Monsignor Vernon's office, and he suddenly offered to show me something. A relic. A relic of his favourite saint, Peter Martyr.'

'A relic?' Balsam said curiously. 'What sort of relic?'

'It was a letter. Just a page. But he told me it was written by St. Peter Martyr. And it was in the same handwriting as the handwriting on the note you showed me Wednesday morning.'

'What did it say?'

'The letter? I haven't the slightest idea. It was in a language I couldn't understand. Almost like Latin, but sort of like Italian, too. I suppose if I'd had time, I could have figured it out.'

'You speak Italian?' Peter couldn't believe his luck.

'And French, and Spanish. I majored in languages in college. So of course I joined the order, and where did they send me? Neilsville, Washington.'

Balsam hardly heard her. 'You really think you could have understood that language?' he asked eagerly.

The nun looked at him, wondering why he was so curious about the relic. 'I don't see why not,' she said thoughtfully. 'My Latin and Italian are both excellent, and since Italian grows directly out of Latin, I shouldn't have any problems with it.'

'What if you *heard* the language?' Peter said.

'Heard it?' Sister Marie laughed. 'Well, that's hardly likely, is it? I mean, who would speak it anymore?'

'But could you understand it?' Peter said urgently. The laughter faded from Sister Marie's voice.

'I suppose so,' she said carefully. 'I can't say. But I can try. I mean, if you aren't just being hypothetical.'

'I'm not,' Peter said. 'Believe me, I'm not.'

For the first time in several days, Peter thought he had a chance of getting to the bottom of the Society of St. Peter Martyr.

Jim Mulvey pulled Karen Morton to him, and squeezed her. A shiver of pleasure ran through her body, but she tried to pull away from him. 'They'll see us, Jim,' she whispered in his ear, gesturing toward the nuns. Sister Elizabeth, the one Karen feared most, had her back to the couple for the moment, but Karen was sure that it wouldn't be more than a few seconds until the sour-faced sister saw them pressed together and moved swiftly to break up the embrace.

'Let them see us,' Jim whispered back, his voice heavy. 'They just wish it was them instead of you,' He pulled her to him again, pressing the swelling of his erection against her. 'Put your hand down there,' he whispered.

She wanted to, but she knew she shouldn't. She resisted the urge to touch him. Instead, she pulled away again.

'Not here,' she hissed. 'Everyone can see.' She glanced around, and sure enough, there was Sister Elizabeth bearing down on them.

'Twelve inches,' Sister Elizabeth said bitterly. 'You know the rule.' She brandished the ruler.

'I know it, but I can't quite manage it,' Jim said innocently. 'Will you settle for eight?'

Sister Elizabeth saw Karen blush a deep red, and wondered if she'd missed something. She glared at Jim, sure that he had gotten the best of her, but uncertain how he'd managed it. She scurried away, leaving Jim grinning triumphantly at Karen.

'That was a terrible thing to say to her,' Karen said.

'Was it?' Jim leered. Then he winked at her. 'Hey, I have an idea. You know that little room where they keep all the gym stuff?'

Karen nodded, remembering the equipment room, no more than a closet, really. 'What about it?'

'Let's go in there,' Jim said. 'It's dark, and private. And no sisters with rulers.'

Karen considered the idea. It'll only be for a couple of minutes, she told herself. What can happen in a couple of minutes?

Jim began dancing her toward the equipment room.

Marilyn Crane felt she was being watched. She told herself that she was only imagining it, that no one was paying any attention to her at all. That thought was even worse. Suddenly her corner became unbearable, and she looked around for refuge. Jeff Bremmer. Of all of them, Jeff was usually the kindest to her. She began working her way across the floor toward the refreshment table, dodging the dancing couples. She stepped aside to let Jim and Karen pass: they ignored her.

She rushed on toward the refreshment table, not speaking to anyone until she reached Jeff. He smiled half-heartedly at her.

'Hot in here,' she said tentatively, dipping herself a cup of punch.

'Too many people,' Penny Anderson said pointedly, staring into her eyes. Marilyn decided to ignore the crack, and turned back to Jeff.

'Can I help you with anything?'

Jeff glanced away from her guiltily, remembering that he'd been at the party when they'd all made her look like a fool. He looked to Penny Anderson for help.

'We can manage fine,' Penny said. Then she relented. 'If you want to get some more ice, it's out in the foyer.' Marilyn's face broke into a smile, and she started toward the main doors. Behind her, she heard Penny's voice.

'She's really pathetic, isn't she?'

The words hit her like a physical blow. Marilyn hurried

toward the door. Only now she knew she wouldn't be back, with or without the ice. She had to get out of the gym, get away from everybody, get to the church.

She had to get to the church. She had to.

The Sorrowful Mother, She had to talk to the Sorrowful Mother. The Virgin had come to her once; maybe she would again.

But then, just as she was about to pass through the doors, her way was blocked. She looked up into the piercing eyes of Monsignor Vernon. He returned her gaze, and seemed about to say something when Sister Elizabeth rushed up. Ignoring Marilyn, the nun spoke to the priest over her head.

'Monsignor,' she said, her voice carrying a heavy burden of outrage. 'It's happened. I knew it would if we let this kind of thing go on, and now it has.'

'What's happened?' the Monsignor replied, his brow suddenly furrowed.

'Jim Mulvey and Karen Morton. I just saw them go into the equipment room together.'

Suddenly, as Marilyn looked on, the Monsignor's face changed from its normally severe mask into a glowering visage of indignation. Thrusting Marilyn to one side. he began striding toward the closed door of the equipment room, scattering the dancers as he went.

Monsignor Vernon grasped the handle of the door of the equipment room, and yanked the door open. The small room was close and dark. The priest groped for the light cord, yanked it, illuminating two startled figures. There, under the naked bulb were Jim Mulvey and Karen Morton, their arms around each other, their bodies pressed close in a passionate kiss. The priest seized them, one with each hand, and thrust them out of the tiny room into the crowded gymnasium. He reached up and found the light cord again. The door began to swing slowly closed, and as he pulled the light switch he was suddenly plunged into darkness. He moved quickly toward the door but his foot caught on something. He tripped.

Monsignor Vernon fell to his knees, and as he caught himself he glimpsed the narrow band of light that came through the slightly open door. Deep inside him, a memory came to life.

Monsignor Vernon froze, staring through the crack in the door. High up in the rafters, the gym's lights glared balefully down on him. He felt himself growing dizzy. And then he saw the girl. She moved into his line of sight, and she seemed to be turning, turning slowly toward him. She had something in her hand. the girl. Something that glinted silver in the light. A knife. It looked like a knife.

Monsignor Vernon lunged to his feet and burst through the door.

Janet Connally, her silver net scarf held high as she danced, paused in mid-step as the priest, his eyes wild, threw the door open.

'Stop it!' he bellowed. Janet froze. The Monsignor stared around him. They were everywhere, the girls, all around him, they all looked alike. They all looked like her, like his sister. 'Sinners!' he cried. 'All of you are sinners!'

The students stared now, and began edging toward the door. Monsignor was angrier than they had ever seen him before.

'No more!' shouted the priest. 'Do you think I don't know you? Do you think I don't recognize you? Do you think I will show you mercy? You do not deserve mercy! Beware for your souls, for you have sinned. Punishment will fall upon you.'

And then across the room, Monsignor Vernon saw Peter Balsam staring at him. The priest raised his hand, and pointed to the teacher.

'Heretic! Punishment will fall upon you,' he bellowed. 'Punishment at the hands of the Lord!'

And then, as quickly as it had come, the rage was over, the memory gone. Nervously, the Monsignor glanced around. A silence had fallen over the room, and when he spoke again, this time in a whisper, everybody in the room heard him.

'The dance is over,' he said.

Five minutes later the room was empty, except for two people. Standing at opposite ends of the gym, as if waiting for the battle to begin, Monsignor Vernon and Peter Balsam stared at each other. And now, thought Peter, it's all going to happen.

He was frightened.

BOOK THREE

Auto-da-Fé

NINETEEN

The cafeteria buzzed with the noise of high-school students at lunch, but Marilyn Crane didn't hear it. She sat alone, surrounded by empty seats, and concentrated on her sandwich. A few feet away from her, at the other end of the same table. Jeff Bremmer also sat alone. Every few seconds he glanced at Marilyn, and tried to figure out what he should say to her.

He knew she'd overheard Penny Anderson's remark on Saturday night. He had intended to follow her out to apologize for Penny. But then Monsignor had found Karen and Jim in the equipment closet, and blown his cool. Jeff shook his head, remembering the priest's outburst.

He glanced at Marilyn again, and decided to use the dance as an opening. 'Boy, that was really something, wasn't it?' he said.

Marilyn looked at him, and wondered if he was talking to her. Then she realized there wasn't anybody else at the table; he *must* be talking to her.

'What was?' she asked warily, searching for a trap.

'The dance,' Jeff said. 'I knew Monsignor was a puritan, but I never expected anything like that.'

'Well, they shouldn't have gone into the equipment closet,' Marilyn said stiffly, allying herself with the priest.

Jeff tried another tack. 'But calling Mr. Balsam a heretic? What was that all about?'

Marilyn shrugged. She didn't see how she could defend the priest against Mr. Balsam; he'd been too nice to her. But she wasn't going to agree with Jeff, either. 'I don't know,' she said carefully. Then she relented. 'It was pretty weird, wasn't it?'

'Weird isn't the word,' Jeff said. 'It was really gross. I mean, just because Mr. Balsam isn't a priest doesn't make him a heretic. Jesus, who uses words like "heretic" anymore, anyway? If you ask me, Mr. Balsam's the best thing to hit this dump in years!'

'He probably won't stay,' Marilyn commented.

'Why would he? Would you?' Without waiting for an answer, Jeff went right on talking. 'But I'm glad he's here now. I like his class; he really makes me think about things.'

'I know,' Marilyn said. 'But sometimes I'm more confused after his class than I was before. I mean, I used to think I understood things pretty well. But since I've been in his class, I just don't know anymore. Those rats are weird. It seems like he can make them do anything.'

'It's just conditioning,' Jeff said smugly. Then he frowned. 'I wonder if you can condition people the same way you condition rats?'

Marilyn shrugged. 'Why don't you ask Mr. Balsam?' There was something else on her mind. 'That isn't really why his class makes me nervous,' she said. 'It just seems like the more I find out about psychology, the worse I feel about myself.' Then, realizing what she'd admitted, Marilyn flushed. But suddenly Jeff was smiling at her.

'I wouldn't worry about it if I were you,' he grinned. 'I mean, you obviously aren't as bad off as some people around here.' He nodded toward the door. Marilyn followed his glance. Judy Nelson was coming into the cafeteria.

The room fell silent. They had all been waiting for this moment; they had all known that Judy was back at school today, that she had spent the morning in Monsignor's office. No one knew what had gone on in there; but no one imagined it had been pleasant. Now here she was, sailing into the cafeteria as if nothing had happened. From the table next to Marilyn and Jeff, Janet Connally called out.

'Over here, Judy.'

While Marilyn and Jeff looked on, Judy slid into a chair and was surrounded by her friends. The questions began.

Judy was enjoying it. They were hanging on her every word, and every couple of minutes someone she hardly knew stopped and welcomed her back to St. Francis Xavier's. They all wanted to know what had happened to her; first in the hospital, then when she got home, and, most important, what had gone on this morning in Monsignor's office.

Judy answered the questions calmly, her voice soft and ethereal. As they listened to her, her friends began to feel that they were talking to a new Judy Nelson, a Judy who had passed through the valley of death and been transformed. It was exactly the impression Judy intended to give.

As Marilyn watched the scene being played at the next table, she began to wonder what had happened to Judy, if the attempt on her own life had really changed her, or if she was putting on an act. Chiding herself for the unkind thought, she turned back to Jeff. He wasn't there.

She glanced quickly back to the table where Judy was still regaling her friends, and saw that Jeff had joined Judy's group, and was hanging on her words along with everyone else. And then, as she watched, Mr. Balsam came into the cafeteria. She looked up hopefully; he always stopped to greet her. But today he walked right past her, intent on something else. Marilyn watched miserably as even Mr. Balsam joined the group around Judy Nelson. A couple of minutes later the teacher rose, and Marilyn's hopes surged again. Now he would pause at her table. But he didn't. Before Marilyn could summon the courage to call out to him, he was gone. Sadly, she turned her attention back to Judy Nelson's table.

Karen Morton had grown restive. She was tired of listening to Judy. Besides, didn't anyone want to hear what had happened to her at the dance? It wasn't fair. Ordinarily, the encounter with the Monsignor would be the major topic for the day, but Judy had eclipsed her. She stared glumly down at her hands. Then inspiration struck.

'Trying to kill yourself isn't such a big deal,' she said breaking into Judy's monologue. She was pleased when Judy fell silent and stared at her.

'Have you tried it?' Judy said knowingly. Karen smiled and held up her hands.

'How do you think I got these?' she said, displaying her palms. The scabs were nearly healed, but still clearly visible.

'Those?' Penny Anderson laughed. 'I thought you said you didn't know how you got those!'

'I just didn't want to admit it,' Karen said. She felt herself losing control of the conversation.

Judy Nelson confirmed the feeling. 'If they weren't even bad enough to put you in the hospital, I don't think they count,' she said acidly. 'Besides, why should you want to kill yourself?'

'I'm not sure,' Karen began, but Penny cut her off.

'I'll give you a reason,' she said. 'I've decided I'm going to take Jim Mulvey away from you.'

Karen's mouth dropped open. All of a sudden it had all gone wrong. All she'd wanted was a little attention. Now they were all laughing at her, and Penny was saying she was going to take Jim away. That wasn't what she'd intended at all. She glared at Penny.

'You have about as much chance of doing that as Marilyn Crane!' she snapped. Then she stood up and walked quickly out of the cafeteria.

The remark hit Marilyn like a slap in the face, and her hand suddenly let go of the sandwich she was eating. She stared down into her lap, and her eyes filled with tears as she surveyed the purple stain that was spreading from the lump of jelly lying on her pale yellow skirt. Now she would have to spend the rest of the day pretending everyone wasn't staring at her dirty skirt. She stuffed the rest of her lunch back into its bag and hurried out of the room.

She started for her locker but suddenly changed her mind. Instead, she made her way to the church, and slipped into the pew in front of the Blessed Virgin. She reached into her purse to pull out her rosary beads. Before she found them her hand closed on something else.

It was the package of razor blades.

Her fingers closed on them and they felt good to her. Then, suddenly frightened, she dropped the blades and found the rosary. She began praying.

When she left the church thirty minutes later, Marilyn had almost succeeded in forgetting about the stain on her skirt. She hurried toward her locker and spun the dial quickly, intent on tossing the remains of her lunch into the metal box, and picking up her books for the afternoon. She pulled open the locker door.

Marilyn Crane screamed, but the scream was cut off as she gagged. A wave of nausea broke over her. Her Bible lay open on the bottom of her locker; on top of it was a white rat, its fur stained by the blood and gore that was oozing from it. Its throat had been slit, and it was disembowelled. The nausea passed, and the tears began. Marilyn Crane sank to the concrete floor, sobbing hysterically. Moments later Sister Marie appeared and gathered Marilyn into her arms. Then she led her slowly away toward the nurse's office.

Peter Balsam sat in his classroom after school, three books spread out in front of him. He was reading snatches from one page, then changing to another book, reading a paragraph here and a paragraph there, then picking up the third book. Slowly he was piecing it all together. And in its own weird way it was starting to make a strange kind of sense. He heard a noise at the door and glanced up. Karen Morton was standing uneasily in the doorframe.

'Can I come in?' she asked tentatively.

'I'm kind of busy,' Balsam said, hoping she'd go away. She stood her ground.

'It'll only take a minute.' Karen advanced into the room. Peter Balsam pushed the books to one side, and glanced at his watch. Maybe he could hold her to the minute.

'What is it?'

'I'm not sure,' Karen said uncertainly. Then, seeing the impatience on Balsam's face, she hurried on. 'It's Judy, I guess. She seems—' She hunted for the right word. '—different I guess.'

Is that all? Balsam thought to himself. 'Well, of course she does,' he said easily. 'But I don't think she is, really. Oh, she may think she is, but don't forget: right now she's the centre of attention around here. It'll all calm down in a couple of days, and things will be back to normal.'

Karen started to say something, but Peter cut her off. 'Look, I'm kind of busy right now. Can this wait till tomorrow?' He picked up one of the books, and had already started to read another paragraph. He had finally found the saint he was looking for, and he promptly put Karen Morton out of his mind.

The girl looked at him for a moment. She needed to talk, but he didn't want to listen. She felt her anger growing, and started out of the room. And then, just as she was at the door, she spun around.

'Maybe I should try to kill myself, like Judy!' she cried. 'Then maybe you'd pay some attention to me.'

The words jarred Peter loose from the book in front of him, but Karen was already gone. He could hear her feet pounding the floor as she ran down the hall. He started to get up to follow her, but another figure appeared in the door of Room 16.

Monsignor Vernon.

The two men faced each other coldly.

'You handled that rather badly,' the priest commented.

'You aren't in any position to criticize,' Balsam said icily, remembering the incident Saturday night.

The Monsignor ignored the remark. 'What happened?' he said, and Peter knew the question was being put as the principal of the school. He explained briefly.

'I should have given her more time, I suppose,' he finished. 'But I'm afraid I was too involved in my reading.'

'Oh?' the priest said, advancing toward the desk. 'What is it that's so fascinating?'

Peter quickly gathered the books together and shoved them into the bottom drawer of his desk.

'It's not that interesting, really,' he said as he closed the drawer firmly. 'Just some old psychology texts.'

The priest seemed to accept his explanation.

'There's going to be a meeting of the Society tonight,' he said. 'At the rectory, the usual time.'

'I won't be there,' Peter said.

The priest stared at him.

'Yes,' he said. 'You will be there. We need you.'

And then he was gone. Peter stared after him. There had been something in the priest's voice, not a note of command, but something else. It was a note of knowledge, as if he didn't feel that he needed to order Peter to attend that night; it was as if the priest had some sort of secret knowledge, a knowledge that told him that something would compel Peter's attendance at the Society of St. Peter Martyr.

Balsam pulled the books out of his desk drawer, and left the school.

Two hours later, when he had finished his reading, it all made sense to him. Crazy sense, a sense he had difficulty accepting, but sense nevertheless. The Monsignor was right: he would attend the meeting of the Society of St. Peter Martyr that evening. But only long enough to confront them with what they were doing, and why.

And then he would leave. If they wanted to go on without him, let them. Peter didn't think they would.

If the conclusions he had come to were correct, they needed him. But they would never have him.

TWENTY

Karen Morton hurried down the front steps of the school, her eyes straight ahead, as if by looking to either side she might tip a delicate balance and give way to the tears that were welling inside her. She wouldn't cry. She would go straight home and spend the rest of the afternoon by herself. If nobody wanted to talk to her, that was fine with her; she certainly wouldn't make them.

It was Judy's fault, she told herself. Judy was supposed to be her friend. Some friend! When Karen had tried to talk about what she had done to herself, about gouging her hands, Judy had laughed at her. Well, maybe not out loud, but inside she had been laughing. And everybody was paying Judy all kinds of attention, even Mr. Balsam. Mr. Balsam should have listened to *her*. Judy's problems were all over with. Couldn't he see that? But what about Karen? Who would talk to her?

Ahead of her, Karen saw Marilyn Crane hurrying down the hill. For the first time, Karen knew how Marilyn must feel. She wanted to call out to her, wanted Marilyn to wait for her. But why should Marilyn wait? Wasn't Karen part of the group that had been making Marilyn's life miserable for years? Maybe she should apologize to Marilyn. No, that wouldn't work either. There was too much to apologize for. Besides, she didn't want to talk to Marilyn. She wanted to talk to a man. She wanted to talk to her father. He would have understood. He would have put his arms around her, and held her, and told her that it was all going to be all right. But he was dead, and there wasn't anybody else...

She heard a car pull up beside her, and recognized the sound of the motor immediately. Jim Mulvey. She kept walking; kept staring straight ahead.

She heard the sound of his horn, then his voice. 'Karen? Hey, Karen?'

She stopped, and turned slowly. He was grinning and waving to her.

'Hop in,' he called. She shook her head and started to turn away.

'Hey,' Jim said, getting out of the car. 'What's wrong? It's me, Jim.' He caught up with her and took her arm. She wanted to shake his hand off, but didn't.

When she turned to face him, Jim realized that something really was wrong with Karen. It looked as though she was about to start crying. The bantering quality left his voice, and it softened.

'Get in the car, Karen,' he said. 'I'll take you home.' Karen let herself be led to the car, and for the first time since she'd known him, Jim Mulvey opened the door for her. She sat staring ahead as he circled the car and slid behind the wheel. They drove in silence.

'Do you want to talk about it?' Jim finally said. Karen shook her head. A minute later he slowed the car and pulled over to the kerb. He turned to face her.

'I heard about what Penny Anderson said at lunch today,' he said. 'If that's what got you upset, forget it.'

'That's not it,' Karen said dully. 'Why don't you just take me home?'

But there was something in her voice that told Jim that she didn't really want to be taken home. He put the car in gear, but instead of driving Karen home, he headed out of town.

'Where are we going?' Karen asked, not really caring.

'Out by the lake.'

'I want to go home.'

'No, you don't,' Jim said definitely. 'You want to talk, so we're going to go sit by the lake and talk.'

'I hate it out there,' Karen complained. 'It smells bad, and there's nothing there but scrub juniper.'

'It's better than nothing,' Jim said.

They finished the ten-minute ride in silence. Jim drove through the picnic area, and parked at the end of the dirt road that led to a primitive boat ramp. The lake was deserted. The silence lengthened, and Jim wondered what he should say. Then he decided not to say anything. Instead, he put his arm around Karen, and pulled her toward him.

She tried to resist when he kissed her, but his arms tightened around her, and his mouth found hers. And then, as the kiss deepened, Karen felt her body responding almost in spite of herself. She needed to be held, she needed to be caressed, she needed to be loved. Her arms went around him.

'Love me, Jim,' she whispered. 'Please love me.' She heard him groan as her hand went to his lap and her fingers touched his erection. She pressed closer to him and helped him as he began undressing her.

'Jesus,' Jim breathed half an hour later. 'I never had it like that before. Let me know the next time you need to talk to someone.' He leered at her, and winked, and Karen felt something break inside her.

He used me, she thought. He doesn't love me. He just wanted to fuck me. Fuck me. Fuck me.

She repeated the words to herself, over and over again, trying to make them take on that meaninglessness that comes when a word is used too often. It didn't work.

She had needed to be loved, and she had only gotten laid. She tried to convince herself that there wasn't any difference, but she knew there was. And now all the things they had been saying about her were true.

'Take me home,' she said quietly.

Jim Mulvey started the car, turned it around, and began driving back to Neilsville.

Twenty minutes later he stopped in front of the Morton house. He let the engine idle, but didn't get out of the car.

'Aren't you going to open the door for me?' Karen asked.

'You can do it yourself,' Jim said. He wasn't sure why, but he was suddenly angry with Karen. All they'd done was get it on, for Christ's sake. It should have made her feel better. And she'd sure acted like she liked it when it was happening. But now, nothing. Well, if she couldn't talk to him, she could damned well open the door herself. He glared at her.

Karen opened the car door, scrambled out, and slammed it behind her. Then, without looking back, she hurried toward the house. Not that it would have made any difference if she had looked back; as soon as the door had slammed, she'd heard the tyres scream as Jim raced away.

Karen went inside, fixed herself a TV dinner, and tried to concentrate on the television. It didn't help. She needed to talk to someone, but there wasn't anybody to talk to. She glanced at the clock – her mother wouldn't be home for a couple of hours yet. But Karen had to talk to her, had to talk to her now. She picked up the phone and called her mother at work.

'Hi, Mom,' she said, trying to keep her voice light.

'What is it?' Harriet Morton asked. All her tables were full; she really didn't have time to talk. 'Are you all right?'

'I'm okay. I was just wondering if you could come home early tonight.'

'If we're going to eat, I have to work,' Harriet snapped. She dropped the phone back on the hook, picked up the coffee pot, and got back to work.

Karen stared at the dead phone, and felt like crying again. Even her mother wouldn't talk to her. She held back the tears and decided not to think about it. She wouldn't think about anything. She'd just watch television till her mother came home, then she'd let it all out. Only a couple more hours. She glanced at the clock.

Almost ten.

Only one more hour.

And then the phone rang. Karen picked it up eagerly; maybe her mother had changed her mind and was coming home.

'Hello?' she said. 'Mother?'

But it wasn't Harriet Morton's voice at all. It was someone else, another voice, a voice Karen thought she recognized.

'You have sinned,' the voice said. 'You are evil. You must repent. Repent!'

And then it was over. The phone went dead in Karen's hand. She dropped it to the floor this time, not even bothering to put it back in its cradle.

So it was already out.

The talking was already starting.

And her mother still wasn't home.

She stared at the clock. Only five after ten.

The desolation swept over Karen Morton, but she still wouldn't let herself cry.

Maybe she should have let herself cry.

Maybe if she had let herself cry, she wouldn't have done what she did next.

Maybe she wouldn't have gone upstairs to the bathroom, locked the door, filled the tub with warm water, and begun cutting herself.

Maybe Karen Morton should have cried instead. But she didn't.

They sat like six birds of prey, the black of their clerical garb accentuating the paleness of their faces. They stared balefully at Peter Balsam, but he maintained his calm, returning them stare for stare, matching the coldness in their eyes with his own icy demeanour.

Inside, Peter Balsam was quavering.

He could tell they didn't believe him; he was sure they thought he had gone crazy.

The silence went on; Peter Balsam was determined not to be the one to break it. He wondered what was going through their minds. Had they simply decided to put what he had told them out of their minds entirely? Or were they thinking about his words, mulling them over, examining them?

'Just what is it you think you're going to tell the Bishop?' Monsignor Vernon finally said.

For the first time, Peter Balsam squirmed. Why had he told them he was going to go to the Bishop? Why hadn't he simply told them he was through with the Society of St. Peter Martyr, and let it go at that?

But they had insisted on knowing why he was leaving, and he had told them.

They had listened in silence as he told them about the chanting; they knew about that. It came to him then that the same things happened to all of them that had happened to him during those weird services: they knew something was happening, but they didn't know what. He tried to tell them. He wanted to tell them that they were all perverts, to detail for them exactly what they were doing during their rituals. But he found he couldn't. They were, after all, still priests. Priests, to be respected. The traditions he had grown up with took over, and he found himself unable to describe for them what went on between them. He merely told them that he had found the whole thing unspeakable.

'But you'll be able to tell it to the Bishop?' Monsignor had said mildly at the end of Balsam's recital.

'I won't have to,' Peter said quietly. 'I have a recording of everything that went on at the last meeting.'

'A recording?' Father Prine said blankly. 'What do you mean, a recording?'

Peter patiently explained it again.

'I wanted to know what goes on at the services,' he said. 'I couldn't remember myself; all I could remember was going into some kind of trance, and it being much later than I thought it should be when I came out of it.'

'Not unusual during times of devotion,' the Monsignor said.

'It had nothing to do with devotion,' Peter replied, his anger rising. 'I don't know what it had to do with, but I wanted to find out what was going on. So I brought a recorder to the meeting, and recorded the whole thing. When I played the tape back, I was sick. Literally sick. If I played the tape for you, you'd all be sick.'

'You're exaggerating, of course,' Monsignor Vernon began, but Peter cut him off.

'I'm not exaggerating,' he snapped. 'The whole thing was absolutely depraved.'

'I think we've heard enough,' Monsignor Vernon said, standing up. 'All you can tell us is that you heard a language that you think – you *think*, mind you, you don't *know* – might be some kind of mixture of Latin and Italian. And that we were all indulging in something you call depraved. Something you won't describe to us.'

'I don't see that it's necessary,' Balsam said. 'I'm sure that when the Bishop hears the tape, he'll be convinced.'

'Convinced?' It was the Monsignor again. He was pacing the room now. 'Convinced of what?'

'Well, for one thing, I think he'll be convinced to put an end to your Society.'

The Monsignor chuckled. 'Convinced by the words of a heretic?' Peter noted that the fanatical light was beginning to come into Vernon's eyes. He told himself to be careful.

'Heretic again,' he said softly. 'Well, at least I know where that's coming from now.'

'You finally figured it out?' The priest's voice was as soft as Peter's own.

Peter nodded gravely. 'That, and a couple of other things.' He stood up. When he spoke again he tried to keep his voice level. 'Monsignor, I don't intend to spend any more time here discussing something that I don't think you're mentally competent to discuss. I know you think I'm a heretic – whatever that word means to you. But *I* think the Bishop is much more likely to come to the conclusion that you're sick. After all, when he hears your voice claiming to be St. Peter Martyr, and calling down the wrath of God on the sinners and heretics, what else can he conclude?'

If he had expected an outburst of protest, Peter Balsam was disappointed. A sudden silence fell over the small study, as the priests exchanged glances. But the atmosphere in the room had changed. No longer was it filled with hostility toward Peter Balsam. Suddenly there was something else. A sense of anticipation, as if something long awaited was about to occur.

Monsignor Vernon had stopped his pacing, and was staring at Balsam. The other five priests all looked uncertainly toward the Monsignor.

'Can it be true?' Balsam heard one of them whisper. But before he could answer the voice of Monsignor Vernon roared over him.

'*What did you say?*'

'I asked what else the Bishop can conclude,' Peter said, trying to ignore the rage in the priest's voice.

'About St. Peter Martyr,' the Monsignor thundered.

'During the last service you claimed to be St. Peter Martyr, and exhorted God to hand down punishment on what you called the sinners and heretics.'

'It's happened,' Father Martinelli breathed.

Peter whirled and stared at the old man. An expression of awe had come over the priest's face, and he was gazing at the Monsignor with adoration.

'What happened?' Peter asked in a low voice, though he was sure he knew the answer.

'He's come to us at last,' Father Prine said softly. 'After all this time, St. Peter Martyr is finally among us.'

Peter Balsam sank back into a chair. It couldn't be happening. And yet it was. They had heard him, but what he had told them hadn't shaken their faith in their young leader. Instead it had deepened it. Peter Balsam remembered the words of the Bishop. '*They want to Believe. They need to lean on each other for support.*' Now, when they should finally have realized that the person they were all leaning on was unbalanced, they only drew closer.

Balsam's eyes moved to the Monsignor. An expression of rapture had come over him, and he was staring upward, his hands clasped in prayer, his lips moving silently. Suddenly he looked at Balsam, and the teacher saw the fierce light in the priest's eyes.

'And still you don't believe?' he said softly.

'No,' Peter said. 'I don't believe any of it.'

'But you *must* believe,' Monsignor Vernon said. 'I tried to tell you so long ago, when we were in school together. But the time wasn't right. But you must have known. It's in the names.'

'The names,' Peter said tiredly. 'You always come back to the names, don't you?' He peered quizzically at the Monsignor; he wasn't sure the priest was listening. But the others were. Balsam looked from one old face to another, and saw the same puzzlement in each of them.

'Hasn't he told you?' he asked them. They stared at him, waiting for him to continue. When he did, Balsam chose his words carefully.

'St. Peter Martyr was a man by the name of Piero da Verona. Peter Vernon, if you want to believe it. And he was killed by another man, a man named Piero da Balsama. Get it?'

'Peter Balsam,' Father Martinelli whispered. 'It's happening all over again! You are St. Acerinus.'

'No!' Peter snapped. 'I'm not St. Acerinus, I'm not Piero da Balsama. Any more than Monsignor Vernon is St. Peter Martyr. It's coincidence. Nothing more!'

And then it happened. Monsignor Vernon's voice was quiet, but it carried throughout the small room.

'I *am* St. Peter Martyr,' he said.

It's a nightmare, Peter Balsam thought to himself. It isn't happening. None of it can be happening.

But it was. Around him, the five priests knelt, staring up at Monsignor Vernon. For them, in that moment, Monsignor Peter Vernon became St. Peter Martyr. Peter Balsam stood up, and his eyes met the Monsignor's over the heads of the kneeling clerics.

'I won't do it,' he said softly. 'I won't carry it any further. I won't be your heretic, and I won't kill you. If you really need a St. Acerinus, you'll have to find him somewhere else.'

But the priest didn't seem to hear him. He stood quietly. His face was calm but the fanatic light gleamed in his eyes.

Peter Balsam walked from the study, and from the rectory. It would have to end now, he told himself. They needed him to sustain the fantasy. But he had withdrawn, and now it would have to end. And then, as he started down the hill, he heard it.

The chanting had begun again.

It had not ended.

Somewhere in Neilsville, a clock was striking the hour. It was ten, and the Society of St. Peter Martyr was holding a service, and Karen Morton was preparing to die.

Karen lay in the tub of warm water, and wondered why it didn't hurt. Judy Nelson was right; there was no pain at all. Only a kind of numbness.

Karen watched the blood flow from her wrists, watched it form strange patterns in the water, then move swiftly around her to turn the entire tub a bright pink.

As the pink slowly deepened into red, Karen wondered if she was doing the right thing. But it was too late. Too many things had gone wrong, and there was no one to talk to. If only there had been someone to talk to, someone to listen to her. But there hadn't been, and as the redness in the tub grew steadily deeper, Karen realized she didn't really care. Not any more.

She began to pray, but she kept her eyes open. She wanted to see the colour of her death, as if perhaps by watching her life stain the water she could figure out why it had all gone wrong.

She never saw the colour of death. Long after her eyes drifted closed, the water continued to darken. When she died, it wasn't from the bleeding.

It was from drowning.

At quarter of eleven, Karen's head disappeared beneath the surface of the crimson water.

At eleven-fifteen Harriet Morton unlocked the front door. 'Karen?' she called. When there was no answer, she called a little louder: 'Karen!?' Still no answer. Yet the house did not seem empty: she was sure Karen had not gone out.

Harriet went upstairs, but didn't call out to Karen again. When she saw the bathroom door, she felt a sudden surge of relief. Karen was in the tub. Of course. That was why she hadn't heard Harriet's first call.

Harriet tapped at the door. 'Karen?' she called. 'Are you in there?'

There was no response, so Harriet tried the door. It was locked. And then the fear hit her.

She pounded on the door, and called out her daughter's name. The silence buffeted against her.

Harriet picked up the telephone in the upstairs hall. The police. She would call the police. But something was wrong with the telephone. There was no dial tone. Only a strange buzzing sound.

Harriet Morton began to scream. She hurled herself against the bathroom door, and it burst inward. The sight of the bathtub, filled with red liquid, choked off her screaming.

At the end of the tub, barely breaking the surface, a foot was visible. The toenails were painted green. Harriet knew that only her daughter had ever painted her toenails green.

The neighbours called the police as soon as Harriet Morton

began crying out into the night; the police called an ambulance. A moment later the night was shattered by the screaming of sirens.

By midnight a doctor had sedated Harriet Morton, and Karen had been taken away. But still the crowd lingered in front of the Morton house, talking quietly among themselves, trying to tell each other what had happened, trying to find a reason for the tragedy that had struck their town. Jim Mulvey was there. He wondered if it had been his fault.

TWENTY-ONE

Peter Balsam sat waiting outside Monsignor's Vernon office the next morning. He was waiting to resign.

There didn't seem to be anything else to do; he had discussed it with Margo late into the night before, then again this morning. They had gone over it all, piece by piece, trying to make some sense out of it. First Judy Nelson. Then the Society of St. Peter Martyr. Now Karen Morton. And Karen was dead.

There had to be a connection. Somehow all the strangeness in Neilsville was coalescing; Judy and Karen were its victims. And Peter was sure that the Society of St. Peter Martyr was involved.

But so was Peter Balsam. Margo had tried to talk him out of it, but all night long his certainty had grown. He had been Judy Nelson's teacher, and she had tried to kill herself. He had joined the Society of St. Peter Martyr, and Karen Morton had killed herself. Another of his students. It was as if whatever force was loose in Neilsville had been intensified first by the arrival of Peter Balsam, and then by his involvement in the Society. And so he would leave. He had already left the Society (for all the good it had done) and now he would leave St. Francis Xavier's and Neilsville.

And he would talk to the Bishop.

But first he would resign, and then he would go to Sister Marie for an exact translation of what was on the tape. He heard the heavy tread of the Monsignor, and stood up.

Monsignor Vernon stepped into the reception room and nodded curtly to Balsam. 'I expected you to be here this morning,' he said. 'How long will it take?'

'What?' Balsam said, his guard dropping a little.

'Why, whatever it is you want to talk about this morning. It's Karen Morton, I assume.'

'Her, among other things,' Balsam said carefully. He felt suddenly off balance, as if he had had an advantage, and lost it.

They moved into the Monsignor's office, and the priest took his seat behind the desk, motioning to Peter to take the visitor's chair.

'No, thanks,' Peter said. 'This won't take long, and I'd rather stand.' He cast around in his mind for the right words, and decided there were none. 'I'm leaving,' he said.

The priest's brows rose a fraction of an inch, but he said nothing. He simply sat in his chair, staring at the teacher, waiting for him to continue.

'I suppose you want to know why,' Balsam said when the silence became unbearable.

'I think I have the right to know, yes,' Monsignor Vernon said calmly. 'I imagine it has something to do with Karen Morton.'

'Among other things.'

'Tell me about them.'

Peter Balsam, without thinking about it, sank into the chair opposite the priest. 'It isn't only Karen, although what happened to her was the final straw. I feel responsible for her death.'

'You're not,' the priest said, almost too definitely.

'Well, it's neither here nor there now, is it? But I do feel responsible. She wanted to talk to me yesterday, and I brushed her off. I shouldn't have done that. I should have known how important it was to her. I'm a psychologist, after all. But I didn't see. And I'm obviously not much of a teacher, either am I? I mean, just look what's happening to my students.' The feeble attempt at black humour failed even for himself.

'I've told you before, and I'm telling you again,' the priest snapped impatiently, 'you aren't responsible for Judy and Karen. You aren't a priest.'

'But it isn't just them,' Peter said softly. 'There's more.'

The priest's head came up and his eyes bored into Peter's. Peter hesitated, but forced himself to say what he'd come to say.

'I'm going to talk to the Bishop about you,' he said, unable to meet the Monsignor's eyes. 'I'm going to see him as soon as I'm released from my position here, to tell him about the Society of St. Peter Martyr. What you and those priests are doing is grounds for excommunication.'

'Indeed?' the priest said incredulously. 'Our prayers may be fervent, but they are still only prayers.'

Something snapped inside Peter; he leaped to his feet and stood towering over the priest.

'Prayers!' he thundered. 'You call that prayer? You have no idea what you're talking about. Fornication! That's what you're up to! You and all of them.'

'*How dare you!*' the Monsignor roared. He was on his feet, his rage almost a palpable force in the room. 'Have you any idea what you're saying?' If it was meant to intimidate Balsam, it failed. The teacher stood his ground, and glared right back at the priest.

'Cocksucker,' he snarled. The priest recoiled.

'What did you say?' There was a look of horror on his face.

'The truth,' Balsam said softly. 'I called you a cocksucker and it's the truth. That's what you do, all of you. You get yourselves stoned some way, and you start in. And the saddest part of it is that you don't even know it.'

The priest sagged into his chair and stared at Peter. 'So that's what you meant last night?' he asked softly. 'When you said we were depraved?' Peter nodded, and the priest shook his head gently. 'Then it's even worse than I thought. I thought you were telling us we were perverted in a religious sense. But it's worse than that, isn't it? It isn't enough for you, is it? Now you have to accuse us of – of—' He broke off, unable to say the words. He stared balefully at Balsam. 'Piero da Balsama,' he said softly, 'you killed me once, and now you try to disgrace me. But you will not do it. This time I shall triumph.'

Now it was Balsam's turn to sag into a chair.

The man was insane. There wasn't any other word for it But how should he deal with it? He tried to remember the books. The books had had the answers, but what were they? *Buy into the insanity.* That was it.

He remembered the technique. It was sometimes used in dealing with paranoia; Balsam was sure the priest was paranoid.

'What makes you think so?' he said now. 'If I beat you last time, what makes you think I won't beat you again? Why should this time be any different?'

The priest's eyes flashed around the room as if he were looking for a hidden weapon.

'I know,' he said softly. 'I just know.'

'Did God tell you?' Balsam sneered the word 'God,' trying to make it sound tainted.

'You don't believe me, do you?' Monsignor Vernon said. 'But why should you? I'd almost forgotten – you're a heretic, aren't you?'

'If you say so,' Balsam said evenly.

The priest continued to glare at him, but then something happened. It was as if a switch had been thrown, and the light suddenly faded from the Monsignor's eyes. He shook himself slightly, as if waking up from a sleep.

'What were we talking about?' he said, totally puzzled. Balsam thought fast; the paranoid state could have passed, or this could be simply another manifestation of it. He'd have to be careful.

'My resignation,' he said. The priest still appeared to be puzzled, but then his face cleared.

'Ah,' he said, clearing his throat. 'Of course.' He smiled genially, and leaned toward Peter. 'Well, of course I can't stop you, but I'm afraid I'm going to have to ask you to wait a while. Oh, not long,' he said quickly as Peter started to protest. 'Just a few weeks. You see, I spoke to the Bishop this morning.'

'The Bishop?' Peter said blankly.

The priest nodded. 'He called me early, about Karen Morton. He's very concerned about the situation here, as am I. He seems to think there's something going on here, that whatever happened, first to Judy Nelson, and then, last night, to Karen Morton, are somehow connected.' The priest's tone suggested that he didn't agree with the Bishop's assessment. 'At any rate, he thinks it would be a good idea if we made the fullest possible use of your background in psychology. For some reason, he seems to think that of everyone here, you're the best qualified to deal with whatever's happening. Not, of course,' he added, almost as an afterthought, 'that anything *is* happening here. However, under the circumstances we're going to have to ask you to stay a while longer.'

Balsam thought it over. The Bishop, of course, was right. His resolution began to waver.

'And there's something else,' the priest said sombrely. 'Were you aware that Karen Morton left a note?'

'A note?' No, Peter certainly wasn't aware of it.

'Yes,' the priest lied. 'A very disturbing note. She said something about us – you and me – to the effect that she thought, and I think I can quote it, "something is going on between them." Nonsense, of course, but if you left right now – well, I'm sure you can see my point. There would be talk, wouldn't there?'

Peter Balsam felt defeat wash over him. Yes, he agreed to himself, it certainly would cause talk. Particularly since it was true. But that 'something' had gone on only in the meeting of the Society of St. Peter Martyr. How could Karen have known about that? Or did she? Maybe she had simply hit a nerve by accident. Not that it mattered. Either way, he was caught. Karen Morton was dead, and Peter Balsam was trapped. He looked up at his superior, and knew he was expected to say something.

'All right,' he agreed. 'I'll stay. But I'm still going to talk to the Bishop about the Society.'

'I assumed you were,' the Monsignor said coldly. 'You'll be wasting your time.' He stood up. 'Is there anything else?'

'No,' Peter said, his voice as cold as the priest's. And then something occurred to him. 'Yes, there is,' he added, eyeing Vernon carefully. 'I was wondering where I might find Sister Marie. There's something I need to talk to her about.'

An odd look passed over the priest's face, and Peter felt a surge of triumph. He had shaken the man. But then the Monsignor's face cleared.

'I'm afraid she's not here,' he said smoothly. 'She'll be away for a while.'

'Away?' Peter asked warily. 'What do you mean, "away"?'

'Periodically, Sister Marie goes into retreat.' He smiled thinly. 'I'm afraid her vocation isn't always as strong as it might be, and we've found, both of us, that it helps her to get away from here now and then. She'll be back.'

'But she didn't tell me she was going away,' Peter protested, his hopes suddenly fading.

'Of course she didn't,' the priest said easily. 'Why would she?'

The interview was over.

'You should celebrate the Mass yourself,' Father Martinelli said. He was sitting in the study of the rectory with Monsignor Vernon, though only he was sitting. The Monsignor was pacing.

'It's a sacrilege,' he muttered.

'I don't see how,' Father Martinelli said emphatically. 'Whatever people may think privately, we know tonight's Mass is not for Karen Morton.'

'That isn't the point,' Monsignor Vernon replied. 'Of course we know the Mass isn't for Karen Morton. How could it be? – she wasn't in a state of grace when she died. The point is that the people intend to *make* it a Mass for Karen. And the only way we can prevent that is to cancel the Mass entirely.'

'And what will that accomplish?' the old man asked, tiredly. 'We'll only face the same thing at the next Mass. There is no way we can stop our parishioners from praying for Karen Morton, and I'm not even sure we should try.'

'But it's wrong,' Monsignor Vernon insisted. 'There's no other way of looking at it. When that girl killed herself she committed a sin beyond redemption. She has no rights within the Church whatsoever.'

Father Martinelli sighed, and his ancient mind tried to sort out the problem. Technically, the Monsignor was right, and yet there was more to the problem. In the church, the parishioners were gathering, expecting to hear Mass, needing to hear Mass. Shouldn't their needs be met? He peered out the window of the rectory, and saw the people still streaming up the hill.

It had begun an hour ago. Ordinarily the turnout for a mid-week Mass was next to zero, even in a parish as devout as St. Francis Xavier. But today was different, and there could be only one reason. The people were coming because of Karen Morton. It had been this way all day. As the word of the girl's suicide spread through Neilsville, the people had begun drifting in and out of the church, praying briefly, and leaving only after silently lighting a candle.

And then, half an hour ago, they had begun arriving for the evening Mass. They kept arriving, until the church was as full as it ever was on Easter Sunday. Two things can fill the church, Father Martinelli reflected – the hope of eternal life, and the fear of unexpected, and inexplicable death. He had watched them stream into the church, and been pleased; Father Martinelli didn't really care about why people came to church. He only cared that they came. But with Monsignor Vernon it was different.

For the Monsignor, it wasn't enough that they were there; they had to be there for the right reasons. And to pray for Karen Morton wasn't, in Monsignor's Vernon strict religion, a suitable person. And so they were discussing the possibility of cancelling the Mass entirely.

'I'll have no part of it,' the Monsignor said in a tone that told Father Martinelli the discussion was over. But then he relented. 'If you want to conduct it yourself, I won't stop you. However, the consequences are your responsibility.' Abruptly, the Monsignor left the room.

As he made his way to the church and began the vesting processes, Father Martinelli wondered what consequences the Monsignor could be talking about.

Peter Balsam dipped his fingers in the font, made the sign of the cross, and slipped into one of the back pews. In front of him, he saw Leona Anderson turn and glare. He pretended not to notice, and picked up his prayer book.

He glanced around the church, recognizing some of the people, just as the organ music surged out of the loft, and the service began.

The first disturbance came when the congregation saw that Monsignor Vernon was not conducting the Mass. They buzzed and whispered among themselves as the stooped figure of Father Martinelli moved unsurely up the aisle. Peter quickly searched for the face of the Monsignor, and was not surprised when he didn't find it.

The Mass began, but it was soon apparent that something was happening. Tonight, the responses, which normally brought only a few garbled murmurs from the congregation, came full-throated from the entire body of the church. Father Martinelli appeared to be unaware of anything unusual, and his quavering voice droned steadily on with the Mass. But Peter tried to locate a focal point for the phenomenon. He found it almost immediately.

Tonight, all of Karen Morton's friends, instead of sitting with their families, were knotted together near the centre of the church. All of them – Judy Nelson, Janet Connally, Penny Anderson, and several others. Apart from them, sitting by herself, was Marilyn Crane.

Marilyn had come alone to the evening service, as she always did, and had taken her usual place near the statue of the Blessed Virgin. She had been engrossed in her prayers, begging the Sorrowful Mother to forgive her for the cruel thoughts she had had about Karen Morton in the past, and asking the Queen of Angels to intercede on behalf of Karen, when she had become aware that the church was filling up around her. Yet no one sat next to her. Suddenly she felt conspicuous, and found it difficult to concentrate on her devotions.

Then it began.

It was soft at first, a barely discernible murmur against the full tones of the organ, but then it began to grow, and, as the last chords of the organ died away, the church was filled with a different kind of music, the music of the human voice.

It was the girls.

They were clustered together, and clasping each other's hands, though otherwise it didn't seem that they were aware of each other's presence. Except for Judy Nelson, all of them were wailing, tears streaming down their faces, their heads tilted upward toward the church ceiling, as if they were searching for something in the heights.

Father Martinelli tried to ignore them and raised his voice to continue the Mass over the growing wail.

But the sound continued to grow, and suddenly the girls were on their feet, swaying together, and crying out in a voice that seemed filled as much with exaltation as grief.

Father Martinelli faltered in the service, then stopped altogether. He glanced around for help, but there was none. Instead, he saw only troubled faces looking to him for leadership. Immediately he went into the benediction, and the organist picked up his cue.

As the girls' keening rose, filling the church, the organ blared out, mixing with the high-pitched lamentations and creating a chaos of sound that made the final words of the benediction inaudible.

It didn't matter. Already the congregation was beginning to move nervously toward the doors, embarrassed to be in the presence of such clearly expressed grief, unnerved by the adolescents' display of emotion.

To Peter Balsam, it was obvious that the girls were caught up in a hysterical response to their friend's death. He rose and moved toward them.

But, as quickly as it had begun, it was over. It was as if the girls had come out of a trance, and the moment they became aware of each other again, they looked at each other, giggled nervously, and hurried out of the church. Behind them, more slowly, Judy Nelson walked up the centre aisle. As she passed the spot where Peter Balsam stood, she suddenly turned to him, and smiled. He supposed it was intended as a friendly smile, but it made him cold. He felt a shiver in his back, and quickly looked away. By the time he got hold of himself, and turned back to face her, she was gone.

Only one figure remained in the church. Marilyn Crane sat huddled in her pew, and seemed unaware of what had been going on.

As, indeed, she was. She had been concentrating on the Sorrowful Mother, and when the strange wailing had begun she was sure it was inside her own head. There was no other explanation for it; such sounds as these were never heard in any church Marilyn Crane had ever attended. And then, when they ended, she realized she was alone in the church. She decided that the Blessed Virgin wanted something from her, and was sending her a sign. She approached the statue, and lit a candle.

She waited for the message.

For a long time nothing happened. Then the urge swept through her. She wanted to put her hand in the flame. She fought the urge, but it grew inside her: this was the message from the Sorrowful Mother; this was the sign.

Marilyn Crane reached out and put the palm of her hand over the flame of the votive light. She lowered her hand until she could see the flame touching her skin. There was no pain. The Virgin was protecting her from pain. It was just as Judy Nelson had told her. It was beautiful.

Marilyn held her hand steady, and didn't remove it from the fire until she smelled the sickly-sweet odour of charring flesh. When she did pull her hand from the flame, she stood still for a few moments, staring awestruck at the wound. Yes, she told herself, Judy was right. There is no such thing as pain.

As she pondered the new truth, Marilyn Crane crossed herself, thanked the Blessed Virgin for the message, and slowly walked from the church.

Peter Balsam had almost reached the sanctuary doors when something caught his eye, and he paused. Then he realized he was staring at one of the saints.

St. Acerinus.

St. Acerinus, the canonized Piero da Balsama.

The saint seemed to be staring down at him accusingly, as if Peter had started something, but not finished it. Peter Balsam told himself that he was being ridiculous, that he was imagining things. He tore himself away from the saint's sightless gaze, and started from the church. But he had a feeling of being watched.

When he turned around, Monsignor Vernon was standing in the chancel, observing him, a look of strange serenity on his face.

TWENTY-TWO

Earlier they had all gone to church; now they were gathered on Main Street, the parents at the drugstore, their children across the street. There was something new in Neilsville – a discotheque – and the St. Francis Xavier crowd had flocked there tonight.

Leona Anderson stabbed fretfully at her banana split, part of her attention focused on the meagre size of the dessert (which she was sure had shrunk by at least fifty percent since she had been a teen-ager), the rest of it silently protesting the noise from across the street.

The Praying Mantis – she wondered how they came up with such a silly name – had opened only a month ago, and Leona's worst fears had been immediately justified, A few of the Neilsville High students had drifted in, but it quickly became obvious that the disco was going to be the headquarters for the youngsters from St. Francis Xavier's. Leona had visions of drug traffic – or worse. She was sure the opening of the Praying Mantis spelled the end of decent living in Neilsville.

'Isn't there a law against making that much noise?' Inez Nelson complained from the opposite side of the booth. Leona shook her head grimly.

'I checked, of course,' she said. 'It's zoned for commercial use. They can do whatever they want.' Her tone implied that she was sure they were doing exactly that, and that 'whatever they want' went far beyond blasting a jukebox at top volume. 'I'm not sure we should allow the girls to go there,' Leona continued. She glared out the window at the offending building, as if by simply staring at it she could make it disappear.

'Oh, I don't know,' Inez Nelson said tentatively. 'Things just aren't the same as they were when we were teen-agers. I suppose you have to bend with the wind. Times change.'

'Do they?' Leona asked crossly. 'Then why are we sitting here in the same drugstore we sat in twenty years ago? It's more than that, Inez. Sometimes I feel as if we've lost control of things.'

Inez stirred her coffee silently, wishing she could deny the truth of what Leona had said. If she had ever been in control, that time was certainly over by now. Ever since Judy had come home from the hospital, Inez had felt like she was walking on eggs. Being manipulated. She knew it was wrong, knew she should be more forceful with her daughter, but she couldn't. She just couldn't. She was too frightened of what might happen. Particularly after last night. Inez knew she'd never forget the look on Harriet Morton's face as they led her out of the house to take her to the hospital.

Leona's right, she thought. We have lost control. She followed Leona's gaze and she, too, began conjuring up images of the bizarre things that must be going on inside the Praying Mantis. A few minutes later the noise became too much for them, and the women fled.

The truth was that not much at all was going on in the discotheque. The jukebox was blaring, but from inside the large room, the music seemed somewhat hollow and desperate.

A few of the teen-agers were dancing, but it was a desultory kind of dancing. For the most part, they were clustered around tables, sitting, the music vibrating against them, trying to forget that Karen Morton was no longer with them.

Except for Janet Connally, whose mother had insisted that she go home right after the services ended, the group of girls who had created the disturbance at the church were there. But they were no longer all together. Judy Nelson was sitting alone, taking in her surroundings unhappily.

It was sleazy, hastily thrown together, without the money to do it right. Rock posters covered the walls; a sensuously sweating Mick Jagger, apparently in a state of sustained orgasm, presided over a gallery of his second- and third-rate imitators.

A makeshift light panel had been tied into the jukebox, but instead of creating the psychedelic visual symphony that had been intended, the crude box could produce no more than an occasional flash of red or green. Because of the poor quality of the light show, another lighting system had been installed, consisting of several strings of outdoor Christmas lights that glowed eerily in the dimness. In the centre of the room, slowly revolving, hung the immense papier-mâché insect for which the place was named. Had Leona Anderson seen the inside of the Praying Mantis, much of her worry would have been displaced by disgust, and she would have wondered why the kids wanted to be there in the first place. But it was, for the students of St. Francis Xavier's the only game in town.

And so they were gathered, trying in their own way to pretend that everything was all right. It might have worked if Jim Mulvey had not been sitting alone at a table, a constant reminder of Karen Morton's absence.

Penny Anderson broke away from the group she had been standing with, and glanced around. She saw Judy Nelson sitting alone, and started across the room to join her. Before she had taken three steps, she realized that Jim Mulvey was also sitting by himself. On an impulse, Penny changed her course and approached Jim's table.

'Hi', she said. He looked up disinterestedly. 'Okay if I sit down?' Without waiting for an answer, she slipped into the chair next to Jim. He glanced at her once more, not smiling, then turned his attention back to his Coke.

'I wanted to talk to you,' Penny said softly. 'About Karen.' She waited for a reaction, and when there was none, she continued talking. 'We're all going to miss her, you know. I mean, Judy and Janet and me. We've always been sort of a foursome, ever since we were little. Of course, in the last year or so—' Penny suddenly broke off. It had been in the last year or so that Karen had started dating Jim Mulvey.

Now Jim looked at her curiously. 'What were you going to say?' he said bitterly. 'Were you going to say that in the last year or so – *ever since she started going with me* – Karen changed?' Jim stared accusingly at Penny.

'N-no—' Penny stammered. 'I wasn't going to say that at all.'

'Yes, you were,' Jim said flatly, leaving no room for argument. 'Don't you think I know what's been going on? Don't you think I've heard the talk? Hell, I started some of it.' He stared sourly into his Coke, and when he spoke again, Penny wasn't sure he was talking to her. 'It's my fault,' he said so quietly Penny could hardly hear him. 'I never treated her the way she wanted to be treated. I never talked to her. I should have talked to her. If I had, none of this would ever have happened.'

Penny reached out and touched his hand. He seemed so unhappy, so unsure of himself. Not at all like the Jim Mulvey she had grown up with. The cockiness, the self-confidence, had vanished.

'It isn't your fault,' she said. Then, as if trying to convince herself, she added, 'It isn't anyone's fault.'

Jim's head snapped up, and he realized he'd been talking out loud. 'Shut up,' he said savagely. 'Just shut up about her, all right?'

Penny felt herself blushing. She wanted to leave the table. But something held her, something told her to stay with Jim. She held his hand a little tighter.

'I just wanted to tell you how sorry I am,' she said desperately. 'I know you were crazy about her, and I know you'll miss her, too.'

Now Jim looked at her, and saw the hurt in her eyes. 'I'm sorry,' he said. 'I just don't want to talk about her. Not now. It's too soon. Maybe not ever.' He looked into Penny's eyes, and thought he saw an invitation. 'I've got to forget her.'

'Then let's talk about something else,' Penny offered.

'What else is there to talk about?' Jim shrugged. 'Look around. It's like a morgue in here. All anybody's thinking about is Karen.'

'I'm not.'

He looked at her questioningly. 'What are you thinking about?'

'You,' Penny said. 'How you aren't at all like I always thought you were. You're really very nice.'

She felt Jim's hand respond under her own. The pressure sent a thrill through her, and she returned the squeeze.

'I like you, too,' Jim said. He looked at her speculatively. Was she telling him what he thought she was telling him? 'Why don't we get out of here?'

Penny started to refuse, but then she looked around the room. Judy Nelson was watching her, as were several of her other friends. What would they think, Penny wondered. What would they think if they saw me leave with Jim Mulvey? Particularly after what I said at lunch – my God, was it really only yesterday? They'd all heard her. They'd all heard her say she was going to take Jim away from Karen. Well,

Karen was gone now, but why wait? If she left with him, wouldn't they think that Jim had been planning to break up with Karen anyway? Karen wouldn't care. She was dead.

'Where would we go?' Penny asked, stalling for time.

Jim shrugged. 'I dunno. Not the drugstore. That place is really gross.' Then he had an idea. 'How about Bill Enders' cabin? I haven't seen Bill in awhile.'

Penny thought it over. She barely knew Bill Enders. Bill was another of her mother's favourite gripes. The young man had built a cabin for himself about a year ago, and because he had long hair and lived alone, Leona Anderson had immediately labelled him a hippie and begun agitating against him all over Neilsville. It turned out Enders had paid cash for the land he'd built his house on, and kept a steady, if modest, balance in the bank. But he kept pretty much to himself, and as far as Penny knew, Jim Mulvey was the only person in town who knew him well enough to drop in on him. The prospect excited her.

'Isn't it a little late?' She half-hoped Jim would agree.

'Not for Bill. He's always up,' Jim smiled at her reassuringly, wondering what her reaction would be when she found out Bill Enders wasn't at the cabin at all.

Penny made up her mind, and stood up. 'Well, what are we waiting for?' As they left, Penny saw Judy Nelson beckoning to her.

'You're not leaving with Jim Mulvey, are you?' she whispered.

Penny, feeling terribly adventurous, did her best to look sophisticated, 'We're just running out to say hello to Bill Enders,' she said, loudly enough to be heard at all the tables in the area. Then, as Judy Nelson's eyes narrowed suspiciously, Penny took Jim Mulvey's arm and walked out of the Praying Mantis.

As they drove out of town a few minutes later, Penny thought she heard it – faintly in the distance, a sound that was becoming familiar to her. She put it out of her mind and turned her attention back to Jim.

But Penny was right; she *had* heard it. Somewhere in the night, an ambulance was wailing through town. The music stopped in the Praying Mantis, and everyone began looking around, trying to assess who was there, and who was not. When they realized what they were doing they became self-conscious, and a nervous buzz of conversation grew in the room as the siren slowly faded.

Penny looked apprehensively at the darkened cabin, tucked away in a tiny stand of cottonwood trees.

'He must have gone to bed,' she said, feeling slightly relieved. All the way out from town, she had been wondering if this was a mistake. Now she relaxed. They would turn around and drive back to Neilsville. But Jim switched off the engine.

'Nah,' he said. 'Too early. He must have gone out for a while. Come on, I know where the key is. We can go in and wait for him to come back.'

Penny wanted to ask him to take her home, but then she told herself that that was silly. She'd come this far, and she wasn't going to chicken out now. Besides, everyone at the disco knew where she'd gone, and who she'd gone with, and if she made Jim take her home, he'd be sure to spread it around. Penny could hear Judy Nelson's caustic remarks about people who talk big and don't follow through.

She got out of the car.

She looked around the cabin curiously, surprised at how neat and cozy it was. It was entirely made of wood, and Bill Enders had obviously known what he was doing. Even the furniture seemed to have been made by hand.

'It's nice,' she said. 'I always thought it was just a shack.'

'That's what your mother wanted everyone to think,' Jim commented. 'Lemme see if Bill has any beer around.' He went to the refrigerator, sure that it would be well stocked. It was. He took out two Olys, and handed one to Penny.

'I've never drunk beer before,' she said hesitantly.

'No time like the present,' Jim said. 'I'll build a fire.'

Penny hadn't realized how cold the night had become. She shivered. A fire would be nice.

Ten minutes later, she and Jim Mulvey were sitting cross-legged on the floor, the flames dancing on the hearth. But the beer was bitter.

'I don't like it,' Penny said, setting the bottle down.

Jim grinned at her. 'I'll fix you something else.'

He went to the kitchen and surveyed the liquor stock. He settled on sloe gin, mixed with ginger ale. He took the drink back to the living room and handed it to Penny. 'Try that.'

Penny tasted it. 'Sweet, but good. What's in it?' she asked.

'Mostly ginger ale, with a little grenadine,' Jim lied. 'They call it a Shirley Temple.'

'Didn't she used to be in the movies?' Penny asked.

'I guess,' Jim said. 'About a hundred years ago.'

Penny giggled, and took another swallow of the drink. She decided she liked it. She drained the glass and held it out to Jim. 'Can I have another one?'

He fixed the second drink, and they sat in front of the fire, enjoying the warmth and the quiet. Penny was beginning to feel much better. She looked at Jim and thought he was terribly handsome in the firelight.

'You're nice,' she blurted. 'I like you a lot.'

Jim turned and gazed at her. 'I like you, too.' Then, after a pause, 'Do you smoke?'

'Smoke?' Penny repeated blankly.

'You know. Grass.'

'God, no!' Penny repeated blankly.

'Well, it's not that bad,' Jim chuckled.

'It's bad enough,' Penny countered.

'How do you know, if you haven't tried it?'

Penny thought it over. She was feeling relaxed – really good – and the idea of smoking some grass didn't seem nearly as shocking as it always had before.

'Why not?' she giggled. Then: 'Do you have any?'

'I don't,' Jim said, winking at her. 'But Bill does.'

He got up and went to one of the drawers that was built

into the wall next to the fireplace. In a minute he was back, two joints in his hand. Penny reached to take one, but Jim held them out of her grasp.

'Not yet,' he said, laughing. 'One at a time, No sense wasting all that good smoke. Just a second, and I'll put on some music.' He chose an Alice Cooper record, and put it on the stereo. Then he rejoined Penny on the floor, and lit one of the joints.

She coughed on the first drag, but Jim showed her how to do it. The second drag went into her lungs, and she held her breath. When she felt her lungs beginning to hurt, she let the air out.

'I don't feel anything,' she said, a little surprised.

'You will,' Jim promised her. 'Take another hit.'

This time she seemed to inhale endlessly before her lungs were full and then she thought she could hold her breath for an eternity. It felt good.

'I'm thirsty,' she said, lazily stretching herself out in front of the fire.

'I'll fix you another,' Jim said softly. 'Finish the joint, and we'll light the other one when I get back.'

When he came back into the room a few minutes later, her drink in his hand, his shirt was off.

'I always get hot when I smoke,' he said. 'Hope you don't mind.'

Penny realized she was staring at his chest. She wondered what it would be like to touch Jim's skin. As if reading her mind, Jim lay down on the floor and put his head in her lap. Her hand fell naturally to his chest and she thought she could feel his heart beating. It was almost as if her fingertips were inside him.

They smoked the second joint and Penny watched the fire, listened to the music, and stroked Jim's chest.

'God, I'm hot,' Jim moaned. Penny looked down at him, and saw him looking hungrily back at her. He reached up and put his hand behind her head. Then he pulled her forward, and kissed her.

It was like an electric shock. She felt his tongue push into her mouth, and suddenly she felt as though she was inside her own mouth, not only feeling the kiss but watching it, helping it. She sucked hungrily at Jim's tongue, wanting it deeper in her mouth.

Then she was lying on her back, and he was on top of her, his body pressing her against the floor. She could feel his hips moving. In the background the music kept time to Jim's movements. By the time his hand touched her breast, she was ready.

'Touch me,' she moaned. 'Oh, God, it feels so good.'

Penny found herself groping for Jim, and she wasn't surprised when she found his jeans unzipped. She slid her hand inside his shorts and touched him.

'Please,' she said. 'Do it to me, Jim. Do it to me.'

He kicked his jeans aside and began removing her clothes. She lay on the floor, the liquor and grass working inside her, dissolving her inhibitions. She felt the heat of the fire, and then the heat of Jim's body. She felt him entering her, felt him pressing against her. And then, painlessly, the membrane broke, and he plunged into her. She gave herself up to the ecstasy, only dimly aware of the sound of Jim's voice calling out near her ear.

'Karen,' he cried. 'Karen ... Karen ... Karen ...'

She knew it was morning even before she opened her eyes. There was a greyness around her, and now she knew she wasn't at home.

She began to remember.

Even through the pounding headache, she could remember it all. The drink. It couldn't have been 'mostly ginger ale.' If it had been, she never would have agreed to try the grass.

And the rest of it. What they had done. She tried to force the images out of her mind, tried to tell herself that it hadn't happened, that what she was remembering was a dream, not a memory. She looked around.

Jim Mulvey, naked, lay next to her on the floor, one hand holding his groin, almost as if he were protecting himself. Penny stared at him for a moment, then leaped to her feet and scrambled into her clothes. She wanted to wake him, but first she wanted to cover him up. She didn't want him to wake up nude, and find her staring down at him. She went into the bedroom and pulled a quilt from the bed.

She took it back into the living room, and threw it over Jim. Then she began shaking him.

'Wake up,' she said. 'Please, Jim, wake up.'

He stirred finally, and looked at her sleepily.

'What time is it?' He jumped up, grabbing the quilt just before it fell away from his body, and picked up his clothes. Then he scuttled into the bedroom.

'It's all right,' he said a couple of minutes later as he emerged from the other room. 'It's just a little after five. If we hurry, you'll be home before anyone even wakes up.'

Penny didn't say anything, nothing at all. She followed him mutely to the car, got in, and huddled miserably in the corner of the seat as he drove her home.

'Stop here,' she said suddenly. They were a block from her house. 'If I get out here, at least no one will see you bringing me home. Then maybe I can convince them I was at Judy's all night.'

Jim let her out, wanting to apologize for what had happened, but unable to find the words. He hadn't meant for the night to end that way, but he had just got too stoned. He hadn't known what he was doing. In fact, he had thought he was making love to Karen. But he didn't tell Penny any of it. Instead, he put the car in gear and drove away. He could understand why she didn't want her parents to see him, but he still resented it.

Penny hurried up the steps and into the house. Her mother, bleary-eyed, gazed at her steadily.

'Where have you been all night?' Leona Anderson demanded.

'At Judy's,' Penny said. She wondered why her mother was looking at her so strangely; it wouldn't have been the first time she had stayed at Judy's overnight without telling her mother. Besides, her mother would have called the Nelsons, and Judy would have covered up for her somehow. And why was her mother still dressed? Hadn't she been to bed at all? Suddenly Penny was frightened.

'Something's happened, hasn't it?' she said.

Leona Anderson, her mouth set, nodded stiffly.

'Well, what is it?' Penny asked. 'Mother, what is it?'

'I've been at the hospital all night,' Leona said. 'As a matter of fact, I just got home myself. Janet Connally tried to hang herself last night.'

Penny stared at her mother for a second, then screamed.

She screamed again.

Something broke inside her, and she crumpled to the floor. Leona Anderson stared at her daughter, then her hands instinctively began working the beads she had taken to the hospital with her.

'Holy Mary, Mother of God, pray for us sinners . . .'

She broke off, unable to finish the prayer. But in her mind the words echoed.

'. . . *now, and at the hour of our death* . . .'

TWENTY-THREE

Penny Anderson's first thought was that it had all been a bad dream. But then she realized she wasn't in her bed; she was on the sofa in the living room, and her mother was staring down at her.

It wasn't a bad dream. It was real. It had all happened. Penny closed her eyes again, trying to shut it all out, but it wouldn't be shut out.

'Janet—' she said finally. 'Is Janet going to be all right?'

'She'll be fine,' Leona snapped. 'Although what's going on in this town I don't know. Ever since that Mr. Balsam got here . . .' She trailed off. No sense going into that now, she reminded herself. 'Do you want to tell me where you were all night?'

'I wasn't anywhere,' Penny said. 'I was just wandering around.'

'No,' Leona said definitely. 'You weren't out "wandering around." You went somewhere with Jim Mulvey, and I want to know where.'

'We were out at the lake, talking.'

'All night? Don't try to fool me, Penelope Louise!'

'He was upset,' Penny replied. 'He wanted to talk about Karen, and he asked me if I'd go for a ride with him, and talk to him for a while.'

'You expect me to believe that?' Leona demanded. 'Jim Mulvey never talked for more than two minutes at a stretch in his life!' She glared at Penny, as if the truth would somehow be pulled out of her by sheer concentration. Penny stared at the floor.

It wasn't that she wanted to lie to her mother. She wanted to tell her mother the truth. In fact, she wanted to throw herself in her mother's arms and cry. But her mother wouldn't understand. Penny was sure of it. Her mother would be horrified by what she'd done. and start yelling at her. Penny couldn't let that happen; she was already too upset. She knew she'd fall apart completely if her mother started yelling at her. Shakily, she got up from the sofa.

'I'm going to take a bath, and go to bed,' she announced. 'I feel awful.'

'I'll bet you do,' Leona agreed. 'And you can take a bath. But you're not going to bed, young lady. You're going to school.'

Penny stared at her mother. School? The way she felt? No. She couldn't go. She wouldn't go. Not after last night. She needed a day by herself; a day to deal with what had happened. A day to forget. But she looked at her mother and knew it was no use. She was going to school.

Tiredly, she started up the stairs. Halfway up she heard her mother's voice again.

'When you get there,' Leona said darkly, 'don't bother to go to your first classes. Go to Monsignor's office. If you won't tell me what happened last night, you can tell him.'

Penny froze on the stairs and listened for the words she didn't want to hear. They came.

'Monsignor will hear your confession.'

Penny could feel people staring at her as she walked up Main Street. She tried to tell herself that they weren't staring at her, that she didn't look any different now than she had yesterday, or the day before, or the day before that. But she could feel the eyes on her, feel people wondering why she was on her way to school so late.

They *were* watching her, and wondering, Neilsville was getting worried. One of their girls was dead. and two others had tried to take their lives. And they were all from the Catholic school on the hill. What was going on up there? So they watched Penny Anderson as she self-consciously walked through town and started up the hill toward St. Francis Xavier's.

She noticed a chill in the air this morning, and glanced up at the leaden sky. Summer was definitely over, and the world seemed to be cloaked in the same grey shroud Penny felt herself suffocating in. She hurried up the steps and through the main door of the school.

Monsignor Vernon was waiting for her, seated at his desk, his fingers drumming impatiently. His lips tightened when he saw Penny Anderson framed in the doorway.

'Your mother has asked me to hear your confession,' he said.

'Couldn't we talk here?' Penny countered. She knew she would have to tell the priest the truth in the confessional. Here, in the office, she could avoid it.

'Shall we go into the church?' Monsignor Vernon said, and Penny knew that he was not asking a question. Silently, she followed the priest out of the school and into the church.

When she was in the tiny confessional, the door latched firmly, Penny knelt and began praying. She heard the shutter open. The priest was waiting for her to begin.

The story came out slowly. But Monsignor Vernon prodded, and poked, dragging it from her detail by detail.

'Did you know it was going to happen?' the priest's voice asked.

'No,' Penny replied.

'Are you sure?'

She tried to remember. 'Not at first,' she said hesitantly.

'But then you knew?'

'When he took his shirt off—'

'How did you feel?'

'I'm – I'm not sure. I wanted to – to—'

'To touch him?' the disembodied voice accused.

'Yes,' Penny hissed. 'Yes, I wanted to touch him.'

'And you wanted him to touch you?'

'Yes,' Penny wailed.

In the other half of the booth, Monsignor Vernon was sweating. It was sinful. What they did was repulsive and sinful. He could see them, the naked boy lying on top of her, her hands on his back, on his buttocks, then reaching around, touching him, touching him. He pictured her hands on the boy's organ, and his own hands began working. He could almost feel the hardness of the boy . . .

'Tell it to me,' he urged her softly. 'Tell me all of it.'

Once more Penny went into the recital of her sins, and the priest felt the wrath of a vengeful God rise in him. A combination of excitement and revulsion. And then it was over. Monsignor Vernon felt a sudden release within himself. Now he would have to deal with the penitent who knelt quietly on the other side of the screen, waiting for him to speak.

He began the prayer of absolution, but was suddenly conscious of a stirring from Penny's side of the confessional. He broke off the prayer.

'Is there more?'

There was a slight hesitation, and then he heard Penny's voice.

'The penance. Father. What is the penance?'

In the dimness of the tiny booth, Monsignor Vernon smiled softly.

'You will know what the penance is,' he whispered. 'When the time comes, you will know what to do.'

Then, as Penny wondered what he meant, Monsignor Vernon absolved her of all her sins.

Monsignor Vernon glanced at one of the hall clocks. 'We're late,' he said, increasing his stride. Penny almost had to run to keep up with him.

'Late for what?'

'Your class,' the priest announced. 'I'm conducting it today.'

Penny stopped in her tracks, the one bright spot in her day ruined. 'Mr. Balsam isn't here today?' she asked. She wondered if she could plead sickness, and go home; she had been looking forward to the psychology class as the one ray of hope; Mr. Balsam always seemed to know what was happening with the kids, and what to say to them. And today he wasn't there.

'He went to the hospital,' Monsignor Vernon said placidly. 'Janet Connally wanted to talk to him, and we thought it best that he go.'

'I see,' Penny said vaguely, though she didn't see at all. They walked the rest of the way to Room 16 in silence.

Penny hesitated at the door, and stared at the empty seats in the front row. Judy Nelson was there, but all the other seats were empty: Karen Morton's, Janet Connally's, and Jim Mulvey's. Where was Jim? she wondered. Home in bed, probably, she thought bitterly.

She started to slip into a vacant seat in the back of the room, but Judy Nelson was signalling to her, so she walked to the front and took the seat next to Judy.

'I had to tell,' Judy whispered urgently. She was speaking so fast Penny could hardly follow her. 'Right after you left with Jim, we heard about Janet. We all went over there, and your mother was already there, and when you weren't with us, and Jim wasn't with us, well – she just put it together. What could I say?' She looked eagerly at Penny. 'What happened? Did you—' But before she could finish her question, Monsignor Vernon rapped on the desk and cleared his throat.

He gazed out over the room, taking note of the empty desks

in the front row. He stared at them for a long time, long enough for the class to be certain what he was thinking. As the silence lengthened, the class began to squirm, and the questions in their minds showed on their faces.

Why is he here?

Where's Mr. Balsam?

What's he going to do?

Monsignor Vernon cleared his throat and the squirming suddenly stopped.

He spoke without preamble, offering no explanation for their teacher's absence. He made a simple announcement.

'Your assignment today will be to write a paper.'

There was a rustling in Room 16. Maybe the hour wouldn't be so bad after all.

'A paper about death,' Monsignor Vernon said. Suddenly the silence in the room was tangible. They stared at him, not sure they had heard him correctly. They had.

'Something is happening in this class,' Monsignor Vernon went on, 'and I don't know too much about it. So I want you, each of you, to tell me. You will spend the rest of this hour writing about death. Specifically, your own deaths.'

Now the students looked terrified. The Monsignor continued.

'You are to look within yourselves. You will decide if there are any circumstances under which you would contemplate committing suicide. If you find that there are, you will describe those circumstances in your papers, and then attempt to reconcile your feelings with the Doctrines of the Church.' He looked out over the class. 'Your papers will be entirely confidential. No one will see them except me and Mr. Balsam. We will read them, evaluate them, and destroy them. They won't be graded, and they won't be recorded. But I think we might be able to get some valuable information about what had been happening to – some of you.'

Suddenly everyone in the class began glancing at Judy Nelson. But Judy sat calmly in her seat, unaffected by what the priest had asked of them.

In the back of the room. Marilyn Crane tried to hold back her tears. To think of killing yourself was a mortal sin! But if it was a sin, surely a priest wouldn't ask you to do it, would he? Then Marilyn realized that the Monsignor had given them an opportunity: if she was honest with herself, she knew that she had thought about it but had always stopped herself. Now she had a chance to think it through, and think it through with a clear conscience. She silently blessed the priest for giving her the assignment, and set to work.

Penny Anderson couldn't think at all. She sat numbly in the front row, and stared at the Monsignor. How could he? With Karen dead and Janet in the hospital, how could he ask them to do such a thing?

Her head was still pounding from the night before, and she felt as though she hadn't slept in a week. She tried to force herself to concentrate. But all she could do was sit and stare at Monsignor Vernon.

And then she realized that he was beckoning to her, signaling her to come to him. She responded to the summons.

'Is something wrong?' the priest asked when she was next to the desk.

'I – I can't seem to concentrate,' Penny stammered.

The priest smiled at her. 'Perhaps you'd better work in the quiet-room,' he said. 'Maybe it would be easier for you if you were alone.'

But I don't want to be alone. Penny's mind cried out. *I want to talk to someone. I want to talk to Mr. Balsam!* Aloud she said:

'I'll try.' Then she repeated it: 'Really, I'll try!' She picked up her things and hurried out of Room 16.

On her way to the basement, where the quiet-room was, Penny hoped she'd find someone else already there. She didn't care who – anyone – just someone she could talk to for a while, to take her mind off herself, off last night, off everything. But the quiet-room was empty, and as Penny closed the door behind her she felt even worse than before.

Resolutely, she put her things down on one of the tables and took out a pen and some paper. She put her name neatly in the upper left-hand corner, and then printed the title of her paper.

WHY SHOULD I KILL MYSELF?

Then, underneath, she wrote something else:

WHY SHOULDN'T I?

Penny stared at the paper for a long time, and after a while the paper blurred in her vision. She began to see other images. She saw Jim Mulvey, his chest glistening in the firelight, his eyes inviting her. She saw herself, kneeling in front of him, tearing at his pants.

And then the image was gone, and Penny saw Karen Morton, She was wearing a white dress – it was her confirmation dress – and she was walking toward Penny. But something was wrong. Penny looked closer. Now she knew what was wrong – Karen was walking toward her from the grave! But Karen was happy; she was smiling, and waving to Penny. How could she be happy? She was dead. Dead! *Dead,* Penny repeated the word to herself over and over again. *Dead.* DEAD! DEAD-DEAD-DEAD-deaddeaddead. And suddenly the word didn't mean anything to her anymore. It was just a sound without any meaning at all. Karen wasn't deaddeaddead. No. Karen was happy. She was wearing her confirmation dress, and she was happy. Penny wanted to be with her . . .

Penny Anderson sat up suddenly, and looked around. Where was she? The quiet-room. Of course. She was in the quiet-room and she was supposed to be writing a paper. What had happened?

She looked at the clock: a few minutes after four o'clock. It must be broken.

But the second hand was moving steadily.

She left her things in the quiet-room and climbed up the stairs to the main floor. The clock on the main floor said the same thing. Seven minutes after four.

It was impossible, of course, She had been downstairs only a few minutes. Then she stopped, and listened. It was quiet. Too quiet. Not the busy quiet of a building full of students, but the awful, deserted silence that comes over a school in late afternoons and on weekends.

Somehow, Penny Anderson had lost most of the day. Shaken, she pushed quickly through the door of the girls' room. As she was washing her hands, she glanced at the mirror. What she saw horrified her.

Her eyes were puffy.

Her whole face seemed to have swollen.

She stared at herself, and began to feel sick at her stomach. Then, as if trying to blot out the image, her fist came up and smashed into the mirror. It shattered, and jagged pieces of glass crashed to the floor at her feet. Shocked, she stared at the mess around her, at the cut that was slowly beginning to ooze blood on her leg. And something clicked in her mind.

The penance.

Something about the penance.

'*You will know what the penance is.*' That was what he had said. '*When the times comes, you will know what to do.*'

Penny Anderson knew what to do.

She reached down and picked up the largest shard. Then she went back into the stall she had just come out of, and carefully latched the door behind her.

She took off her shoes and her pantyhose.

She sat on the plumbing above the toilet, and carefully put both feel in the toilet bowl.

She grasped the fragment of broken mirror and reached down.

The blood came slowly at first, then faster, running down her ankles into the bowl. She stared at the red water, then flushed the toilet. A moment later, the bowl refilled with clean water, but that, too, soon turned red.

Over and over again, Penny slashed at herself with the broken glass, lacerating her legs until the blood poured from them as from a tap. Then she let the glass fall to the floor.

She watched the blood flow into the toilet bowl, and when

it again turned red, she reached down once more and pressed on the lever. She watched her life swirl down into the sewers, watched the clean water bubble into the bowl, watched her blood mix into it once more.

The fifth time she reached for the lever, she was too weak to press it. Instead she sat, resting her weight on one hand, watching the red fluid rise in the bowl. And she thought she heard music, somewhere in the background. It sounded like the nuns chanting vespers, but she knew it was too early for that. Or was it? It seemed to be getting darker.

She slipped from the toilet to the floor, and gave herself up to the darkness. She thought she saw a tunnel. At its end Karen Morton was waiting for her, still in her confirmation dress, beckoning to her. And in the background, the chanting continued, sending Penny onward.

In the room next to Room 16 – not a room, really, but an oversized storeroom that had been converted into a makeshift laboratory – Marilyn Crane was patiently working with the white rat. She had set up a particularly difficult maze, with two routes through it – one shorter, but complicated, the other much longer, but much simpler. She was trying to determine if the rat would discover both routes, explore them, and then choose one. So far, the results had been inconclusive. The rat had made his way through the maze several times, but he seemed to take just as long by either route, and so far hadn't shown any preference for either.

Marilyn had made herself come to the laboratory that afternoon. Until two days ago she had enjoyed working with the rats. Now, every time she was with them, the image of the disembowelled creature loomed up in front of her, and she had to force herself to pick up the live animals. Gingerly, she reached down and picked up the wriggling creature.

I should have gone home, she thought. Why did I stay? But she knew why she'd stayed. It had been the essay for Monsignor Vernon that morning. What she'd written had frightened her, and she was afraid her fear showed. She didn't want her mother to ask her what had happened that day, so she'd decided to stay after school until she calmed down. It hadn't helped.

She was about to drop the rat back at the beginning of the maze when she felt it. Hot. Wet. Instantly she knew what had happened. Marilyn cried out in disgust and dropped the rat. It missed the maze entirely, hit the floor, and scuttled off into a corner, where it sat looking curiously at Marilyn. But Marilyn was staring at the yellow fluid that was running off her hand onto the floor.

The rat had – had *peed* on her!

Mortified, she ran out of the room and down the hall to the girls' room.

She knew something was wrong as soon as she opened the door. Glass all over the floor. She decided to ignore it, and began to pick her way carefully around it to use the other wash basin.

Then she saw the blood. At first, she thought it was just a drop, but then she realized it was a puddle of blood, oozing slowly toward the drain in the middle of the floor.

Almost against her will, her eyes followed the blood toward its source. It was coming from a closed stall.

'Is someone here?' Marilyn said softly, knowing there would be no answer. The silence only increased her fear. She pushed at the door. It didn't give.

She knelt down, carefully avoiding the glass and blood, and looked under the door.

Penny Anderson, her eyes open and vacant, stared back at her.

Marilyn felt the sickness rise.

Moving with a strange calm, she let herself into the end stall, bent down, and threw up into the toilet. Then, detached, wondering why she was behaving as she was, she waited for the sickness to subside, washed out her mouth, and left the girls' room. She returned to Room 16, gathered her things, and left the school.

The fresh air hit her like a bucket of water, and she knew what had happened. Penny had killed herself. But why was she so calm? Why wasn't she screaming? Why wasn't she running, calling for help? Maybe Penny was still alive. Maybe if she did something, they could still save Penny.

And then she realized that Penny wouldn't want her to do that, that Penny would want her to stay calm, and walk down the hill. And leave her alone.

Marilyn started down the steps, and away from the school. Suddenly it all seemed to be closing in on her, and she felt the pressure building in her, the pressure she had been fighting against for so long – the pressure to do what should be done, instead of what she wanted to do. Now she was going to do what she wanted to do. She was going to listen to the voices.

She was not going to tell anybody what she had seen in the restroom.

She passed the rectory, glancing at it as she passed. Then she stopped and looked more closely. Smoke was coming out of the chimney. It struck her as strange, since the afternoon was still warm. The evening would be cold, but not yet.

Then she heard the chanting. At first she thought it must be coming from the convent. Then she knew it wasn't. It was coming from the rectory.

And it was telling her the same things the voices inside her were telling her. She listened for a moment, then hurried down the hill.

TWENTY-FOUR

Margo looked surreptitiously across the table at Peter, trying to see him with his guard down, trying to decide whether he looked strained, or whether it was her imagination. He was concentrating on his food, unaware of her scrutiny.

'I'm not going to stay tonight,' Margo said, breaking the silence that had reigned over the table since they had sat down for dinner. Peter looked up from his steak.

'Don't ask me why,' she went on, anticipating the question. 'I couldn't tell you. I just have a feeling I'm going to be needed at the hospital tonight.'

'It's the atmosphere around here lately,' Peter said, putting down his fork. 'I've felt the same way all day, ever since I talked to Janet Connally.'

'Can you tell me what she said, or is it confidential?' Margo wanted to know. She had already heard about Peter's visit with Janet from Dr. Shields, but she wanted to hear it again, first-hand, from Peter. If his story differed much from the one Dr. Shields had told her, it might help her make up her mind.

Peter looked at her wryly. 'It's not confidential,' he said. 'As a matter of fact, I'd like to hear what you think of it. The whole day, not just the visit with Janet.' He cast around in his mind, trying to decide where to start.

'There was a note in my box, just before the psych class. It was from Monsignor, and it told me to go to the hospital right away, that Janet wanted to talk to me. He said he'd take over my class, and I should leave as soon as I found the note. I stopped by his office to see if there were any details but he wasn't there. So I left...'

He walked into the hospital just after eleven, and asked for Janet Connally's room number. The nurse looked slightly annoyed; then, when he identified himself, her annoyance grew.

'Well, you certainly took long enough.' She didn't seem to expect an answer, so Peter followed her silently down the hall. He was relieved when they passed the room Judy Nelson had been in, and turned into the next one. Janet was propped up on a pillow, watching television. As soon as she saw him she reached over and snapped the TV off.

'You certainly took long enough,' she echoed the nurse. 'I was beginning to think you weren't coming at all.'

Peter sat down in the chair at the foot of the bed and looked at Janet in puzzlement. 'The nurse said the same thing, that I "certainly took long enough." I came as soon as I got the message.'

'It must be the school, then,' Janet complained. 'I called at seven-thirty this morning, and talked to Monsignor. He promised he'd give you the message as soon as you got there.' She smiled sheepishly. 'I really did a number on him, Mr. Balsam. I tried to make it sound like I was dying, and that if you didn't come instantly, terrible things were going to happen to me. But I guess he didn't believe me.'

Or, more likely, chose to ignore it, Peter thought. He looked at Janet carefully, trying to determine if she was as well as she appeared to be.

Last night this girl had tried to hang herself.

Today she was the same as she had always seemed – happy, cheerful, with no apparent problems. Or were the problems just too well concealed for his eyes to see?

'I look too good, don't I?' Janet said. Her perceptiveness startled Balsam and made him wary.

'I don't know,' he said evasively. 'How do you feel?'

'No different than ever,' Janet responded immediately. Then, realizing the answer could have a double meaning, she clarified it. 'That means fine. I feel fine now, and I felt fine yesterday.'

'Then why are you here?' Peter said, trying to approach the issue obliquely. Janet, in her straightforward way, hit it head on.

'Because I hung myself last night. Or tried to. I've been trying all morning to decide if an attempt counts. I mean, since I'm not dead or anything, do I say "I hung myself," or "I *tried* to hang myself"?'

Peter bit his lip, suddenly nervous. She must be covering up something. She *had* to be. But what? He decided to be as forthright as she.

'Janet,' he said sombrely, 'it isn't funny. You hung yourself – or if you want to be absolutely correct, "hanged yourself" – last night. If your father hadn't gotten to you as quickly as he did, you'd be dead right now. As it is, you're lucky you didn't suffer any brain damage.'

The grin vanished from Janet's face, and she shifted in the bed. When she spoke, the lightness had gone from her voice.

'I know it isn't funny,' she said. 'But right now it's the only way I can cope with it. If I don't make fun of it, I think I'll go crazy. I might be crazy anyway.'

Peter Balsam's brows arched, and she took the expression as a question.

'That's why I called you. I suppose I should talk to Dr. Shields, but I just can't. He's nice, but I don't know him, and he doesn't know me. You've seen me every day this semester—'

'Which has barely begun,' Peter broke in.

'All right, so it's barely begun. But you've seen me every day, and you know what I'm like. Or, anyway, better than Dr. Shields does. Dr. Shields is sure to think I'm some kind of a nut. I mean, what else can he think? Anybody'd have to be crazy to do what I did.'

Peter decided to take a gamble. 'Then by your own terms, you're crazy.'

She stared at him for a moment, then nodded.

'I know. That's why I called you. You decide if I'm crazy.'

'I'm not qualified,' Peter protested.

'I don't care,' Janet said. 'You're the one I want to talk to. There isn't anybody else I can talk to. Don't you see? Dr. Shields has to think I'm crazy, and why shouldn't he? And everybody else – well, you know what it's like around here. Particularly at school. All they'll do is tell me I'm a sinner, and give me a penance. But I'm *not* a sinner.'

Peter moved his chair closer to the bed and took Janet's hand. 'All right,' he said gently. 'What happened?'

'First, I didn't try to kill myself.'

'You didn't?'

'No, I didn't. Oh, yes, I *did*, I know, but I didn't *really*.' Her face twisted in frustration. 'I'm sorry,' she went on, forcing herself to relax. 'I know none of this makes sense, but just listen to me, then you try to figure out what happened. I've tried, and I can't, and I'm scared. So please, help me?' For the first time since he'd gotten there, Peter Balsam saw the part of Janet Connally that was still a small child. He wanted to hold her and comfort her. 'I'll listen,' he said softly. 'Tell me what happened.'

'I keep telling you,' Janet said. 'I don't know what happened. Where shall I start?' Without waiting for an answer she went right on talking. 'Everything was fine yesterday, or as fine as it could be, what with Karen and all. I don't know how I got caught up in what happened at church. In fact, I can barely remember it. We must have sounded like a bunch of Holy Rollers. Anyway, after it was over with, I went home with my parents, and we watched television for a while. Then I went up to do my homework.' She stopped talking. Peter waited patiently for her to resume the story. Finally he prompted her.

'And?'

She looked at him bleakly. 'And that's when it happened. I was studying, and all of a sudden I got this crazy urge to hang myself. At first I told myself it was ridiculous, that there wasn't a reason in the world why I should want to kill myself. But I still wanted to. So I sat there for about an hour, and argued with myself. I mean, I literally argued with myself. But the feeling wouldn't go away.'

'But why?' There must have been some reason why you wanted to kill yourself.'

'That's the part that makes me think I must be crazy. There wasn't any reason. Just this incredible urge to hang myself. And I did.'

Balsam nodded gravely. 'This may sound strange, but do you remember what it was like?'

'It wasn't *like* anything. I mean, there I was, getting a chair, and putting it under the chandelier in my room, and taking an extension cord, and tying it around my neck. And all the time wondering why I was doing it, and trying to make myself stop. But I couldn't.'

'It must have been frightening.'

'That's what I kept thinking, too. But it wasn't. All the time, there was just this strange sense of not being able to control myself. Like a puppet. It was just like someone was pulling strings, and I had to do whatever they wanted me to do.' Her voice suddenly became bitter. 'So I stood up on the chair, and tied the cord around my neck, and kicked the chair away.' The blood drained from her face as she remembered it. 'What if they hadn't been home? What if Mom and Dad had gone out last night?' Janet Connally shuddered, and fell silent.

Peter Balsam turned the story over in his mind. It all seemed preposterous, and if it had been anybody but Janet telling him, he would have been inclined to discount it. But not Janet. Her assessment of herself coincided exactly with his own, and the story had the ring of truth. Or of what Janet thought was the truth. Then her voice interrupted his thoughts.

'Mr. Balsam,' she said, almost pleading, 'am I crazy?'

'Do you feel crazy?' he countered.

'No.'

'And you don't look crazy, and you don't sound crazy. Granted, the story sounds crazy, but you don't. So,' he went on, more lightly, 'I think we can assume that, since you don't feel like a duck, look like a duck, or sound like a duck, you probably aren't a duck.'

'Probably,' she said, repeating the qualifying word.

Peter Balsam shrugged. 'Would you believe me if I said "absolutely"?' He was pleased when she smiled again.

'No. And "probably" is a lot better than I was doing by myself.' Silence. Then: 'Mr. Balsam, what am I going to do?' Again, the plaintive, childlike quality in the voice.

Balsam had been expecting the question. But when it came, he had no ready answer. All he could offer was some reassurance.

'Try not to worry,' he said. 'Just relax, try to stop worrying, and I'll go talk to Dr. Shields and see if I can convince him that you aren't quite ready for the looney bin yet.' And talk to him about a few other things, he silently added to himself. He squeezed Janet's hand one last time, and stood up. 'Do you need anything?'

Janet shook her head. She started to speak, stopped, then started again. 'Mr. Balsam? Thanks for coming. I feel better just talking about it to someone.'

'There's lots of people you can talk to about it,' he said.

Janet smiled wanly. 'I suppose so. But not around here.' Then, as if to preclude any answer, she reached out and switched the television set back on. Peter Balsam stood in the doorway for a second or two longer, then turned and left the room.

He approached the nurses' station and waited for the nurse to finish with the chart she was working on. Finally, she looked up and put on a practised smile.

'Can you tell me where Dr. Shields's office is?'

'I'd better show you.' She stood up and led him down the hall. 'You're the psychology teacher, aren't you?' Her voice stayed carefully neutral, and Peter wondered whether the question was hostile.

'Yes.'

'And all these girls ... they're in your class, aren't they?'

'I'm afraid they are.'

The nurse smiled tightly. 'Must be some class,' she observed. Then, before Peter could respond, she was pointing to a door. 'Dr. Shields's office is right through there.' And she was gone. Peter watched her until she turned a corner and disappeared from view, then went into the reception room she had indicated, and tapped on the inner door, half-hoping Margo would come out. Instead, Dr. Shields himself opened the door.

'Excuse me,' Peter said. 'I don't know if you remember me. I'm—'

'Peter Balsam,' Dr. Shields said, opening the door wide. 'I've been expecting you.' He held the door until Peter was inside the inner office, then closed it firmly. Instead of taking the chair behind the desk, he seated himself in one of the armchairs that flanked a small table, and gestured for Peter to take the other.

'Expecting me?' Balsam asked.

'Janet Connally. Ever since she was admitted she's been saying you were the only one she wanted to talk to. So this morning we gave in, and let her call you. I assumed that as a matter of – what shall we call it? professional courtesy? – you'd drop by to see me after you talked to her.'

'I have a few questions of my own.'

'I'll do my best,' Dr. Shields said, observing Balsam behind a smile.

As Balsam related the conversation he'd had with Janet Connally, Dr. Shields found himself putting all his attention on what the girl had said. When Balsam finished the story, Shields's first question was, 'Will she tell me the same story?'

Balsam nodded. 'I told her I was going to try to convince you that she's not crazy.'

'You don't think she is?'

'I don't.'

'What about her story? Do you believe it?'

'I don't know,' Balsam said carefully. 'I guess I'd have to say that I do. In fact, that's what I wanted to talk to you about. The control thing. It sounded as though she thinks she's a victim of some kind of mind control.' Peter's expression grew intense, and his voice took on a note of urgency. 'Is it possible? I mean suppose, just suppose, that a group of people was trying to exercise its will on others. Without the others knowing what was happening. Could it be done?'

Why doesn't he say it? Dr. Shields wondered. Why doesn't he say he's thinking of the Society of St. Peter Martyr? Aloud he said:

'Who knows? I suppose anything's possible. But I'd say it's highly improbable. I don't think anything of the sort is going on.'

'Something's going on,' Peter stated.

'Of course it is,' Dr. Shields agreed. 'Answer this: Are they all friends? Judy Nelson? Karen Morton? Janet Connally?'

'Close friends. And there's one more in the group. A girl named Penny Anderson.'

'Then it's pretty obvious what's happening,' Dr. Shields said. 'It's called a suicide contagion.'

Peter Balsam had heard the term before, but wasn't sure what it meant. 'A what?'

'Suicide contagion. Put simply, the urge to self-destruction passing from one person to another. It's not unusual, in fact. But it almost always happens in an institutional environment. Read "hospital" for that. And it's almost always restricted to teen-aged girls. There's even a term for them – "slashers." In some places, it's gotten so bad that entire wards of teen-age girls have had to be put under physical restriction to keep them from cutting themselves.'

Balsam's eyes widened in surprise. 'But what causes it?'

'It's a hysterical condition,' Dr Shields explained. 'As far as I know, though, it only occurs in hospitals, and the victims are always pretty unstable types to begin with.' He paused, considering. 'But what's happening up at St. Francis Xavier's sounds like a suicide contagion to me.'

'But couldn't it be something else?' Peter Balsam felt himself grabbing at straws. 'You said they were called slashers. That certainly fits Judy Nelson and Karen Morton. But what about Janet? She didn't cut herself.'

Dr. Shields shrugged expressively. 'I don't know. Until today, I hadn't even considered the possibility of a suicide contagion. Now, I have to. But mind control? I don't think so.'

When he left the psychiatrist's office a few minutes later, Peter Balsam felt more alone than ever. Alone, and frightened...

'The whole thing sounds too bizarre to be believed,' Margo said.

'It is too bizarre to be believed,' Peter said, 'but it's happening.'

Margo fell silent, thinking. Dr. Shields had already told her Peter's story. But Dr. Shields had gone further, and Margo decided it was time to tell Peter about it.

'You should talk to Dr. Shields about the Society,' she said. 'Since he already knows about it.'

'He knows about it? How?'

Suddenly Margo felt guilty, as if she had betrayed a trust. But she hadn't talked to the psychiatrist to betray Peter; only to gain some insight.

'I told him,' she said. 'I've been talking to him a lot lately, about you... about us.'

'And about the Society?' It was almost an accusation.

'Of course about the Society. Peter, the Society has been a pretty big thing between us.'

'How much did you tell him?' Peter felt embarrassed, as if a private part of him had been exposed for public scrutiny.

'Not much,' Margo hastened to assure him. 'As little as possible, really.' She smiled at Peter wryly. 'I guess I didn't want him to think we were both crazy.'

'Is that what you think?'

'You know it isn't.' Hurt edged Margo's voice and Peter was immediately sorry. Before he could apologize, the telephone rang.

'It's for you,' Peter said a moment later. 'Your boss, He sounds upset.'

Margo took the receiver and carried on a one-sided conversation. Though she said very little, Peter knew something was wrong. Her complexion turned chalky. Finally, after what seemed an eternity, she hung up and turned to him.

'It can't be . . .' she began.

'What—?'

'Penny Anderson. They found her half an hour ago. Peter, she's dead.'

'Oh, Jesus.' Peter sank back into his chair, and buried his face in his hands. Then, forcing himself, he looked up at Margo again.

'How?'

'She – she cut herself. At the school. In the restroom.' Margo was already gathering her things together. 'I have to go to the hospital. Leona's there – she's in pretty bad shape – and Dr. Shields says there are other people there, too. All of them suffering from all kinds of strange symptoms. He says it's hysteria, and it seems like it's all over the place.'

Peter pulled himself together. 'I'll go with you.'

'No!' Margo said the word too sharply, and immediately regretted it. Dr. Shields had warned her. Some of the people were saying the whole mess was Peter Balsam's fault; whatever she did, she mustn't let him come to the hospital with her. 'I – I'd rather go by myself,' Margo stammered.

'I see,' Peter said, the situation suddenly becoming clear to him. 'Yes, I suppose I should stay here.' He looked mutely at Margo, and she wanted to go to him, hold him, stay with him.

Instead, she turned, and hurried out of his apartment.

Peter washed the dishes, then tried to read. He tried the television next, then turned it off and went back to his book. Finally he went to bed. But before he turned off the lights he made sure to lock and bolt the front door. Then, as an afterthought, and feeling silly, he moved a chair in front of the door as well.

Just before he turned off the lights, he wondered whether he'd taken the precautions to keep others out, or himself in. But he put the thought out of his mind, and went to bed.

He woke up the next morning more tired than he had been the night before. He felt restless, and sweaty, as if he'd been running all night. He'd had bad dreams. Dreams about the Society of St. Peter Martyr.

In the dreams he'd been back in the rectory, back with the priests, and they had been doing things to him. Things he didn't want to think about. He'd tried to keep it from happening but there were six of them, and only one of him, and they could do anything they wanted to. Anything. And they did.

He lay in bed, thinking about the dream, then decided to put it out of his mind. He rose from the bed, threw on a robe, and went into the living room.

The chair had been moved away from the door.

The chain hung loose.

The door was unlocked.

Peter tried to tell himself it wasn't true, that he must have done it himself, in one of the restless periods during the night. But he knew he didn't remember it. No, something else had happened.

Something unspeakable.

He went quickly to the bathroom and dropped the robe from his shoulders.

His back was covered with the strange red welts.

TWENTY-FIVE

Marilyn Crane hadn't slept all night. She covered a yawn as best she could and seated herself at the table. Her father didn't even glance up from his paper, but her mother surveyed her critically. Marilyn wondered what she'd done wrong now.

'Dressed for school?' Geraldine asked.

Marilyn looked at her curiously. Was today a holiday? She searched her mind rapidly. 'Shouldn't I be?' For some reason she felt vaguely guilty.

'I don't see why,' Geraldine Crane said a little too sharply. 'You're not going.'

'Of course I'm going to school,' Marilyn protested.

Geraldine set down the frying pan she had been holding and faced her daughter.

'Not today,' she said. 'Not after what happened yesterday. Imagine, that poor child lying there all afternoon. It must have been terrible.' She clucked her tongue, her head bobbing sympathetically.

Terrible for whom? Marilyn wondered. Certainly not for Penny Anderson. Why did everyone worry so much about what happened to people when they were already dead? It wasn't as if Penny had been in pain. Penny's face appeared before her again, the eyes wide open, the features frozen. Penny had looked almost happy.

Marilyn kept her thoughts to herself. After all, nobody knew she had seen Penny.

'But I want to go to school.'

Her father lowered his newspaper and looked at her curiously.

'I'd think you'd want to stay as far away from there as possible,' he remarked. 'Anyway, it doesn't matter. There isn't going to be any school today, at least not at St. Francis Xavier's. I don't know what they're doing at the public school.' He shook the paper out again, prepared to drop the subject, but Marilyn didn't want to let it go.

'Just because of Penny?' The newspaper went down again, and at the stove Geraldine froze.

'*Just* because of Penny?' her father repeated, emphasizing the first word. 'Marilyn, she killed herself.'

It was the first time anyone had actually used those words, at least in front of her, and they echoed in her ears. '*Killed herself . . . killed herself . . . killed herself . . .*' Until that moment, it hadn't been real for her. Now it was. Penny had killed herself. By her own hand. Penny was *dead*. Marilyn looked from one of her parents to the other, then, wordlessly, left the table. A few seconds later they heard her tread on the stairs. Geraldine glanced toward the ceiling, as if her eyes could bore through the plaster and wood, and detect what was happening in the mind of the girl above. Then she shifted her gaze to her husband, whose interest was back on his newspaper.

'Bill,' she said quietly, 'something's wrong.'

He looked up at her, faintly annoyed. 'You're just catching on?'

Geraldine ignored the sarcastic tone. 'I'm not just talking about Karen and Penny,' she began.

'And Janet Connally, and the Nelson girl,' her husband interjected.

'I'm talking about Marilyn,' Geraldine said.

'There's nothing wrong with Marilyn.' Bill's nose was buried in the paper again. 'Just growing pains.'

'I don't know,' Geraldine protested. 'I think it's something more.'

'If something's bothering her, she'll tell us about it. Greta always did. Why should Marilyn be any different?'

Geraldine shook her head now, as if trying to jar loose a thought that was nagging at her. 'They aren't the same. They're really quite different. And something's happening to Marilyn. Maybe I should talk to Monsignor about her.'

Bill Crane turned the page of his newspaper. 'Good idea. Why don't you do that?'

No one had told him school was cancelled for the day. He had simply arrived at St. Francis Xavier's to find the place deserted. The sisters were nowhere to be seen. Monsignor Vernon, if he was around, wasn't in his office. Peter had started to check his mail, then changed his mind. What if there was a message there? A message from the Monsignor? Better not to check at all.

He hurried down the hill, aware of the strange silence that had fallen over Neilsville. Everywhere he looked, there were clusters of people, talking softly among themselves, and looking up now and then, suspiciously, as if by quick furtive glances they would be able to catch a glimpse of the evil in their midst.

Peter felt the glances piercing him. They were looking at him, and wondering. Nothing much had ever happened in Neilsville until he came along. But since he had arrived, things had started going bad. How long would it be before the entire town became infected with whatever it was that was infecting the girls from St. Francis Xavier's? The only thing they could pinpoint was the outsider. Peter Balsam. The stranger. Not to be trusted.

As he passed each group the silence deepened, and he could sense that he was the focus of it. Then, after he passed, the talk would begin again, the heads drawn more closely together, lips close to ears, but the eyes, always the eyes, following him as he made his way down Main Street.

As soon as he got to his apartment, he called Margo.

'Peter? Is that you?' He hadn't spoken, and was pleased at the anxiety in her voice. He tried to mask his fears about the night before.

'Want to go for a ride? I've got the day off.'

'I didn't sleep all night—' Margo hesitated.

'Who did? But they cancelled school, and I decided to go see the Bishop. I was going to borrow your car, but why don't you come with me?'

She almost refused, almost told him she was going to spend the day in bed. But she didn't.

'I'll pick you up in twenty minutes,' she said. Then, as an afterthought: 'Are you going to take the tape?'

'I – I don't know,' Peter hedged. 'I hadn't thought about it.'

A silence, then Margo's voice, very confident.

'You don't have to tell him one of the voices is yours,' she pointed out, pinpointing his hesitation. 'The only voice that's recognizable is Monsignor Vernon's.'

What she said was true, but still he hesitated, wishing there was some other way. He knew there wasn't. Without the tape, how could he expect the Bishop to believe him? He made up his mind.

'I'll be waiting,' he said. 'With the tape.'

He hung up the phone, and opened the bottom drawer of the desk. He reached into the back of the drawer, groping for the tiny cassette. His fingers couldn't find it. He pulled the drawer out further, and felt again.

He was still searching when Margo arrived twenty minutes later. All the drawers had been emptied, and he was methodically going through their contents, though he knew it was useless. As soon as Margo saw what was happening, she knew.

'It's gone, isn't it?'

Peter nodded mutely.

'Was it hidden?'

Again, he nodded. 'But no one searched for it. They knew exactly where it was.' Margo's face clouded: was he accusing her?

'Only one person knew where the tape was,' Peter went on. He looked at her with an anguish that tore at her. Whatever he was going through, he wasn't accusing her.

'Who?' She wasn't sure she wanted to know the answer.

'Me,' Peter said bitterly. 'I'm the only one who knew where that tape was. So I must have taken it myself.'

He told her about the night before, about locking himself in and chaining the door. Then about putting a chair in front of the door, to be extra sure. Then about the dreams, the dream in which he had been at the rectory, been back with the Society.

'This morning the door was unlocked,' he finished. 'The chain was loose, the chair was back over there . . . And I was a mess.'

Margo sank onto the sofa, despair washing over her like a wave.

'And you took them the tape?' she said softly. 'Is that what happened?'

'What else could have happened?' Peter answered, spreading his hands in a gesture of frustration. 'The only thing I had on them, and I gave it to them myself.'

'Maybe you didn't,' Margo said suddenly, standing up. 'Maybe you just hid it somewhere else, and forgot.' She began searching the room, methodically at first, but then more and more frantically, as Peter looked on. As suddenly as she had begun searching, she stopped. She looked at him, and for the first time Peter saw fear reflected in the depths of her eyes.

'It's no good, is it?' she said bleakly. 'I won't find it here, will I?'

'No,' Peter said softly. 'I don't think you will.' He went to her and put his arms around her. She stiffened, then let go, her arms curling around him, holding on to him.

'Oh, God, Peter, are they going to get you too?'

She believes me, he thought. At least she believes me. But he didn't have an answer for her question.

Father Duncan looked up at them and smiled.

'Mr. Balsam,' he said. 'What a pleasant surprise.' But something in his face told Peter it wasn't pleasant at all. A surprise, yes. But not pleasant. He could almost see the young priest trying to sneak a look at the calendar on his desk, hoping he had not made a mistake, hoping his name was not there.

'It's all right,' he said, trying to put him at his ease. 'I don't have an appointment.'

It was the right thing to say. Father Duncan relaxed in his chair, and his smile suddenly became genuine.

'Well, that's a relief. Usually people come in here without an apppointment, demand to see His Eminence, then insist that they set up an appointment two weeks ago.'

'Then I can't see him?'

'I didn't say that,' the secretary grinned. 'Honesty should be rewarded.' He pressed the key on the intercom. 'Mr. Balsam is here for his ten-o'clock appointment,' he said smoothly. He winked at Peter, then included Margo in the wink. There was an ominous silence from the intercom, then the Bishop's voice crackled through.

'I don't see his name on my calendar,' he barked.

'Really?' Father Duncan said smoothly. 'My mistake; I must have forgotten. But we can't take that out on Mr. Balsam, can we?'

'Whom *can* we take it out on?' the Bishop's voice came back.

'Your next appointment,' Father Duncan said. 'It's Mrs. Chambers. She wants to arrange for you to give some spiritual guidance to her Girl Scouts.'

'Little green trolls,' the Bishop muttered. 'All right, show Balsam in.'

Margo settled herself in the secretary's office to wait, and Father Duncan ushered Peter into the inner office. The Bishop was on his feet, his hand out.

'Nice to see you again, young man, however, unexpectedly.' He tried to direct a severe look at Father Duncan and failed. 'Any idea how long you can keep Mrs. Chambers at bay?'

'She won't wait more than twenty minutes,' the secretary warned.

'Then let's count on at least an hour's chat, shall we? Sit down, Mr. Balsam, sit down.' The Bishop waited until Father Duncan was out of the room, then turned twinkling eyes back to Peter.

'He's terrific,' he said. 'Always manages to get the people I want to see in, and keep the others out. But Mrs. Chambers won't be easy.'

'I'm sorry,' Peter apologized. 'I should have made an appointment, but I didn't know I'd have any free time till just a couple of hours ago.'

'Of course you should have, but it doesn't matter. I was going to have Father Duncan call you today anyway.' The sparkle left his eyes. 'What's going on in Neilsville?'

'That's what I want to talk to you about.'

It took nearly thirty minutes for Peter to reconstruct the entire story for the Bishop. He tried to make the realities of the Society of St. Peter Martyr as palatable as possible, but the Bishop prodded him. 'Out with it, young man. I'm not a prude, and I've been around.'

Peter told him as much as he could remember, and everything he and Margo had been able to piece together from the tape. The Bishop listened in silence.

'And you think the Society is connected with the suicides in Neilsville?'

'I do.'

'It sounds pretty farfetched.'

'I know it does. But what happened last night is pretty farfetched, too. I'm sure I wound up in the rectory last night, and I know I didn't want to go. I don't remember going, I don't remember being there, and I don't remember coming home again. But I'm sure that's where I was.'

'And you think they got you there by using some kind of mind control.' The Bishop turned it over in his mind. 'Frankly, I don't think it's possible.'

'I wouldn't have either, a few days ago. But when nothing makes any sense. you have to believe whatever the facts point to. Nothing else makes any sense at all – it's got to be some form of mind control or hypnotism . . . or something.'

'You make it all sound rather sinister,' the Bishop commented.

'It is sinister. Two girls are dead. Two more nearly died. At first I thought the Society was just a sick pastime for some unbalanced priests. But it isn't, Your Eminence. It's something else entirely. Monsignor Vernon believes he *is* Peter Martyr – his reincarnation. And they think I'm a reincarnation of St. Acerinus, a man named Piero da Balsama, the man who killed St. Peter Martyr. At first I thought it was harmless, but I don't think so any more. I think they're all very sick, and I think they've found some way to inflict their sickness on everyone else.'

Bishop O'Malley leaned forward slightly.

'I wish I could agree with you,' he said gravely, 'but I'm afraid I can't. I talked to a—' He consulted a pad on his desk. '– Dr. Shields this morning.'

'I know him.'

'He thinks Neilsville is experiencing a suicide contagion.'

'I know,' Peter said shortly.

'Then you should also know that I agree with him,' the Bishop said. 'It is quite obvious to me that what's going on at St. Francis Xavier's is a hysterical phenomenon. And, quite frankly, it doesn't surprise me. Dr. Shields told me that the sort of thing we seem to be experiencing usually – almost without exception – occurs in mental hospitals.' The Bishop paused, considering. 'Unfortunately, in small towns, parochial schools can become very institutional. I think we're going to have to begin making some rather radical changes in the structure of the school.'

'Will that include Monsignor Vernon's dismissal?' Peter asked. He supposed the question was rude, or at best impertinent, but he didn't care. He felt his stomach tighten when the Bishop shook his head.

'I don't see that I can go that far,' he said gently. 'Not right away, at least. It may become necessary if he refuses to go along with the changes I have in mind. But not now.'

Peter stared at the Bishop. When he finally found his tongue the words tumbled out.

'But he's a danger now! It's now that he's doing whatever it is he's doing! I had it all on the tape!'

'But you don't have the tape, do you?'

Peter could only shake his head.

The Bishop stood up. 'I'm sorry Mr. Balsam – Peter. May I call you Peter?' Balsam nodded. 'Peter, I just don't see that anyone in the world would believe the story you just told me. I don't believe it myself. I grant you that I don't think much of the Society of St. Peter Martyr, but all you've given me are a lot of impressions about things you can't even remember. After all, you could be wrong.'

It was over, Peter walked numbly through Father Duncan's office, and Margo fell in step behind him.

'It didn't go well, did it?' she asked, knowing by his face that it had not. 'What are you going to do?'

He didn't answer the question for a long time. Instead, as he drove back toward Neilsville, he watched the barren countryside, and remembered how foreign it had looked to him when he had come in on the train only a few weeks earlier. Now, it all seemed terribly familiar. Now the countryside around Neilsville looked every bit as bleak as Peter Balsam felt.

Beside him, Margo Henderson maintained the silence. She, too, watched the desert go by, and wondered if there would ever be anything else for her. She was getting tired of desert; she'd lived in it too long. She'd hoped Peter Balsam would take her out of it. Instead, he was getting caught by it.

As they approached the outskirts of Neilsville, he suddenly took her hand. 'I know what I'm going to do.' He said it so quietly she almost didn't realize what he was talking about. Then, remembering, she looked at him questioningly.

'I'm going to play my part,' Peter said quietly. 'I'm going to be St. Acerinus.'

BOOK FOUR

St. Acerinus

TWENTY-SIX

Leona Anderson sat in her living room, staring vacantly ahead, trying to understand it. She had sat like that all day, wordlessly, not hearing the condolences of her friends.

She had listened to Monsignor Vernon that morning, heard him telling her why her daughter could not be buried in sanctified ground. She had known it, of course, but until the priest had come to tell her, she had not believed it.

'It's that teacher,' she said bitterly, shattering the silence that had fallen over the room.

One of the women glanced at Leona, then away.

'It is,' Leona insisted quietly. 'They were all in his class, all of them. Judy and Karen, and Janet and – and —' she broke off, knowing that if she said her daughter's name she would lose control. She must not cry. Not yet. First, she must destroy Peter Balsam. 'When I first met him I knew there was something wrong. And look what's happened to us.' She looked desolately from one face to another.

'Leona, we don't know what's happening,' one of the women said soothingly. Leona Anderson turned to the woman who had spoken, and a hardness came into her eyes.

'Don't we, Marie?' Then, remembering that only a few days ago Marie Connally had come close to going through what she was going through now. Leona spoke more softly: 'But what if Janet had died? How would you feel then?'

Marie Connally smiled. 'But she didn't die, and she isn't going to. She's home, and she's feeling fine. And that's largely because of Peter Balsam. I'm sorry, Leona, but if you want to attack Mr. Balsam, please don't do it in front of me.'

'Think what you like,' Leona said stiffly. 'But mark my

words. It isn't over yet. As long as Peter Balsam is in this town, it won't be over.'

The object of Leona's bitterness emerged from the church into the darkness of night, and began making his way back down the hill.

Below him he watched the scattered lights of Neilsville glowing dimly in the night. It crossed his mind that the lights of Neilsville were as dim as his own faith. He had spent two hours in the church, seeking guidance and solace, and had found none. Instead, he had found himself.

A few minutes later he was on Main Street. But it was a different Main Street than the one he had walked up two hours earlier. Or he was different.

Now, as he felt the eyes of strangers on him, he met their glances, and smiled at them. They turned away, embarrassed. Once he heard a voice shouting at him from a doorway.

'Go away, teacher,' a woman shouted. 'Leave us in peace!'

Peter turned around to confront the source of the shout, but the woman was gone, faded back into the cloak of the evening.

In the middle of town, music throbbed from the Praying Mantis, and Peter found himself drawn to it. He paused at the door, then made up his mind. He pulled the door open, and stepped into the shabby discotheque.

In the flickering light the faces seemed gaunt and hollow and there was a heavy silence behind the blaring music. It was a moment before Peter realized that there were no girls in the room: the girls seemed to have disappeared from the face of the earth. He knew why. None of them would be allowed to go out tonight. They would all be home, their parents keeping a watchful eye on them.

Someone waved to Peter, and he started across the floor.

Sitting together at a table were Jim Mulvey, Lyle Crandall, and Jeff Bremmer. Without waiting for an invitation, Peter seated himself in the fourth chair at their table. All three boys looked at him. He could see fear in their eyes.

'It isn't all that bad,' he said softly. 'It's almost over now.'

'What is?' Lyle Crandall asked. He looked curiously at the teacher, and thought the man looked different. It was the eyes. There was something about Mr. Balsam's eyes that had changed.

'The dying,' Peter Balsam said. 'It won't go on much longer. It can't.'

Jeff Bremmer stared at him. 'Mr. Balsam, what's going on?'

Peter smiled at the boy, a warm smile. 'I wish I could tell you, Jeff.'

'But you know, don't you?' Jeff said, more as a statement than as a question.

Balsam shrugged. 'As much as anybody knows, I guess.'

'It's my fault,' Jim Mulvey said suddenly. Peter shifted in his chair to look squarely at the boy.

'Don't believe that,' he said. 'Don't ever believe that. Whoever's to blame, it isn't you. It isn't any of you. Children don't do things like what's being done here.'

'But they do,' Jeff Bremmer said softly. 'My dad says it's called a suicide contagion, and it happens all the time.'

'In mental hospitals,' Balsam said. 'That only happens in mental hospitals.'

'Then what is it?' Lyle asked. All three boys were staring at Balsam.

'It's a game,' Peter said, more to himself than to the boys. They looked at each other, puzzled.

'A game?' It was Jim Mulvey, and now he, too, saw that something had changed in their teacher. 'What kind of a game?'

'A religious game, I suppose you might say.' He was about to say something else, but he was interrupted.

The sound tore through the room like a knife, cutting through the music, through what little conversation was going on, through each of the people who heard it.

It was the siren, wailing through Neilsville.

'Oh, Jesus, not again.'

No one knew who had spoken, and no one cared. It was the thought that had come to all of them, and all of them knew it was too late.

Somewhere in Neilsville, 'again' had happened. As if an order had been given, all the people in the Praying Mantis moved out into the street, where they were swallowed up by the crowd that had emerged as if from nowhere in response to the eerie cry of the speeding ambulance.

Peter Balsam spoke to no one, and no one spoke to him. He made his way quickly through the crowd, and started once more up Cathedral Hill, moving faster as he climbed, until, by the time he reached the top, he was running.

He didn't stop till he reached the rectory.

He looked up.

Smoke was curling from the chimney. The sound of chanting drifted through the night.

Marie Connally was trying to hurry her husband as they walked home from the Andersons'.

'Can't you walk a little faster?' Marie asked, increasing her pace.

Dick Connally's arm tightened around his wife's shoulder. 'There's nothing wrong. No need to hurry,' he said with a conviction he didn't feel.

'But she's only been out of the hospital a day. I just don't like the idea of leaving her alone.'

'She's not alone,' Dick reminded her. 'Your mother's with her.'

'Well, I just don't like it. Janet should have us—'

She broke off as the sound of the siren reached them. They stopped on the sidewalk and stared at each other, listening. Then, as the siren grew steadily louder, they began running.

Lights blazed from their house.

The ambulance was parked in the driveway, its red lights still flashing.

'Stay back,' someone called to them. 'Don't go in!'

They ignored the warning.

Marie Connally's mother stood numbly at the foot of the

stairs, stairs, her face pale, her whole body shaking. She stared hollowly at her daughter and son-in-law, then one hand reached toward them, grasping at them.

'I fell asleep,' she muttered. 'I was watching television, and I fell asleep.' No one heard her: Marie and Dick were already halfway up the stairs.

And so they saw her again. It was like a recurring nightmare. She looked exactly the same, her limp body suspended from the fixture in the ceiling, an extension cord knotted around her neck.

Only this time it was too late. Her skin was bluish, and her eyes bulged. Her face, which had always been so pretty, was no longer recognizable.

From her wrists, blood was still dripping to the floor.

Marie Connally began screaming.

Her husband put his arms around her, and tried to pull her from the room. But it was no use; she remained rooted to the spot, staring at Janet, screaming.

She stayed that way for almost five minutes, until one of the paramedics prepared a shot and administered it to her.

The shot could stop the crying, but it could never erase the image. For the rest of her life, Marie Connally would live with the vision of her daughter hanging dead from a light cord.

Just before she fell under the deadening influence of the sedative, Marie Connally decided that Leona Anderson had been right.

It was Peter Balsam. It must have been. There could be no other answer.

In Neilsville that night, no one slept.

TWENTY-SEVEN

There was an uncomfortable stillness in the auditorium. It was as if they had been anaesthetized and were waiting for the stimulant that would bring them awake again. When Monsignor Vernon moved to the lectern they looked at him expectantly; for years they had been trained to look to their religious superiors for guidance. Now, the teaching sisters of St. Francis Xavier's rustled their habits; all over the room beads were suddenly released from tight grips.

Monsignor Vernon looked from face to face, trying to gauge the mood of the sisters. With a few exceptions, they looked confused. Concerned, and confused. Sister Elizabeth, however, looked angry as did Sister Kathleen. And Sister Marie, back from retreat, seemed to be entirely closed down, her face impassive, a glaze in her eyes that gave no clue as to what might be going on in her mind.

'I wish I could say "good morning," Monsignor Vernon began gravely. 'But there isn't very much good about this morning.'

'Monsignor—' It was a hesitant voice from the back of the room, and the priest smiled at the elderly nun whose face seemed particularly drawn. She had been teaching at St. Francis Xavier's for nearly forty years, and the parents of most of the students had been students of hers. Leona Anderson, in fact, had named her daughter for the nun.

'Yes, Sister Penelope?'

'I – I—' the old sister faltered, trying not to cry. 'It's just all so terrible. What's happening to us?'

'We don't know,' Monsignor Vernon said calmly. 'That's why I wanted all of you here this morning, to try to tell you what little we do know, and to decide what to do.'

'Penny,' Sister Penelope said, her voice breaking, 'I need to know about Penny. She was always my favourite – always.'

One of the other sisters reached out to pat Sister Penelope gently on the hand, and whisper a word or two in her ear.

'I wish I could tell you what happened,' Monsignor said sorrowfully. 'All we know is that she left her things in the quiet-room.'

'What about Janet?'

Now Monsignor Vernon frowned slightly. 'Again, we don't know exactly what happened. But Janet did leave a note.'

A ripple passed through the room as the sisters looked at each other, murmuring among themselves. At last, there was something.

'She said she didn't know exactly why she was doing ... what she did. She said she was having very strange feelings lately, feelings she didn't understand. It was almost like – and I'm quoting her now – "someone outside is making me want to kill myself".'

The nuns looked at each other. None of it made any sense to them. They turned their attention back to the Monsignor.

'She went on to say that she was feeling more and more hopeless, and even though she really didn't want to kill herself, she was being forced to anyway. She asked to be forgiven for what she did.'

'Forgiven?' Sister Elizabeth asked stiffly. 'By whom?'

Monsignor Vernon's eyes met those of the nun, and a look of understanding passed between them: The Church is a rock and cannot be bent. 'I don't know,' the priest said softly. 'Perhaps she forgot she would not be dying in a state of grace.' Another murmur buzzed through the room as the nuns considered the state of Janet's soul. Monsignor Vernon let it go on for a moment, then cleared his throat to regain their attention.

'We don't know, of course, what is going on here. I confess I'm as baffled as any of you. And I also find I'm forced to go outside the Church for help.'

'Outside the Church?' Sister Kathleen said in a manner that

made her opinion clear: there could not possibly be any help outside the Church.

'I – we – are put in a very difficult situation,' the priest said with unease. 'My faith, of course, lies in the Church, and the Church places full responsibility for suicide on the person who commits it. And yet, we are faced with a unique situation. Three of our girls have died, and a fourth one has tried to kill herself. Can it be that each of these girls came to the same decision independently?' Though he had intended the question rhetorically, Sister Elizabeth had an answer.

'They were all friends,' she said emphatically. 'Close friends. Ever since they were small, what one of those girls did, all of them did. That's why we have always tried to keep them apart.'

'I'm aware of that, Sister,' Monsignor Vernon said. 'And I'm afraid that closeness is part of the problem. Dr. Shields—'

'Who?' It was Sister Penelope again.

'Dr. Shields,' the priest repeated the name. 'He's a psychiatrist at the hospital. And he tells me that, despite what the Church teaches, there is a phenomenon called suicide contagion.'

Suddenly the nuns were frowning and staring at each other as Monsignor Vernon explained the term.

'But what can be done about it?' Elizabeth demanded.

'I don't know. When it happens in a mental institution, the solution is easy. They simply put the girls under physical restraint until the hysteria that causes the syndrome passes. That, of course, is impossible in this situation. It simply isn't feasible to put all the girls in the school under physical restraint. Although,' he added, 'there have been times when I wished I could do exactly that.'

An appreciative chuckle passed over the room, and some of the tension seemed to ease. Then Sister Kathleen made a small gesture.

'Monsignor?'

'Yes, Sister?'

'You've only mentioned girls. What about the boys?'

'According to Dr. Shields this sort of hysteria only affects adolescent girls. Our boys are quite safe.'

'But what do we do?' one of the sisters asked.

Monsignor Vernon shrugged. 'There isn't too much we can do. But,' he warned, 'we must stay calm. We must carry on as always. School will be in session tomorrow, and the parents of every child who isn't there will be contacted, and urged very strongly to keep their children in school.'

'Are you sure that's wise?' It was Sister Marie, and it was the first time she had spoken that morning.

'It's the only thing we can do,' Monsignor Vernon said. 'If the children are here we can watch them. If they aren't . . .' The Monsignor's voice trailed off, as if the consequences he had been about to name were too dire to be articulated. 'We must watch them,' he repeated, 'we must watch the girls.' He paused, then added crisply, 'If you notice anything out of the ordinary, anything at all, I want you to report it to me at once.'

The sisters digested this, and wondered just what was to be considered "out of the ordinary." Lately, everything had begun to look out of the ordinary.

'Monsignor,' Sister Marie asked suddenly, 'why isn't Peter Balsam here?'

'I asked him to stay home today, and perhaps tomorrow as well. This whole thing has been very difficult for him, and it seemed to me that he needed some rest.'

It was as if a dam had burst in the room. The sisters were suddenly talking animatedly among themselves, glancing at Monsignor Vernon every now and then, then whispering to each other once more. Only Sister Marie remained aloof from the buzzing. She sat almost isolated in the hubbub, her eyes fixed on Monsignor Vernon. She still wore that slightly glazed, unfathomable look. Then, as quickly as it had begun, the nuns' talk subsided. Sister Elizabeth stood. It was apparent she had become the spokeman for them all.

'Monsignor,' she said, 'we have some questions about Mr. Balsam. I'm not sure how to begin,' she went on, though it was obvious that she certainly did know how to begin. 'I'm afraid, though, that we all think there has to be some connection between Mr. Balsam and what's happening to the girls. Particularly in light of what Janet Connally said in her note. About someone putting thoughts into her head. Who else could it be but Mr. Balsam? Certainly, before he came, we never had any trouble like this. And before he came, those four girls were never in a class together. But now he's here, and the four girls were all in his class, and of course we all know what kind of class he teaches –' She paused significantly, as thought the conclusion was inescapable; the psychology class was somehow responsible for the deaths of the girls. '– and it seems to us that the most obvious way to put a stop to all this . . . this madness is to put a stop to Mr. Balsam and his psychology class.'

She sat down again, her expression telling the world that as far as she was concerned, the matter was closed. She, and the rest of the sisters, had placed Peter Balsam in the centre of the horror around them, and it was now up to Monsignor Vernon to expel the offender from their midst.

'I can understand your concerns,' he said carefully, trying to read the mood of the sisters as accurately as he could. He would have to tread lightly. 'As a matter of fact, I share some of them. It certainly does seem strange that all this is happening to girls in one class, particularly a psychology class. But I think we have to be very careful not to judge – not to make quick decisions based more on feelings than on facts. Of course, I realize it must seem a bit strange to all of you, asking a man with Peter Balsam's background to instruct adolescent girls on the subject of psychology—'

'His background?' Sister Elizabeth was on her feet again. 'What about his background?'

'Well, I just mean that all things considered, it strikes me as being a bit peculiar that Peter Balsam should be involved with so many girls killing themselves. Considering his history, I mean.'

'What history?' Sister Elizabeth demanded. 'What about his background? Monsignor, what are you talking about?'

The priest stared at them. 'You mean you didn't know?'

he said, as if genuinely puzzled. 'But I thought I'd told you long ago.'

'Told us *what*?' Monsignor Vernon could see the swing of Sister Elizabeth's habit as her foot tapped impatiently beneath the heavy skirts.

'I'm sorry,' he said contritely. 'I thought you were all familiar with Peter Balsam's background. But I can see that you're not.' He looked from one face to the next, as if trying to make up his mind whether to go on. He made his decision. 'But since you aren't,' he said, 'I think it would be highly inappropriate of me to talk about him just now. Highly inappropriate.' He turned, and a moment later had left the room. The nuns, left to themselves, huddled together, trying to decide what the priest had been talking about.

All but Sister Marie. Sister Marie remained in her seat, her eyes fixed on the door through which Monsignor Vernon had just passed.

Peter Balsam spent most of that day alone in his apartment. In the middle of the morning he had gone out, gone downtown, just because the walls had begun closing in on him. Downtown, it was worse. Downtown, Neilsville closed in on him.

They were staring at him openly now. There was no silence as he passed. Now, they raised their voices to be sure he heard what they were saying. Much of the talk was about Janet Connally:

'Why did they let her out of the hospital?'

'They thought she was all right. *He* said she was all right!' (A not very surreptitious look at Peter Balsam.)

'*He* went to see her, you know.'

'And they let him? Well, I never!'

'Lord knows what he told her, but after that note she left —'

The talk that wasn't about Janet Connally was about him:

'Comes from Philadelphia—'

'Studied for the priesthood, but they threw him out—'

'You know, he's seeing Margo Henderson!'

'But she's *divorced*—'

'Ever since he came to Neilsville—'

That was the summation. Everywhere he went, Peter Balsam felt it bearing down on him. 'Ever since he came to Neilsville—' The sentence was never finished, always left hanging to be completed by the listener. By noon he was back in his apartment, the door locked, the draperies drawn. He was beginning to feel like a caged animal, and he was sure he could sense them outside; the small-town people, passing by his building and looking at the closed-up apartment, and wondering what he was doing inside, what he might be planning in the darkness.

He had not been accused. He had not been tried.

But he had been judged, and found guilty.

Peter Balsam wanted to leave Neilsville, wanted to pack his clothes and flee. It would be easy. He could simply walk once more through the town, and go to the train station. There would be a train at six o'clock. Once, he went so far as to pull his suitcases down from the closet shelf and open them on the bed.

But he couldn't do it. Not this time. He'd run away before – from the priesthood, then from his marriage. Besides, this time there was more to think about than himself. There were the children. If he left, it would go on and on, and nobody would know how to stop it.

Nobody would even understand it. And why would they? It was simply too bizarre.

Too bizarre. The words rang in his head. It *was* too bizarre. There had to be something more. Something he was overlooking. In the middle of the afternoon, he went back to his books.

First the story of the saints. He reviewed it all, what little there was.

He read briefly over the paragraphs about Piero da Verona, the fanatical Dominican priest who had roamed Italy during the early years of the Inquisition, persecuting heretics and sinners, in the name of the True Faith and the Mother Church.

Then he came to the man whose name was so similar to his own – Piero da Balsama, the heretic who had finally been driven too far, and waited in ambush one night to crush Verona's head with a stone.

Not that the killing had accomplished anything, Balsam realized. The Medieval Church had elevated its murdered Inquisitor to the status of saint, named hım St. Peter Martyr, and used his martyrdom to carry on the Inquisition. And apparently it had worked very nicely, for the murderer, poor Peiro da Balsama, had repented, and joined an order himself. Eventually he had even joined his Inquisitor in the ranks of the saints.

Piero da Balsama had become St. Acerinus.

Was it all really happening again? Balsam wondered. Had his old friend Pete Vernon really come to believe that the two of them were the ancient saints in reincarnation?

He went over their histories in his mind. Certainly there were parallels beyond the simple coincidence of their names. Pete Vernon, since his elevation to Monsignor, had certainly taken on the sort of fanatical dedication to the Church that had been the hallmark of the Dominican Inquisitors.

And Peter Balsam had certainly undergone some profound doubts of his own faith, the sort of doubts that once, long ago, would have branded him a heretic. But that was long ago. In the modern Church, questioning such as his was common. Many Catholic theologians, Balsam knew, had proposed more radical ideas than he ever had. But not in Neilsville. With a chill that turned his body to ice, Balsam remembered the massive black-clad figure of the Monsignor standing in the gym, pointing at him; remembered the light in his eyes and the word he had used: *heretic*.

He remembered all the times he had tried to confront the priest, and all the times he had backed off in the face of the priest's hypnotic wrath.

Hypnotic.

It was like a light had been switched on, and the darkness cleared away. The word stood out in Balsam's mind, and images began to swirl around it.

The flickering candlelight.

The steady rhythms of the chanting.

The memory lapses, when time had been telescoped, and hours had been compressed into minutes.

The things Janet had told him: 'I'm being forced to do things I don't want to do.' 'It's as if something's controlling me, making me do things.'

It had to be a form of hypnosis, but a form that went beyond the normal.

Feverishly, Peter began going through his books; not the texts, but the odd volumes he had been collecting over the years, the flotsam and jetsam of parapsychology, psychic phenomena, and speculation.

He picked up a piece here, a bit there. It was like fitting together extra pieces from several jigsaw puzzles to form something new. And when he was finished, it made a certain kind of sense.

Monsignor Vernon had found a way to control minds.

In his fanaticism he had stumbled onto a method of using the combined concentration of several minds to inflict his will on others. And it was working.

The girls were dying.

But why? Peter Balsam spent the rest of the afternoon worrying at the problem, turning it over in his mind, trying to fathom the motivations of the priest.

He knew it had to do with the girls. But was it just the four girls who had been victimized so far, or would there be more?

And there was the problem of his own role. He tried to figure out how he fit into the scheme.

He was sure that he did. Too many times Monsignor Vernon had insisted that he was vital to the Society of St. Peter Martyr, although he certainly didn't share their fanatical opinions. It was something else. It had to be.

Something clicked in his mind, Something from his past, but way back in his past, when he had first come to the convent. There was something about one of the boys, something none of them was supposed to talk about. Could it have been about Pete Vernon? His thoughts were interrupted by the telephone.

Margo's voice brought him out of his reverie, and he glanced at the clock. The day was gone.

'Want me to bring over some dinner?'

'Yes. And I want you to spend the night,'

There was a silence. Margo thought she detected something different in Peter's voice, a sureness that she had never heard before.

'Are you all right?' she asked.

'I'm fine,' Peter replied. 'I finally put it all together, Margo. I know what's happening around here.'

'Are you sure?'

'I'm positive. The only thing I don't know is why it's happening, but I'll find that out, too. And then I'll put an end to it all.'

The confidence in his voice made up her mind for her. For the first time, Peter Balsam sounded as she had hoped he would sound.

'I'll bring some steaks. And my toothbrush.'

While Peter Balsam and Margo Henderson ate dinner that night, and made love, and were happy together, Marilyn Crane found herself in turmoil. She tried to read, and she tried to watch television. Then she went up to her room, and tried to study. She couldn't concentrate.

She heard things in hei mind. She heard a strange chanting, and voices calling to her. She imagined the voices were angels, and they wanted her to come to them.

She knew she couldn't. If the angels wanted her, they would have to come for her. She wished they would.

She listened to the angels call out to her.

She wanted to respond, wanted to heed their call.

But it was sinful, and Marilyn didn't want to sin. The Sorrowful Mother hated sin.

Marilyn Crane forced herself not to listen to the voices.

From the chimney on the roof of the rectory, smoke curled slowly into the sky.

No one in Neilsville noticed it. They were all at home, worrying about their children, and watching them.

TWENTY-EIGHT

A somnolence lay over the town, and it was centred on Cathedral Hill, where the buildings of the church, the school, and the convent had taken on the air of a fortress. People moved slowly, forcing themselves through the motions of the day, as if by keeping up the appearance of normality they could somehow achieve it.

They watched each other, all of them, In every class, lessons came to a sudden halt as the teachers found themselves studying the faces of their students, searching for a clue as to who would be next.

The students, too, watched each other, and gossiped together between classes. But with them, there was almost a sense of anticipation, an excitement, as if they were spectators at a macabre circus. With the confidence of youth, each of them was sure that whatever force was striking out at them would inevitably hit someone else. Who?

There was an unspoken consensus.

As she moved through the day. Marilyn Crane could feel it. As long as she could remember, she had felt people watching her, felt them talking about her, felt them snickering silently at her. Now, she was sure, they had decided she was next, and they were watching her more intently than ever.

It didn't matter where she went; she could feel the curious eyes on her, examining her as if she were an exotic insect. And it wasn't just her classmates, it was the Sisters, too. She heard the rustling of habits as the nuns began to keep a vigil over her. Every time she turned around one of them was there: a figure in black disappearing around a corner, or seeming to be busy with something else, or bending close to another black-garbed figure, whispering something into an invisible ear.

The days went by and her turmoil grew. As her emotions became more chaotic and her thoughts more confused, they knew. They knew, and they were waiting.

She began spending more time in church. She stopped eating lunch, preferring to spend the hour in the sanctuary, losing herself in the Madonna, silently crying out to the serene figure to help her.

She was rarely alone in the church; always there were two or three people scattered among the pews, each of them lost in his own meditations. Often they were the families of the girls who had already died, privately seeking solace for their loss, praying for understanding.

Peter Balsam, at his own insistence, had returned to the school after only one day's absence. But he had changed, and everyone noticed the change. They were watching him almost as closely as they were watching Marilyn Crane, and he knew why. Just as they thought Marilyn Crane would be the next victim, they thought he was responsible. Leona Anderson, in her grief, had done her work.

Everywhere he went the watching eyes, the hostile stares, of the people of Neilsville frightened him. The nuns too, had changed, had hardened toward him. He had tried to find out why, but none of them would tell him. They merely stared at him, as if to say 'you know better than we.'

Except Sister Marie. She came to him the day he returned to St. Francis Xavier's, and offered to help him.

'Help?' he asked blankly. 'Help with what?'

'Before I left, you wanted me to translate something for you. Or at least try.'

Peter remembered. The tape. 'I'm sorry,' he said. 'It's too late.' Then: 'Sister Marie, why did you leave?'

A small frown crossed her brow. 'I don't know really,' she said. 'Just one of Monsignor's quirks, I guess.'

'Monsignor's?'

'He ordered me into retreat.' Sister Marie's infectious grin suddenly lit up her face. 'I don't think he likes me. I'm afraid I just don't take things seriously enough for him. Every time he thinks I'm getting out of hand – my words, not his – he sends me off to spend a few days in retreat. Believe me, if you'd ever had to maintain the Silence for three days, you'd come back feeling more serious about everything, too.'

Peter tried to remember exactly what Monsignor Vernon had told him about Sister Marie's sudden absence. No, there was no conflict between what the priest had told him and what the nun was telling him now.

'I'm sorry I had to go just then,' he heard the nun saying. 'Was it terribly important? Whatever it was you wanted me to translate?'

Peter shook his head briefly, and tried to smile. 'I don't think so,' he said. 'I thought it was, but now I'm not sure. Anyway, it's too late.'

'Peter,' Sister Marie said slowly, as if having a difficult time making up her mind to speak. 'What you wanted me to translate – did it have anything to do with – with what's been going on? The girls?'

'I thought it did. But now I'm not sure.'

'Do you know what's going on?' Sister Marie asked bluntly.

'I think I do,' Peter said uncertainly, wondering whether to take her into his confidence.

Sister Marie chewed her lower lip. When she looked at him again there wasn't a trace of her usual merriment left in her eyes.

'A lot of people here think—' She broke off, embarrassed.

'That I'm responsible for what's happened to the girls?'

She nodded.

'What do you think?' Peter said softly.

She stared at him, and Peter saw tears brimming in her eyes. 'I – I don't know what to think,' she blurted finally. Then she turned, and hurried away from him.

Sister Marie hadn't spoken to him since, nor had Peter sought her out.

Every day he was growing more exhausted. Only on the nights that Margo Henderson stayed with him did he let himself sleep, and there had only been two of those nights. When she wasn't with him, he stayed up, keeping himself awake with coffee, afraid to sleep alone. The exhaustion was showing in his eyes, and he knew it was not going unnoticed in Neilsville.

He knew Leona Anderson had gone to Monsignor Vernon, demanding that Peter be dismissed immediately; he knew that the priest had refused. But he didn't know why the Monsignor had refused – the chill between the two men had grown to the point where they rarely spoke now, and the obvious tension between them served only to give the town one more thing to whisper about.

Occasionally Balsam himself wondered why he stayed, but each day he told himself that this would be the day he would find a way to be alone in the rectory, to search the study for whatever might be there that would fit the last piece into his puzzle. If there was anything, he had decided, it would be in the study, for it was in the study that the horror took place. Then, when he knew why the horror was perpetrated, he would know how to stop it.

His only solace was Margo Henderson. They began to spend each evening together; each evening Peter would reiterate his theory to Margo. And she would listen.

But nothing was happening. Neilsville was quiet. The days were beginning to take on the dull sameness they had always had, and Margo found it a relief. The town was still restless, people were still talking, but the tension was easing.

Except that each evening Peter Balsam would tell her again that what they were going through was only a respite, that the horror would begin again.

'But how can you be so sure?' she demanded one night. 'I mean, if anything's going to happen, why isn't it happening?'

'I don't know,' Peter said doggedly. 'But I know it isn't over yet. I won't be able to end it until I know why it's happening.'

Margo looked at his pale complexion and haggard eyes.

It was becoming an obsession with him. Their evenings weren't fun anymore; he was too wrapped up in a problem Margo was no longer sure even existed.

'Even if you find out, what makes you so sure you can do anything about it?' She tried to keep her voice level, but her own growing doubts about Peter came through.

'You don't believe me, do you?' Peter asked.

Margo saw no point in denying it. The doubts had been growing for days.

'I don't know,' she said, compromising with herself. 'I *want* to believe you, Peter. But it's all so—' She groped for the right word. '– so farfetched. Peter, it just isn't rational.'

'I never said it was,' Peter countered.

'No, you didn't,' Margo complained. 'Maybe if you had tried to make the whole thing sound reasonable it would be easier. But you don't. You just insist that I believe you. You know, there really isn't any difference between you and Monsignor.'

The words stung, and Peter winced. 'I'm sorry you feel that way,' he said stiffly.

'So am I,' Margo said coldly. 'But it's the way I feel, and I can't do anything about it.'

Peter rose from his chair and went to the kitchen to fix himself a drink. As he pried the ice loose, and measured the liquor, he reflected on the fragility of the threads of faith. His faith in the Church had broken, and he had turned to himself. Now the carefully nurtured threads between himself and Margo had broken, too. Where could he turn now?

He returned to the living room.

Margo was gone.

Peter Balsam was alone.

It was on Tuesday that Peter Balsam overheard Marilyn Crane. He was sitting behind his desk in Room 16, trying to grade Latin exams. In the small room adjoining Room 16, Marilyn Crane and Jeff Bremmer were working with the rats. Peter had been vaguely aware of their conversation as they worked, but it wasn't until Marilyn suddenly began talking about the rats that Peter gave up trying to concentrate on his work and began listening to the two adolescents in the next room.

'They aren't any good anymore,' Marilyn suddenly commented.

Jeff Bremmer glanced at her, annoyed first that he had been assigned to work on the experiment with Marilyn, and currently because now she was insisting on talking, instead of simply getting on with it.

'What's that supposed to mean?'

Marilyn ignored the implied rebuke.

'Look at them. They don't even try anymore. It doesn't matter what you do; they just plod along until they get through the maze. A few days ago, you could tell them apart. But not anymore. Now they're all alike. It's like their personalities are gone.'

'They never had any personalities,' Jeff said, his irritation growing. 'They're just rats, for Christ's sake!'

Marilyn shot him a look. 'You shouldn't talk that way.'

'What way?'

'Swearing.'

'Oh, Jesus,' Jeff said deliberately.

Marilyn didn't hear him this time; her attention was back on the rats.

'Why do they do it?' she mused. 'Why don't they just sit in a corner and wait it out? All they get for finding their way through the maze is a little piece of food, and they'd get that anyway.'

'They don't know that,' Jeff said, anxious to get back to work. 'For all they know, if they sit down and do nothing, they'll starve to death.'

Marilyn didn't seem to hear him. 'Sometimes I feel just like them,' she said. Her voice had taken on a dreamy quality, and Jeff was no longer sure if she was talking to him, or to herself. 'Sometimes I feel like my life is just like that maze, and every time I figure out what I'm supposed to do, somebody changes the rules, and I have to start all over again.'

In Room 16, Peter Balsam put down the exam he had been working on, and devoted his full attention to Marilyn.

'Why do I bother to do it?' she was saying. 'Why don't I just quit? I mean, what could happen to me? I'm just like the rats.' Her voice grew bitter. 'They keep going, and I keep going, and they're all starting to seem alike, and I'm starting to seem like all the rest of them. It must have been the same for them. They must have felt just like I do, like someone else is running their lives for them. But they all gave in, and did what they were supposed to do. Except Judy. But she never does what she's supposed to do.'

Jeff Bremmer had stopped working, and was gaping at Marilyn. She no longer seemed to be aware of his presence, or even of where she was. Though she was still staring down into the maze, her eyes had taken on a faraway look, and Jeff wasn't sure she even saw the rats. Her voice continued to drone through the sudden quiet that had fallen over the two rooms.

'Janet tried to fight it, too; she just wasn't as strong as Judy is. But she was stronger than me. If she couldn't hold out against him, how can I? And why should I? It would be a lot easier just to give in to him, and get it over with.'

Jeff picked up on the word. 'Him.' She had said 'him.' He reached out and grabbed Marilyn's arm.

'Who?' he said. 'Give in to who?'

Marilyn didn't respond for a second or two, but then her eyes focused on Jeff, and her body stiffened. She hadn't realized she'd been talking out loud. She'd been thinking. Only thinking. But Jeff had heard.

She shifted her gaze, and looked through the open door to Room 16. Mr. Balsam was staring at her too. Everything she'd been thinking – no, said – they'd heard. Now they'd think she was crazy. She had to get out. Get out of the room. Get out of the school.

She wrenched her arm free of Jeff's grasp, and bolted toward the door. As she passed through Room 16 her tears began to come, and she tried to force back the sob that was in her throat. She began to run, out of the room, down the hall.

Out.

She had to get out. By the time the wracking sob tore loose from her throat, Marilyn Crane was halfway down Cathedral Hill.

She hadn't even noticed the smoke curling up from the roof of the rectory. She was only aware of her own sobbing, and the noises in her head. The sounds. The awful, compelling sounds.

By the time Peter Balsam could react, she was gone. He hurried to the door of the room, but she had disappeared around the corner; all he could hear was the pounding of her feet. He went slowly back into Room 16. Jeff Bremmer was waiting for him.

'What did she mean?' Jeff asked. 'It sounded like—'

'Never mind what it sounded like,' Peter snapped. Immediately he regretted his tone; he hadn't been thinking when he spoke. He tried to ease the hurt that had sprung into Jeff's face.

'I'm sorry,' he said. 'I was worried about Marilyn.'

'She's getting worse,' Jeff commented.

'Worse? What do you mean, worse?'

Jeff fidgeted uncomfortably. Maybe he shouldn't have said that. 'Well, she was always a little, you know, weird. But lately it's really gotten bad. I mean, most of the kids think—' He broke off, unwilling to condemn a peer in front of an adult, even if the peer was Marilyn Crane.

'Think what?' Peter asked. Then: 'Never mind. I know what they think.'

Jeff looked at his teacher curiously, remembering the word Marilyn had used. 'Him.' And then, when she had seen Mr. Balsam looking at her, she had run.

'You,' Jeff said suddenly. 'She was talking about you, wasn't she?'

'Me?' Balsam said blankly.

'When she was talking about giving in. She said something about giving in to "him." She was talking about you, wasn't she?'

'No,' Peter said definitely. 'She wasn't talking about me.'

But there was something in his eyes, something in his face, that made Jeff doubt him. When he left the room, Jeff Bremmer was sure that whatever had happened to all the girls – what was happening now to Marilyn Crane – Mr. Balsam was to blame.

Peter Balsam sat alone in the room for several minutes, trying to decide what to do. Whatever he did, he would have to do it alone. There was no one left to turn to.

He made up his mind. He would call Marilyn's mother. He would warn her, tell her to watch out for Marilyn, to talk to her.

Peter gathered his things together, locked the uncorrected quizzes into his desk, and left the room. His mind was so occupied with trying to decide exactly what to say to Mrs. Crane that he passed the rectory without even looking up.

No one answered the telephone at the Crane's home until nearly nine o'clock, and as the hour grew later, Peter became more and more worried. Maybe he was too late. Maybe something had already happened to Marilyn. But when the phone was finally answered, the voice speaking in his ear sounded normal.

'Yes?'

'Mrs. Crane?'

'Yes. Who is this?'

'We haven't met, Mrs. Crane. I'm one of Marilyn's teachers.'

Geraldine Crane's impulse was to hang up. How dared he call her? Didn't he know what everyone was saying about him?

'Mrs. Crane, are you still there?'

'What do you want?' Geraldine asked coldly.

'I'm calling about Marilyn. Is she there?'

'Of course she's here. Where else would she be?'

'Mrs. Crane, I'm very worried about Marilyn. I think she may be in danger, and I don't know what to do.'

'Danger?' Geraldine Crane held the receiver away from her ear and stared at it. What was the man talking about?

'She was working in the lab this afternoon, and I – well, I don't know how to put it exactly—'

'I suggest you put it the way it happened, whatever it was.'

'Well, she was sort of talking to herself.'

'Marilyn? Don't be ridiculous.' Geraldine was finding the man more annoying every minute.

'I'm sorry, maybe I put it badly.' He told her what he'd overheard, and what had happened after Marilyn realized she'd been talking out loud.

'I tried to go after her,' Peter finished. 'But by the time I got to the hall, she was gone.'

'Well, I can assure you, she's quite all right now,' Mrs. Crane said icily. 'She came home this afternoon, and we all went out for dinner. Right now she's upstairs, doing her homework.'

'Mrs. Crane, I know it sounds like a strange request, but I think you ought to spend some time with Marilyn. Talk to her. Try to find out what's bothering her.'

Geraldine Crane lost her patience. 'Mr. Balsam, apparently you don't know who you're talking to. I happen to be her mother. I talk to Marilyn every day. You spend perhaps one hour with her each day, and now you presume to tell me how to behave with my daughter. I know you claim to be a psychologist, but I have to tell you that I don't have much faith in that sort of thing. I never have, and after what's been happening in Neilsville since you arrived, I have even less. As far as I'm concerned, I think it might be best for everyone if you spent a lot less time meddling in the affairs of your students, and stuck entirely to your classes.'

'Mrs. Crane—'

'Mr. Balsam, I'll appreciate it if you don't interrupt me. Marilyn isn't like any of the other children in Neilsville. She's always, since she was a baby, been somewhat withdrawn. I don't know why, but it's always been that way. So you see,' she went on, her voice dripping with sarcasm, 'your wonderful perceptions are no news to me. I'm aware that Marilyn has been upset lately, but why wouldn't she be? My Lord, Mr. Balsam, she's lost three of her best friends. I don't know if you're aware of it, but Marilyn was very close to those girls. She visited Judy Nelson in the hospital, and Karen Morton had Marilyn at her party. So of course she's upset. She's a normal teen-ager. Mr. Balsam, and I would think you'd understand that.' Without waiting for a reply, Geraldine Crane firmly placed the receiver back in its cradle.

Peter Balsam stared at the dead phone in his hand, and wondered what to do. But there didn't seem to be anything left. He put on the coffee pot, and took one of the pills that helped him stay awake. It was going to be a long night.

Geraldine Crane sat seething for several minutes after she hung up on Peter Balsam, and congratulated herself on how well she'd handled the impudent teacher. Then, as her anger eased, she remembered what he'd said. Could he have been right? Was something bothering Marilyn?

Marilyn was on her bed, a book open in front of her. She looked up when her mother came into the room, but didn't close the book.

'Marilyn?' Geraldine's voice was tentative, as if she weren't quite sure how to approach her daughter.

'I'm studying, Mother.' There was a flatness to Marilyn's voice.

'I just thought you might like to talk awhile.'

'I don't. I talk too much. Can't you just leave me alone?' Marilyn turned her attention back to her book.

Geraldine stood helplessly at the door, wondering what she should do. Then, following the path of least resistance, she started out of the room.

'Marilyn? If you need to talk, I'm here.'

'I know, Mother.' But it was a dismissal, and Geraldine knew it. She left her daughter, and went back downstairs.

Marilyn got up and closed the door to her room. Why couldn't they leave her alone? All of them? It was Mr. Balsam on the telephone. She was sure of it. If it wasn't him, who else would have called and induced her mother to try to talk to her?

She couldn't talk to them. What could she talk to them

about? The strange things she wanted to do to herself? They wouldn't understand. She didn't even understand it herself, so how could they?

Maybe they wanted her to be upset. Maybe it all was Mr. Balsam, or he was part of it, whatever it was. But it couldn't be him, could it?

She would pray. She would pray for guidance, and the Blessed Virgin would tell her what to do.

She began praying. She prayed all through the night. And all through the night, the voices howled in her mind, calling to her, chanting to her.

The night was long, but for Marilyn Crane it wasn't nearly long enough.

TWENTY-NINE

Peter Balsam watched the sun come up, watched the black horizon turn first to a pearly grey, then to a pale rose as the first rays crept above the hills. The long night was over.

He'd sat up through the endless hours, concentrating his depleted energy on resisting the strang impulses within him. Hour after hour, he had heard the chanting echoing in his mind, reaching out to him like invisible fingers, pulling at him, demanding that he leave his home and go – where?

He was sure he knew. He was sure the Society of St. Peter Martyr was reaching out to him, trying to draw him to the rectory, trying to ply its evil on him once again.

The telephone had rung several times during the night, its jarring clangour breaking into his intense concentration, sending waves of fear through him. He wouldn't answer, wouldn't leave the chair he clung to. Each time it rang, it seemed louder, and went on longer. The last call had been just before dawn, and went on endlessly, the steadily paced rhythm of the bell breaking in on him, rattling on his nerves, shaking him.

Now, as the sun rose over Neilsville, Peter Balsam dragged himself into the tiny bathroom. He stared at himself in the mirror, and wondered if the image he saw was truly himself, or if something else was being reflected there.

The eyes were rimmed in red from lack of sleep, and at the corners, crow's feet were beginning to show starkly against his pale skin. His whole face seemed to sag under the weariness he felt. He wondered how long he could go on.

Today, he decided. Today, somehow, he must find a way to get into the rectory, to search the study. Whatever he was looking for, it had to be there. If it wasn't, there was no hope at all.

He began dressing, fighting off the tiredness. An irrational idea grew in his mind, and he reached up to the highest shelf of his closet, and pulled a large box from the depths. He set it on the bed, and opened it. His monastic robes lay inside, relics from a more secure past. He put on the unfamiliar articles, one by one.

He knew the exhaustion was overtaking him, knew that he shouldn't be doing what he was doing. He tried to tell himself to take off the vestments, to put on his ordinary clothing. But his body wouldn't obey, and once again he heard the chanting voices reaching out to grasp his mind. Only now he had no more resources left. His fight was done. As the unspoken commands came into his mind, his body numbly obeyed.

In his black robes, a crucifix swinging from his waist, an exhausted Peter Balsam left his apartment and began walking toward Main Street.

Marilyn Crane, too, had fought against the voices through the long night, her beads clutched in her hands, counting out the decades over and over, praying for her soul. As the sun climbed into the sky above Neilsville, Marilyn put the rosary aside, and looked at her fingers. They had grown red during the night, and had swollen. Blisters showed where she had squeezed the beads, as if through pressure alone she could find strength. Her legs ached, and at first she could barely move. She sat on the edge of the bed, flexing first one knee, then the other. She tried to close out the chaos that still raged in her mind, and concentrated instead on the sounds of her family preparing for the day.

She heard her mother calling her, and forced herself to get up from the bed, and move through the door of her room, and down the stairs.

In the kitchen, her mother stared at her.

'You're not dressed,' the voice accused. One more accusing voice. One more fragment of disapproval, adding itself to the confusion.

'I'm staying home today.' Her voice was flat, drained by the long hours of whispered prayer.

'Don't be silly.' Geraldine looked sharply at her younger daughter. 'Are you sick?'

'No. Just tired.'

'Well, I'm sorry. You shouldn't have studied so late. But that's your fault and no one else's. You'll go to school.'

The words rang in Marilyn's mind as she slowly plodded up the stairs. 'Your fault. Your fault. Your fault.' Everything was her fault. Everything that went wrong was her fault. The chaos in her mind grew, and Marilyn Crane stopped thinking.

She dressed slowly, almost dreamily, and when she was finished, she gazed at herself in the mirror.

'I'm pretty, she thought. I'm really very pretty.

She went downstairs, and presented herself to her mother. Geraldine surveyed her daughter critically.

'White?' she asked. 'For school? That's a Sunday dress.'

'But I want to wear it today.'

Why not? Geraldine Crane asked herself. She looks so tired, and if it'll make her feel better, why not? She kissed her daughter on the cheek, and Marilyn left the house.

She walked slowly, almost unaware of her surroundings. Suddenly she felt at peace, and the voices in her head were no longer calling to her so stridently; now they were singing to her, caressing her spirit.

She got to Main Street, but instead of turning to start up the long hill to the school, she turned the other way, and began walking into Neilsville, her soft white skirt floating around her, the morning sun bathing her face.

Far ahead, as if at the end of a tunnel, she saw a shape moving toward her. She concentrated on the shape, and her focus seemed to narrow until she was no longer aware of anything else: only the dark shape coming slowly closer. Marilyn clutched her purse to her abdomen with one hand, and with the other once again began counting the decades of the rosary.

Peter Balsam trudged slowly up Main Street, vaguely aware that people were staring at him. He knew he must be an odd spectacle in his robes, his face unshaven, his eyes swollen and red. He wanted to go back, to go home and lock himself in once more. But it was too late. The chanting had a firm grasp on his mind now, and he could only keep walking, his pace steady, one foot carefully placed in front of the other.

Then, far ahead, he saw a figure in white coming toward him. He felt his pace pick up, and idly wondered why. The white figure wavered in front of him, and he realized that it wasn't the figure that wavered; it was himself. He steadied himself, pausing for a moment to regain his balance. Ahead of him the figure in white seemed to pause too.

Peter strained his eyes, trying to make out who it was. Then he knew.

It was Marilyn Crane.

She should have been going the same way he was going, up the hill, to the school. Instead, she was coming toward him.

Something was wrong. He forced his exhausted mind to begin functioning again. Marilyn was coming toward him, and something was wrong.

Now he tried consciously to hurry; his feet refused to obey him. But he had to get to her.

He raised his black-robed arm and waved.

Marilyn saw the dark shape coming closer, and then she saw the uplifted arm. It was beckoning to her. Beckoning, as the voices in her head had beckoned.

Suddenly she knew what the figure was.

Clothed in black, Death was coming for her.

She wanted to run, wanted to fling herself into the arms of the spectre, and let him carry her away.

But there was something she had to do first. There was some act she had to commit, some symbolic gesture she was required to make to let the figure know that she was ready to accept Him.

Her right hand dropped the rosary beads, and the crucifix clattered to the sidewalk. Marilyn knelt, reached into her purse, her eyes fastened on the black figure before her. Her fingers closed on the package. The razor blades that had been with her for so long. She fumbled at them.

Peter stopped suddenly, realizing that Marilyn was no longer coming toward him. He saw the crucifix and beads fall to the sidewalk, and his hand went to his waist, his fingers tightening on his own rosary.

She was kneeling now, and had dropped her purse near her beads.

And then the redness began to flow from her wrist, and Peter knew what was happening. He began to run.

Marilyn watched the blood spurt from her left wrist, and quickly transferred the blade to her other hand. She began hacking clumsily at the arteries of her right wrist. Suddenly the blade met its mark; skin and flesh parted. She stared at the throbbing artery for a split second, then plunged the razor deep into it. A crimson fountain gushed forth, splashing against the white of her dress, and dribbling slowly to the pavement beneath her.

She looked up, away from the blood. She had been right. Death was coming for her now, hurrying toward her, and she must go to meet Him. She began running, her arms stretched out toward her approaching Death, the blood spewing from her wrists.

The truck was coming toward Main Street on First Street. For once, the light – Neilsville's only traffic light – was green. The driver pressed on the accelerator and the engine surged. He would make the light.

It happened so fast the driver had no time to respond.

From the left, a figure ran in front of the truck, a blur of red and blinding white. He moved his foot to the brake, but before the truck even began to slow he heard the dull thump, and the scream.

He brought the truck to a halt, and leaped from the cab. He threw up on the pavement.

Her head caught under the left front wheel, her neck broken Marilyn Crane lay in a crimson heap. Only the blood, still being slowly pumped from her wrists, signified that she was still alive.

Peter Balsam saw it happen, saw Marilyn dashing across the street toward him, too intent on him to notice that the light was wrong, and that the truck was coming. If she saw it before it hit her, she gave no sign. She didn't try to veer away, she didn't try to stop.

She screamed once, but that was a reflex.

He never knew whether he paused, or whether he took in the scene as he ran. But suddenly he was beside her, on his knees, her blood soaking the heavy material of his robes.

Peter Balsam, his mind reeling, began praying over the broken and dying body of Marilyn Crane.

From out of his past, from somewhere in his memory, Peter began administering the Last Rites to Marilyn.

The crowd gathered slowly, until there was a solid mass of people surrounding Peter as he prayed for Marilyn's soul. The crowd was in shock, but finally one of them broke away and found a telephone.

A few moments later, the ambulance screamed through Neilszille.

In the rectory, Monsignor Vernon stared into the last coals of the dying fire. An intense satisfaction filled him, and he stood up. He moved to the window, drawing the curtain open to the suhlight. With the sunshine came the howl of the siren.

The priest smiled softly. At last, the long night was over. He began to prepare for the day ahead.

THIRTY

The story was sweeping through Neilsville even before the ambulance had taken Marilyn Crane and Peter Balsam to the hospital.

Neilsville stopped functioning. For the first time, each one of them, as he heard the story, felt personally touched. Until that day they had talked, spoken in whispers, wondered about the girls who had died. But that day, they had seen it,watched from the sidewalks, from the windows, as the evil among them spilled out into the street. By noon, everyone in town had heard the story, and told it, and heard it again. For each of them it was as if they had seen it themselves; by afternoon each of them believed he had seen it.

School was cancelled before it even began that day, and the Sisters retired to their private chapel to spend the day in prayer. The children went home, but on their way home they talked, and by the time they reached their homes, all of them were sure that they had seen Marilyn Crane die.

She was dead by the time the ambulance reached the hospital, but still, in the manner of hospitals, they tried to act as if she was not. They worked over her for nearly an hour, and all the time they worked, Peter Balsam sat numbly looking on, knowing they were not treating Marilyn, but treating themselves, avoiding by simple activity the truth of what had happened, what was happening.

Margo Henderson walked briskly into the emergency room, but when she saw why she had been called she came to an abrupt halt. She stared at the spectre before her, not wanting to believe her eyes. But then the professionalism born of years in the hospital came to the fore, and she steeled herself. She approached Peter Balsam.

'Peter?' There was no answer, and she realized he was in shock. She repeated his name: 'Peter.'

'I have to end it,' he murmured. 'I have to end it.' He kept repeating the phrase as Margo led him through the halls.

Dr. Shields gave him a shot, and he slowly came out of it. He gazed first at Margo, then at the doctor.

'She's dead,' he said, neither asking a question nor stating a fact.

'What happened?' Dr. Shields asked gently. 'Can you talk about it?'

'Nothing to talk about,' Peter said thickly. 'I have to end it, that's all.'

'Peter, there's nothing for you to do,' Margo said. Suddenly an image flashed in her mind, an image of the attractive young man she had met on the train such a short time ago. Could this haggard being, his bloody robe hanging limply from stooped shoulders, be the same young man?

No, she decided, it could not. Biting her lips to hold back her tears, she hurried from the room. Peter watched her go, and knew that this time she was gone forever. It didn't matter. The only thing that mattered was that he must end the horror. He tried to focus on the doctor.

'I have to sleep,' he said. 'Can you give me something to sleep? If I sleep, I'll be all right.'

Dr. Shields nodded. 'Why don't I admit you to the hospital?

'They'll watch me?' Peter asked.

'Watch you?'

'While I sleep. They'll watch me while I sleep?'

Dr. Shields nodded.

'If they'll watch me,' Peter said vaguely. 'I can't sleep alone, you know.'

Dr. Shields nodded understandingly, though he hadn't the vaguest idea of what the young man was talking about.

'I'll see to it,' he promised.

Thirty minutes later Peter Balsam was asleep in Neilsville Memorial Hospital, a nurse sitting by his bed. She watched him for an hour, checking his breathing and his pulse. When she decided all was well with him, she silently left the room to go about her duties.

He woke to the sound of church bells pealing, and knew what it meant.

All over Neilsville the churches were holding special services. The people had asked for them, needing something to take their minds off the horror of the day, needing something to tell them that soon all would be well among them again.

Peter lay in his hospital bed, thinking that it was curious. The bells were sounding for Marilyn, all of them except St. Francis Xavier's. The bells of St. Francis Xavier were sounding as usual, calling the faithful to evening Mass. Usually, on a weeknight, attendance would be light. But not tonight, he was sure. Tonight they would all be there, praying guiltily for the soul of Marilyn Crane, knowing in their minds that they should not, that Marilyn was no longer worthy of their prayers, but praying for her nonetheless.

He glanced at the clock. Thirty minutes, he thought, and they'll all be in church. All of us, except those of us here, or in the grave.

All of us. He repeated the words to himself. All of us. Peter Balsam sat up in bed, the last vestiges of sleep falling away as his mind suddenly became alert. Now was the time. If ever there was going to be a time, it would be now.

He rose from his bed and shuffled into the tiny bathroom wedged economically between his room and the next. He splashed cold water on his face and looked in the mirror.

His eyes were better, and the crow's feet had faded. He needed a shave but it didn't matter. No one was going to see him anyway.

He found the bloodstained robes hanging in the closet. Loathing them, he put them on. Then he sat down to wait.

He waited until the bells died away, and silence fell over Neilsville. Then he left his room. Without speaking to anyone, Peter Balsam walked out of the hospital.

No one tried to stop him. Perhaps it was the strange figure he presented, barefoot, his bloodstained robes trailing the floor, his crucifix clutched tightly in his hand. The orderlies looked at the nurses, and the nurses looked at the resident, but none of them spoke. Dr. Shields had admitted him, but had said nothing about keeping him there. 'Make sure he sleeps.' That's what the doctor had ordered, and that's what they had done. Peter Balsam had slept, and now he was going home.

But he didn't go home. Instead he walked slowly up Cathedral Hill, listening to the sounds of the choirs that were raising their voices to God all over Neilsville. No one was in sight, but he could sense them around him, praying quietly in the churches.

He mounted the steps to the rectory, and let himself in the front door. He picked up the silver bell and shook it, then shook it again. Its tinkle echoed through the dimly lit house, and Peter knew he was alone. He walked quickly down the hall to the door of the study.

He paused there, suddenly frightened. He had to remind himself that the room on the other side of the door was empty, that there were no strange rituals being performed, that tonight no one was reaching out to draw him to this room. Tonight, he had come on his own.

He opened the door, and entered the small room. He found the light switch, and the room was filled with a yellow glow that seemed to change its configuration, washing away the gloom.

He began his search of the desk, opening and closing the drawers rapidly. He wasn't sure what he was looking for. He would recognize it when he saw it.

There was nothing in the desk, and he moved to a small filing cabinet that was built into one of the walls. He opened the top drawer, and began going through the files. Nothing.

Nothing in the second.

In the third, he found what he was looking for.

It was a large sealed envelope, wedged behind the last of the files. Peter pulled it from its hiding place, and tore open the envelope. A scrapbook. A scrapbook and a file folder. He opened the file folder.

On top was a single sheet of paper; on it was written a list of names. Five of them had been scratched out.

Judy Nelson
Karen Morton
Penny Anderson
Janet Connally
Marilyn Crane

At the end of the list, Judy Nelson's name appeared again, with no line though it.

Peter Balsam had found what he was looking for.

He slipped the file folder back in the envelope, and closed the drawer of the cabinet. He let himself out of the study, snapping the light off as he went, then, carrying the bulging envelope, walked out of the rectory into the fading light of evening.

For the first time in several days the dusk held no fear for Peter. This night he would complete the puzzle. This night would end the terror, both for him and for Neilsville.

As he hurried down the hill the bells of St. Francis Xavier began to peal once again. Mass was over.

In his apartment, Peter began going through the scrapbook. He leafed through the pages quickly. They were all moie or less the same: filled with yellowed newspaper clippings, each clipping headlined in bold type:

GIRL SLAYS PARENTS, SELF

MODERN LIZZIE BORDEN WILL NEVER STAND TRIAL

CHILD WATCHES AS FAMILY DIES

There were nearly fifty clippings in the scrapbook, from brief articles less than a column long to major features spread over several pages. All of them were about the same crime, all of them were from the same time. Peter Balsam subtracted quickly. He would have been two or three at the time the crime took place.

He went back to the first page of the scrapbook, and began reading the articles carefully.

Most of them gave simply the bare facts:

A man and his wife had been found in bed, murdered. In the same room their daughter was discovered hanging from a light fixture. When the room was thoroughly searched, the couple's small son was found hiding in the closet of the bedroom, in shock.

The tabloids had spread the story over several pages, and it was in the clippings from the tabloids that Peter Balsam was able to glean the details of the bizarre crime.

The couple had been murdered while in the act of making love. Their daughter had walked in on them and hacked them with a cleaver. The weapon indicated premeditation. The motive was unclear. There was some speculation that the girl was reacting badly to her own misfortune – an autopsy had revealed that she was pregnant.

But what the tabloids played up most was the little boy – the little boy who was thought to have watched the entire thing from the closet, from the moment when his parents came into the room and began making love – not knowing they were being observed – to the moment when his sixteen-year-old sister brought the cleaver into the bedroom, hacked her parents to death, then hanged herself from the light fixture.

He had been in shock when he was found, and had been rushed to a hospital. There, it was discovered that the child had no living relatives. In the end he had been anonymously placed in a convent.

The convent was unnamed, but Balsam was sure he knew which one it was. What he had just read was the story that had been whispered about when he was a child. None of the children at the convent had known the facts. Now Peter Balsam knew them all.

He searched through the papers.

The name. Where was the name of the family?

The name was not given. Nowhere. In every story the names of everyone involved in the crime had been carefully deleted, as if whoever had compiled the scrapbook had wanted the story known, but the identities kept secret. Nor were the papers themselves identified. Each clipping had been carefully cut from its page.

In only one story was there even a clue. In one story, someone had slipped. The child's name was Peter.

Suddenly it all made sense. He had never gotten over the shock. It had festered in him all the time he was growing up, all the time he had studied for the priesthood. And then, sometime, not too long ago, the shock had caught up with him.

He had begun to hate adolescent girls. And why shouldn't he? Hadn't one of them taken his parents away from him? Taken his home away from him? Left him with nothing? If one of them could do that, why not all of them? His hatred had grown, had turned into an obsession.

And Peter Vernon – now Monsignor Vernon – had acted on his obsession. He had gathered together the forces at his disposal, and begun to strike back, taking revenge on the children his injured mind blamed for the loss of his parents.

Balsam leafed through the scrapbook. He could understand it, now, and for the first time he felt a trace of sympathy for the priest.

He wondered what to do with the scrapbook. Should he

take it to the police? But what would they do? All right, so the Monsignor kept a scrapbook about a crime more than thirty years old. So what? If it was your family, wouldn't you have kept a scrapbook too? Those girls killed themselves, mister, and the fact that a priest's older sister did the same thing thirty years ago is just one of those coincidences.

The Bishop. He could take it to the Bishop, Even if the Bishop didn't believe the Monsignor had anything to do with the suicides, at least the scrapbook would prove that something had gone wrong in the Monsignor's early life, and that the priest should at least be carefully observed. The Bishop could order the Monsignor to undergo observation. From there, the psychiatrists could take over. It would all come out.

The door suddenly opened.

Monsignor Vernon stood framed in the door, a small smile playing around his lips; a smile that was betrayed by the burning fire in his eyes.

'I went to see you at the hospital,' he said. 'But you'd left.'

'Yes, I did,' Peter said blankly, his mind whirling.

'May I come in?' The burning eyes bored into Peter, and without waiting for an answer the priest entered the room and closed the door behind him.

'You found my scrapbook,' he said softly. His eyes darted around the room, coming to rest on the open scrapbook on the desk.

'It was you we all talked about, wasn't it? When we were kids?'

'Yes, it was me,' the priest said. 'But I didn't know it, not until five years ago.'

'Five years ago?'

'Someone sent me that scrapbook. I don't know who, and I don't know why. But it explained a lot to me. It made me see what I had to do.'

'Do?' Peter Balsam felt his heart beat faster.

'I had to punish them. All of them.'

'You mean the girls?'

'They're evil,' the priest said. 'They're evil with their minds, and with their bodies. The Lord wants me to punish them.'

'I thought it was St. Peter Martyr,' Balsam said softly.

'Of course you did. That's what I wanted you to think. And that's what I wanted the members of the Society to think. It makes it much easier that way.'

'I see,' said Peter. 'The Society never had anything to do with religion, did it?'

'What is religion? It has to do with my religion, and with St. Peter Martyr's religion. But not with the religion of the Church. The Church has no religion any more. It has become weak. It tolerates.'

'And you do not.'

'I don't need to,' the priest said. The fire in his eyes was raging now, and Peter Balsam was suddenly afraid, But he had to know.

'Me,' he said. 'Why did you need me?'

Monsignor Vernon smiled now.

'You think I'm insane, don't you?' he asked.

'Are you?'

'If I were, I wouldn't do what I've done.'

The fear stabbed at Balsam again. 'Done? What do you mean?'

'You,' the priest said simply. 'You've figured out everything else, but you haven't figured out your own part in it, have you?'

'I'm to be St. Acerinus,' Peter said. 'I'm supposed to kill you, and then repent. But I won't do it.'

'No, you won't,' the Monsignor said. 'You've done everything else admirably, but I don't expect you to kill me. That was never part of the plan. That was the way it happened the first time. This time St. Peter takes his revenge.'

'I'm not sure I'm following you,' Balsam said. It was all getting confused again. Did the priest really believe, after all, that he was St. Peter Martyr's reincarnation? And then the truth struck. Of course he did. He had to, or the guilt would be too much for him. If he weren't Peter Vernon – if he were St. Peter Martyr – then everything was different. He was punishing heretics and sinners, carrying on the work of the Lord, and protecting the Mother Church. He was no longer just Peter Vernon, insanely avenging the death of his parents.

'I'm going to kill you,' Monsignor Vernon said in the silence.

Balsam stared at him. 'You can't,' he protested.

'Can't I?' The priest's eyes had grown cold. 'What will happen if I do? They'll think it was suicide.' He picked a letter opener off Peter Balsam's desk, and began twirling it in his hands as he talked.

'When they find you, what will they find? A young man, a psychologist, a teacher. Wearing monastic robes stained with blood.'

The letter opener glittered as it reflected the light from the desk lamp. Peter Balsam blinked as the flashes of light struck his eyes.

'And who is this young man? His name is Peter. He grew up in a convent, after a tragedy in his youth.' The priest touched the scrapbook with the point of the letter opener. 'And he was a failure at nearly everything.'

The letter opener glinted again. Peter Balsam watched it, unable to force his eyes away from the lamplight reflecting on the blade.

'His students have been dying, one by one,' Monsignor Vernon's voice went on inexorably. 'But has he been trying to help them? No. Instead, he's been busying himself by spreading preposterous tales about a simple religious study group. And he's been acting very strangely.'

The light seemed to bounce off the blade directly into Peter's brain.

He felt the sleepiness overcoming him, felt the heaviness in his limbs that he knew marked the first stages of hypnosis.

He tried to fight it, tried to summon his last reserves of energy to rouse himself, to look away from the flashing light, and block out the voice of the priest. But he couldn't tear his eyes away from the blade; the voice was relentless.

'They'll find the scrapbook, of course, and they'll read about what happened to the little boy – the little boy Peter – who grew up and became a psychologist, and whose students began to kill themselves.

'They'll put it all together, Peter. They'll call your death a suicide. Your work is done, Peter. Mine is just beginning.'

Peter saw the priest come toward him, the letter opener held almost carelessly in his right hand. Still the light flashed in his eyes. He told his body to do something, to move, to react, but there was nothing. His brain cried out in its weariness, but his body would not respond.

'Would you like to watch yourself die, Peter? It won't hurt, I promise you. There won't be any pain, Peter. No pain at all. The blade will simply slide into you, and it will all end.'

The point of the letter opener was against his chest now, its tip lost in the folds of his robe. And still he watched it, his eyes drawn to the blade in fascination.

Is this how it ends, he wondered, staring at the polished blade. Is this what they felt – Karen and Penny and Janet and Marilyn? Did they see the shining metal, coming for them? He tried to rouse himself from the awful torpor that had claimed him. It was too late.

He felt a slight pressure, but Monsignor Vernon was right. It wasn't pain, not really. What he'd been feeling the last few days had been pain. This was release.

He gave himself up to it, and began praying silently for redemption.

Peter Balsam watched as the blade slid into his chest, but he felt nothing. Only a sense of anticipation, and a sense of gladness. For him, finally, the horror was truly over.

Ten minutes later Monsignor Vernon left Peter Balsam's apartment, and began walking back to the rectory. He took the side streets. No one saw him as he moved deliberately through Neilsville. Not that it would have mattered had he been seen; the tall authoritarian figure of the Monsignor was a familiar sight in Neilsville. They believed in him. They leaned on him.

THIRTY-ONE

They buried him a week later, in an unmarked grave. They tried to reach his wife, but she had disappeared. They weren't sure that even if they found her, she would want him. Not after hearing what they would have to tell her.

In the manner of small towns, everyone in Neilsville knew where the grave was. And they went; the Catholics secretly, the others openly. They covered it with filth, as if by desecrating his grave they could wipe him out of their memories. Each day the filth was cleaned away, and each night it reappeared.

It took nearly a year, but eventually they forgot, or buried their memories deep in the backs of their minds. Peter Balsam's grave lay clean, unvisited, unattended. For a while.

For Judy Nelson, that year was the most difficult of her life. She had always felt set apart from the town, but during that year it was worse than ever. Her friends were gone, and she was unable to make new ones. It was as if she was tainted; as if whatever had brushed against her, then attacked her friends, might still be in Neilsville, ready to strike again.

Judy was haunted by the memory of Marilyn Crane. Late at night, when she should have been sleeping, she would remember. She hadn't intended for the pranks to go as far as they had. She had only been teasing Marilyn. She hadn't meant for Marilyn to die. But Marilyn had died, and Judy knew that, whatever had happened to the other girls, with Marilyn it had been different. She, Judy, had driven her to her death. Her mind would not let her forget.

On the anniversary of Peter Balsam's death, the memory of Marilyn Crane loomed larger than ever in Judy's mind. She woke out of a sound sleep, and Marilyn was singing to her, calling her. She left her bed and moved to her closet. From the top shelf she removed the box that contained her confirmation dress. She opened the box and shook the dress out.

She put it on.

She left the house quietly, and walked through the streets of Neilsville. She entered the graveyard, and went to the spot where Marilyn Crane lay buried. She stood for a long time, staring down at the grave and praying.

Then, as the first grey of dawn showed in the eastern sky, Judy moved to Peter Balsam's grave. There, too, she stood for a long while, praying once more. As she prayed, the music – a sort of chanting – grew in her ears.

She began searching in the rubble around the grave until she found a piece of broken glass.

With the shard of glass she began to cut herself.

They found her late that morning. She was lying on Peter Balsam's grave, face down, her arms spread wide, as if trying to embrace the decaying remains that lay below. Pools of blood soaked the earth beneath her palms, and her rosary lay broken, the beads scattered in the mud where the headstone should have been.

They removed Peter Balsam's bones from the ground and burned them.

But it happened again, and yet again.

The people of Neilsville wondered, and were frightened.

They grew expectant, and each year, about the same time, they began watching their daughters, looking for a sign. But there was never a sign, never a clue. But each year, sometime in the fall, one of their children would be missed from her home. She would always be found in the same place, reaching out as if to embrace the empty grave.

And each year, in the rectory of the Church of St. Francis Xavier, the Society of St. Peter Martyr met.

Six priests, meeting in the glow of the firelight, praying to their patron saint.

On each of those nights, very late, the flames would begin to dance in a slow rhythm, and the voice would speak to them.

'Give praise unto the Lord, my servants. Strike down the heretics, and punish the sinners.'

Each year the will of St. Peter Martyr was carried out, and the sins of the faithful were punished.

JOAN SAMSON

THE AUCTIONEER

Harrowing tensions explode in a series of events that could happen anywhere, to anyone, just as they do to John Moore – whose days of freedom run out, who is stripped of his possessions, his courage, and his hopes, by the ominous presence of a stranger impossible to resist . . .

'The creeping horror is so frightening for its plausibility that everyone will find some parallels in their own life . . . the heavy claustrophobic terror that this book strikes in our hearts is welcome for its warning.'
Yorkshire Post

'Explosive . . . chilling . . . I challenge anyone to resist it after reading the first few pages.'
New York Times

CORONET BOOKS

ROBERT CALDER

THE DOGS

In the small town of Covington, a divorced college professor named Alex Bauer finds an abandoned puppy, takes it home, and grows to love it – unaware that at an experimental canine development installation a hundred miles away a very specially bred pup is missing.

Then one day a sudden, savage incident drives the dog into the woods, where among outcasts and strays he reverts to the primal instincts of his species, to kill.

So begins Covington's ordeal and Alex Bauer's private hell. The pack of killer dogs sets off a cataclysm of horror which sweeps a countryside – the chilling vortex will grip the reader with a shock of recognition that reverberates long past the final page . . . not because it could happen, but because it is happening. Now!

CORONET BOOKS

JOHN SAUL

SUFFER THE CHILDREN

One hundred years ago in Port Arbello a pretty little girl began to scream. And struggle. And die. No one heard. No one saw. Just one man whose guilty heart burst in pain as he dashed himself to death in the sea...

Now something peculiar is happening in Port Arbello. The children are disappearing, one by one. An evil history is repeating itself. And one strange, terrified child has ended her silence with a scream that began a hundred years ago.

A novel of unnatural passion and supernatural terror.

CORONET BOOKS